Figuring the Woman Author in Contemporary Fiction

Figuring the Woman Author in Contemporary Fiction

Mary Eagleton

First published in 2005 by
PALGRAVE MACMILLAN
Houndmills, Basingstoke, Hampshire RG21 6XS and
175 Fifth Avenue, New York, N.Y. 10010
Companies and representatives throughout the world.

PALGRAVE MACMILLAN is the global academic imprint of the Palgrave
Macmillan division of St. Martin's Press, LLC and of Palgrave Macmillan Ltd.
Macmillan® is a registered trademark in the United States, United Kingdom
and other countries. Palgrave is a registered trademark in the European
Union and other countries.

ISBN-13: 978–1–4039–0391–4 hardback
ISBN-10: 1–4039–0391–3   hardback

This book is printed on paper suitable for recycling and made from fully
managed and sustained forest sources.

A catalogue record for this book is available from the British Library.

Library of Congress Cataloging-in-Publication Data

Eagleton, Mary.
    Figuring the woman author in contemporary fiction / Mary Eagleton.
        p. cm.
    Includes bibliographical references and index.
    ISBN 1–4039–0391–3
    1. English fiction – Women authors – History and criticism. 2. Women
authors in literature. 3. Feminism and literature – English-speaking
countries – History – 20th century. 4. Women and literature – English-
speaking countries – History – 20th century. 5. American fiction – Women
authors – History and criticism. 6. American fiction – 20th century –
History and criticism. 7. English fiction – 20th century – History and
criticism. 8. Feminist fiction, American – History and criticism. 9. Feminist
fiction, English – History and criticism. 10. Authors in literature. I. Title.

PR888.W6E15 2005
823'.9109352—dc22   2005049049

10 9 8 7 6 5 4 3 2 1
14 13 12 11 10 09 08 07 06 05

Printed and bound in Great Britain by
Antony Rowe Ltd, Chippenham and Eastbourne

Rosaleen Eagleton (1913–2002)

Contents

Acknowledgements

I am indebted to Leeds Metropolitan University which provided me with a sabbatical during the writing of this book and, particularly, to Gordon Johnston and Simon Gunn within the School of Cultural Studies; their good management and supportiveness have been invaluable. The Arts and Humanities Research Board generously funded me under the auspices of their Research Leave Scheme and made the timely completion of this project possible.

Many colleagues and friends have helped in ways academic and non-academic. I am very grateful to Linda Anderson and Cora Kaplan for their encouraging response to my original proposal; to Christine Bousfield, Kristyn Gorton and Susan Watkins who read sections and offered much useful comment; to colleagues and friends at a number of universities – among which, Birkbeck College, London, Edinburgh University, the University of Leicester, the University Rovira I Virgili, Tarragona, Liverpool John Moores, the University of Stockholm and the University of York – whose invitations to lecture or give conference papers greatly helped the development of my ideas during the formative stage; to Palgrave's anonymous readers who gave me some excellent advice, particularly in the final stage, which I was happy to follow. In the production of the book, the word-processing skills of Pat Cook and Marianne Huntley and the editorial guidance of Paula Kennedy have been indispensable. I am especially grateful to Vidhya Jayaprakash for her exemplary professionalism. My major debt is to David Pierce for always being interested and always being steadfast.

In several chapters I draw on material from earlier publications: in Chapter 2, from 'Feminism and the Death of the Author: Margaret Atwood's *The Handmaid's Tale'*, *British Journal of Canadian Studies* 12:2 (1997), pp. 281–97; in Chapter 4 from 'Carol Shields and Pierre Bourdieu: Reading *Swann'*, *Critique: Studies in Contemporary Fiction*, Vol. 44, No. 3 (Spring, 2003), pp. 313–28, reprinted with permission of the Helen Dwight Reid Educational Foundation and published by Heldref Publications, 1319 18th Street, NW, Washington DC 20036–1802. www.heldref.org. Copyright © 2002; in Chapter 6, from 'The Danger of Intellectual Masters: Lessons from Harry Potter and Antonia Byatt', *Revista Canaria de Estudios Ingleses*, No. 48 (2004), pp. 61–75; in Chapter 8 from Helen Graham, Ann Kaloski, Ali Neilson, Emma Robertson (eds) *The Feminist Seventies* York, UK: Raw Nerve Books, 2003. (Website http://www.feminist-seventies.net.) I am grateful to the editors involved for their permission to reprint material here.

1
Introduction
Birth, Death and Resurrection

> It would scarcely be an exaggeration to say that the struggles of feminism have been primarily a struggle for authorship – understood in the widest sense as the arena in which culture attempts to define itself.
>
> Seán Burke, *Authorship: From Plato to the Postmodern*[1]

Seán Burke is surely right in suggesting the importance of authorship for feminism whether as a practice, an identity or a concept. Second-wave feminism always presumed that access for women applied to the cultural sphere as much as any other and the reshaping in the last thirty years of our cultural history, the establishment of feminist publishing companies or of feminist listings within mainstream companies, the importance of feminism as an academic discourse and the current visibility of women as not only writers but as artists, musicians, cultural workers generally are all testament to that. In this book I sometimes make mention of – to use Umberto Eco's term – the 'empirical authors', female and male, who write the texts I discuss but that is not my major focus. My concern is with the figure of the woman author who appears so frequently and in a number of guises as a character in contemporary fiction and with 'figuring out' what she signifies. I do not limit my brief to high-status literary writers. They certainly feature in the figure of the critically respected poet, Mary Swann, in Carol Shields's novel of that name, or the successful novelist, Fleur Talbot, in Muriel Spark's *Loitering with Intent* or the feminist literary critic, Maud Bailey in Antonia Byatt's *Possession*.[2] But we also encounter less prestigious authors and less prestigious literary forms: the slave woman who tells her oral narrative in Sherley Anne Williams's *Dessa Rose*, or Joan Foster, the writer of popular Gothic romances in Margaret Atwood's *Lady Oracle*, or the unpublished

memoirs of the unnamed narrator in Ursula Le Guin's 'Sur'.[3] In Alice
Walker's 'Everyday Use' and Byatt's 'Art Work', the women are artists,
producing quilts and fabric sculptures, and Fleur Talbot, although writing fiction, refers to herself as 'an artist'.[4] But I use the term 'author'
rather than 'artist' or 'cultural producer' or 'cultural worker' as the
generic term because it contains within its etymology connotations of
'authorising' and 'authority', both of which have been highly problematic concepts for women in the cultural sphere and for the development
of a feminist cultural criticism.[5] Even if one quibbled with Burke about
the *primacy* of authorship for feminism – I imagine feminist economists
or political theorists would have a rather different view – the need for
women to claim cultural legitimacy through authorising themselves in
various ways is indisputable.

Every woman writer, artist or narrator we will consider in this study
has some issue with authorising and authority. As is indicated in the
renewed interest in the female *Künstlerroman*, the female author is achiev-
ing a sense of her coming-into-being and her validity in what is represented as both a self-authorising and a wider social acceptance.[6] Ruth
Parkin-Gounelas, commenting on the popularity of post-1960s women's
writing, talks of these 'fictions of the female self' and the movement 'out
of silence into obsessive self-definition'.[7] But that process, constantly
replayed in recent years in both fiction and criticism, is not without
ambiguities. For Shields's author-heroine in *Unless*, writing is both com-
pulsive and imperative; it is the 'richest territory', concludes Reta, 'the
remaking of an untenable world through the nib of a pen; it matters so
much I can't stop doing it'.[8] Yet elsewhere in the novel, Reta notices
accounts of literary history constructed as a 'testicular hit list of literary
big cats' (164) and her own relegation in a review to the position of a
'miniaturist' of fiction. For Spark's Fleur Talbot, authorship is an unmit-
igated delight: 'How wonderful it feels to be an artist and a woman in
the twentieth century' (19). For the poor, timid, murdered poet, Mary
Swann, 'the anxiety of authorship' that Sandra Gilbert and Susan Gubar
situated in the nineteenth century evidently continues well into the
twentieth.[9] Whereas for Fleur becoming the woman author is to secure
her place in the culture and she reflects on a successful literary career,
Lorna Sage describes the woman author as still looking for a place in 'the
house of fiction' and often 'homeless'.[10]

How this 'authorising' might link to a stronger sense of 'authority' has
been one of the dominant narratives in feminist literary criticism over
the last thirty or more years. While some feminists in the late 1960s and
the 1970s looked for the instatement of alternative canons of women

writers or women artists to establish that authority, others resisted either because of a caution about aesthetic hierarchies generally or because of a specific anti-individualist, anti-heroic objection to privileging some women above others. While some agitated for access to that wide cultural arena that Burke speaks of, others espoused the marginal. While some linked authorship to identity and political agency, others found a progressive politics in a *rapprochement* between feminism and post-structuralism's questioning of identity politics or the possibility of a coherent and knowable subjectivity. Moreover, the blunter version of post-feminism would claim that there is no longer any need to posit 'the woman author' as a distinct figure since the battle has been won. Women authors fill the book shelves, have literary prizes devoted to them, are read as frequently as male authors in reading groups and, according to a recent piece of research in the United kingdom, compose the most favoured courses in Higher Education.[11] To insist on a special place for the woman author is essentialist, anachronistic and ties her to victimhood.

This twin impulse both to give birth to the woman author and to bury her found a particular expression in the ironies that surrounded the publication and dissemination of Roland Barthes's influential essay, 'The Death of the Author'. Originally published in 1967 in the American magazine, *Aspen*, Barthes's essay did not reach an extensive Anglophone audience until 1977 with its publication in Stephen Heath's edited collection of Barthes's essays, *Image-Music-Text*.[12] Since then it has been frequently discussed, cited and anthologised and the title has become the catch phrase for a wider set of arguments. But 1977 was also the year in which Barbara Smith published 'Toward a Black Feminist Criticism', Luce Irigaray the French edition of *This Sex Which Is Not One* and Elaine Showalter *A Literature of Their Own*. The year before, Hélène Cixous had published 'The Laugh of the Medusa' in the American journal, *Signs*; a year after, the Marxist-Feminist Literature Collective in the United kingdom published an essay that reassessed Victorian woman writers; and two years after Barthes's essay, in 1979, a much larger reassessment of the Victorian period was published in Sandra Gilbert and Susan Gubar's *The Madwoman in the Attic*.[13] These texts – and one could list many more – indicate a curious contradiction in intellectual history, how one group of academics was declaring the 'death' of the author as a figure of origin, meaning and power at precisely the same moment as another group, from varying feminist positions, was looking for the 'birth' of the author in terms of a reclamation of women's literary history and an exhortation to women to claim a voice. Even if one believes with Samuel Beckett that we give birth astride a grave, no one expected birth and death to be quite so proximate.

It is also clear, though, that any opposition between Barthes and feminism needs to be complicated. The 'death' of the author never did mean the death of writing and, from many feminist positions, the 'birth' of the woman author never meant cultural dominance or control of meaning. Furthermore, many feminists have found ways of embracing Barthes's argument, particularly with respect to identity and the danger of an authority that has traditionally excluded women and other subordinated groups. In the 1980s, the argument about 'the death of the Author' rapidly became an orthodoxy and one of those 'small local imperialisms' that Barthes himself rejected and yet, during the same period, the expansion of academic publishing and the focus on women's writing meant a lucrative and commercially driven 'birth' of new authors. The popularising of Barthes's essay and its separation from his other work has rendered it far more absolute than it actually is. In Barthes's work 'birth' and 'death' are closely aligned. Indeed, the author is not 'dead' but repeatedly returns in various guises, though never as essence, authority or solution. As Eugen Simion was quick to point out, the author is doomed to 'ritualistic resurrection' rather than 'ritualistic death'.[14] Lorna Sage uses the same vocabulary for the woman author. Speaking of Atwood, she comments on 'a pattern of deaths and resurrections, a way of surviving as an author through the artificial miracle of mutation', a strategy which, as we shall see in Chapter 7, certainly applies to Joan Foster in *Lady Oracle*, as it does to the fiendishly orchestrated deaths and resurrections of authors in Gilbert Adair's *The Death of the Author* (chapter 2).[15] Not surprisingly, the creative writer has been keen to keep the author alive. In the texts featured in this book, published between 1973 and 2000, the figure of the woman author constantly reappears carrying with her a lot of unfinished business. If anything, creative writers have been stimulated by the 'death of the Author' thesis rather than stifled, delighted rather than defensive, and the 1980s revealed a particular flowering of texts with author-protagonists as Barthes's argument became better known and part of wider metafictional interests. Generally, authors wanted to reaffirm a role – definitely more living than dead – and there was a particular disquiet about the author's ethical responsibility; in this respect the signature of the author is crucial.[16] But the idea of the author as a questionable figure, not identifiable with the person who writes, possibly mendacious and close relative of Jekyll and Hyde came as no news to the creative writer.[17]

Three further factors work to establish the current interest in the figure of the woman author. First and inevitably, some of the impetus is biographical. Though not everyone is as mischievous as Muriel Spark who uses her fictional author, Fleur Talbot, to respond to critiques made of her own writing and one would not want to present all fiction as merely veiled autobiography, the figure of the woman author provides the living woman author with opportunities to explore, to some extent at least, her own situation, her aspirations and anxieties. A number of texts play on that notion of the creation of a 'real' authorial life by their use of biographical and autobiographical modes. Shields in *Unless* talks about this writerly self-reflexiveness as 'incestuous waters' (208); Linda Hutcheon about its 'narcissism'.[18] Second, the academic background of many of the empirical authors featuring in this study – not only Byatt and Adair but also J. M. Coetzee, Alison Lurie, Anita Brookner, David Lodge, Amanda Cross (pen name of Carolyn Heilbrun) – encourages a theoretical interest in authorship which they bring to the fiction. All these authors have at least a good knowledge of, some a deep intellectual engagement with, theories of authorship and in certain texts, *Possession* by Byatt, *The Death of the Author* by Adair, *Foe* by Coetzee, a dialogue between fiction and theory is central to the plot and the novel's metafictional narrative.[19] Third, the political perspectives of feminism, post-colonialism and anti-racism – movements in which many post-1970's writers have been sympathetically or actively involved – often draw writers to the figure of the woman author whose subaltern status alongside her potential for critical expression makes her a figure of rich narrative interest. From both theoretical and political viewpoints, the woman author is frequently seen as the key figure for exploring problems of authorial power. A recurrent theme in the texts we shall be considering is how the loss of a woman's authority over her work, in terms of content, form and legal ownership, results not in a dispersal of power and a liberating deposing of 'the Author' but in a redistribution of power which confirms existing hierarchies of gender, class and race.[20] Conversely, an equally favoured theme is the resistance of the woman author and the subversive undermining of male authorial power. Subtending both responses is, necessarily, an identity as 'the author'.

Outline of chapters

The problem of the authorial subject, the 'I' who writes, and its relation to gender is the focus of Chapter 2, 'Feminism and the Death of the Author'. It is not only Barthes's essay that is considered here but also Michel Foucault's 'What Is An Author?' in which he argues that authorship is discursively produced. Neither of these essays gives any consideration to the woman author specifically or to gender generally. That gap is filled in the work of Peggy Kamuf and Nancy Miller who, in a series of essays throughout the 1980s, supplemented Barthes and Foucault and discussed between themselves the relevance – or not – of Barthes's and Foucault's work for feminism. Kamuf is the more approving and an astute exponent of the anti-identity position. She is suspicious of both categories, 'women' and 'women's writing': 'If the inaugural gesture of this feminist criticism is the reduction of the literary work to its signature and to the tautological assumption that a feminine "identity" is one which signs itself with a feminine name, then it will be able to produce only tautological statements of dubious value: women's writing is writing signed by women.'[21] Miller's equally telling argument wants to retain these categories. Metafictional play with the 'death of the Author' thesis will not necessarily do much to upset the social and legal status of the successful author; indeed, depending on the level of success, such self-consciousness can add considerably to the author's symbolic and economic capital. But for the underrepresented author, the thesis can work to invalidate her/his legitimacy at a time when it has been achieved only recently and tentatively and, even then, only within certain parts of the globe. One should not work for the 'death', goes this argument, when so many authors from our literary history and present have barely been 'born'.

The indispensable nature of the authorial 'I' is discovered by the author in Shields's short story, 'Absence', whose writing is fundamentally inhibited by the loss of the letter 'i' from her keyboard; however much she circumvents the problem, the 'i' demands to be reinstated.[22] The intransigence of the authorial 'I' becomes evident also to Léopold Sfax in Adair's *The Death of the Author* since Sfax actually survives his own death and is 'resurrected' – twice. The details of Sfax's life are closely modelled on those of Paul de Man and the revelations that provoked much heart-searching in the academic community. Both hide a collaborationist past and advocate a thorough deconstruction of authorship. The question of Adair's novel is: are these two facts connected? Sfax extends his undermining of the author to the point of complete ethical irresponsibility; if the signature has no authority it also has no accountability. In Sfax's case, the 'death' of the author signifies the eradication of responsibility for a series of murders, among which is the woman author who is intending to write his biography. The third text considered in this chapter, Atwood's *The Handmaid's Tale*, shows some of the consequences for the woman author if ethical and political needs are insufficiently recognised.[23] If the handmaid, Offred, had been able to authorise her own story she would not necessarily have been an authority but she might have been less vulnerable before the dubious interventions of Professor Pieixoto. Reading Offred and Pieixoto in the context of Barthes and Foucault somewhat surprisingly reveals Pieixoto, the academic, as theoretically more conservative than Offred, the abused handmaid. He is keen to maintain the position of 'the Author' since he can gain considerable status by discussing the lost author and being the authority on this anonymous text. But, crucially, Offred's more theoretically progressive response to authorship – her uncertain relation to her own position as an author, her questioning of the signature, literary form and the act of reading – is that of the amateur and springs from a lack of power rather than a deconstruction of power. Let us not be 'too confident that nondiscursive practices will respond correctly to the correct theory of discursive practices' is Miller's warning.[24] There is no neat correspondence to be had between good politics, good theory and an equitable distribution of power.

The texts that feature in Chapters 3 and 4 are discussed chiefly with respect to the making of the woman author, how she is created within the cultural field through the efforts of agents within publishing or the media or the art world or literary criticism as much as through her own efforts, and how her authorship may be constrained by certain historical conditions, facilitated by others. The major theoretical underpinning to these chapters comes from the materialist analysis of Pierre Bourdieu. Though Bourdieu has been concerned in his own work largely with male authors of the second half of the nineteenth century, his approach is equally applicable to female authors of the twentieth and twenty-first centuries.[25] He brings together in his work a number of strands: a macro dimension in mapping out large and complex cultural fields; a micro dimension in an understanding of the details and subtle shifts within fields; an analysis of 'the author' or 'the artist' not as a charismatic individual but as a relation between a position offered within the field and the necessary dispositions of the individual; and a vehement denunciation of the violence of aesthetic categories which sanction various forms of social exclusion and cultural impoverishment. In the short stories by Alice Walker and Antonia Byatt in Chapter 3, three women artists, Mama and Maggie in Walker's 'Everyday Use' and Mrs Brown in Byatt's 'Art Work', are on the verge of being authorised, culturally sanctioned. This is remarkable since in terms of gender, race and, particularly, class, they are unlikely candidates. Their social positions have denied them the cultural experience, the capitals and competencies usually associated with authorship. But they are also possible candidates since cultural fields are constantly shifting, the commercial interest looks always for innovation, and women, black or working-class people can suddenly become marketable.

These stories teeter at a point of cultural change where the benefits and debits are unknown. Nobody in these stories, not least Mama, Maggie and Mrs Brown, can look upon the women unequivocally as 'artists'. It is, precisely, the production and the validation of this position that is in dispute. Equally nobody is sure that what the women create is 'art'. Not only does it border on 'craft', it also eludes distinctions between dominant and popular aesthetics in terms of both form and function. Finally, it is difficult to authorise what Mama and Maggie and Mrs Brown produce because both they and their work are uncertainly located. They have had no experience of the institutions of art production – art schools, galleries and museums – although now, with changes in the art market, galleries and museums look interested in consecrating their work. At the same time, the location they do know, the domestic, is being re-evaluated as a space for cultural production and is being integrated into both a 'high' and a commercial aesthetics. Mrs Brown sees potential in this flux. The changes could indicate a democratising of the cultural field; this might be the moment when she can claim an authority she has never known before. But Mama is wary. The reinterpretation of her and Maggie's quilting as an art form would, in some ways, dignify it and aestheticise it but it would also locate it within a different set of values and a different economy. I return to this figure of the reluctant woman author in Chapter 8.

The paired texts in Chapter 4, Shields's *Mary Swann* and Spark's *Loitering with Intent*, are concerned with the establishment of the woman author at a specific historical moment and both employ the lost text as a key trope. Finding, owning and controlling the texts are, it seems, intrinsic to establishing one's position as 'Author' or, even, 'author'. In Shields's novel, loss and absence take a number of forms, most strikingly in the insubstantiality of Mary Swann's life and the disputed authorship of her poetry, but common to both texts is the significance of loss as theft. In *Loitering with Intent*, Fleur Talbot's novel is stolen but retrieved by the author; in *Mary Swann* the entire literary production and associated memorabilia of the poet, Mary Swann, disappears. The chapter considers how Foucault's understanding of the author-function and Bourdieu's analysis of both *habitus* and the workings of the literary field can explain the construction of the author and the fiercely competitive behaviour of the critics attending the first Mary Swann conference. Forms of capital are at stake, economic, cultural and symbolic, and all the critics are aware, as Pieixoto is with respect to Offred, how warmly they may bask in reflected glory if they establish the distinction of *their* author and their position as 'Critic'. Mary Swann's position is much less secure. When the dispositions and the material conditions of the puta-tive author are so removed from what we conventionally associate with 'the Author', when the life and texts of the author are so nebulous, when the actions of the literary field are so questionable if not disreputable, what does one eventually find – the figure of the lost woman author or a game of smoke and mirrors? As in *The Handmaid's Tale*, it is in the haunting trace of the woman author that loss is at its most poignant.

Fleur Talbot in *Loitering with Intent* is nobody's victim. In face of the loss or theft of her work, Fleur is in no doubt that the author needs a secure place in the literary field and a strong measure of authorial control; her production of the text cannot conform to the strictures of others and her ownership must be assured. But, alongside this, Fleur as author is playful, unpredictable, non-realist, refuses to explain and dances with the devil as often as the angels. Spark recognises the post-war literary field in which Fleur struggles to get a start but, ultimately, Fleur's making as an author is a self-making and in creating herself she mocks moder-nity and rejects a socially conscious authorship or any identification as 'a woman author'. The literary field she aspires to is male-dominated, the constructions of femininity she sees around her are unattractive to her and she has no interest in positioning herself within a female liter-ary tradition. It is fruitful here, I suggest, to compare Fleur's position on authorship (and Spark's since the two are difficult to separate at this point) with Virginia Woolf. In common is a stylistic lightness of touch, a caution about easy identifications with others, a position of critical disengagement and a devastating use of satire and ridicule. But, unlike Woolf, Fleur cannot ally herself with the figure of the woman author since, in the first place, such a move could associate her with a position of victimhood or with propagandising, both of which Fleur trenchantly resists and, second, it demands a view of history as, in Raymond Williams's words, 'a long revolution'.[26] Fleur's success as she describes it is as 'a woman' and 'an artist', not as 'a woman artist'. It is more localised, the product of individual initiative within small, well-placed, class-based networks, at a specific historical moment.

In Chapters 5, 6 and 7, I discuss three particular materialisations of the figure of the woman author – the oral narrator, the academic author and the writer of romantic fiction. In each case the figure of the woman author acts, in part, as a catalyst for problems of textuality and 'literari-ness'. The women narrators in Chapter 5 are in hazardous positions: Susan Barton, in Coetzee's *Foe*, an imagined prequel to Daniel Defoe's

Robinson Crusoe, is penniless and homeless in London, trying to sell her story of life as a castaway; Dessa Rose in Williams's novel has escaped from prison and is on the run with other members of a slave coffle; Grace Marks in Atwood's *Alias Grace* is in prison for murder.[27] The texts raise fundamental questions about narrative. First, should these women's stories ever be told since, however carefully they are narrated or sympathetically received by some, they will expose the women to dangerously unsympathetic attention from others? Second, can the stories be told? Susan in *Foe* is defeated not merely by the greater cultural power of the male author, Cruso, but by the demands of the market for a certain kind of narrative and, most particularly, by the disturbing silence of the slave, Friday. If, as Salman Rushdie has remarked, 'all stories are haunted by the ghosts of the stories they might have been', some of those ghosts can, it appears, disable the dominant narratives.[28] Third, who should author the tale? In each of the texts, the move from oral narration to possible written format entails a shift from female to male author and a battle about ownership, access to the public sphere and the authenticity of the story. This is expressed in part through disputes about form and the respective merits of oral versus written narratives, or personal testimony versus scientific enquiry or factual account versus fiction.

Dessa Rose and *Alias Grace* offer examples of what I referred to earlier as the subversive undermining of male authorial power. In both texts the male author watches, listens to and makes notes on the female narrator. The seeing and hearing are about knowing, interpreting, exerting control but they are also, it is revealed, about an inability to do this effectively; the men can see and hear only what conforms to their world-view. The subaltern woman, on the other hand, *has* to see and hear outside her own perspective so as to protect herself from an abusive power. She learns how to understand others, how she might be constructed by others and, hence, how best to employ her own looks and words. The defensive strategies are present also in the women's reactions to the scene of writing itself. Applying Claude Lévi-Strauss's comments on 'A Writing Lesson' and Jacques Derrida's response in *Of Grammatology*, we can read Dessa Rose and Grace as neither ignorant of writing nor corrupted by it but, rather, perceptive in their use of it.[29] On the other hand, Susan in *Foe* is unable to take the high moral ground and unable, ultimately, to suit writing to her own purposes. The relations between the white woman and the black man in *Foe* and the black woman and the white woman in *Dessa Rose* are, as we shall see, complex relations of 'asymmetry' and 'reciprocity', to use terms discussed by Gayatri

Chakravorty Spivak, David Attwell and Iris Marion Young.[30] What is possible and impossible in terms of sustaining relationships illustrates how distributions of power with respect to authorship are just as tortuous within the margins as between margin and centre.

In Chapter 6, the author in question is the academic woman author. Elaine Showalter has claimed that this figure, in the guise specifically of the feminist literary critic, is the most likely heroine in 'the New British Woman novel' of the 1990s.[31] Showalter's remark harks back to the New Woman novels of the 1890s and the historical reference gives some sense of the kind of disruption this figure embodies. She brings the challenge of her own femininity into traditional academic communities; she might unsettle the orthodoxies in which other characters and, often, the author her/himself were educated; she sometimes brings the challenge of feminism and, in a text consciously written within that context, she will be the focus for debates within the discourse. Certainly in campus novels it is almost *de rigueur* to include a feminist professor to wage war in the battle of the theories. She has also adapted well to detective fiction. The hunting for clues, the assembling of evidence, the present-ing of a clear case are skills common to both the researcher and the detective. As Maud Bailey, literary sleuth as well as literary critic, says, '[l]iterary critics make natural detectives' (237).

The academic woman author offers a twin provocation in both her authorship and her intellectualism. For the author figures discussed in this chapter, there is a further dilemma in trying to reconcile their intel-lectualism, their femininity and, in some cases, their feminism. The problems of the professional woman, which the women psychoanalysts described in the 1930s, are still being lived through, it seems, at the turn of the millennium. These women authors have varying degrees of affin-ity to feminism. Maud Bailey or Robyn Penrose, the literary critic in David Lodge's *Nice Work*, or Polly Alter, the art biographer in Lurie's *The Truth about Lorin* Jones, are emphatic in their commitment; Vinnie Miner in Lurie's *Foreign Affairs*, Beatrice Nest in *Possession* and Janet Mandelbaum in Amanda Cross's *Death in a Tenured Position* are, by turns, indifferent or apprehensive or trenchantly opposed.[32] But all are affected by a culture in which the academic woman author will be positioned with relation to feminism whether she likes it or not. As Janet Mandelbaum discovers, if you do not find feminism, feminism will still find you. The chapter examines in two ways this impossible conjunction for the academic woman author between intellectualism, femininity and feminism: first, by considering Michèle Le Dœuff's concept of 'eroticotheoretical transference', an unconscious strategy on the part of the academic woman to ease the relation between intellectualism and femininity by revering the intellectual master; and, second, through an examination of the intellectual work of Maud Bailey and her colleagues and how Byatt engages 'the literary', in terms of literary theory and literary form, as a way of providing a tentative resolution.[33]

Maud, steeped in high theory, finds it difficult to bring romance into her life but, unexpectedly, so too do the authors of romantic fiction we see in Chapter 7, Edith Hope in Brookner's *Hotel du Lac*, Mary Fisher in Fay Weldon's *The Life and Loves of a She Devil* and Joan Foster in Atwood's *Lady Oracle*.[34] Though commonly dismissed as purveyors of 'trash', these authors also turn to culture and matters of textuality, to language, narrative, signification and myth, as ways of trying to give expression to love and the elusiveness of the object of desire, and as ways of understanding their own positions as authors of romantic fiction. Desire and textuality are intrinsically related. As Sue Vice says, 'Desire is always already textual; and expecting to be satisfied is like expecting to reach the signified at the end of a chain of signifiers in a text. Thus unrequited – or unrequitable – love is desire's most authentic expression.'[35] And the grip of desire is tenacious. These romantic fiction authors question the legitimacy of romantic discourse and their own role as authors while remaining entranced by the form.

Catherine Belsey's argument, discussed in this chapter, concerning the inadequacy of the language of love suggests another aspect of textuality and poses a real problem for the authors of romantic fiction.[36] The language is always derivative, hackneyed, inauthentic. In face of this, Edith, the most honourable of our authors, is driven to silence, Mary cynically plays with the clichés of romance and then becomes a victim of them, while Joan relishes the language and conventions with little thought for value or discrimination and, thus, with disastrous consequences for herself. The authors are aware of both romance and their own roles as authors of romance as constructed amidst a range of cultural narratives and signs. Hence, Edith is as knowledgeable about canonical literature as she is about romantic fiction and she is sustained by Aesop's fable of the tortoise and the hare while Joan is alarmingly susceptible to every cultural image and narrative and ricochets between roles which she dramatically performs. The proliferation of signs in Joan's world throws into unexpected relation numerous narratives of romance and numerous figures of the author, none of whom could be designated 'Author' with a capital 'A'. A recent study by psychologists in Ohio, picked up by the popular press in the United Kingdom, criticised romantic fiction for encouraging unsafe sex and the spread of sexually transmitted diseases. Joan Foster could have told them that this is woefully beside the point. The romantic fiction author in the form of Joan, or even the eminently respectable Edith Hope, is propelled by unconscious forces and is immune to rational argument. Mary Fisher's nemesis, the wronged wife Ruth, certainly knows this. She has the opportunity to make herself as an author of romantic fiction but deliberately refuses that role. To be an author of romance, she believes, is not to promote 'hope' but lies. Her response is, again, textual. She re-fashions herself through a process of judicious selection amongst cultural myths and literary forms of power, autonomy and self-creation.

The dominant narrative of feminist cultural criticism has concerned women gaining access to the cultural sphere, being seen and heard and establishing some level of cultural authority. But the fiction has told an interesting counter narrative – a reluctance about authorship because of a combination of indifference to the dominant order of production and circulation and a fear that for women there is little to profit and much to lose. There is an irony in the frequency with which real authors, most of them female, create fictional women characters who, with some difficulty, become authors but, then, keep asking the question, 'Do I want to be here?'. Some, such as Mama in Alice Walker's 'Everday Use', come to the conclusion that rejection is the best policy; others, such as Mrs Brown in 'Art Work' or Dessa Rose, take a chance on a carefully orchestrated *entrée* into public culture. These women cannot conceive of themselves as 'Authors' in the Barthesian sense, are hesitant about thinking of themselves even as 'authors' and, depending on their circumstances, view the cultural field as a place of either threat or absurd pretension. In Chapter 8, I focus on this authorial reluctance. Annie, the author heroine in Jane Gardam's 'The Sidmouth Letters' is highly conscious of women's exposure in the literary market and the ease with which they can be exploited and, thus, destroys some recently discovered letters of Jane Austen even though they could have contributed greatly to her own literary and financial status.[37] The woman author in Ursula Le Guin's short story, 'Sur', fears that publishing her account of the discovery of the South Pole by herself and a group of South American ladies years before Roald Amundsen would provoke scandal and, consequently, she keeps it in a trunk in the attic. Finally, in Michèle Roberts's, *The Looking Glass*, the female literary activity is varied and abundant but unrealised in terms of publication or, in some cases, in terms of writing itself.[38]

The chapter accounts for the women's reluctance to publish in two main ways. It considers the relevance of Joan Riviere's concept of the 'female masquerade'.[39] The narrator in 'Sur', for example, is fearful of retribution and wants to preserve the propriety of her middle-class life and the sense of superiority of her menfolk. But, more provocatively, she uses the masquerade in a way Riviere did not anticipate, as a façade behind which women's desires can find expression. Annie in 'The Sidmouth Letters' has a similar strategic awareness in her dealings with her ex-professor, Shorty Shenfold, who is planning to buy the Austen letters and use them for his own advancement. All three texts also relate to Hélène Cixous's understanding of 'a feminine economy' with respect to authorship and though the stories are, in some ways, structured around an opposition of masculine and feminine economies they show as well how each transaction, each act of giving or taking, has to be deconstructed in terms of motives and consequences, the kinds of profits produced and their dissemination.[40] The women tread a tricky line between, on the one hand, indifference to the dominant economy of profit, both monetary and symbolic, alongside a self-protective caution about becoming the victim of that economy; in so doing, they develop a skill in negotiating different economies. Like the women storytellers of Chapter 5 they recognise the politics involved in seeing, knowing and possessing.

In Michèle Roberts's *The Looking Glass*, there are many female writers and storytellers employing a wide diversity of literary forms and expressing a catalogue of critical positions on the production of writing, none of whom becomes 'the author' in the sense of being published and publicly recognised. Their absence can be explained materially in the context of the French literary field in the early years of the twentieth century and in the context, as we saw with the other texts, of their own reluctance, their attachment to other values and practices. But this does not explain why some of the women find not merely publishing but writing itself impossible. Here the novel invites a psychoanalytical reading in the struggle, expressed through the servant girl Geneviève, between the semiotic and the symbolic, the lost mother and the paternal order, the unspoken and 'the Word'. What this reluctance means to the politics of feminism is the question with which this chapter ends. In each of the texts, the withdrawal from the public sphere has cemented relations among the women, relations that are forged around secrecy, conspiracy and a sense of superiority over men. This is sustaining, one of the pleasures the subordinated enjoy, but does it link to what Nietzsche sees as a form of *ressentiment* which ultimately mires the slave in her/his oppression?[41] Is it the lesson that structural and ideological barriers, and personal reluctance have all to be overcome and that women have to take the risk of authorship?

2
Feminism and the Death of the Author

> Every six months or so, when the letter 'I' on my keyboard gets too sticky, I have a fit of the ab-dabs over what a waste of precious time I am and email all my union men/anti-globalisation girl compadres for facts and figures that might help take my mind off my everlasting self.
>
> Julie Burchill, *The Guardian*[1]

The woman author in Carol Shields's short story 'Absence' has a similar problem to Julie Burchill.[2] The letter 'i' on her keyboard is not merely sticky but actually broken. How can she write without the 'i'? Shields's story does not only narrate the problem, it enacts it; there is no letter 'i' in the course of the story. The first clue to this absence comes at the end of the opening paragraph when the narrator describes the letter rather than writing it: 'a vowel, the very letter that attaches to the hungry self' (108). This impediment in the process of writing leads the narrator to an exploration of the significance of 'i'. Its loss frustrates the rhythm of her writing; her grammar is affected, particularly in preventing the use of the gerund that the author finds so indispensable; her vocabulary is constrained; the very sound of her writing is altered. To this extent, the story is a light-hearted *jeu d'esprit* or a kind of writing exercise for budding authors. But the story pursues the problem further. It also suggests the political, philosophical and aesthetic problems concerning the centrality and significance of the writing subject, the signature and the authorial 'I'. It is at this point we move from the small 'i' to the capital 'I' that provokes Burchill and her 'everlasting self'. The question now for Shields's author is not how can she write without the 'i' but how can she write without the 'I', the authorial subject. At one point she thinks this is possible. She forgets her sense of self and '*became* the walls, and

15

also the clean roof overhead and the powerful black sky' (112) but immediately she recognises there is no escape – 'the words she actually set down came from the dark eye of her eye' (112); 'eye' is the best she can do to suggest the 'I' that cannot be evaded. And this 'I' is a gendered 'I'. The substitute for the pronoun 'I' in the final sentence of the story is a gendered noun: ' "A woman sat down and wrote," she wrote' (112). One could read the certainty of this comment as a riposte to Jorge Luis Borges's final sentence in 'Borges and I': 'I do not know which of us has written this page.'[3]

Other women authors have had problems with the letter 'I' and these problems are often framed by questions of gender. Famously, the narrator in Virginia Woolf's *A Room of One's Own* soon becomes bored with the 'I' of a male author she reads. His presence is 'a straight dark bar, a shadow shaped something like the letter "I" ' and lies oppressively across the page. The narrator realises how this authorial subject is obliterating a female figure we might interpret as the putative female author; she is so insubstantial, 'shapeless as mist', that she is unable to claim any 'I' at all.[4] For Maxine Hong Kingston, it was partly gender and partly cultural difference that made 'I' 'unsayable' for her as a schoolgirl and the adoption of an authorial 'I' so difficult. On the one hand, she confronts the Chinese word for the female 'I' which means 'slave' – 'Break the women with their own tongues!', comments Hong Kingston sardonically.[5] On the other hand, as with Woolf, the phallic associations of the erect 'I' render it alien and its ideographic appearance of all-American assurance is puzzling and intimidating to Hong Kingston:

> The Chinese 'I' has seven strokes, intricacies. How could the American 'I', assuredly wearing a hat like the Chinese, have only three strokes, the middle so straight? Was it out of politeness that this writer left off strokes the way a Chinese has to write her own name small and crooked? No, it was not politeness; 'I' is a capital and 'you' is lower-case. (150)

Thus the burden of these comments is sometimes in agreement, sometimes at odds with those of Roland Barthes in 'The Death of the Author' and of Michel Foucault in 'What Is an Author?'. Where these women writers would agree with Barthes and Foucault is in acknowledging the trickiness of the writing subject; there is no easy identification for the writing 'I', no innocent position to adopt. One way in which they would differ is in their common awareness of the play of gender. In each of the examples above an effective female authorial 'I' has to establish itself against male prescripts. Barthes, however, is able to withdraw from the figure of the author. 'Writing', he tells us is 'that neutral, composite, oblique space where our subject slips away, the negative where all identity is lost, starting with the very identity of the body writing'.[6] In the course of his essay the 'Author' is replaced with the 'scriptor', literature by 'writing' and that intensely personal material of 'passions, humours, feelings, impressions' by the impersonal quotations culled from the scriptor's 'immense dictionary' (147). A similar line of argument can be taken with Foucault. Just as Barthes begins his essay with the question 'Who is speaking thus?' (142) and finds this an impossible question to answer, so Foucault ends his essay with the question 'What difference does it make who is speaking?' and gives this suggestion all the impact of a concluding statement.[7]

This – in Foucault's word – 'indifference' to the author has been immensely problematic for feminism. If we accept the loss of 'the very identity of the body writing' then certain conclusions follow: the name and gender of the author become irrelevant; the fact that all the authors mentioned by Barthes are male and that only three of the more than forty authors mentioned by Foucault are female is inconsequential; and the preoccupation of literary feminists to find lost women authors and to focus on women's literary production has been misplaced. Following Barthes and Foucault during the 1980s, the period in which these essays had a major impact within the Anglophone academy, seemed tantamount to pressing the self-destruct button for literary feminism based on a recognition of the category of 'women's writing', or for any feminist endeavour based on the category of 'women'. How could feminism take heed of the insights of post-structuralism and postmodernism without jettisoning its political project? A series of essays published by Peggy Kamuf and Nancy Miller during that period engages with this difficulty. They pursue the points made by Barthes and Foucault concerning the significance of the signature and the author's identity but, unlike Barthes and Foucault, they relate those points to the project of feminism.[8] In 'The Text's Heroine: A Feminist Critic and Her Fictions', Miller trenchantly responds to Foucault's concluding question:

> This sovereign indifference, I would argue, is one of the 'masks ... behind which phallocentrism hides its fictions'; the authorizing function of its own discourse authorizes the 'end of woman' without consulting her.[9]

The comment constitutes a reply also to Kamuf whom Miller quotes – in fact, slightly misquotes – in the above. What Kamuf actually writes is:

> If ... by 'feminist' one understands a way of reading texts that points to the masks of truth with which phallocentrism hides its fictions, then one place to begin such a reading is by looking behind the mask of the proper name, the sign that secures our patriarchal heritage: the father's name and the index of sexual identity.[10]

Clearly, Kamuf feels she *has* been consulted on this issue and that an indifference to the female signature has feminist potential.

In a later essay, 'Changing the Subject: Authorship, Writing, and the Reader', Miller situates her remarks in response to the writing of Barthes, most notably 'The Death of the Author'. Miller questions 'stories of textuality which trade in universals – the Author or the Reader' and insists that our analysis of the authorial subject should be 'recomplicated by the historical, political, and figurative body of the woman writer'. To do so, Miller believes, will move us away from a 'metaphysics of reading' to 'reading as a politics'.[11] The central passage in her argument, much quoted subsequently, is as follows:

> The postmodernist decision that the Author is Dead and the subject along with him does not, I will argue, necessarily hold for women, and prematurely forecloses the question of agency for them. Because women have not had the same historical relation of identity to origin, institution, production that men have had, they have not, I think, (collectively) felt burdened by *too much* Self, Ego, Cogito, etc. Because the female subject has juridically been excluded from the polis, hence decentered, 'disoriginated', deinstitutionalized etc., her relation to integrity and textuality, desire and authority, displays structurally important differences from that universal position.[12]

Unlike Kamuf, Miller wants to retain the signature and to focus on the ways in which it has operated historically. Miller's view is that discussions about the death of the Author have to be gendered and particularised. The struggle of women in Western culture to gain access to literary production and women's relation to authority, both legal and textual, have been so distinct as to make impossible their straightforward inclusion in the concept of 'Author'. This is a generic concept which in a patriarchal society will always at root signify *male* author. Kamuf sees in the notion of 'women's writing' or 'a female tradition' a tautological danger as 'women's writing' becomes merely any writing by women. For Miller, though, the political need for the visibility of the woman author remains uppermost. Far from being a move beyond authority, to dispense with the figure and signature of the woman author is itself an act of high-handedness. Miller speaks as 'one who believes that "we women" must continue to work for the woman who has been writing, because not to do so will reauthorize our oblivion'.[13] While for Kamuf it is vital to reject an emphasis on the proper name, the mark of sexual identity, a 'common sense' view of authorship as tokens of the order feminists wish to overthrow, Miller presents such a move as dangerous and precipitate.

When in 1988 Miller collected her essays in *Subject to Change: Reading Feminist Writing*, she commented somewhat regretfully on the dialogue with Kamuf and noted how it had perpetuated an unhelpfully schematic and antagonistic relation, what she called 'the current sclerosis of "French/American" positions'.[14] Despite Miller's hope that such opposition could be confined to its historical moment, the 1990s brought little relief: Anglo-American versus French, humanist versus post-structuralist, metaphysical versus political, sociological versus poetic remained the dominant structure of many debates. For feminism, continuing to steer a perilous route between the Scylla of post-structuralism, postmodernism, anti-essentialism and the Charybdis of humanism, Enlightened modernity, identity politics, the meaning and role of the author was often a point of contact and conflict. Reina Lewis, for example, discusses a personal illustration of the problem when she recounts being asked by the editor of her chapter to 'adopt an experiential tone' and to write in a way with which the reader could identify while the content of her chapter critiques just such an identification.[15] At the end of the 1990s, Toril Moi looked back with wonder on the post-structuralist argument that the positing of a coherent self and a gendered identity as 'woman' or 'man' was somehow politically abhorrent and ineffective: 'these are puzzling claims, since the whole liberal tradition and indeed the Marxist humanist tradition, with their antediluvian views on individual agency, freedom, and choice, were quite capable of fighting racism, sexism, and capitalism before poststructuralism came along'.[16] And not surprisingly the creative writer, as much as the critic, continues to have an interest in 'the very identity of the body writing'. In what follows in this chapter, two figurings of the author are to the fore both of which turn on issues of identity, namely the author as ethically responsible and the continuing need for the author to retain a representative identity as, in this case, 'the woman author'. The two interconnect since, as we shall see, an absence of ethics by one author can lead to the loss of identity, both corporeal and cultural, for another. The 'death of the Author' becomes embroiled in the death of the author.

The life or 'the Life': death or 'Death'

The conceptual death of the authorial 'I' is often revisited when the real death of the author takes place. In 1992, Lorna Sage wrote about the death that year of her friend, Angela Carter. The piece, entitled 'Death of the Author', makes explicit reference to Barthes's essay. 'Writers' lives merely distract us from the true slipperiness and anonymity of any text worth its salt', says Sage. 'A text is a text is a text. Angela, of course, was of the generation nourished on the Death of the Author (Barthes, 1968 vintage), as was I.'[17] Sage is aware, as she says these words, that she is quoting a party line that has already been challenged. She affirms: 'for the first time I see there's at least one virtue in literary biography: a "Life" can demythologize the work in the best sense, preserving its fallibility, which is also the condition for its brilliance' (235). She now understands Carter's Barthesian- and Foucaudian-influenced impersonality, a rejection of any autobiographical or confessional writing, as 'entirely personal at base – a refusal to be placed or characterized or *saved* from oneself' (254). Nine years later Sage herself died prematurely and, in the tributes that followed, the problem of the relation between the life and the work was again reassessed. Marina Warner in her introduction to Sage's posthumously published collection of essays, *Moments of Truth*, refers to Sage's piece on Carter, to the importance of Barthes's 'Death of the Author' and to the developing interest in life-writing in the 1990s including Sage's memoir of her girlhood, *Bad Blood*, which was published, to great acclaim, just before her death. Warner concludes that the argument throughout Sage's *Moments of Truth* is that 'you can't have the work without the life or, more pointedly, the life without the work, nor the work or the life without the art'.[18]

Thus, under the impact of physical death, Barthes's claims are re-evaluated. Rather than the person or life of the author functioning 'to impose a limit on that text, to furnish it with a final signified, to close the writing' (147), it can, argues Sage, open new insights into the text; rather than 'the personal' being a narcissistic preoccupation with, to return to Burchill, an 'everlasting self', it can be the impetus in forming a mode of impersonality; rather than the work or the art relegating the life, each might be enmeshed in the other. Sage believes that the death of the author allows the reader to read the work 'backwards, sideways, whatever because now it's an *oeuvre*, truly finished' (235). Thus, death is both the 'final signified' – there will be no new work from this author – and the event that permits the most open and flexible reading. With the finality is also, of course, the loss. The work left without the author is not the same as the work with the author. The death brings to the fore the sense of the person, who s/he was and the essential features of the author are confirmed in the obituaries or pieces written shortly after death. Paradoxically, in the corporeal death we always have the strongest sense of the life while the metaphorical death of the author is unable to escape from a sense of the insistent presence of the author.

Much more sensationally, the death of Paul de Man in 1983 and the revelation of his writings in the collaborationist Belgian newspaper *Le Soir* revived discussion of the ethical consequences of the conceptual death of the author. One function of the signature is to ensure the author's accountability; the 'death' of the author, in this sense, might be merely an evasion of responsibility.[19] John Banville talks of a 'welter of personal, impersonal, impersonating pronouns'.[20] It is when we move into the area of the 'impersonating' and the pretence of an ethical 'I' that problems ensue. Such a situation is explored in Gilbert Adair's *The Death of the Author*.[21] The biography of his hero, Leo Sfax, is closely reminiscent of Paul de Man's: Leo is born in 1918, de Man in 1919; Leo writes for the collaborationist *Je suis partout* between 1941 and 1943 (though the dates, like most things about Leo, are a little uncertain) just as de Man writes his articles between 1940 and 1942; Leo writes under the pseudonym Hermes and it is the password that he gives to a computer file that eventually reveals his murderous actions while de Man set up a publishing house called Édition Hèrmes after the war; Leo's family tries to escape to Spain as did de Man and his wife; Leo emigrates to the States in 1949, de Man in 1948; Leo becomes an eminent theoretician and essayist, based at New Harbor, de Man had a similarly renowned career at Yale (New Haven); both are brought low by the activities of a research student.[22] Other aspects of Adair's creation link him with Nabokov, Derrida, Baudrillard and, in the title and Sfax's own grossly self-serving version of the 'death of the Author' thesis, with Barthes.

Sfax is torn between publication, fame and the resulting revelation which would certainly mean the 'death' of the celebrated author he is impersonating, and a self-protective retreat. His mad stratagem is to publish *The Vicious Spiral*. This, he knows, would hasten the revelation of himself as the author Hermes, the Nazi collaborator but, through a devilishly clever deconstructive turn in its argument, Sfax thinks it would also exonerate him of all responsibility. Consequently, in his critical essays, he writes of the absence of the author, the uselessness of a biographical or situated view of the author, the disconnection between texts and any 'real' world, the insistence with which the text undermines what it appears to be saying and the *aporia* that confronts any attempt to decipher meaning. Such a theory, Sfax believes, would irrefutably ensure that Hermes had no existence, had produced no texts of any meaning, with no relevance to the real world and betraying no support for a Nazi ideology. How then could Leo Sfax bear any responsibility? Quoting Christopher Norris's list of possible responses to the discovery of de Man's wartime writings, Seán Burke adds: 'There is at least one more form of possible response, that of a radical anti-authorialism which would affirm that "Paul de Man" signifies nothing, and that consequently there is no oeuvre. To the best of my knowledge, however – and for all the theoretical insistence on the death of the author – no-one has risked this particular line of argument.'[23] But this *is* Sfax's line: there is no Hermes so there are no texts and, even if there were, they would be either indecipherable or meaning the opposite of what they said.

The woman author, Astrid Hunneker, is both the nemesis and the victim in Sfax's deluded world. She comes to Sfax as a research student with a feminist thesis on Wilkie Collins and the omniscient author; unfortunately for Sfax, she must, therefore, be interested in both detecting and knowing all. Soon enraptured by Sfax she embraces 'the Theory', publishes her thesis with a feminist publisher – dismissed by Sfax as 'limp and sandpapery booklettes' (40) – and then embarks, much to Sfax's horror, on his biography with an advance from a major New York publisher to make it possible. Sfax knows that all will be revealed through Astrid's detecting: like the troublesome women of a Wilkie Collins's novel, Astrid has to be silenced. The death of this woman author is at once real and theoretically audacious. If the living presence bears no relation to the conceptual absence of the author, why should not the converse apply and the absence of a motive disguise the presence of a motive? Thus Sfax commits the motiveless crime of bludgeoning to death with a bust of Shakespeare his lovable colleague, Gillingwater, to hide the 'motiveful' murder of Astrid whom he bludgeons to death with his own bust that she had been modelling: 'I couldn't entrust my head to her', says Sfax (5, 45, 99). 'Head' signifies the incriminating memories and records of events that would be revealed in the biography, while we could read the sculptured head as another example of the inanimate 'author' annihilating the living author. Astrid's boyfriend, Ralph, uncovers the crimes and then carries out a further death of an author by shooting Sfax and making it appear as suicide. At the same time, Ralph ensures that Sfax's true history and crimes are revealed on his computer.

De Man describes the dominant figure of the epitaphic or autobiographical discourse – and Sfax's first-person narration of his life and death fits both these categories – as 'the prosopopeia, the fiction of the voice-from-beyond-the-grave'.[24] This is given a literal twist in Adair's text when Sfax continues writing as the trigger is pulled and then beyond his death to reveal the apprehension of Ralph, exposed because he could not adequately pastiche Sfax's style in his suicide note, and the ongoing critical debates about his own life and work. Much against his own theories, it seems that Sfax has become an omniscient author, knowing and seeing everything. Sfax had once before seen himself 'die' and yet continue to live. As a child he had watched his grandfather's coffin buried with their common name, Léopold Sfax, engraved on the coffin lid. Why should not this death also be followed by a resurrection? At last he discovers the truth of de Man's dictum, that 'death *is* merely the displaced name for a linguistic predicament' (135). On the final page of the book, as Sfax again dies, so the words diminish and fade. In 'Autobiography as De-Facement', de Man looks at the etymology of prosopopoeia and links voice and face: '*prosopon poien*, to confer a mask or a face (*prosopon*)'. The word 'face' then suggests 'deface, *figure*, figuration and disfiguration' (76). Sfax's Machiavellian tricks indicate another range of meanings, the mask as an active deception, 'face' as 'two-faced' or, as Banville indicates, the impersonating pronoun.

Offred and theories of authorship

Margaret Atwood's *The Handmaid's Tale* similarly puts ethical questions to the fore and, again, it is the Professor who is the most ethically suspect. At the end of the novel, Professor Pieixoto lectures on *The Handmaid's Tale* and the determination with which he and his colleague, Professor Wade, have appropriated the story of the desperate handmaiden, Offred, is revealed.[25] The novel also raises Miller's question about the political importance of maintaining 'the woman author' as an identifiable figure. Considering authorship from Offred's perspective suggests that the identity of the author *is* relevant and that the loss of a female signature is a loss of power for women; it reminds us of the significance of the woman author as a material presence and not only, *à la* Foucault – or Sfax – as an impersonalised function; it indicates that the female author's relation to authority is structurally different from the male's and that the controlling authorial position, on which Barthes and Foucault focus, has rarely been the position of the woman author. In short, the text affirms that for the female author the problem may not be the need for 'death' but the fact that she has barely lived and, thus, the critic should not help with her euthanasia.

We could turn again to the debate between Miller and Kamuf to consider the importance – or not – of the signature for Offred. How would the questions posed by Barthes, 'Who is speaking thus?', and by Foucault, 'What difference does it make who is speaking?' relate to Offred? Kamuf agrees with Foucault in arguing for a position of 'indifference' to the signature of the author. In her essay on the problematic authorship of the *Portuguese Letters*, Kamuf writes against the critical work of Leo Spitzer and his attempts to name the author. She rejects Spitzer's attempt 'to give this text a father, some "deliberate" poet ... who can confer with his name and his art a legitimacy on these unsigned letters'.[26] For Kamuf the uncertainty surrounding the text's authorship allows her to move away from the tyranny of authorship and any *ad hominem* or *ad feminam* arguments. Even if the *Portuguese Letters* had turned out to be written by a real Portuguese nun, to name the author of the text is still, in Kamuf's terms, to 'contain an unlimited textual system, install a measure of protection between this boundlessness and one's own power to know, to be this power and to know that one is this power' (297). Conversely, Miller, concerned with the woman author's specific historical and political position and her relation to authority and the signature, would want to find the author and name her. In her view the need is not for '*in*difference' but for a finer sense of 'difference'. It is not that the name of the author determines the text but, equally, it is not that the name of the author is irrelevant to the text.

Kamuf's objection to the proper name as 'the sign that secures our patriarchal heritage: the father's name and the index of sexual identity' is supported most clearly in *The Handmaid's Tale* in the crude naming of the handmaids – Offred, belonging to Fred, the sexual chattel of Fred and similarly Ofglen, Ofwarren (286). But Offred's own response to the signature is neither indifference nor a desire for anonymity. In her distress at being unnamed, Offred tries to convince herself that names do not matter but concludes that, in fact, they do:

> My name isn't Offred, I have another name, which nobody uses now because it's forbidden. I tell myself it doesn't matter, your name is like your telephone number, useful only to others; but what I tell myself is wrong, it does matter. I keep the knowledge of this name like something hidden, some treasure I'll come back to dig up, one day. I think of this name as buried. This name has an aura around it, like an amulet, some charm that's survived from an unimaginably distant

past. I lie in my single bed at night, with my eyes closed, and the name floats there behind my eyes, not quite within reach, shining in the dark. (94)

Kamuf's understanding of the signature as systematising and codifying, as something which corrals the text is far removed from the doubting, reluctant and troubled authorship of Offred. The sense of magic which Offred finds in her name is not like that which surrounds 'Shakespeare' or any canonical author. Though her earlier name was doubtless also marked by the father, Offred has to hold onto her name as part of a hopeless, existential struggle to retain some semblance of an enabling subjecthood. She speaks her name in the reckless intimacy with Nick – 'I tell him my real name, and feel that therefore I am known' – and it is embedded in the text for future attentive listeners/readers to discern (282 and 14). In a similar way, Janine is brought back to a tenuous stability by Moira's insistence on a name and an identity: 'Look at me. My name is Moira and this is the Red Centre. Look at me' (228). Both Offred and Moira are conscious of the vulnerability and, yet, the necessity of these gestures.[27]

Like Miller, Offred wants also to particularise the reader. She must construct in her listener/reader a living identity for the people she has lost:

> By telling you anything at all I'm at least believing in you, I believe you're there, I believe you into being. Because I'm telling you this story I will your existence. I tell, therefore you are. (279)

In devising for Moira a narrative voice she recreates her: 'I've tried to make it sound as much like her as I can. It's a way of keeping her alive' (256). Offred is willing to accept the author and reader as constructed but not as mere linguistic effects. For Barthes the reader is a 'space on which all the quotations which make up a writing are inscribed' (148). For Offred with her urgent need for contact the reader must be a pre-cisely realised presence. While Barthes appears to deny the reader an identity only to fill the 'space' immediately with a male, generic subject – 'the reader is without history, biography, psychology; he is simply that *someone* who holds together in a single field all the traces by which the written text is constituted' (148) – Offred and the handmaids con-sciously seek out female readers and find their own clandestine modes of communication. The pig-Latin of the previous handmaid, '*nolite te bastardes carborundorum*', becomes for Offred a 'taboo message (which) made it through, to at least one other person' (62) and then later, more despondently and impenetrably, 'a code in Braille' and 'an ancient hieroglyph to which the key's been lost' (156). Offred repeats the message to herself, traces her fingers over the words, visualises the author. The graffitti in the toilets at the 'Rachel and Lea Re-education Center' and the shared 'whispering of obscenities' (234), the cushion embroidered with the single word, 'FAITH', the decoding of 'Mayday', the abbreviated conversations, 'like a telegram, a verbal semaphore. Amputated speech' (211) – all these are examples of clandestine acts of specifically female authorship and readership. The ending offers the possibility that Offred makes her escape from one safe house to another. Prefiguring that move, the telling and hearing of stories and information function as a kind of escape 'in the form of one voice to another' (144). Offred becomes part of a chain of authors and readers, a chain of links and resistance.

Offred's view of authorship is at odds with most of Barthes and Foucault's propositions. She would not want to claim or look forward to 'the death of the Author' – a phrase which would have only a terrible literal meaning for her; she could not see authorship as a cultural function separate from a personal need for survival; she has not the social and academic power to adopt a smooth, self-assured authorial command – the 'Author', as Barthes indicates, with an upper-case 'A'; she would not want to mythologise a role which carries for her a concrete immediacy. The 'virtuous' authors for Barthes – Mallarmé, Valéry, Proust, Flaubert, Brecht – are those who contribute to the 'desacrilization of the image of the Author' and, thus, make way for their own demise, transform the Author-God into the subject of enunciation (144). Having never enjoyed or aspired to such status this deconstruction is irrelevant to Offred.

Her ambiguous relation to authorship reveals itself both in her unwillingness to become an author – at different moments she owns and disowns the story she is telling – and in her uncertainty about the mode of writing she is producing. Offred is not sure whether she is the author of fiction or of history or of autobiography. At times she maintains a demarcation between fiction and history and places her experience in the realm of 'fiction'. Remembering how her daughter had been taken away from her, she comments:

> I would like to believe this is a story I'm telling. I need to believe it. I must believe it. Those who can believe that such stories are only stories have a better chance.
>
> If it's a story I'm telling, then I have control over the ending. Then there will be an ending, to the story, and real life will come after it. I can pick up where I left off. (49)

Later, thinking of a film she had seen as a child of the Nazi concentration camps, she remarks: 'I thought someone had made it up. I suppose all children think that about any history before their own. If it's only a story, it becomes less frightening' (154). To inhabit the house of fiction gives Offred the possibility of a control absent in her life. She tries to use fiction defensively and opportunistically. If it's 'only a story' you can dismiss the knowledge you cannot bear to hear. A too painful story can be stopped and other stories interposed: 'Here is a different story, a better one. This is the story of what happened to Moira' (138). Stories have a short time-span and the author decides the ending, possibly a happy one; if not happy, 'normal' life can still be resumed as soon as possible. Varied versions of a story can be rehearsed – for example, Offred's creation of three narratives for Luke – so that whatever happens, the author will have anticipated and have been prepared. Consequently, Offred deliberately uses the concept of 'fiction' as a protection, a bulwark against the invasion of material reality and an engulfment by her own defencelessness. Scheherazade told stories to keep herself alive; Offred tells stories to keep herself sane.

At other times Offred is recalled to history and the story becomes a testimony in which she will have to recount her own sad experience, her complicity and of which she is a witness and an unwilling transmitter: 'I don't want to be telling this story', she says on more than one occasion (237, 285 and a similar sentence on 60). In that strategy common to dystopian writing and historiographic metafiction, the distinction between fiction and history becomes confused. Offred believes she has to hold fast to an historical memory and to keep it distinct from fiction. Yet, despite this, she feels the temptation to divest herself of her obligations, to lose herself in the security of the father – for instance, in the form of the blandishments of the TV news commentator: 'I sway towards him, like one hypnotized. If only it were true. If only I could believe' (93). Or Offred might try to distance herself temporarily from both the story and the history to inhabit a fragile marginal space:

> We were the people who were not in the papers. We lived in the blank white spaces at the edges of print. It gave us more freedom. We lived in the gaps between the stories. (66–7)

At these moments, for the woman to be 'hidden from history' is not a problem of exclusion as feminism would usually judge but a welcome escape from a threatening involvement. Offred is unable either to enjoy the surety of authorial mastery or to reject the responsibilities of authorship. Unwillingly, she is forced into an authorial role which veers between political strategy, an ethical obligation to bear witness, and a personal psychological need.

Where Offred is in accord with Barthes and Foucault is in her questioning of the validity of the autobiographical voice and in her own self-conscious authorship, highly aware of narrative as constructed and of the contingency of her control. Offred recognises how the bifurcation of the 'I' who is telling and the 'I' who is told about opens up all manner of possibilities for omission, evasion, exaggeration, acts of convenient hindsight:

> It's impossible to say a thing exactly the way it was, because what you say can never be exact, you always have to leave something out, there are too many parts, sides, crosscurrents, nuances (144)

Sometimes she encourages the imagined reader to be suspicious about her confessional voice. She admits to some fictions, discovers some self-deceptions so there may be others. Chapter 23 begins with, 'This is a reconstruction. All of it is reconstruction' and ends with, 'That is a reconstruction too'. The account of her passionate meeting with Nick is interrupted with, 'I made that up. It didn't happen that way. Here is what happened' (273). The subsequent retelling ends with, 'It didn't happen that way either. I'm not sure how it happened, not exactly. All I can hope for is a reconstruction: the way love feels is always only approximate' (275). Where Offred's situation differs from Barthes's is on the question of power. While Barthes divests his 'Author' of power so as to democratise writing, Offred must try to claim power so as to assert a subjecthood capable of effective action and to write the history which the State of Gilead would like to eradicate. Miller's description earlier of the female subject as 'juridically ... excluded from the polis, hence decentered, "disoriginated", deinstitutionalized etc. (with the result that) her relation to integrity and textuality, desire and authority, displays structurally important differences from that universal position' is especially true of Offred as the female subject *in extremis* in a fundamentalist, patriarchal state.

At the end of 'What Is an Author?', Foucault rejects a number of familiar questions about this figure of the author:

> 'Who really spoke? Is it really he and not someone else? With what authenticity or originality? And what part of his deepest self did he express in his discourse?'

He turns instead to some new questions:

> 'What are the modes of existence of this discourse? Where has it been used, how can it circulate, and who can appropriate it for himself? What are the places in it where there is room for possible subjects? Who can assume these various subject-functions?' (160)

Which of these questions is relevant to ask of Offred and her story? Certainly the second set about the construction, utilisation and circulation of discourse is important. The question 'who can appropriate it for himself', elsewhere translated as 'Who controls it?', has, as we shall see, a particular resonance for Offred.[28] But can we afford to dispense with the first set of questions, those that look for the 'real' author? In putting these two sets in opposition, Foucault seems to be working on some dubious assumptions. For example, that the reader will want to take part in this either/or dichotomy: either you believe in the endless circulation and repositioning of discourse or you believe in the author as an originating source. Then again, he implies that if you have an interest in the person of the author, you must have accepted, unquestioningly, the view of the author as prime-mover and arch-controller and, equally, an idealist approach to creativity as the expression of either a deep, intuitive self or a universal, transcendent perception. Offred's authorship suggests that the importance of the second set of questions does not obliterate the need for the first or, indeed, for a whole series of less polarised, intermediary questioning. We end the book sad at the disappearance of Offred, not because we see her in any theological sense as the origin and source of meaning, not because we assess her as a creative genius or an individual of exceptional insight, not because we believe her to be uniquely heroic, but because we recognise how she has been dispossessed of a story and a subjecthood and because her personal dispossession is representative of many others throughout history. Thus the job of the critic must be to reinstate the woman author, but without making her into an icon, and to reaffirm the woman's story, but without making it into a sacred text.

Pieixoto and theories of authorship

Unfortunately, the critics, Pieixoto and Wade, do not see their task in this way. Their activities, like those of Sfax, are founded on a desire for control and a disregard of the ethical implications of their practice.

In both *The Handmaid's Tale* and *The Death of the Author* the woman author is an obstacle to be overcome and *The Handmaid's Tale* particularly reveals how the woman author can be so easily lost to history and the potentially feminist text all too readily accommodated and recuperated by patriarchy. Pieixoto and Wade, however, hold to a traditional view of authorship, far removed from Sfax's theoretical gymnastics and ripe for Barthes and Foucault's deconstruction. Not only are Pieixoto and Wade concerned to establish themselves as 'Authors' with a capital 'A', they act as an exemplum for Barthes and Foucault's arguments in their search for 'the Author', their investment in their role as critics and their construction of 'the work'.

Barthes's descriptions of 'work' and 'Text' in his essay 'From Work to Text' indicate that Pieixoto and Wade are firmly involved with the former rather than the latter.[29] Barthes describes the work as something concrete, something that can fit on a library shelf; as tied to the signified; as needing to be interpreted; as involved with 'sources' and 'influences'; as an object of consumption. Evidently, Barthes's essay did not survive the Gileadean revolution, for while Barthes rejects the work in favour of the pluralistic, playful, democratic Text, Pieixoto and Wade seem to sub-scribe, unquestioningly, to all the attributes Barthes critiques. Where they differ from Barthes's schema – as we shall see, for reasons related to gender – is in what Barthes refers to as the 'process of filiation', where 'the author is reputed the father and the owner of his work', both in terms of the legality of ownership and in recognising and respecting the importance of authorial intention (160). In 'What Is an Author?', Foucault does not make the same semantic distinction between 'work' and 'Text' and uses the terms interchangeably but he does point out how the intractability of the author is related to the concept of a work/Text. The significance of the writing is dependent on the establishment of an author and, without an author, the writings that an individual may produce cannot constitute a work/Text. As Foucault asks, 'When Sade was not considered an author, what was the status of his papers? Were they simply rolls of paper onto which he ceaselessly uncoiled his fantasies during his imprisonment?' (143). At the end of *The Handmaid's Tale*, we see Professors Pieixoto and Wade involved in a variety of ways in creating what Barthes would recognise as a 'work'. In the first instance, they have constructed the material artefact, transcribing the tapes, making judgements about the meaning of problematic words and ordering the thirty tapes into what they believe to be the correct narrative structure. The material construction of the work is also, of course, an act of interpretation. Pieixoto and Wade have imposed their coherence on the work, at once opening it to certain possibilities while closing it to others. The process of building an interpretative context continued by annotating the work and, in Pieixoto's lecture, by providing a range of historical, cultural and literary detail about the Gileadean and pre-Gileadean periods and stylistic comment about the work itself, all of which, again, necessarily circumscribe how the work might be read.

Pieixoto wants to endow *The Handmaid's Tale* with an author since this figure is essential not only in establishing the work but also in validating his research activity. Foucault points out how the author-function 'does not develop spontaneously' but is rather 'the result of a complex operation which constructs a certain rational being that we call "author" ' (150). In several ways Pieixoto's lecture describes a search for someone who will fulfil the author functions that Barthes and Foucault outline. One pressing need is for the 'explanatory' function of the author, someone who could tell us about sources and influences. Barthes describes this function as follows:

The *explanation* of a work is always sought in the man or woman who produced it, as if it were always in the end, through the more or less transparent allegory of the fiction, the voice of a single person, the *author* 'confiding' in us. (143)

Foucault claims:

the author provides the basis for explaining not only the presence of certain events in the work, but also their transformations, distortions, and diverse modifications (151)

With remarkable accord Pieixoto affirms:

If we could establish an identity for the narrator, we felt, we might be well on the way to an explanation of how this document – let me call it that for the sake of brevity – came into being. (315)

In addition, Pieixoto is concerned with the 'classificatory' function which, according to Foucault, 'permits one to group together a certain number of texts', 'establishes a relationship among the texts' and 'serves to characterize a certain mode of being of discourse' (147). Foucault finds this classificatory function operating in the author's name. For this anonymous, spoken text, Pieixoto finds the classificatory function in the author's voice. Described by the voiceprint experts as 'the same one throughout', this voice gives unity and consistency to a collection of fragmentary recordings (314).

Though Pieixoto and Wade believe that Offred's voice can authenticate the work, its reconstruction as *written* text which will circulate within an academic discourse is intrinsic to their research process.[30] As Foucault suggests, one cannot simply ditch the concept of 'author' and focus on the work itself since 'the word "work" and the unity that it designates are probably as problematic as the status of the author's individuality' (144). Pieixoto and Wade do not even have 'rolls of paper' on which to base their claims; what they are dealing with is a jumble of music cassettes, some mislabelled, into which the speaking voice intrudes. At the start of the lecture, the tale's appellation as a 'manuscript' is only *'soi-disant'* for, as Pieixoto explains, 'what we have before us is not the item in its original form. Strictly speaking, it was not a manuscript at all when first discovered, and bore no title' (312–13). A paragraph later he refers to 'this item – I hesitate to use the word *document*' (313); later again, it becomes 'blocks of speech' (314); then, as we saw in the earlier quotation on the explanatory function of the author, the word 'document' reappears, once more with a qualification about the legitimacy of the description.[31] Only when Offred's words have been transposed into a written text, a medium of greater durability, and put into a sequence in the way that Pieixoto and Wade feel best, can they begin to make their critical analysis:

> Once we had the transcription in hand – and we had to go over it several times, owing to the difficulties posed by accent, obscure referents, and archaisms – we had to make some decision as to the nature of the material we had thus so laboriously acquired. (314)

Even here quite what the 'material' constitutes is unsure but in changing it from Offred's spoken voice to their written text they have established a control, made it ready for their exegesis. The obvious danger is that the heroine, having escaped being 'of-Fred' simply becomes 'of-Pieixoto and Wade'; they own her text as the Commander had owned her body.

The sexist asides and salacious innuendo in Pieixoto's lecture are the clearest indication that Pieixoto and Wade may not construct the work, or the author, in any way that the feminist reader would find satisfactory. The audience response to Pieixoto's jokes – laughter, applause, mock groans of despair – leads one to wonder about the nature of the institutional and academic community within which Offred's life is being discussed. Both Barthes and Foucault comment on the critic's role of finding the author, a process which at once defines the text and confirms the critic's activity:

> To give a text an Author is to impose a limit on that text, to furnish it with a final signified, to close the writing. Such a conception suits criticism very well, the latter then allotting itself the important task of discovering the Author (or its hypostases: society, history, psyché, liberty) beneath the work: when the Author has been found, the text is 'explained' – victory to the critic. (Barthes, 147)

> And if a text should be discovered in a state of anonymity – whether as a consequence of an accident or the author's explicit wish – the game becomes one of rediscovering the author. Since literary anonymity is not tolerable, we can accept it only in the guise of an enigma. (Foucault, 149–50)

Pieixoto and Wade do, indeed, take up the required role and act as literary detectives to solve the puzzle. However, beyond a certain point, the trail turns cold and this, according to Pieixoto, is because of the deficiency of Offred who is lacking in 'the instincts of a reporter or a spy' (322). Thirty recordings from a desperate woman are, apparently, not as relevant to history as twenty pages of printout from a powerful man. Offred's narrative is disappointing for Pieixoto; she does not tell him what he wants to hear. Perhaps it is too much a woman's story about motherhood, daughterhood, female friendship, the female body. Moreover, Offred cannot adequately fulfil the explanatory function which Pieixoto and Wade look for in the author. As Foucault tells us, the explanation of the text comes 'through (the author's) biography, the determination of his individual perspective, the analysis of his social position, and the revelation of his basic design' (151). In Offred's case most of this remains shady and uncertain.

Undaunted, Pieixoto and Wade are able to turn to their advantage the elusiveness of the author and the instability of her text. In Kamuf's analysis of Spitzer she discovers three putative fathers for the *Portuguese Letters* – Guilleragues, a minor poet of the period whom critics do now agree to be the likely author of the letters; Abelard, who in his letters to Heloise provides a literary precedent; the French officer, the lover of the Portuguese nun and the recipient of the letters. A similar process is at play in Pieixoto's lecture on *The Handmaid's Tale*. Here too a number of men are produced to legitimise an unsigned text, reclaim it for the father, dispose of the unsatisfactory voice of the woman author. First, as we have seen above, it is Waterford who is the author Pieixoto would much prefer to examine and a significant part of his lecture is concerned with debating the respective merits of Judd and Waterford as the unnamed Commander from the tale. Then, just as Spitzer names Abelard, Wade discovers for the handmaid a *male* literary precursor in Chaucer; indeed, the handmaid's tale is so called 'in homage to the great Geoffrey Chaucer' (313).[32] Above all, with their ordering, transcribing, interpreting, contextualising, lecturing, naming, publicising, their academic status, it is Pieixoto and Wade who emerge as the triumphant authors of the tale. Barthes points out how the 'Author' and the 'Critic' work in tandem to mutually advantageous effect – 'the reign of the Author has also been that of the Critic' (147). For Pieixoto and Wade it is equally advantageous to collapse the distinction between the two roles and become at once 'Author' and 'Critic'. The female author cannot be recovered – she is dead, unknown, subordinate – and, in Pieixoto and Wade's version, does not need to be recovered; the 'process of filiation' that Barthes spoke of is now effectively centred on them. They have become 'the father and the owner of [the] work' (160).

We see, then how Offred's loss of authorship does not dispel the notion of authority but rather repositions it in the hands of influential, professional men. Or, to put that point another way, the authority of Pieixoto and Wade is contingent on the exclusion of Offred. Though ostensibly looking for the lost woman author, it is actually essential that they do not find her so that they may take over her role. *Her* story never was in the public domain. It is the story as constructed by Pieixoto and Wade that has become the matter of articles and conferences, and in this story the subject position available to Offred is not that of 'Author' or even 'author' but, variously, that of a quasi-Chaucerian character, or the butt of jokes, or historical enigma, or inadequate reporter, or mythological tragic heroine. Pieixoto's lecture masterfully takes control of the text. One can imagine that in some copiously edited and footnoted edition of *The Handmaid's Tale* subsequently published it would be the names of Pieixoto and Wade which would appear prominently on the title page while Offred's name would feature as an insignificant 'Anon.'.

The dominant reading effect of the 'Historical Notes' is a sense of the absence of Offred's voice. As Pieixoto moves to the crescendo of his lecture, he returns with a series of questions and hypotheses to the figure of Offred, her obscurity and silence. His ending waxes grandiloquent:

> We may call Eurydice forth from the world of the dead, but we cannot make her answer; and when we turn to look at her we glimpse her

only for a moment, before she slips from our grasp and flees. As all historians know, the past is a great darkness, and filled with echoes. Voices may reach us from it; but what they say to us is imbued with the obscurity of the matrix out of which they come; and try as we may, we cannot always decipher them precisely in the clearer light of our own day. (324)

The 'we' in this passage places Pieixoto, Wade and their audience in the position of Orpheus; as he tried to reclaim Eurydice from the dark underworld so 'we' try to reclaim Offred.[33] What Pieixoto glosses over here is any suggestion that it could be the failure of Orpheus which condemns Eurydice to the 'great darkness' and, concomitantly, that he and Wade may have played a part in the loss of Offred. Feminist interest in the Orpheus and Eurydice tale has focused on Eurydice's relation to the male poet, on Orpheus's look as a fatal act of mastery, on how to understand the silenced figure of Eurydice. In Atwood's poem 'Orpheus (1)', the speaking voice of Eurydice complains that Orpheus constituted himself through her so that she became *his* Muse, *his* 'hallucination', *his* 'echo'.[34] Similarly in 'Eurydice' the poetic voice comments:

> This love of his is not something
> he can do if you aren't there (109)

But Atwood offers an interesting twist to the conventional interpretations of the parting of Orpheus and Eurydice. In her version the separation takes place not through Orpheus's 'mistake' but through Eurydice's necessary rejection of Orpheus's narcissism. So in 'Orpheus (1)' she writes:

> Though I knew how this failure
> would hurt you, I had to
> fold like a gray moth and let go.
>
> You could not believe I was more than your echo (107)

And in 'Eurydice':

> *Go back*, you whisper,
>
> but he wants to be fed again
> by you. O handful of gauze, little
> bandage, handful of cold

air, it is not through him
you will get your freedom. (109)

Like Orpheus, Pieixoto and Wade attempt to create in Offred the woman they need – 'Before your eyes you held steady/the image of what you wanted/me to become ...' (106). Like Eurydice, Offred ultimately evades the male grasp but only at a price; she slips towards the void, the edge of non-representation. A feminist reader might feel that both Offred and Eurydice deserve more sympathetic interpreters, not uncritical, but sensitive to the palpable anguish of their tales. Pieixoto's determination to construct Offred as a particular form of author renders him deaf to her desiring, fearing voice. Equally, his cultural relativism, duly applauded by the audience, conveniently exonerates him from any identification with Offred and from making political and ethical judgements about what happened to her. 'Our job is not to censure but to understand', he says (315). Disappointed by Offred as author and as access to a detailed recreation of Gilead, Pieixoto can only mythologise, elevate, even sentimentalise her. History becomes 'a great darkness'; the material presence of Offred reverts to an echo or a disembodied voice; Offred will never be known, only glimpsed. At the moment when she is, possibly, rescued by Nick, Offred wonders if she is stepping 'into the darkness within; or else the light' (307). Once again, as with Eurydice, she is poised between two worlds. Pieixoto's reading has confined her, if not in the darkness, then in the shadow of his own search for authorial status.

3
Playing the Field
Women's Access to Cultural Production

> **Carr:** ... What is an artist? For every thousand people there's nine hundred doing the work, ninety doing well, nine doing good, and one lucky bastard who's the artist.
>
> Tom Stoppard, *Travesties*[1]

Generally speaking, the women artist or the woman author has not considered herself or been considered by others as the one lucky bastard in a thousand. The wonderful cartoon by Guerilla Girls, entitled 'Advantages', features a woman artist, brush in one hand, looking intently at her canvas. She is also pregnant, has a saucepan on her head and a toddler pulling at her skirts. The caption reads: 'Why have there been no great women artists? – "Great questions by great men" series'. Moreover, in the two stories that are the focus of this chapter, Alice Walker's 'Everyday Use' and Antonia Byatt's 'Art Work', it is not clear if the women involved are 'artists' or their work 'art'.[2] Whether it is possible or desirable to construct the women and their work in this way is precisely the problem the stories confront. Becoming that figure or earning that title for one's work is intimately connected with being able to authorise oneself and one's activities. Walker's story concerns some quilts, their production, their multiple meanings and their rightful ownership. Dee, the successful, educated daughter of a poor, black family from the Southern States, makes one of her infrequent trips back to her mother's house to claim the quilts which she wants to display in her own home. In the *dénouement* Mama confounds Dee's presumption, takes back the quilts and gives them to Maggie, the 'backward', rural daughter who, along with Mama, is the quilt maker. The story leads the reader to consider the politics and ethics of this decision. Byatt's story deals with the domestic relations of an 'artistic family' – Robin, who is a

37

full-time artist and his wife, Debbie, trained in graphic design and now working as a design editor on a woman's magazine – and the unexpected discovery of the artistic ability of the family's cleaner, Mrs Brown. The story ends with Mrs Brown having an exhibition at a gallery where Robin had hoped to exhibit and this precipitates some serious reappraisals on the part of Robin and Debbie. The uncertain status of Mama, Maggie and Mrs Brown as 'artists' relates as much to their class positions and their racial and ethnic identities as their gender. (Mrs Brown is part Guyanese, part-Irish.) These women have no foothold in the artistic field. Their understanding of its demands is limited and the artefacts they produce – not only Mama and Maggie's quilts but Mrs Brown's bizarre 'sculptures' made of knitting and crochet – do not accord with conventional aesthetic norms. If you can become 'an artist' only by knowing how to operate as an artist and by being recognised as such by the community which is in a position to authorise you, then Mama, Maggie and Mrs Brown have a long road to travel.

In both stories what Pierre Bourdieu would call 'the dominated aesthetic' is becoming mobile and changing its status. The works of these women are beginning to acquire symbolic capital and to climb a hierarchy of legitimacy.[3] The reader encounters them at that perilous juncture when the common, popular, domestic, craft-come-hobby is edging towards a cultivated, distinctive, public art and so being transformed into symbolic power. 'The science of works', writes Bourdieu, 'takes as object not only the material production of the work but also the production of the value of the work or, what amounts to the same thing, of the belief in the value of the work'.[4] We see that collective belief being formed and the characters are actively reassessing the objects before them. The stories ask at what moment, at what levels of legitimacy, through which agencies, with what consequences, amidst which value systems will Mama or Maggie or Mrs Brown ever become 'artists'. In Byatt's story similar preoccupations relate to Debbie whose return to her woodcuts at the end of the story might signal a move to a new identity as 'artist' while Robin's difficulties in getting his work placed indicate a loss of status. As the objects reveal their potential to move up or down a hierarchy of legitimacy, they are also caught in what Bourdieu sees as a 'trial by market'.[5] Though Mama would never articulate the issue in this way, she has a strong suspicion of the market place as fatally compromised and Robin too is ambiguous, at once wanting recognition, anxious about the process of offering his work for evaluation and disdainful of the current values by which he is being assessed. Yet, both stories illustrate that success can enhance status: 'the market is accepted more and more as a legitimate means of legitimation' (27).[6] This is seen particularly in 'Art Work' where the active marketing of Mrs Brown through an exhibition, TV appearance and a magazine article seems set to confirm her aesthetic aspirations whereas the current failure of Robin to succeed in the market lowers his legitimacy.

Bourdieu's concept of 'the field' is integral to his understanding of the violence of social relations in the creation of 'the artist' or 'the author' and the legitimisation of the work. Here is one of his many explanations of the term from *On Television and Journalism*:

> A field is a structured social space, a field of forces, a force field. It contains people who dominate and others who are dominated. Constant, permanent relationships of inequality operate inside this space, which at the same time becomes a space in which the various actors struggle for the transformation or preservation of the field. All the individuals in this universe bring to the competition all the (relative) power at their disposal. It is this power that defines their position in the field and, as a result, their strategies. (40)

We can see in the language that the term 'field' has no bucolic associations: this is 'the field' as in field of war with forces and struggles for power between the dominant and the dominated.[7] On other occasions Bourdieu uses the language of game-playing but serious, competitive and strategic game-playing like chess or poker. He mentions 'players', 'tokens', 'hands', 'clues', 'bluff', 'stakes', 'trump cards'.[8] The 'normal' vicissitudes of social relations mask a battle for power, a desire to amass the relevant forms of capital and, hence, dominance in the field. The arguments, insecurities, tensions, jealousies exhibited in these stories indicate that this is no easy engagement. Where forms of capital are at stake, the struggle will always be, in Brecht's words, 'contradictory, fiercely fought over, full of violence'.[9] The dramatic highpoints of these narratives are, indeed moments of intense 'transformation or preservation'.

The form of cultural investment expressed by the characters in these stories is not that of the superior art-lover of the dominant aesthetic who thinks himself 'perfectly disinterested, unblemished by any cynical or mercenary use of culture' and who instinctively and without calculation pursues his love of art, blind to the symbolic profits he is earning.[10] For many of our characters, the cultural investment is conscious, cunning, opportunist, needy and seen most obviously in the bald determination of Dee to possess the quilts. Dee's acquisition of educational capital has produced increased economic capital and certain cultural competences which she mercilessly impresses on Mama and Maggie. Power struggles are also present in the complex quadrille that takes place between the characters of 'Art Work'. They are evident in the marital disagreements of Robin and Debbie, for instance, or the triangular relationship of Robin, Debbie and Mrs Brown, or in Debbie's unsuccessful and Mrs Brown's successful negotiations with the gallery dealer, Shona McRury. All these disputes are in large part about access to and power within the artistic field but the position of agents in the field is never static even when significant power is achieved. The field is constantly in motion: the different positions and position-takings, the varied quantities and kinds of capital and changing valuations of different capitals mean that all is in flux. Through 'the logic of action and reaction' delightful reversals can take place when the character/agent with significant capital (Dee, for example) profits least from her machinations and a character/agent with little capital (Mrs Brown, for example) profits most.[11] Dee's demise can be viewed as both a failure to supplement her power within the field and a gratifying example of literary *schadenfreude*.[12]

In this chapter, I want to explore the figures of, particularly, Mama, Maggie and Mrs Brown who respond differently to their encounters with the aesthetic field and to the possibility of a heightened consciousness of themselves as authors of their work. Entering that field of aesthetic and economic evaluation offers both opportunities and dangers. An understanding of what the work signifies and the women's authorial significance can be enhanced or undermined. The initiative depends not only on the women; we see the field as well constructing the artist, the work of art and the appropriate location for art. Within this volatile field, we can judge what possibilities are available for a progressive discourse, such as feminism, in supporting the woman artist in authorising her work or in validating her decision to withdraw from the game.

Who is the artist?

One of the curiosities of these two stories, replete with artists, is that only one of them actually accepts the designation. For Mama and Maggie such a role with its connotations of symbolic capital and magical status is beyond their ken. This is not to say that they are without aesthetic competences or values; rather that these attributes are understood differently by them. Mrs Brown starts from a similar position but, at the end of 'Art Work', she is tentatively moving towards some redefinition of herself as 'an artist'. Though still referring to herself in her TV interview as 'a cleaning lady' (86), one feels that the way she describes her work and her earlier pursuit of Shona McRury are pointers to her assuming a new identity. Debbie, though, is dangerously close to becoming one of feminism's lost women artists, her talent in graphic design leading her into employment and away from the woodcuts which her fingers ache to produce. She acknowledges the title 'artist', would like to have it but, for most of the story, recognises that the daily conditions of her life remove her from it. It is Robin – the man, the product of a fine art training, dedicated to his artistic pursuits – who sees himself as 'the artist'. His artistic involvement is treated, especially by him, as a more serious and engaging activity than anyone else's and his expectation is that other people (female) will run the home and even provide the family income so as to save him from inconsequential details. He aspires to being the charismatic artist and is infuriated that the world in the form of Mrs Brown's cleaning and maddening remarks might impinge on his ethereal activities. At the same time, Robin at heart knows that his work is out of fashion; his histrionic over-performance of the role of artist is a product of his insecurity and part of the story's comic effect. Robin's vulnerable psyche could just about cope with being the *artiste maudit*, the 'cursed artist' whose true value is unappreciated at the time he is producing. What he cannot cope with is being the 'failed artist'.[13]

Equally, characters seem to have difficulty in authorising each other as 'the artist' and these difficulties are always riven by difference. Debbie experiences a quiet, sad, persistent hatred for Robin and his failure to appreciate or even think of the artistic aspirations she has abandoned. She is not 'the artist', nor is she Robin's muse but she has assumed that other traditional, and chafing, role of wifely support to the gifted husband. Until the knowledge is forced upon them, no one thinks of Mrs Brown as 'the artist' since her class position places her outside that category. Both she and Debbie are quite sure that Robin is 'the artist' but their weary accommodation of his role satirically undercuts its charismatic status. While Debbie anxiously placates and Mrs Brown reluctantly tolerates his demands, neither is blind to the fact that it is their mutual ordering of daily life in the home and Debbie's economic support that allow Robin to think of himself as 'the artist'. Both view Robin with a 'disenchanted female gaze', well aware of the games they are playing in bolstering the male ego.[14] As Debbie guiltily recognises, 'she is beginning to treat (Robin) like a backward and stupid child' (76). In Walker's story, Dee likes the *idea* of Southern, black culture, what it might represent in the history of black people; she likes it as a lifestyle to be sampled periodically or as a cultural sign. She is less delighted with personal encounters with the, to her, intransigent producers of the quilts. They merit only small quantities of her time but large quantities of her exasperated ire. Dee has no desire to claim her mother and sister as women artists since to take that position would demand a serious regard on her part towards the very people she is trying to deny. She would like to grant cultural consecration to the art object but without doing the same for the art producers.

In the eyes of Dee, Robin and Debbie, uneducated, unsophisticated, working-class women, such as Mama, Maggie and Mrs Brown, could not be artists since they lack that essential quality, 'taste'. No follower of the 'high' aesthetic could see Dee's taste as 'pure' since it is far too compromised by a deep desire for self-advancement. Yet, from her own perspective, Dee has no doubt as to the righteousness of her judgement on the wilful behaviour of Mama and Maggie. Similarly, Robin vehemently complains of Mrs Brown's 'filth' (58), her lack of capacity for distinguishing between aesthetically important and unimportant objects, her ignorance of form and colour. He believes in a 'pure gaze', 'a quasi-creative power which sets the aesthete apart from the common herd' and this provokes his rantings against the 'barbarous' taste of Mrs Brown.[15] 'Aesthetic intolerance can be terribly violent', warns Bourdieu and there are explosions of anger in both stories when the 'barbarous' refuse to accept the so-called inadequacy of their views.[16] In a comparable but less personally aggressive way, Debbie wonders at the bizarre nature of Mrs Brown's clothes – Robin thinks these are 'the epitome of tat' (59) – and agonises over what to do with her unacceptable home-made gifts for the children which to Debbie problematically muddy the employer/ employee relationship. Debbie also repeatedly confirms Robin's views on taste, partly to mollify him but partly because she does accept as valid the aesthetic problems he sets himself. As people comment, with varying degrees of enthusiasm, about Robin's work: ' "He's *got* something", or more dubiously, "He's got *something*" ' (56).

Mama, Maggie and Mrs Brown are victims of what Bourdieu calls 'symbolic violence', the mechanisms by which 'the infallible taste of the "taste-maker" ' seeks to expose 'the uncertain tastes of the possessors of an "ill-gotten" culture'.[17] Disdainful of her origins and eager for increased legitimacy, Dee has long experience of marshalling the forces of symbolic violence against Mama and Maggie:

> She used to read to us without pity; forcing words, lies, other folks' habits, whole lives upon us two, sitting trapped and ignorant

underneath her voice. She washed us in a river of make-believe, burned us with a lot of knowledge we didn't necessarily need to know. Pressed us to her with the serious way she read, to shove us away at just the moment, like dim wits, we seemed about to understand. (50)

It is Mama's sad fantasy that, on something like the Johnny Carson show, she will be reunited with Dee who, amidst smiles and tears, will acknowledge her true value. The bitingly critical emphasis of Walker's language is not too distant from the impassioned indignation with which Bourdieu himself describes symbolic violence towards the end of *Distinction*. In both cases the language leaves no doubt as to the real effects of this form of violence:

> If there is terrorism, it is in the peremptory verdicts which, in the name of taste, condemn to ridicule, indignity, shame, silence ... men and women who simply fall short, in the eyes of their judges, of the right way of being and doing.[18]

Bourdieu could be admonishing Dee or Robin at this point but is, in fact, talking of dominant groups in French culture. Though the American equivalent, WASP culture, is not open to Dee, she has enjoyed the benefits of social mobility for educated blacks in a post-Civil Rights United States and is cleverly employing her newly-acquired capital in a world of upwardly mobile, middle-class blacks in what she acknowledges as 'a new day for us' (59). While Dee's symbolic violence over her mother and sister is brutally clear to the reader, its full significance only gradually becomes evident to Mama. Symbolic violence is, as Beate Krais says, 'a subtle, euphemized, invisible mode of domination', not perceived as violence.[19] To Mama and Maggie, Dee's behaviour is irritating but 'misrecognized'; it is just the way Dee is. The dramatic turn in the story when Mama snatches the quilts back from Dee's grasp and gives them to Maggie is the moment when the scales fall from Mama's eyes. The symbolic violence and its false legitimacy are perceived for what they are; the emperor has no clothes. Mrs Brown largely accommodates Robin's savage judgements within her realistic understanding of the sexual politics of the family: this is what husbands are like, particularly artistic husbands, and Debbie needs her help. There is also, of course, a powerful economic reason for Mrs Brown not to internalise the unpleasantness of Robin's comments. Yet, in this story too, the uneasy *modus operandi* is sometimes upset. Robin's behaviour can become too cruelly explicit, Mrs Brown takes offence and Debbie has to bridge-build.

From the viewpoint of the most conservative wing of the dominant aesthetic Mama, Maggie and Mrs Brown simply do not have what it takes to be 'the artist'. They do not belong to the right sex, race/ethnic group or class; they do not have the right competences, aesthetic sense, innate talent; they have none of the necessary capitals – cultural, educational, social, symbolic. The only position they could take up within the dominant culture would be as a *miraculée*.[20] For Dee, eager to establish the difference between herself and her family, what she perceives as the progressiveness of her view against the regressiveness of theirs, Mama and Maggie have to be excluded as embarrassingly inadequate to her notion of 'artist'.[21] For Shona McRury, however, there are no family hang-ups to exorcise and she has an astute sense of the market's readiness for invention and, specifically, feminist invention. Thus, she has no qualms in appreciating with equal relish the aesthetic and financial potential in Mrs Brown and can become the key person who, in Bourdieu's words, 'creates the "creator" '.[22] By focalising through Debbie, the narrator captures the puzzle of that moment when, contrary to class norms and all social expectations, the cleaner accosts the gallery dealer. Her behaviour is, at best, inexplicable; at worst, intrusive and pushy or, even, treacherous:

> Mrs Brown, in her trench-coat, catches up with Shona McRury. Mrs Brown's hair stands up like a wiry plant in a pot, inside a coil of plaited scarves, orange and lime. Mrs Brown says something to Shona McRury who varies her pace, turns her head, answers. Mrs Brown says something else. What can Mrs Brown have to say to Shona McRury? (75)

Whatever Mrs Brown says results in a sudden increase in her stock of social and symbolic capital. To Shona the idiosyncrasy of Mrs Brown is not a problem but a bankable asset and her visibility – soon to be evidenced in the exhibition notes, the complimentary magazine interview, the TV appearance – is to be encouraged.

As Mrs Brown embarks on the rocky road to possible legitimacy, forms of aesthetic distancing come into play. Bourdieu describes how the true aesthete assumes a position of 'detachment, disinterestedness, indifference' far removed from the ' "vulgar" surrender to easy seduction and collective enthusiasm' of the uninitiated.[23] There is, of course, 'an interest in disinterestedness' and the aesthete has much to gain from taking up this position.[24] The distance is both intellectual in the adoption of a certain aloof mindset, 'the refusal to invest oneself and take things seriously' and bodily:[25] Bourdieu compares the different vocal and gestural responses of audiences at, among other locations, concerts in churches, football matches and jazz.[26] In appropriating popular forms, the aesthete 'introduces a distance, a gap', shifting interest from content and character 'to the form, to the specifically artistic effects which are only appreciated relationally, through a comparison with other works'.[27] The move is one of objectification and control and the immediacy of 'everyday use' has to be reconstructed if the object is to be worthy of the aesthete's attention.

But not only the object. In this story we see how the producer too is distanced within the field and for Mrs Brown this distancing works to her advantage in offering her a new status. In the family, she moves out of the invisibility of her domestic role and, in so doing, becomes more remarkable. In this instance new social space entails a new physical space since she will no longer be available for domestic work in the home. It also entails a new symbolic space as, in the course of the story, Mrs Brown is transformed from 'person' to 'representation'. The family now have to view her in ways that are not face-to-face but mediated through the television, the magazine article, the gallery exhibition and this entails a conscious reassessment of who she is. This repositioning of Mrs Brown and the attention given to her life, thoughts, artwork produces fresh information about her – her first name, for example, which, despite years of daily intimacy, had been unknown within the family. As Debbie muses, '... if we had been friends, she would have shown *me* her things. But we weren't. I only thought we were' (88). It is a measure of Mrs Brown's 'becoming' as an artist that the family start to see her with an unaccustomed regard.

What is a work of art?

A key reason why the women cannot be readily authorised as 'artists' is because their work cannot be readily recognised as 'art'; there has to be some agreement between the producer and the object produced. For instance, what are quilts? Are they utilitarian objects, as Walker's title indicates, for 'everyday use' with the function of keeping people warm; are they 'collectors' curios or historical and ethnographic documents' from which we can discover about their domestic production, quilting bees, local styles and significance; are they political banners for feminism, anti-racism or AIDS causes?[28] Or are they works of art and, if so, do they operate within the dominant aesthetic or within the dominated aesthetic of devalued, oppressed groups, and does their reproduction on postcards, tablecloths, calendars signify a 'play of cultured allusions and analogies' or merely a degraded commercialism predicated on notions of folksy Americana?[29] The answer, of course, is that they can be all of these and some of these in different contexts at different moments with different effects. Though few objects operate within so many discourses as the quilt, Mrs Brown's work in fabric and Robin's paintings are also variously understood.

Bourdieu's position in *Distinction* on the difference between dominant and popular aesthetics is commented on by John Frow:

> Whereas the dominant aesthetic is associated with an autotelic formalism, a refusal of practical or ethical function, a refusal of the facile and the vulgar, and with intertextual rather than mimetic modes of reference, the 'popular' aesthetic is defined as having a primarily ethical basis and as subordinating artistic practice to socially regulated functions (for example, working-class people use photography above all for the ritual celebration of family unity).[30]

Though this can be seen as the major aesthetic opposition in French culture during the period Bourdieu was writing *Distinction*, Bourdieu also recognises the mobility of the aesthetic as a category. In these stories, the aesthetic conforms to some extent to this summary and to some extent deviates from it. The quilts in 'Everday Use' are the product of female domestic labour. They have been pieced, hung and hand sewn by Grandma, Big Dee and Mama. For Mama and Maggie the scraps of fabric evoke a family and cultural history. They remember from whose clothes the scraps came and the piece from Great Grandpa Ezra's Civil War uniform suggests a larger history. The quilts' value for Mama and Maggie is diverse and, certainly, the practical, social and ethical are significant. They will be used by Maggie, repaired and when necessary replaced; acting as a memorial to family members and events, the quilts carry important 'socially regulated functions'; they are the focus of ethical values about respect, integrity, family feeling and, thus, Mama's concern about their ownership. However, the quilts are also for Mama and Maggie aesthetically pleasing. There *is* a recognition of the formal qualities of the quilts since this is partly why these particular quilts have been carefully kept for Maggie's bottom drawer and, as we know, quilt designs – some of which are specifically named in the story – have been established intertextually through a long history of collective quilt making and pattern sharing. It is not that Mama sees the quilts as *merely* useful, a commodity like any other. Rather it is that she refuses the opposition; the quilts are both of 'everyday use' *and* worthy of particular regard.[31]

Dee's place in the field is notably difficult. Her plan for the quilts entails a shift from function to form and she is irritated that Mama and Maggie will continue putting the quilts to 'everyday use'. Yet, at the same time, it is vital for Dee that she does not lose contact with the 'mimetic modes of reference' that Frow mentions. Indeed, with respect to the black discourse within which she is now operating, that link is important as a sign of both authentic roots and the distance she has travelled; it is at once a validation for her new politics but also, to Dee, an irksome reminder of her past. Walker is most critical about how Dee will use the quilts to testify to her radical chic and to contribute to her kudos and political 'right-onness'. Dee wants to be both 'in' the culture of her past and 'out' of it, to possess selected cultural products and significances but only on her terms. Her frustration, her moments of self-serving memory (for example, in the re-evaluation of the furniture of her childhood) or self-serving amnesia (for example, in the fact that she had been offered the quilts when she went away to college and rejected them as old-fashioned) testify to the absence of any easy sense of justification and, hence, the falseness of her intimacy upon returning home. Photography is her chosen aesthetic mode but she does not use it, as Frow says, 'for the ritual celebration of family unity'. Rather the photographs Dee takes of family, house and passing cow constitute a carefully staged reincarnation of her origins with an audience in mind from outside the family. Her actions result in a re-reading of the functional to render it either, as we have seen, a sign of political credibility or that which is 'quaint'. The extent to which Dee has moved towards these other modes of valuation is evident in the eagle-eyed assessment which she carries out on the house and its objects. Not only are the items photographed but provenances carefully recalled through family narratives about the making of furniture and household equipment. In the asset-stripping which follows, the objects of her childhood are transformed into the 'collectors' curios' of which Bourdieu speaks. Behaving like some unreconstructed anthropologist, Dee wants to remove the objects from their native origins to 'safe keeping' in the metropolis.

Astonishingly, Mrs Brown, a cleaning lady with a penchant for knitting and sewing in garish colours, evades almost all Bourdieu's categories for the dominated aesthetic. Her work is neither functional, mimetic nor, in her own mind, particularly ethical or socially relevant. It is others who see her work ethically, socially, and within a feminist politics. To complicate matters further, these same people also view her work intertextually. The author of the magazine article links it to Richard Dadd and Kaffe Fasset. Though both are attempts to dignify

Mrs Brown's work, these references fall on different sides of traditional aesthetic distinctions with Dadd signifying 'art' and Fasset signifying 'craft', albeit the artistic end of 'craft'. Unexpectedly, Mrs Brown approximates a 'pure' aesthetic view, talking of her work in terms of form, as 'soft sculpture', of making 'box-like things as well as squashy ones' (84). While her description of her aesthetic sensibility as 'a kind of coloured rush' (85) might for the purest, Kantian aesthete hint at unwelcome connotations of the sensuous and the bodily, it is still far removed from the feet-on-the-ground practicality of Bourdieu's dominated aesthetic. Moreover, any resistance on the part of the popular aesthetic towards ambiguity, symbolism, the abstract, the absurd in favour of identification, immediate gratification, linear narrative structures does not accommodate Mrs Brown. Her work is non-realist, some would say surreal, full of irony and metaphor. If Walker's quilt suggests a utopian balance and harmony with disparate elements formally held together, Byatt's story points to a postmodern proliferation and, in Mrs Brown's work, a cultural and historical ragbag, spilling out profuse meanings, startling juxtapositions, transpositions and multilayerings. Certainly not 'facile' in its range of associations, its form and scale also demand public rather than private exhibition. In short, far from an opposition of dominant and dominated what we see repeatedly in these stories is a complex criss-crossing of concepts, positionings, readings.[32]

Byatt takes this instability even further. In 'Art Work' the aesthetic has become rampant. A kind of wild deregularisation of the aesthetic is in operation so that not only is Mrs Brown's work commented on in aesthetic terms but also clothes, household objects and decor, make-up, the colour of people's hair and skin. This strategy could be contained within the dominant aesthetic. Bourdieu points out the distinctiveness of those who can 'apply the principles of the "pure" aesthetic in the most everyday choices of everyday life, in cooking, dress or decoration, for example'.[33] Yet, in 'Art Work' this aestheticisation moves promiscuously across from high culture to popular culture, from the 'pure' to the commercial and consumerist in a way that would horrify the aesthete. At one moment we are hearing about Mrs Brown's theory of colour, based on her knitting of a set of pink and orange, circular cushions; at the next, it is the turn of Robin's colour theory expressed in a series of fastidiously placed objects referred to as 'fetishes' and 'icons' (62). Art is without distinctions or boundaries, hierarchy or specific contexts; it is simply everywhere. As Mrs Brown says, 'you can see things *anywhere at all* to make things up from' (86). It is indiscriminate and amoral. Even the effects of the domestic violence Mrs Brown suffers are described as a composition in colour: 'Mrs Brown's bruises, the chocolate and violet stains on the gold skin, the bloody cushions in her hair and the wine-coloured efflorescence on her lips' (44). Where discrimination enters Byatt's story is in the political agenda. It is still not usual for a female, working-class, part Guyanese, part-Irish, middle-aged cleaner to be transformed suddenly into 'an artist'.

Where is art located?

Mama, Maggie and Mrs Brown have difficulty in being artists in the terms of the dominant aesthetic because they have little or no access to the locations of art – the art school, the studio, the gallery, the museum. In line with feminist art criticism of recent years, Walker's and Byatt's stories suggest that the domestic should be reappraised as a creative space and the dailiness of life as suitable, artistic material. Both indicate that art, particularly women's art, might be produced from a domestic setting, employ materials and skills common to the domestic and could constitute a transformation of the domestic. But both also question, as many feminist critics have, the neatness of the traditional model – that is, 'art' signifies art school and studio as places of production with ultimate consecration in a museum or public art gallery and an audience with all the relevant competences; while 'craft' signifies the home as the place of female production with the status only of ephemera or the functional and the family and local community as the audience. 'Domestic art', a term expressing a striking conflation of concepts, is produced at the point where the division between high and low culture, public and private, male and female has become blurred.

Walker's work has been much concerned with 'womanist' and matrilineal perspectives and with reaffirming the value of cultural experiences outside the pale of the dominant order; she wants to honour these experiences without doing violence to them.[34] In 'Everyday Use' it appears that that recognition can truly take place only within the culture that produced the quilts. The possibility of the quilts being relocated to a museum or gallery is not discussed in the story, though it is likely to be in the mind of many readers, while the possibility of moving them from one domestic setting, Mama's and Maggie's, to another, Dee's, is strongly critiqued. In Mama's (and Walker's) eyes, Dee's claim to the quilts fails not simply because she already has so much in terms of material goods but because she is not a proper custodian for the quilts, lacking the necessary regard for the history and values they embody. Furthermore, Dee's wish to exhibit the quilts in her home, thus framing them within a particular space, will mark them not only as 'art' but specifically as private art. Under her ownership, the quilts *could* enter a market economy of galleries, dealers, antique shops, auctions and she makes clear that she is well aware of the relative merits for this economy of hand stitching versus machine stitching. Dee's furious cry at the end of the story – 'But they're *priceless!*' (57) – can be read as both an aesthetic and an economic evaluation. She is just as concerned with what the quilts could produce in terms of cultural and symbolic capital and with the distinction and reputation these objects will earn for her amongst her new friends.

Walker is not averse to the display of quilts in museums and galleries. In 'In Search of Our Mothers' Gardens', she recalls being much moved by seeing a quilt in the Smithsonian.

> It is considered rare beyond price. Though it follows no known pattern of quilt-making, and though it is made of bits and pieces of worthless rags, it is obviously the work of a person of powerful imagination and deep spiritual feeling. Below this quilt I saw a note that says it was made by 'an anonymous Black woman in Alabama, a hundred years ago'.
>
> If we could locate this 'anonymous' black woman from Alabama, she would turn out to be one of our grandmothers – an artist who left her mark in the only materials she could afford, and in the only medium her position in society allowed her to use.[35]

Commenting on Walker's essay, Elaine Showalter points out that the maker of the quilt is in fact known, namely Harriet Powers (1836–1911), born a slave in Georgia. She adds, 'For Walker, genuine imagination and feeling can be recognized without the legitimacy conferred by the labels of "art" or the approval of museums', and then continues, 'Paradoxically this heritage survives because it has been preserved in museums; but it can be a living art only if it is practiced.'[36] These remarks illustrate some of the ambiguities surrounding museum location. Though Walker and Showalter feel that the legitimising function of museums is suspect, Walker values the Powers quilt in just the terms the Smithsonian would itself use, that is the quilt's rarity value, its imaginative and spiritual qualities, the artist's control over form and materials. Thus, Showalter's remark is incorrect in suggesting that Walker has rejected the legitimising function of the concept of 'art' as that function is embedded in her language. Unlike Dee, Walker is at pains to unite the maker and the object and to confer on the maker the title of 'artist': 'an artist who left her mark in the only materials she could afford, and in the only medium her position in society allowed her to use'. She is not so much rejecting the legitimising function of the concept of 'art' as questioning its premises and extending its domain. In so doing she risks the inconsistency of being at the same time *for* the special aesthetic qualities of quilt making and other domestic crafts and *against* the privileged position of 'art'. Bourdieu notes the double-bind inherent in such a position, how struggles against the legitimate aesthetic hierarchy are 'precisely what creates legitimacy, by creating belief not in the value of this or that stake but in the value of the game in which the value of all the stakes is produced and reproduced'.[37]

The preservation function of museums is also in question. Showalter's point is that quilts can be most effectively remembered, their value most fully acknowledged only if they are preserved, though her caveat about their production hints at some lingering use value. Though Mama has kept her quilts unused, she is quite happy with the idea of using even these special quilts to the point of disintegration since Maggie can always make more. Mama is working within a different economy from Dee. She has no interest in acquisitiveness or reification but, at the same time, her attitude is neither careless nor disposable. While Dee would privatise the quilts, fetishise them and impose a finality on them as finished items, Mama views them as part of a frugal recycling but their contingency in no way undermines their value. Her concern is for what one might call the 'performance' of the quilt in making and in use and she certainly prefers to see the quilts used rather than preserved within a context which wrenches them from a network of meaningful associations. Placing the quilts in a public museum undoubtedly suggests that their significance can be appreciated by a numerically larger audience than the restricted community of the quilt makers but the museum audience will be very differently constituted. As Bourdieu points out: 'If it is indisputable that our society offers to all the *pure possibility* of taking advantage of the works on display in museums, it remains the case that only some have the *real possibility* of doing so.'[38] That 'some' are likely to be 'among the fractions (relatively) richest in cultural capital and (relatively) poorest in economic capital' and such a selection will have obvious consequences in terms of class and race.[39] The museum, especially one of the status of the Smithsonian, holds 'the power to grant cultural consecration'; in keeping the quilt in good repair it will 'conserve the capital of symbolic goods'; in defining what constitutes art, who are the notable artists and who are the suitably informed viewers, it takes part in 'the legitimate exercise of symbolic violence'.[40] But it is not certain that any of this serves the interests of quilt makers such as Mama and Maggie.

In 'Art Work', all the artists or potential artists spend considerable amounts of their time within a domestic sphere and, with the exception of a visit by Debbie to the gallery where Mrs Brown is exhibiting, all the action of the narrative takes place in the home. But this is a middle-class, contemporary British home where shifts in work practices, new discourses in the culture around women's and feminist art and the changing aspirations of individuals have led to important rethinking on the meaning of domestic art and the home as a place of artistic production. The title of the magazine Debbie works for, *A Woman's Place*, both suggests and disputes that the woman's place *is* in the home. As a professional woman and the family's breadwinner, Debbie's place is in the office but it is also in the home as mother, wife, domestic organiser and, on occasions, homeworker. Mrs Brown's place is certainly in the home, in her own but in other people's homes as well where she serves as domestic labour. Still somewhat unusually for contemporary Britain, Robin's place too is in the home but, notably, without any domestic responsibility.

The demarcation of space within the home is both gendered and classed but with some knowing, quirky variations by Byatt. Thus we discover that an important stage in the artistic development of Mrs Brown was the acquisition of 'a room of one's own' but certainly not Virginia Woolf's traditional study, supported in the values of 1929 by an ample £500 a year; rather it is a lockup room in the basement of her block of council flats, acquired through an unspecified arrangement with the caretaker. Robin, on the contrary, inhabits an attic space but in this story it is neither the attic of demented, oppressed women nor the garret of impoverished Bohemian male artists but what sounds like an estate-agent's dream – 'the whole third floor' with 'large pivoting windows' and cream and terracotta blinds that can precisely adjust the quality and angle of the light (45). Robin is not separate from the home in a studio but occupies a privileged sanctum within the home. In contrast Debbie's domestic workspace is cramped and frequently dark since, when her drawing board in not in use, she has to prop it against the window. By the end of the story she has also found a place somewhere in her little workspace to return to her wood-engravings. While Robin is fixed in his studio, both Debbie and Mrs Brown are itinerant, passing up and down between the floors attending to varied needs – housework, frequent, loud protests from Robin, doorbells, sick child. As the cleaner, Mrs Brown is expected to be both on the move, doing her job and considerate in her use of space; therefore, it causes some concern for Debbie when she does not immediately leave Robin's studio upon the arrival of Shona McRury. Hence the domestic has become a more complicated space. It is still the space of family life, of unpaid female labour (the wife), of poorly paid female labour (the cleaner) and of gender and class inequalities. But it is also the domestic in 1990s, middle-class mode where men do not have to be the chief link with the public world and where homeworkers are not necessarily the exploited on piecework but highly paid, middle-class women with the appropriate technology.

In Byatt's story, the home is, again, a location for artistic production and that production is integrated into the domestic in diverse ways, most radically in Byatt's infusion of the domestic and the familiar with an aesthetic sense. If, as Toril Moi says, 'Bourdieu makes sociological theory out of *everything*', then Byatt makes art out of everything.[41] At the beginning of the story Byatt's narrator refers to a representation of Matisse's 'Le Silence habité des maisons' in Lawrence Gowing's *Matisse*.[42] The illustration in Gowing's study is in black and white, as Byatt remarks, 'a dark little image on the page, charcoal-grey, slate-grey, soft pale pencil-grey, subdued, demure' (32). It appears in more colourful form on the cover of *The Matisse Stories*. She imagines what it would look like 'flaming, in carmine or vermilion, or swaying in indigo darkness, or perhaps – outdoors – gold and green' (32). This interplay between the quiescent and the brilliant is central to Byatt's story. The narrative is, on the one hand, a conventional story of the social relations, sexual politics and emotional reticence of English middle-class life: the husband is over-sensitive and immature, hence demanding and hectoring; the wife is self-contained and long-suffering; she and Mrs Brown barely need to articulate their common understanding of strategies for coping. The women's negotiations concerning gender and class are also well within the familiar realm of realism. So, Mrs Brown will help Debbie with her post-natal depression and Debbie will help Mrs Brown with her experience of domestic violence but each refers to the other by her married title. Similarly, though Mrs Brown knows a lot about the intimacies of her employer's life, as all domestics do, she is reserved about her own. There is a genuine alliance between Debbie and Mrs Brown brokered around gender but, equally, because of class difference, this alliance has its limitations.

As in Walker's story, domestic materials are often employed for artistic purposes. Thus Debbie comments in one of her articles about 'an artist called Brenda Murphy, who works in the kitchen with her children, using *their* materials, crayons and felt-tips on paper' (69) and Mrs Brown proves herself to be wonderfully inventive with her knitting machine and what she culls from 'skips, jumble sales, cast-offs, going through other people's rubbish, clearing up after school fêtes' (83–4), the flotsam and jetsam of the homes in which she cleans. Yet, the aesthetic also penetrates the domestic in less conscious ways. Byatt presents us with another world, dramatic, heightened, full of sensory intensity, which seethes alongside and interacts with the everyday. The sounds of commonplace objects – typewriter, children's electric toys, record player, washing machine, phone – produce a cacophony of noise. The Hoover manipulated by Mrs Brown is like some fearful monster, wheezing, groaning and snoring up and down the stairs, just as in Mrs Brown's installation the central fantastical figure is a kind of dragon and a kind of Hoover. In turn the figure is rather like the Muppets that Jamie, the young son, watches on the television and, perhaps, not entirely unconnected with the 'grotesque merman' or 'human-headed dragon' breathing fire that appears on one of Robin's artistic 'fetishes'. Jamie's body being covered with calamine lotion becomes like a little plaster manikin; the bedcovers of the daughter, Natasha, are reminiscent of Matisse designs; the detritus of domestic life collected by Mrs Brown in Robin's bowl, which he sees as an affront to his aesthetic sense, becomes the boxes and drawers spilling threads in her art work; Jamie's chicken-pox is described as patterns of shape and colour; the tonal balance of the clothes of Shona McRury is as carefully constructed as a painting ... and on and on.

In 'Art Work', the domestic is not outside the aesthetic or inferior to the privileged locations for the aesthetic. Rather the vapidity of the everyday world is aestheticised: as Baudrillard comments, 'everything that redoubles itself, even ordinary, everyday reality, falls in the same stroke under the sign of art, and becomes aesthetic'.[43] Thus Debbie writes in her magazine copy, 'new moulding techniques give new streamlined shapes to the most banal objects. Sink trays and storage jars ...' (44–5). Mrs Brown's art is the quintessential expression of this dialogue, metamorphosising unwanted materials and the homely skills of knitting, crochet and sewing into a vibrant, intense aesthetic. Gowing's shades of grey do, indeed, become carmine, vermilion, indigo, gold and green through the efforts of Mrs Brown. Her installation reveals the domestic as both darker, somewhat Gothic and unsettling, but also brighter, less flattened by convention, more redolent with possibility. In Byatt's social comedy it is the latter mode which wins out. As Mrs Brown steps onto the ladder of fame, Debbie returns to her woodcarvings and Robin introduces not only the image of Mrs Brown into his work but also a more upbeat, less controlled style that he could have learned from her. Aesthetic oppositions are resolved in a productive interplay and the 'barbarous' Mrs Brown ends up enhancing the artistic competence of Robin, 'the artist'.[44]

Feminist responses

Walker's story suggests that there may be more to lose than to gain in becoming 'the artist'. Mama fully comprehends the questions of Virginia Woolf's narrator in *Three Guineas* – '[D]o we wish to join that procession or don't we? On what terms shall we join that procession? Above all, where is it leading us, the procession of educated men?'[45] – and answers: 'No, we don't. The terms aren't good enough. The procession may well lead us away from what we most value.' Her separatist response leaves her and Maggie with the quilts, sitting in their yard, taking snuff and 'just enjoying, until it was time to go in the house and go to bed' (59). Mama's decision is deliberate, based on a rejection of the assumptions of the game and a principled refusal to collude with the position Dee has allotted to her. The aspiration of Walker's story is that women, aware that their capacity to generate symbolic capital is limited, can refuse entry into the field, remain in happy self-sufficiency and operate within a different economy. We will see in Chapter 8 some similar doubts about entering the cultural field and an exploration of other economies with respect to the production and circulation of texts. Luce Irigaray's words could act as a commentary on the ending of 'Everyday Use':

> Use and exchange would be indistinguishable. The greatest value would be at the same the least kept in reserve. Nature's resources would be expended without depletion, exchanged without labor, freely given, exempt from masculine transactions: enjoyment without a fee, well-being without pain, pleasure without possession. As for the strategies and savings, the appropriations tantamount to theft and rape, the laborious accumulation of capital, how ironic all that would be.[46]

Mama and Maggie would circulate the quilts in woman-to-woman, non-exploitative exchanges, an economy of giving; Dee's 'laborious accumulation of capital' would have no credibility.

Though Bourdieu would never present the problem as merely one of voluntarist choice, his comment on little- or undifferentiated societies has further relevance for Mama's situation. In such societies,

> access to the means of appropriation of the cultural heritage is fairly equally distributed, so that culture is fairly equally mastered by all

members of the group and cannot function as cultural capital, i.e., as an instrument of domination, or only so within very narrow limits and with a high degree of euphemization.[47]

Mama has to keep out of the procession so as to ensure that the quilts do not become, through Dee's agency, 'an instrument of domination'. Irigaray follows her extract quoted above with the comment 'Utopia? Perhaps'. This is, of course, the problem of Walker's story, that it might fall before the charges of utopianism, idealism and nostalgia. While Mama and Maggie sit in the backyard, history will pass them by and consign them to the scrap-heap. The least savoury character in the story has the forward-looking energy; the most ethical characters are, for the dominant culture, the most disposable. Mama's action might be a laudable but ineffective gesture. As Beverley Skeggs remarks: 'The capitals already exist. They can be disavowed on an interpersonal level but this does not have any negative consequences for their cultural and social valuing.'[48]

Mrs Brown's response to Woolf's questions is a canny 'yes'. She enters the field to trade her limited capital and enjoy her, at least, fifteen minutes of fame. She and Shona come together partly through a shared concept of temporality: *carpe diem* could be the motto for both of them. Mrs Brown is, from one perspective, a naïve artist, 'one who almost stumbles into the field, without paying the entry fee, the toll'; a lot of what happens to her is by chance.[49] But it is unlikely that she will ever be a parvenu and she does not have Dee's desperate need to be accepted. She is prepared to chance her hand in the game and is rapidly acquiring knowledge of its laws but one feels that if it all soon ended she would not be greatly fazed by the turn of events. Though Byatt's story does not pursue Mrs Brown beyond her first successful step, the happy ending suggests another common feminist trope, namely that the shrewd woman might beat the field and claim the spoils without compromising her values. On the other hand, Mrs Brown might be co-opted into the game, won over or victimised, despite all her wise-woman attributes and the critical force of her artwork fully absorbed.

The issues posed in these two stories are not dissimilar to the questions commentators ask about Bourdieu's own work when discussing what some see as his determinist tendencies: can one stop playing the game, play a different game, transform the game or are we all held within its inexorable rules?[50] Both Mama and Mrs Brown know the power of the dominant order but are not totally determined by it. They have begun the kind of reflexive analysis Bourdieu himself advocates which will 'open up the possibility of identifying true sights of freedom'.[51] While Bourdieu believes the scope of human freedom to be fairly limited, a position which his critics have found dispiriting, marginal women like Mama, Maggie and Mrs Brown have to believe it will be large enough for them. In the following chapter, another two creative women, the poet, Mary Swann, and the novelist, Fleur Talbot, are established in the literary field where the existing members sometimes help, sometimes hinder and nearly always pursue their own self-interested ends.

4
Lost and Found
The Making of the Woman Author

> The thought came to me in a most articulate way: 'How wonderful it feels to be an artist and a woman in the twentieth century.' That I was a woman and living in the twentieth century were plain facts. That I was an artist was a conviction so strong that I never thought of doubting it then or since; and so, as I stood on the pathway in Hyde Park in that September of 1949, there were as good as three facts converging quite miraculously upon myself and I went on my way rejoicing.
>
> Muriel Spark, *Loitering with Intent*[1]

Three facts converge – gender, being an artist and historical moment. In *Loitering with Intent*, we read Fleur Talbot's autobiography as she looks back to a decisive period of ten months, from September 1949 to the end of June 1950, when she acted as secretary to Sir Quentin Oliver's Autobiographical Association and had accepted for publication her first novel, *Warrender Chase*. Fleur repeats this thought about the wonder of being a woman and an artist in the middle of the twentieth century on two further occasions. Her adaptation of Beneventuto Cellini's comment, 'I am now going on my way rejoicing', is repeated with slight amendments a further five times. Like Fleur, Muriel Spark quotes Cellini. Her autobiography, *Curriculum Vitae*, also ends with the publication of a first novel, *The Comforters*. Reading the laudatory reviews that her editor, Alan Maclean had brought for her to see, Spark comments: 'However, I took great heart from what he said and went on my way rejoicing'.[2] *The Comforters* too is a novel from the mid-century, finished in late 1955 and published in 1957. It concerns a literary critic, Caroline Rose (another character whose name signifies flower), who is about to write her first novel, precisely Spark's situation at that time and close to Fleur's situation in *Loitering With Intent*. As Spark says in *Curriculum Vitae*, *The Comforters* was the novel she had to write to know she could be a novelist: 'I didn't feel like "a novelist" and before I could square it with my literary conscience to write a novel, I had to work out a novel-writing process, peculiar to myself, and moreover, perform this act within the very novel I proposed to write' (206). Thus, Spark's characteristic self-referentiality permits the three texts – fictional autobiography, autobiography and novel – to converge around this founding moment of a woman author producing her first novel in the middle of the twentieth century.

Such breezy optimism about the life of the woman artist is not possible for Mary Swann, the poet in Carol Shields's novel of that name.[3] Shields is equally precise with her dating. Swann's only publication, a book of poems entitled *Swann's Songs*, comes a little later in the century, 1966. It is, indeed, a swan song as Mary had been murdered by her husband in December 1965 after a life of rural poverty in Ontario, Canada. An article written by feminist critic, Sarah Maloney, in the early 1980s is instrumental in initiating Swann studies; five years later the first Swann symposium takes place. Both *Loitering with Intent* and *Mary Swann* reflect on the creation of a woman author at a particular historical moment. Shields's novel, located in the late 1980s, shows how the market and the literary field take up Swann twenty years after her death and construct her to suit their own purposes. As we saw in previous chapters, ethical and aesthetic dilemmas about the nature of authorship and the production of a text, and the struggle, both personal and collective, to create an author are central. In both of the novels we consider here, an important trope is the loss or theft of literary material and the implications of this for authorial power, that power's necessity and its danger. Though Fleur remarks on the convergence of three facts, it is not clear whether the wonder of being 'a woman' and 'an artist' in the middle of the twentieth century extends to the wonder of being 'a woman artist'. The construction of Byatt's Mrs Brown and Shields's Mary Swann within the context of a feminist discourse provides a language for speaking about the woman artist. But Spark's post-war focus points to a period in which it would be difficult to see oneself, or be seen, as a woman artist in anything other than a pejorative or ironic way. Though terms such as 'a lady novelist' or 'a poetesse' would have been used in a self-consciously archaic manner, there was at this period no developed discourse around women's writing with which Fleur could have associated herself. Moreover, looking back on her life from thirty odd years later, Fleur has no desire to raise that situation as a problem, for reasons which we shall consider later.

Lost ...

At the end of *Mary Swann* a group of participants at the Mary Swann symposium gathers to reconstruct one of her poems, entitled 'Lost Things', a poem which has itself been almost lost by the curious disappearance of all the volumes of Swann's poetry. Almost lost but not quite since the group is composed of Swann fans, some of whom know her poems by heart, and, thus, with a bit of cross-checking amongst themselves, they can resurrect the poem. In the course of the novel we see important literary items deliberately cast aside or accidentally and irreparably damaged. By the end, seemingly everything connected with Mary Swann's literary production is lost – not only the copies of her one book of poems, 250 of which were published by a small press, but the lectures, notes and papers of three critics, Syd Buswell, Morton Jimroy and Willard Lang, Mary Swann's unpublished notebook, rhyming dictionary and the Parker 51 pen with which she wrote, numerous library holdings of her work and related papers, the single clear photograph of Mary Swann, a file concerning the publication of Swann's work and the original Swann manuscript itself. Morton Jimroy also believes, though with no evidence to support his supposition, that 'confiding letters' were sent by Swann but carelessly lost by her daughter, Frances Moore. Jimroy himself intends deliberately to exclude reference to two Swann letters in the biography of her he is writing while some love letters, reputed to be in the possession of Willard Lang, have yet to be revealed.[4] All these letters are, thus, by one means or other, lost to public view.

But is 'lost' the proper word? Throughout the novel a lexicon of terms is attributed to the disappearance of different objects. Things are 'stolen', 'loaned', 'mislaid', 'neglected', 'burgled', 'misplaced', 'spirited away', 'smuggled', 'removed'. By the time the symposium meets, Sarah Maloney and Frederic Cruzzi, Swann's publisher, are even talking with disbelief about loss through 'conspiracy' or 'academic piracy' (282) and the story does reveal a major academic fraud as Brownie, a bookseller and ex-lover of Sarah, schemes with Lang to appropriate, through fair means or foul, the entire Swann *oeuvre*. At what stage do things that are mislaid or neglected actually become 'lost' and can they be fully reclaimed? What is the difference between an accidental and a deliberate loss, an innocent or a malicious loss; indeed, can loss ever be intentional? When is a loss significant, when not; after all, the inconsequential 'lost things' of Swann's poem – a book, a picture, a coin, a spoon – take on a weighty, more metaphysical order of meaning by the end of the poem. On occasion things *are* just plain lost but the simple loss is often complicated with a more problematic form of loss, frequently loss through theft. So Jimroy's luggage is lost en route to California but in the luggage is the 'lost' photo of Mary Swann which was, in fact, stolen by Jimroy from the Nadeau Museum which has a display of Swann memorabilia. The luggage and photo are returned only for the photo to disappear a short time later from Jimroy's house. Then part of Jimroy's luggage, his briefcase, is lost again at the conference. It contains not only his notes, lecture and symposium materials but also 'a very valuable fountain pen' (254), valuable since it is the Mary Swann pen that Jimroy had stolen from the house of Frances Moore. Other things are feared lost but turn out not to be. The reader thinks that the remaining, blurred photo of Mary Swann might be lost when Rose Hindmarch, a neighbour of Mary Swann's and in charge of the local library, is in an embarrassed flurry to show it to Frederic Cruzzi and cannot, at first, find it in her suitcase. (Jimroy also has something of a problem in finding the stolen photo in his returned luggage.) Rose's photo is then nearly stolen from the glass exhibition case at the symposium and, finally, removed to Sarah Maloney's room for safe keeping. Similarly in 1965, Cruzzi is panicked to think that the Swann manuscript has been burnt by his wife. To his joy, it has not but then, to his fury, he discovers that it has been wrapped round wet fish and rendered, in part, illegible and, thus, 'lost'. This loss is replicated at the symposium when Brownie steals yet more material, puts it in a pillowcase and throws it out of the window. The pages that fall in the snow will become, like the manuscript of the poems, soggy and indecipherable.

While literary objects come and go, and the reader has to work hard to keep track of them, characters are bedevilled too with memory loss, their own and others. At the end of busy days, memories suddenly return. Sarah Maloney, getting ready for bed, is struck, after a day's nagging sense of 'neglect or loss' (29), with the thought that she has not seen Swann's notebook for some time. Rose is unable to settle in her bed until she clearly remembers what has been bothering her, namely, the unexpected invitation to the symposium. Jimroy, anxious that his life as well as his memory is falling apart, is pleased to wake up in the middle of the night and remember the word 'sporran'; he is also pleased that, despite losing his luggage and forgetting words, he always remembers the telephone number of his ex-wife so that he can make silent, nighttime calls to her. On the other hand, Jimroy is not at all pleased with the memory losses of Frances Moore who seems unable to recollect anything her mother said and explicitly refuses to remember any information about her father, especially that crucial event, his murder of her mother. It is fitting, therefore, that one of the lines of Swann's verse that

Jimroy recalls very well refers to 'stories of damage and loss' (108) and it is fortunate that the group gathered at the end of the story remembers Swann's work so effectively. Rose remembers with wondrous clarity a number of events, meetings, conversations with and relating to Swann and tries to charm the misogynist Jimroy with her information: unfortunately, all the memories are completely false. Memory for the other middle-aged and elderly neighbours of Mary Swann is not so clear but, at least, honest and, in a desultory way, they attempt to recall details of her looks, manner and verse.

Loss, then, is associated with both economic and symbolic gain within the field of Swann studies. To reinforce the developing symbolic status of Swann, certain items have deliberately to be lost because they do not accord with the owner's view of who Mary Swann, the poet, should be. Thus Sarah, having been given by Rose Mary Swann's copy of *Spratt's New Improved Rhyming Dictionary for Practising Poets*, drops it into a roadside litterbin. Though Sarah can accept Swann as a poor, oppressed farmer's wife, uneducated and far removed from literary circles – indeed, that biography fits rather well into Sarah's feminist critique – the thought that she might have got her rhymes from a rhyming dictionary is too crass to be accepted. Even her recollection that Sylvia Plath consulted a thesaurus is insufficient balm. Sarah's motives are a combination of the self-interested and the selfless. The dictionary might have explained why so many critics had found Swann's rhymes deplorable and, hence, it could have been of use to the critical field but, at the same time, it would have undermined Sarah's clever, and already published, argument concerning the rhymes. Sarah is highly protective of Swann and would not want her disdained but she is also keen to protect her investment. Such rapid calculations of the debits and credits of certain actions are common amongst the critics. Jimroy is omitting from his biography Swann's letter to a mail-order company about returning underwear and has ' "misplaced" another, which referred to a "nigger family" the astonished Mary Swann saw in Elgin one summer' (88). Neither Swann's racism nor her ordinariness and definitely not references to underwear can be accommodated in Jimroy's elevated view of his biographical art.[5]

Shields reveals how the competitive nature of literary fields is such that everyone is involved in literal or metaphorical forms of theft, a continuous round of loss for some and gain for others. As we saw in Chapter 3, the field, as Bourdieu conceives it, is a space of conflict involving all forms of capital whether the economic that motivates Brownie, the symbolic capital that spurs the critics or the cultural capital for which Rose hopes. Sarah is aware how the gains of her research in terms of new knowledge might depend on a kind of theft. She says about Rose: 'As she talked, I took notes, feeling like a thief but not missing a word' (42). The gain is not only for the critic but for all participants in the game who take part in 'countless small acts of deception' (163) and 'subtle thefts and acts of cannibalism' (231). Both members of the symposium and the neighbours back in Nadeau feed, to a greater or lesser extent, on the life and work of Mary Swann, hoping to touch the hem of greatness. Jimroy, Brownie and Lang are involved in theft in more direct ways both to augment their capitals and as a product of their troubled psychologies. Gain through theft can compensate – at least temporarily – for an inner sense of loss and substitute a sense of power and satisfaction. Brownie recalls losing some stamps as a child and feeling 'stupid and careless and unworthy' (38). Presumably, gain through money or theft will make him feel clever and in control and of value. In Jimroy's case there is the added delight of 'perverse pleasure' (140) in imagining the distress of his victim but that power and pleasure have to be risked repeatedly so as to reaffirm them. The criminal acts of Jimroy, Brownie and Lang are but the most extreme examples of a widespread process whereby characters take from others for their own varied benefits. Disinterestedness is always shown to have an interest which in the worst cases 'can lead to the most brutally interested and egoistic confrontations'. Bourdieu mentions as his example 'the forgery of scientific results'.[6] *Mary Swann* provides its own share of examples, not only of theft but tampering with material, editing that borders on re-writing, numerous deceptions, self-deceptions and sleights of hand.

Not surprisingly, then, Swann's poem that is reconstructed at the end of the symposium links loss not with gain but with shame. The 'larger loss' is likened in the poem's final line to 'moments of shame' (313) and it is this line that Cruzzi contributes to the group's collective reconstruction of the poem. Cruzzi has cause to link 'loss' and 'shame'. On discovering that his wife, Hildë, had been responsible for the wet fish incident, he had lashed out violently causing her to fall and cut her chin. 'Something snapped' (221) in him at just about the same moment as it did in Angus Swann: *both* of them could have been wife murderers. While the nature of the lost things and the manner of their loss vary, so also do the motivations and levels of culpability of those involved, and so does the significance of the loss. A different set of synonyms for 'lost' come to mind – lost as 'excluded' or 'expropriated' or, as Bourdieu would suggest, lost through symbolic violence. The historical loss of Mary Swann is compounded by all these other losses. One of the reading effects of the novel is that the real reader, like the critics and the readers at the symposium, is forced to peer through the miasma of loss and uncertainty so as to piece together the scraps and clues to reinstate Swann.

Fleur Talbot in Spark's *Loitering with Intent* is alive and feisty enough to fight her own corner as an author. In dialogue throughout the book with the autobiographical practice of not only Cellini but also John Henry Newman, Fleur produces her own *apologia pro vita sua* as a writer: she does not need the critics to do this for her. But, like the Swann community, Fleur does have to cope with repeated losses as she finds herself in the middle of a frantic game of theft and counter-theft; she struggles to maintain control of her literary production and defeat the machinations of her employer, Sir Quentin Oliver. Sir Quentin keeps under lock and key the memoirs of the Autobiographical Association, a group of – to him – highly distinguished friends who are in the process of writing their life-stories. Fleur perceives at once the potential in this situation for blackmail though she later learns that Sir Quentin's goal is not money but power. Fearful that he is being revealed in Fleur's novel, Sir Quentin attempts to destroy her book and, under his influence, Dottie, Fleur's friend, steals the manuscript of *Warrender Chase* from Fleur's room. Fleur consoles herself with the thought that the typescript and proofs are still with her publisher, Revisson Doe, but he has already been leant on by Sir Quentin and not only disposed of the only typescript and the proofs but broken up the type. A second set of proofs which was earlier sent to Fleur's literary friends, Theo and Audrey, has been returned to the publisher and destroyed with the rest of the material while a further set which Fleur spied in Sir Quentin's desk drawer has been burnt. Fleur eventually steals back the manuscript from Dottie's room, replicating the strategy Dottie used, and in fevered haste produces two typed copies which she lodges with her friend, Solly, while she retains the manuscript and one new transcript. To act as leverage during this period, Fleur steals from Sir Quentin's office the memoirs of the Autobiographical Association which Sir Quentin has a professional burglar steal back; Edwina, Sir Quentin's mother, subsequently destroys them. And Edwina steals pages from Sir Quentin's diary and passes them to Fleur. These pages conclusively prove Sir Quentin's manipulative corruption. Fleur types a fair copy to show to Sir Quentin, who believes she must have employed a professional burglar, while keeping the original.

The twists and turns of the plot and the proliferation of references – to the manuscript, the original manuscript, the handwritten manuscript, the manuscript copy, the foolscap manuscript, the proofs, the printed proofs, the new transcript, the typescript, the carbon copies of the type-script, the typeset and so on – are, in part, a literary in-joke about the complexity of book production in a pre-computer age. The events further convey Fleur's increasing desperation as the product of each stage in the production process evaporates before her eyes. But, more fundamentally, the loss of literary material in both *Mary Swann* and *Loitering with Intent* raises questions about authorial control. If the author is not controlling the material, who is and for what purpose? Furthermore, in both texts, the prolific loss generates an anxiety on the part of the reader as s/he tracks the 'lost things', the author and the texts. What are we all looking for? Is it some origin, a Holy Grail? Why do we want to know the author? Are we sure the text should be owned and controlled? Why do we want to tie the text to the author? Though the movements of theft and counter-theft are, at times, reminiscent of a French farce or a pantomime, there is no doubt that this is a deadly serious game about authorial control and, particularly in Fleur's mind, about literary truth.

... and Found

Swann's poem suggests that lost things 'have withdrawn/ Into them-selves'. They are 'without history,/ Waiting out of sight'. They are 'Without a name/ Or definition or form' (313). This could be a description not of a lost *thing* but of a lost *person* – the woman author, outside liter-ary tradition and needing to be reinstated; for the critics at the sympo-sium, this could be a figure for Mary Swann herself. As Shields's critics have indicated, *Mary Swann* creates a strong sense of both the absence and presence of the woman poet. She is absent in being dead, in the doubtful authorship of her one text, in the paucity of records that have been left (her notebook, for example, or the lack of a driving license or medical records), in the fuzziness of others' memories, in the lack of a social network in which to situate her. Even those who make careers out of her presence can find themselves close to defeat. To Sarah Moloney, Swann is 'maddeningly enigmatic' (191); to Jimroy, her biographer, she reveals 'one of the dullest lives ever lived' (76); to Willard Lang, she is 'narrowly rural' (18). Often with no proof or against what little there is, the field of critics and readers make strenuous efforts to establish Swann within various discourses, such as feminism, postcolonialism – specifically, as a Canadian author – and within recognised literary forms or a presti-gious literary genealogy; Burns, Jane Austen, Rilke, Stevie Smith, Rashid and Emily Dickinson are all mentioned as relevant antecedents.[7] Rose, who is not a literary critic, can provide the personal memoir and be the living link with the past. These discourses permit Swann's making as 'a poet', a position which in 1966 would have been near to impossible for a woman in her situation. Her only position then would have been as a local celebrity – and she had sent in poems to the local paper – or, as Lang's comment indicates, as a regionalist, or as a *poète naïve* if she had been taken up by the literary establishment of the time.

One way to understand Swann's creation as a poet is in relation to Foucault's author-function, particularly its third characteristic which is that the author-function 'does not develop spontaneously as the attribution of a discourse to an individual. It is, rather, the result of a complex operation which constructs a certain rational being that we call "author".'[8] Though the critics in *Mary Swann* are capable of 'analyzing the subject as a variable and complex function of discourse', and Sarah especially can see how Lang's emphasis on 'rusticity' and Jimroy's grandiose attitude to biography place Swann in a particular way, none of the critics is quite willing to join in 'depriving the subject (or its substitute) of its role as originator' (158). This is because the critics are keen to support the developing status of both Swann as 'author' and, as we saw in earlier chapters with respect to Pieixoto and Offred and to Shona McRury and Mrs Brown, of themselves as 'creator of the creator'.[9] Precisely as Foucault predicts, the critics and readers look to the figure of 'the author', Mary Swann, as the explicator of the text, each feeling they have special access to her meaning, and all work to ensure the unity and homogeneity of her writing, hence, the need to 'lose' unsavoury letters or the rhyming dictionary. Though Foucault recognises that the incompatible can be 'tied together or organized around a fundamental or originating contradiction' (151), having a recognised author with a penchant for reading the Bobbsey Twins and Edna Ferber is a contradiction too far.

Foucault makes clear that talking about the author and the author-function is distinct from talking about the writer: 'It would be just as wrong to equate the author with the real writer as to equate him with the fictitious speaker; the author-function is carried out and operates in the scission itself, in this division and this distance' (152). What we see in *Mary Swann* is not only that 'complex operation' for constructing 'the author' and the attribution of a text to this figure in the most speculative circumstances but also the problem of constructing 'the author' in the absence of 'the writer'. Despite their allegiance to their particular critical approaches, the elusiveness of 'the writer' Mary Swann inhibits and, at times, exasperates the critics. Authorship cannot be solely a discursive production, the text suggests; there has to be some credible link with an historical, embodied presence. Furthermore, while 'the writer' cannot be found in any extensive way, the attempts of the critics to establish 'the author' are repeatedly unsettled by Shields and this in three respects. First, the satire of the academic field undermines the discourses – feminist, postcolonial, biographical – that the critics are using to confirm 'the author'; second, the status of *Swann's Songs* is so dubious that the reader does not know who the 'real writer' is and the determination of the critics to link Mary Swann to the post of 'author' only serves to emphasise the contrived nature of the process; third, the critics cannot reconcile certain traces of 'the writer', for example, her popular reading tastes or the scraps of lined paper on which she wrote, as these do not easily fit with the construction of a consecrated author.

We could link Foucault's approach to authorship with that of Bourdieu. Bourdieu's interest is not only in the positions that an author may take up in the literary field, as we saw in the previous chapter, but in the *dispositions*, intellectual and bodily, that the individual brings to the activity. These dispositions may give us a way of understanding those traces of the writer or, as Foucault says, 'the scission' between the author and the writer. What we learn from Cruzzi, Rose and the neighbours in Nadeau about the timidity of Swann and her gaucheness, places her outside the expected dispositions of 'the author' but also suggests the pathos of her situation, that sad aspiration to be what she was not meant to be. Rose, sharing to some extent Swann's *habitus*, can understand her situation more readily than Jimroy. Bourdieu describes *habitus* as 'the product of a *practical* sense' and as 'a socially constituted "sense of the game" '.[10] It is our finely tuned understanding of how to behave appropriately within the fields we inhabit, 'a sort of ontological complicity, a subconscious and pre-reflexive fit'; the shrewd calculations of the critics, mentioned earlier, would be an example of *habitus* at work.[11] While Jimroy tries to inflate Swann's absence from church into a sign of some primitive spirituality outside the bounds of established institutions, Rose prosaically indicates that it was more likely due to Swann not having any decent clothes. And when he suggests that Swann's blood poem is about the sacrament of Holy Communion, Rose thinks, but dares not say, that it is rather more likely to be about menstruation. For Jimroy there would be no way to find a 'fit' between the bodily hexis of a menstruating woman and the post of a poet of distinction. Swann's bodily dispositions – the scant hair, the lost teeth, the hesitant speech – confirm her oppression and poverty and, again, limit her likely possibilities as an author to that of the minor or eccentric.

But Bourdieu talks also of how the body '*enacts* the past, bringing it back to life' and Cruzzi has recognised that.[12] In his reference to the 'sensual' (213) in Swann's mannerisms and to something 'intimate and dignified' (215) in her voice is a trace, that of a lost allure. Speaking of Susanna Moodie, Shields remarks: 'How do you retrieve someone who is dead and try to build up with the nib of your pen a personality who was voiceless about things that mattered? ... it's a little bit like the resurrection of Mary in *Swann: A Mystery*. How can you ever know anything about a person who's been so effectively erased from the world?'[13] Bourdieu offers a parallel example in his description of the naïve artist, le Douanier Rousseau, who 'has no "biography" in the sense of a life story worthy of being recounted and transcribed' and is 'literally *created* by the artistic field'.[14] In Swann's resurrection, Shields encourages the reader to be suspect about the construction of 'the author' by the literary field and of 'the writer' by the people of Nadeau but to continue looking for Mary Swann in the sketchiness, absences and uncertain memories of the biography.

If Mary Swann is identified with an absence that can be redeemed only partially or artificially, Fleur Talbot has a commanding and self-activating presence. On 28 May 1950, Fleur thinks of the opening scene of *Warrender Chase* in which the death of Warrender in a car crash is announced and then hears the next day that her enemy, Sir Quentin, had been killed in a head-on collision at just about that moment; on 1 July she gets a letter from Triad Press and learns at the following meeting that they are to publish her novel; in the weeks after publication a series of positive reviews, media contacts and the selling of American rights, paperback rights, film and foreign rights establish Fleur as an economically independent and successful author. As is the case with Caroline in *The Comforters*, Fleur becomes 'the author' as she writes and lives through the production of her book and her writing entails a meditation, a disputation, on the nature of novel writing and life-writing. In her characters, Fleur is not looking for 'constancy' and 'steadiness' or unity as do the members of the Autobiographical Association or for the spurious 'frankness' that Sir Quentin admires but, instead, for the contradictory, the paradoxical, 'bits of invented patchwork' (30). Fleur's authorial position is similarly ambiguous. On the one hand, we see her trying to get her first toehold in the literary field, on the other, she is reflecting on thirty years as a successful writer; on the one hand, she loses all control of her manuscript, on the other, she tenaciously and deviously retrieves it and both the character of Fleur and the momentum of the text leaves the reader in no doubt that she will be victorious. In terms of the production and ownership of her work, Fleur insists on being 'the author'; in terms of the artistic process she is accepting of the inexplicable and serendipitous in the fluid relation between fiction and reality and the osmotic manner in which the artist, sometimes consciously and sometimes unconsciously, absorbs the turns of phrase and the mannerisms of the people around her. Her comments on the role of the artist approximate a Romantic view; the artist is concerned with 'truth', magically transforms reality, has a vocation and a prophetic perception. But these comments are delivered in an offhand manner that undercuts any portentousness and Fleur never loses contact with an economic base of poorly paid jobs and slender means.

Fleur refuses to provide motives for her characters or to help the reader 'know whose side they were supposed to be on … indicating what the reader should think' (53). She never wants to curry favour with the reader; her presumption is that the ideal reader is self-sufficient. This resistance to determining everything and the openness to multiple meanings is, Barthes tells us, 'an anti-theological activity, an activity that is truly revolutionary since to refuse to fix meaning is, in the end, to refuse God and his hypostases – reason, science, law'.[15] Yet it is just as difficult to 'fix' Fleur as a refuser of totalising meanings as to 'fix' her as a promoter. She does critique the dogmatic and controlling, particularly through her evaluations of Sir Quentin and his housekeeper, Mrs Tims, but, at the same time, she uses a moral vocabulary which can speak absolutely of truth versus falsity, good versus evil, and, yet again, she can employ a playful narrative method and a style of wit, wryness, lightness of touch. What Malcolm Bradbury has said of Spark applies equally to Fleur: '[I]t is the relation between the chaotic and contingent and the possibility of a meaning and a teleology that guides both her artistic and moral interests.'[16] That 'relation' is not a reconciling or synthesising of contradictions; it is more an acceptance of parallel universes. Like Spark, Fleur is a proponent of the 'nevertheless principle', a way of viewing the world which builds a bridge from the known to the unlikely.[17]

Fleur is, at once, the author-as-God and the author-as-jester. She is also the author-as-devil. Bryan Cheyette remarks on how Spark's later fiction was 'to mischievously encourage the idea of a demonic narrator who could represent with aggressive honesty, the absurdity of contemporary life as well as the dark forces underpinning the writer's imagination'.[18] Fleur has no doubt that she is writing in opposition to Sir Quentin for *her* writing is concerned with 'ideas of truth and wonder' (59) while Sir Quentin embodies 'pure evil' (120 and 148) and produces 'falsity' (83) in the writings of the Autobiographical Association. But the reader is alerted from the start of the novel to the fact that Fleur has a 'demon' inside her and this links her to Sir Quentin rather than distinguishes her (8).

She understands his purposes as quite different from her own, 'yet at the same time they coincided' (27). Like Sir Quentin, she uses blackmail and theft; like him, she is involved in autobiography, that most omniscient of forms that foregrounds the relation between life (*bios*) and writing (*graphe*); like him, she amends the memoirs of the Autobiographical Association members and uses them for her own purposes in her writing career; like him, she has done her own dangerous tampering in introducing Dottie to the Autobiographical Association. Sir Quentin may have his 'little sect' (142) but Fleur, her publishers predict, will have 'a small cult-following' (153). The moral values of Fleur's autobiography are constantly unsettled. We are uneasy about Fleur's allegiance to truth and good; what is morally 'good' can also be a self-serving manoeuvre. We identify with Fleur's assertion that Sir Quentin is false and evil but recall that Dottie associates Sir Quentin with goodness. Then we remember how none of Dottie's views are ever endorsed in the text but, equally, how Fleur is always 'loitering with intent'. Spark leads the reader to hope for Fleur's success as an author but also to wonder what monster has been created.

Why not 'a woman artist'?

Until the acceptance of her first novel, Fleur's position has been much less secure and she ekes out a living 'on the grubby edge of the literary world' (78); her friends are mostly writers or they know writers or they think that with a bit of effort they could be a writer. Publishing is about gentleman publishers, small magazines and even smaller returns. Sitting in a pub one night with her poet friend, Gray Mauser, Fleur notes:

> There were one or two well-known poets at the bar at whom we glanced from our respectful distance, for they were far beyond our sphere. I think the poets at the bar on that occasion were Dylan Thomas and Roy Campbell, or it could have been Louis MacNeice and someone else; it made no difference for the point was we felt the atmosphere was as good as the Cornish pasties and beer, and we could talk. (73)

In one sense, Fleur is right, the names make no difference; they interchangeably signify 'poet' and 'literary status'. But in Spark's career the name of specifically Louis MacNeice is significant. Martin McQuillan has written of the four occasions in which Spark returns in her writing to an event in the Summer of 1944 when, caught in a London air raid, she had been invited to shelter in a house, only to discover during the evening that this was the house of Louis MacNeice, though MacNeice himself was not at home. McQuillan remarks that 'the name of Louis MacNeice in these fragments is the rehearsal and a condensation of a complex social and cultural process which brings Spark to writing'.[19] As with the mid-century publication of a first novel, that I mentioned at the beginning of this chapter, Spark sees this event as a founding moment and writes of it in *Curriculum Vitae*: 'I felt I had truly entered the world of literature; it had symbolically materialized; it was real' (162). But, interestingly, McQuillan characterises Spark's returns to this incident as signifying loss as much as a becoming: 'As Spark's writing career unfolds each fragment mourns the lost subjectivity which is the theme of the preceding texts' (90). Once again, the coming into being of the woman author is a series of births, deaths and resurrections.

At this point in Fleur's career, 'Louis MacNeice' expresses a longing or the unattainable. One notes too the fact that all the named poets are male. Fleur is in awe of a literary field of Thomas, Campbell and MacNeice, not Elizabeth Jennings, Kathleen Raine and Anne Ridler or, if she were to think of women novelists of the period, Elizabeth Taylor or Barbara Pym or Rosamond Lehmann, and in this absence is another sense of loss. In *Curriculum Vitae*, Spark mentions male authors in a similar, notable way, not only MacNeice but Edmund Blunden who tries to arrange a date with her and Evelyn Waugh whom she describes, in words close to Fleur's on the famous poets, as 'someone quite outside of my orbit' (207). Fleur does not see the absence of a female literary tradition as an issue. As I pointed out earlier, the specific problems and possibilities of 'the woman artist' are not mentioned at the end of the novel when Fleur reflects on her career.

In addition, though we know that Fleur thinks this is a 'wonderful' time to be a woman – presumably because of the developing possibilities for a single, independent, creative life for women – the gender critique that emerges in the novel situates Fleur as at odds with femininity. It is antipathetic to the constructs of femininity of the period and is acutely aware of femininity as a performance linked to artificiality and manipulation. Irritated at Dottie, Fleur plays at the hysteric: 'To show her I was a woman I tore up the pages of my novel and stuffed them into the wastepaper basket, burst out crying and threw her out, roughly and noisily, so that Mr Alexander looked over the banisters and complained' (53). She satirises the performance by both Dottie and Mrs Tims, of 'the English Rose', the dominant construct of middle-class femininity in the post-war period, and she makes this the title of her third novel.

Mrs Tims, banging about to get attention at a meeting of the Autobiographical Association, is derided by Fleur: 'It seemed that as she was being overlooked as a woman she was determined to behave as a man' (31). Especially important for Fleur is to reject the conventional, gendered implications for women's authorship; she admits that she writes with a 'light and heartless hand' (59) and refuses any suggestion that the author has an obligation to charm.[20] Thus, for Fleur to become 'a woman artist', rather than 'a woman' and 'an artist', as indicated in the epigraph to this chapter, it would have to be without the support of a female literary tradition, against the dominant constructs of femininity and against her own disposition as a satiric but admiring spectator on the margin of a male-dominated literary field – not an easy task.

Despite the austerity of post-war life, evident in the novel in the references to petrol and food rationing, utility coats, bombed out buildings or the black market, Fleur can, at least, look to making herself as a writer within the conditions of modernity. As both she and Sir Quentin declare, they are living in 'modern times' (10 and 27) – another connection between the two – but, then, the flippancy of Fleur's tone and the pomposity of Sir Quentin's make that proposition doubtful as well. Fleur's strategy of ridicule links to Spark's writing philosophy as outlined in 'The Desegregation of Art' where she refers to ridicule as 'the only honourable weapon we have left'.[21] Spark is placing herself in opposition to what she terms 'socially-conscious art' where the victim, in various forms, is defended against the oppressor. Such art draws both authors and audiences into 'a cult of the victim' (24), what she sees as a false sense of involvement in the social world, a false catharsis and a condition of hypocrisy. Fleur too resents as hypocritical the artist's vicarious identification – 'No matter what is described it seems to me a sort of hypocrisy for a writer to pretend to undergo tragic experiences when obviously one is sitting in relative comfort with a pen and paper or before a typewriter' (59) – and her own writing, as we hear it in her ruminations on her work-in-progress, is not socially conscious in any explicit way. Spark turns to satire, mockery, cunning as more effective and more democratic aesthetic modes. This is very much Fleur's authorial position as well. She not only ridicules popular constructs of femininity but Sir Quentin's dark power, Dottie's rabid Catholicism and the literary scene she is, at the same time, trying to enter. Only Edwina and Solly remain touchstones of value.

Fleur keeps distinct the designations, 'woman' and 'artist', so as to avoid taking on the consequences of women's social and aesthetic exclusion. To be 'the woman artist' risks either becoming involved in that victimised position which she has rejected or in a proselytising role associated with the doctrinaire which, again, both Spark and Fleur find unappealing. However, rejecting this seems to necessitate in Fleur's mind a rejection also of any group identity and a common history; indeed, her confidence depends on not recognising a history of 'women artists'. Given this position, it is surprising to find in Fleur's (and Spark's) aesthetic views and narrative methods, echoes of that great advocate for women's writing, Virginia Woolf. For instance, Fleur is interested in 'what [she] saw out of the corners of [her] eyes' (27). The critique of gender emerges in the use of the indirect, the apparently inconsequential or the elliptical comment and, to this extent, Fleur and Spark *are* in a line of female writers.[22] Consider not only Woolf herself but the suggestion of Woolf's narrator in *A Room of One's Own* that the only way for Mary Carmichael to write the story of Chloe and Elizabeth 'would be to talk of something else, looking steadily out of the window' or, indeed, Emily Dickinson's advice to 'tell all the truth but tell it slant'.[23]

In addition, Fleur, Spark and Woolf all agree on the emotional and political dangers in an unconsidered identification with others and on the effectiveness of satire and ridicule as aesthetic modes. In *Three Guineas*, Woolf comments on the number of books being written by the educated middle class about the working class, just as in *A Room of One's Own* she had noted the number of men writing about women. Whereas in the latter case the presiding emotions seemed to be anger and fear on the part of the male author, the working class offers to the socially conscious middle-class 'glamour' and 'the emotional relief afforded by adopting its cause'.[24] This is reminiscent of Spark's comment on the cathartic effect of feeling 'absolved' (24) as the readers' 'moral responsibilities are sufficiently fulfilled by the emotions they have been induced to feel' (23) and Fleur's remark on the hypocrisy of writers. Like Woolf, Fleur and Spark see such emotional outpouring as essentially conservative. Purged of the distress, the reader or theatre goer 'rises refreshed, more determined than ever to be the overdog', says Spark (24). Finally, both Spark in 'The Desegregation of Art' and Woolf in *Three Guineas* are stirred by the same political crisis. Spark writes of the goose-stepping and posturing of Hitler and Mussolini and their troops which, she believes, could have been fatally disturbed by the derision of massed crowds. In *Three Guineas*, published on the eve of the Second World War, Woolf advocates laughing at power, indifference to power, a refusal to reinforce it by acknowledging it and the adoption of an 'outsider' position. The adequacy of these aesthetic modes as a political response and the ease with which ridicule of the powerful can extend into a more general disdain have been critiqued; both Woolf and Spark have been accused of snobbishness. Spark's political intent in 'The Desegregation of Art' is clear; she wants an effective politics, not a turning away from politics. But the role she gives to culture, the bringing about of 'a mental environment of honesty and self-knowledge, a sense of the absurd and a general looking-lively' (26) is not only distinct from what one would conventionally see as politically engaged but looks a weak response in face of the forces of fascism. Woolf's *Three Guineas* met similar objections.

At the same time, we need to be cautious about pressing too emphatically the relation to Woolf. Despite the dangers, Woolf saw the need to name 'the woman artist'. She was politically more involved, had a developed analysis of patriarchy and a different understanding of history. As we see through Fleur, Spark understands history as historical moment, all those precisely dated events from 1949–50, and there is a strong sense of historical period in the depiction of a post-war social life. Fleur is placed in history but she does not come to us with a history; we simply encounter her in the graveyard, learn about ten months of her writing career and a very sketchy *resumé* of what follows. Elizabeth Dipple believes that Spark's situating of the novel in the middle of the century and, one could add, in the middle of Fleur's life is an example of 'a metafictional parody of the ancient idea of epic narrative begun *in medias res* [which] connects her heroine's artistic life with the tremendous fictional structures of the past'.[25] This may help us to see Fleur within one kind of more extended history but Spark is not interested in Woolf's sense of a longer history as a narrative of struggle and of social change. Spark can make no sense of the longer movements of history since history to her is 'absurd'; what we have to deal with, she believes, is 'the ridiculous nature of the reality before us' (26).

I considered, at the start of this chapter, some of the meanings of 'loss' with respect to *Mary Swann*. The nature of the loss varies. It is affected by motives; it signifies in material, psychological and bodily ways; it operates in an economy of debit and credit in the relations of the critics; and there are different inflections of meaning between related and synonymous terms. Dominick LaCapra explores semantic and conceptual differences in the distinctions and relations between 'loss', 'absence' and 'lack'. '[L]oss is situated on a historical level and is the consequence of particular events.' He stresses that 'it is important not to hypostatize particular historical losses or lacks and present them as mere instantiations of some inevitable absence or constitutive feature of existence'.[26] Locating loss in the historical is to recognise the meaning of specific events or the consequences for specific people and to enable a working-through of the problem in the present and the future. Loss is the term we can attach to Mary Swann. Her figure becomes intelligible within a particular social and literary history – that is, the situation of women, working-class and postcolonial writers in the middle of the twentieth century – and within a particular cultural milieu that leaves Swann reliant on the dubious activities of a literary field in which she has no part. 'Lack', remarks LaCapra, 'indicates a felt need or a deficiency; it refers to something that ought to be there but is missing' (703). This too can function within the historical. It does not have to signify a personal inadequacy; as Shields conceives it, 'lack' could apply to the figure of Mary Swann and the fragmented history of women writers.

But it is more difficult to relate Fleur's coming to authorship to such a model. Spark's comic mode works against the tragedy of 'loss' and 'lack' and, as we have seen, Fleur does not see women's authorship as framed by a history of prohibition and a struggle for access, though she is conscious of the workings of gender and class. Spark describes her own political position, inherited from her Edinburgh upbringing, as 'a haughty and remote anarchism' with no faith in politics and politicians but, it would seem, with a high degree of individualism.[27] One could describe Fleur in the same way. Fleur eschews a political vocabulary of 'justice' and 'rights' in favour of a moral vocabulary of 'truth' and 'good'. This vocabulary is suggestive of the absolute, the transhistorical and the metaphysical that LaCapra associates with 'absence'. For Fleur, though, the moral sense helps to establish her presence. Fleur tells us that the 'three facts converging' to make her career as a writer possible are gender, being an artist and historical moment. But, having read her story, one could look again at that passage and interpret it rather differently. What makes authorship possible for Fleur is, first, a faith in 'truth' and 'good', second, a belief in personal initiative and 'conviction' – and we see in her much of that determined, valiant individual – and, third, an ahistorical intervention of the miraculous and the fortuitous. These 'facts' could never produce 'the woman artist' with her sense of a collective and political identity but they do lead to much rejoicing as 'a woman' and as 'an artist'.

5
Tell Me a Story
Women Oral Narrators

> I write my letters, I seal them, I drop them in the box. One day
> when we are departed you will tip them out and glance through
> them. 'Better had there been only Cruso and Friday,' you will
> murmur to yourself: 'Better without the woman.' Yet where
> would you be without the woman?
>
> J. M. Coetzee, *Foe*[1]

> I have been unwritten. Written out. Written off. Therefore I am
> not even dead. I never was. I am non-existent. There is no I.
>
> Michèle Roberts, *In the Red Kitchen*[2]

In the following three chapters, I consider three specific incarnations of
the figure of the woman author. Issues about the role of the author, the
power to authorise and about access to the cultural field continue to
be relevant for these women but so also are matters of textuality.
The woman author is embroiled in problems about genre, literary form
and language and solving these problems is important in maintaining
her independence and her autonomy as an author. A major dilemma for
the women authors figuring in this chapter lies in the movement of their
stories from oral to written format, a move which, in each case, is from
female to male author. Susan Barton in J. M. Coetzee's *Foe*, an imagined
prequel to Daniel Defoe's *Robinson Crusoe*, is written out of history like
Michèle Roberts's female pharaoh who dreams of her defaced sepulchre
where all the painted scenes of her triumphant reign and the hiero-
glyphs spelling her name are obliterated. Rescued with Cruso and Friday
from the desert island on which they have been cast away, Susan tells
her story to the ship's captain who has no doubt about its uniqueness
and suggests, encouragingly, that the booksellers will be able to 'hire a
man to set your story to rights, and put in a dash of colour too, here and

there', an idea that Susan indignantly rejects in the name of 'truth' (40). Susan's determination to 'be the author of my own story' (40) and her conviction, after the death of Cruso on board the ship returning to England, that she now owns the island narrative are views that are sorely challenged and yet persist. Though she learns to doubt the possibility of her story being written without Friday's, she remains sure that the author, Foe, must write under her direction, that she has the power 'to guide and amend. Above all to withhold', and that she must be 'father' to the story (123).[3] Susan's response to Foe's tale of an Irishwoman about to be hanged at Tyburn who, compulsively, kept confessing proves apposite: 'If I were the Irishwoman, I should rest most uneasy in my grave knowing to what interpreter the story of my last hours has been consigned' (124). Susan has every reason to rest uneasy. Not only does the story that has come down to us in Defoe's novel make no mention of her, it transforms the characters of Cruso and Friday and the island setting itself. And, to rub salt into the wound, it is Susan's personality – enquiring, resilient, reflective, self-sufficient – that has been bestowed on Defoe's Crusoe; the person Susan knew was taciturn, disinterested, without desire. In addition, the story of Susan's life in Bahia looking for her lost daughter, which Susan did not want told, appears in Defoe's *Roxana*.[4] As Coetzee shows, the relation of fiction to 'truth' is complex, male writers in the early eighteenth-century book trade were wily creatures and the chances of an aspiring woman author getting the better of them were few.[5]

Susan misses out on her chance for fame and fortune but in Sherley Anne Williams's *Dessa Rose* and Margaret Atwood's *Alias Grace* the situation is more hazardous. In *Dessa Rose*, Adam Nehemiah questions the slave woman, Dessa, about her part in a slave rebellion. Already a successful author of *The Master's Complete Guide to Dealing with Slaves and Other Dependents*, Nehemiah is now at work on *The Roots of Rebellion in the Slave Population and Some Means of Eradicating Them*. The new book, he feels, will establish him as an important Southern author though he is aware that too close a knowledge of slave management would bar him from the planter society he hopes to join: slave trading is 'something from which every gentleman would profit but which no gentleman would admit knowledge of'.[6] During the period of these interviews, the pregnant Dessa is imprisoned in a root cellar, expecting to be hanged after the birth of her baby. In Margaret Atwood's *Alias Grace* interviews are also taking place as Dr Simon Jordan questions Grace Marks about her role in the murders of Thomas Kinnear, her employer, and his housekeeper and mistress, Nancy Montgomery. Though unable to remember any of the salient events from the day of the murder, Grace is serving a life sentence in Kingston Penitentiary. Jordan hopes that he will be able to unlock her memory by his use of a kind of 'talking cure' and a process of association and suggestion and that his writing-up of the case will both advance his professional interests and, maybe, effect for Grace a pardon.

A number of factors, then, are common to the three texts. In each case, a woman in a parlous situation is telling her story to a male interlocutor who has a real expectation of becoming the published author of her narrative and sees the writing as contributing to his social advancement. The male/female relationship is riven by inequalities of gender, class, access to the public sphere and, in the case of Dessa and Nehemiah, by race; in each case, the woman is protective of her story and apprehensive about the motives of the man. But Susan is distinct from Dessa and Grace by being 'a free woman' – obviously, 'free' in the sense that she is not imprisoned as are the other two but 'free' also in that she identifies with a colonial ethic of unrestricted movement, entrepreneurial initiative and optimistic self-determination. I suspect that Susan could have talked very intelligently to Nehemiah about the problems of handling slaves. Dessa and Grace, on the other hand, know in their bones that freedom, in either its limited or fullest sense, is unlikely to be theirs. They are framed by discourses and historical conditions that position the woman as deviant, dangerous, unreliable, licentious, the man as rational, knowing, controlled. It is Nehemiah and Jordan who are the investigating subjects, Dessa and Grace who are the investigated.

However, in the course of these three novels, the distribution of power shifts and important questions about authorship and textuality occupy centre stage in that movement. Can the woman's story ever be told, who should tell it, how and through what interventions? *Dessa Rose* and *Alias Grace* explore the modes of resistance open to the investigated and the consequences these have on the telling, understanding and dissemination of the tales. We witness in *Dessa Rose* and *Alias Grace* an undercutting of the male author, his narrative, research methods and purpose. The woman, it seems, can turn to good effect the man's miscomprehension and his inability really to 'hear' her story and she can, then, structure her own narrative accordingly. For Dessa or Grace, the story telling, always a source of danger, holds out a possibility of some power. Conversely, Susan's belief in control is increasingly challenged as Coetzee's novel develops. Her personal defeat through Foe's manipulation and knowledge of the market is but one example from a literary history of exclusion. But, at least equally, Susan is defeated by the issue of market demands bearing on the problem of representation itself. How can she sell a castaway narrative that tells only of a bleak island inhabited by two men who have no desire to leave and who spend their time moving boulders? Susan VanZanten Gallagher shows how the point at issue is not only the story's content but also its structure, its lack of, in Edward Said's phrase, 'genealogical connections'.[7] It is these that Foe offers in his suggested rewriting of her story in terms of 'loss, then quest, then recovery; beginning, then middle, then end' (117). Particularly, Susan wonders, how she can make sense of either her own story or Cruso's without understanding the silence embodied in Friday. It is not that Susan does not want to tell her story or does not hold to her belief in the author as the origin and controller of the text; she wants to be the modern subject not the postmodern. But, increasingly, she simply does not know how it can be done. In exploring this struggle between oral narrator and professional author, I want to focus on three points of contact – relations of hearing and seeing, the scene of writing and the power negotiations within the margins of the culture that impact on authorship.

Hearing and seeing: *Dessa Rose* and *Alias Grace*

> 'I could tell what happened. But no one listened to me.' There is a small, thin sobbing. 'I was not heard' ... 'You're the same, you won't listen to me, you don't believe me, you want it your own way, you won't hear'
>
> Margaret Atwood, *Alias Grace*[8]

Just as Pieixoto's literary criticism carried infinitely more status than Offred's fragmentary recordings, as we saw in Chapter 2, so Nehemiah and Jordan's production in writing of 'scientific' evidence, whether as management manuals or medical papers, has more renown than Dessa and Grace's oral narratives. For the male authors the discourses and social formations in which they operate determine how they see their subjects and how they hear their stories. Immersed in the racist discourses of slavery, keen for some kind of recognition and unsettled by both fear of and desire for 'the other' in the form of Dessa, Nehemiah is steadfast in making all events fit his script and cannot really hear or understand anything Dessa says to him. He is, by turns, repulsed by her and yet 'oddly arrested' (38), irritated while also 'fascinated' (37), impressed by her 'cunning stubbornness' but also by her 'playfulness' (42).

Similarly, as Jordan loses control, he begins to see in Grace concealment, 'cunning', a 'passive stubborn strength against him' (362). Nehemiah's dominance over Dessa and yet unease concerning her is evident in the somatic relations between them, his proximity to or distance from her, his sitting in a position above her, his sense of an offensive smell which later – as a further example of the twin responses of revulsion and attraction – becomes 'a pungent, musky odor that reminded him of sun-warmed currants and freshly turned earth' (39), and in the extended reference, developed throughout the book, to eyes and looking. Nehemiah sees Dessa's eyes at first as 'wide and black ... unmarred by that rheumy color characteristic of so many darkies' (20), while Dessa recoils from his eyes which seem to her 'covered by some film, milky and blank' (49). From Nehemiah's perspective, Dessa's 'flicking' of her eyes away from him is an insult which provokes him to violence and he strikes her (30 and 36); to Dessa, her 'cutting' of her eyes towards him is a way of checking Nehemiah's expectations (56). Nehemiah at first delights in what is to him the devilish and, hence, marketable potential of Dessa's eyes, 'the ghostly gleam of the Darky's eyes in the dimness' (21). Dessa, though, reminds herself of the danger of looking into the eyes of whites: 'There was only emptiness in them; the unwary would fall into the well of their eyes and drown' (49).[9] Thus, what each sees and sees in the other, how their eyes look and look to the other, all trace a network of comprehension, miscomprehension, authority, subordination and subversion.

Atwood's comment on Grace applies equally to Dessa and, as we have seen, to Susan Barton: 'In my fiction, Grace, too – whatever else she is – is a storyteller, with strong motives to narrate but also strong motives to withhold; the only power left to her as a convicted and imprisoned criminal comes from a blend of these two motives.'[10] Dessa's strategies of response prevent Nehemiah from learning anything about the methods the slaves used in their escape from the coffle or about conspiracy, or who might still be free and where they might be hiding. She works within her own field of possibilities and constraints. Her impoverished and restricted life and her lack of education mean that often she cannot answer Nehemiah's questions; she understands generally the menace of his questioning but not the import or context of specific questions. But she also has at her disposal the strategies of the subaltern, ploys to thwart her interrogator. Her silence, her dialect, the circularity of her comment, her sullenness, the guardedness of her expression, her ability to 'turn his own questions back upon themselves' (60) are either deliberate acts of resistance or become acts of resistance because of the effect they have on Nehemiah.[11] Grace too shows caution, self-censorship, a shrewd understanding of the dynamics and power play of the interview process.[12] Both Dessa and Grace are expert in the 'good stupid look' (AG 38). Grace withholds knowledge so as to preserve some privacy or to revenge herself on Jordan when he has offended her or because she thinks it would not interest him. She remembers the advice of her friend, Mary Whitney, that 'a little white lie such as the angels tell is a small price to pay for peace and quiet' (458). At other times, she tells Jordan things simply to please him. Because he brought her a radish she wanted, Grace gives 'a sort of return gift' in telling her story as interestingly as she could and 'rich in incident' (247). Though it is painful for her, Dessa deliberately recounts the story of her husband, Kaine, and his murder by their master so as to stop herself from accidentally revealing anything about the escape. But the more Dessa and Grace tell their interrogators, the less Nehemiah and Jordan are able to keep a grip on the narrative. For Jordan, Grace's detail confuses rather than leads to any coherence or certainty. As Jordan comes to realise, 'the very plenitude of her recollections may be a sort of distraction, a way of drawing the mind away from some hidden but essential fact' (185).

For their survival, Dessa and Grace *have* to be able to see and hear their questioners, *have* to understand as far as they can the discourses of power. And from this position of partial ignorance and partial perception they sometimes see into the heart of things. For instance, Dessa's challenge to Nehemiah about his status as a white man – 'Kaine say it be's white men what don't talk white man talk. You one like that, huh?' (66) – puts him on the defensive and undermines his project. Nehemiah increasingly fears that he cannot perform whiteness as he would like. 'I *teach* your master and his kind how to speak' (66), he says in response to Dessa's accusation but if he cannot control one uppity black woman slave or her story, he cannot really speak as a white man. Occasionally the tables are turned and the eyes reveal it. Preparing for his first interview with Grace, Jordan looks at an engraving of her from a pamphlet distributed at the time of the murders. He sees 'the vapid pensiveness of a Magdalene with the large eyes gazing at nothing' (58). He thinks that by now she must be quite changed, become 'more dishevelled; less self-contained; more like a suppliant; quite possibly insane' (59). His first face-to-face look, however, positions her as 'a nun in a cloister, a maiden in a towered dungeon'; he sees 'the eyes, enormous in the pale face and dilated with fear, or with mute pleading' and thinks 'all was as it should be' (59). She now reminds him of the hysterics he had seen in the Salpêtrière in Paris. A moment later she becomes much more ordinary, nondescript in appearance and her eyes, as Jordan notices, 'were unusually large, it was true, but they were far from insane. Instead they were frankly assessing him. It was as if she were contemplating the subject of some unexplained experiment; as if it were he and not she who were under scrutiny' (60). The roles of investigator and investigated had, momentarily, been reversed.

The inability of Nehemiah and Jordan not only to hear but to differentiate between what they hear and hence to understand is fatal. Nehemiah cannot interpret other sign systems with which Dessa is familiar and cannot differentiate between signs. He is frequently irritated by Dessa's humming but the 'humming' also sounds to him like 'moaning' and the noise that sounds to Nehemiah like 'some kind of dirge' sounds to Hughes, the slave owner and sheriff, like 'a happy nigger' (29). 'You make no distinction between moaning and singing?' Nehemiah asks Hughes. To which Hughes replies; 'Why should I?.... . The niggers don't' (29). Similarly, Grace comments on Jordan: 'he does not understand much of what I say, although I try to put things as clearly as I can. It's as if he is deaf, and has not yet learnt to read lips. But at other times he appears to understand quite well, although like most gentlemen he often wants a thing to mean more than it does' (243). At one point Jordan becomes a rather slow-learning child: 'I try to put things as clearly as I can.' At the next, he is dismissed as fanciful: 'like most gentlemen he often wants a thing to mean more than it does'. Jordan might like to think of himself as Simon Peter, casting his net into deep waters, but, as Grace points out, 'there is also Simple Simon' (379). Sometimes he hears too much, over-interprets; at other times, he does not hear at all.

Cloth-eared to whatever does not fit their expectations, Nehemiah and Jordan miss moments of possible revelation. Thus, when Nehemiah appears at Dessa's prison window, about to leave with the Sheriff on a search for a maroon settlement and promising, threateningly, to return, he interrupts Dessa's participation in 'a call'.[13] Exchanging verses and refrains from a spiritual with other slaves outside the prison, she prophesises her escape but Nehemiah cannot hear it; when he returns some days later, she has gone. And Jordan, despite his pretensions, cannot hear the language of the unconscious; he cannot understand Grace's dreams (he never picks up on the meaning of the red peonies, for instance) or her methods for blocking him or his own counter-transference and psycho-sexual attachment to the figure of the servant girl. As his life slips into increasing disarray through his involvement with his landlady, Mrs Humphrey, he is unable to hear even commonplace remarks: 'For a moment, he thinks he's gone deaf, or suffered a small stroke: he can see her [Grace's] lips moving but he can't interpret any of the words' (291). Nor can he understand that the hypnotic powers of the mysterious Dr Jerome DuPont, at various times, mesmerist, ventrilo-quist, showman, peddler and always friend of Grace, constitute 'another language'; as DuPont says, 'if one speaks it, one takes it simply for granted. It is others who find it remarkable' (83). Like Nehemiah, Jordan's determination to shore up his own language renders him deaf to others and, thus, he does not perceive the degree of possible collusion between Jerome and Grace.

In two ways, then, Jacques Derrida's comments on the significance of the ear in Nietzsche's work connect to the position of Nehemiah and Jordan. Neither has 'a keen ear ... an ear that perceives differences'.[14] Derrida talks of the importance of hearing differences in political dis-course. Nehemiah and Jordan want only to bolster a fixed, limited sense of difference – that between black as inferior and white as superior for Nehemiah, hierarchies within class and gender for Jordan and, for both, the difference between the knowing subject and the ignorant object of investigation. For Nehemiah and Jordan, 'words of difference serve to legitimate a discourse instead of delaying its authority to infinity'.[15] To maintain this position demands deafness to the voices of Dessa and Grace and the range of difference incorporated within these women and within their cultures. Furthermore, Nietzsche's signature becomes effec-tive, says Derrida, 'not at the moment it apparently takes place, but only later, when ears will have managed to receive the message ... when the other comes to sign with him, to join with him in alliance and, in order to do so, to hear and understand him' (50–1). Again this is precisely what Nehemiah and Jordan cannot do. Though on one level, it is impor-tant for the production of their texts that Dessa and Grace tell them their stories since they can contribute the inside knowledge and the dramatic immediacy of the rebellion or the murders, at another level, the men's whole purpose is *not* to hear the message, *not* to make the women's signature effective but to deprive them of it. Discussing *Dessa Rose* and Toni Morrison's *Beloved*, Anne E. Goldman points out the invidious position of the white author, constructing himself as subject on the basis of the black woman's words. He wants to establish his dif-ference but is, of necessity, indebted. Consequently, says Goldman, 'he needs to continue consuming – that is, seizing bodies and words as quickly as they are created, to obliterate the evidence of the laborer whose work would articulate her own authority'.[16] The same relation applies to the class division that separates Jordan and Grace. Textualising in written and published form Dessa and Grace's narratives is the way to ensure the repeated display of the authority of Nehemiah and Jordan. But that authority is always at risk. Hearing, properly hearing, the stories of Dessa and Grace would destroy it but, at the same time, they do not completely fail to hear what Dessa and Grace tell them either in their words or in their withholding of words. They hear enough to know that something essential escapes them, that something is beyond their control. For this reason, the anguished Jordan writes to his friend, '*Not to know* – to snatch at hints and portents, at intimations, at tantalizing whispers – it is as bad as being haunted' (424).

A writing lesson: *Dessa Rose* and *Alias Grace*

Although Dessa and Grace cannot tell their stories so as to be heard by the dominant order, they can certainly be effective in undermining that order and, in so doing, their attack on Nehemiah and Jordan's writing is key. Some of the perils and potential involved here can be seen if we compare with another encounter between the literate and the illiterate as related in the chapter 'A Writing Lesson' in Claude Lévi-Strauss's *Tristes Tropiques*.[17] Lévi-Strauss recounts how, in an exchange of gifts with the Nambikwara Indians, he distributed sheets of paper and pencils. The next day he sees the Indians drawing wavy lines on their paper in imitation of his writing. But the chief does more. He asks Lévi-Strauss for a writing pad and then writes with him; if Lévi-Strauss asks him a question, the chief 'writes' an answer in reply. He then extends his competence further by 'reading' to the other Indians from a list and so organising the exchange of gifts. This masquerade of reading and writing goes on for a very long two hours. Lévi-Strauss comments: 'Most probably he wanted to astonish his companions, to convince them that he was acting as an intermediary agent for the exchange of the goods, that he was in alliance with the white man and shared his secrets' (296). In a shorter illustration, Lévi-Strauss mentions the role of the scribe whom he had observed in small villages in eastern Pakistan: '[H]is knowledge is accompanied by power, with the result that the same individual is often both scribe and money-lender; not just because he needs to be able to read and write to carry on his business, but because he thus happens to be, on two different counts, someone who *has a hold* over others' (298). Both examples convey Lévi-Strauss's anxiety about what he sees as the corrupting effect of writing and about his own culpability as the bringer of writing to illiterate cultures; his 'gift' might be a curse. We could read his comments, also in this chapter, on the decimating effects of flu and gonorrhoea-related illness as springing from the same source. In his discussion of the evolution of writing, Lévi-Strauss is at pains to play down writing's contribution to progress, for example, in agriculture or architecture. Instead he stresses its link to 'the exploita-tion of human beings rather than their enlightenment' (299) and remarks that 'the primary function of written communication is to facilitate slavery' (299); that 'it was perhaps indispensable for the strengthening of dominion' (300); that it 'connected with an increase in governmental authority over the citizens' (300); that, through writing, native peoples 'become vulnerable to the still greater proportion of lies propagated in printed documents' (300). Lévi-Strauss describes the peo-ple who, after this show of 'reading', did not follow the chief's line as 'the most sensible' (300), but he also has admiration for both the chief and the insubordinates for both seem to have intuitively understood something essential about writing – for the chief, that writing could aug-ment his power and, for the doubters, 'that writing and deceit had pen-etrated simultaneously into their midst' (300). In this particular encounter, the doubters win the day as they withdraw their support from the chief and he is abandoned.

To some extent, Nehemiah and Jordan act like bad anthropologists. They are privileged investigators of 'the native', playing a punitive role – without much awareness in Jordan's case – and using either crudely reac-tionary and oppressive discourses (Nehemiah) or therapeutic and reform discourses (Jordan) to position 'the other' as uncivilised and dangerous (Dessa) or needy and grateful (Grace). Though Dessa and Grace obviously know about writing and Grace has some degree of literacy, Nehemiah and Jordan can still use writing to 'have a hold' over the women since their greater cultural capital has power to reinforce hierarchies of status, knowl-edge and economy. All Lévi-Strauss's fears about the connections between writing and power, dominion, authority, exploitation and, in a very par-ticular way, the facilitating of slavery have credibility.[18] The women are vulnerable to, in Derrida's phrase, 'the violence of the letter' and neither of the options open to the Nambikwara is possible for Dessa or Grace.[19] They cannot be 'sensible' and leave the scene; nor can they risk unprob-lematically allying themselves with the writing since they recognise all too well its menace. Specifically they cannot aspire, as the chief does, to be the intermediary since that would be, in Dessa's case, an impossible betrayal of her community and, for the isolated Grace, there is no one for whom she can be intermediary unless it is to protect Jeremiah.

In his analysis in *Of Grammatology* of Lévi-Strauss's chapter, Derrida has no doubt as to the validity of Lévi-Strauss's link between writing on the one hand and violence, hierarchies, political, economic and technical power on the other, but he does critique Lévi-Strauss for seeing power as always oppressive, for failing to 'distinguish between hierarchization and domination, between political authority and oppression' (131). Moreover, Derrida's deconstructive reading of Lévi-Strauss's work reveals that the Nambikwara were not innocent of writing either as a sign system or as 'arche-writing'.[20] Lévi-Strauss obscures what the Indians know about writing and what he himself – though not consciously – knows they know. If the Nambikwara already know about hierarchies and power, then their understanding of the relations inherent in writing cannot have been 'instantaneous', as Lévi-Strauss suggests, nor is it possible to idealise their previous, face-to-face encounters as uncontaminated by difference. What Derrida refutes is, as Christopher Norris says, 'the moment of harking back to a "natural" state of mankind and society before the fateful advent of writing' (128).

Dessa and Grace also know much more about writing than Nehemiah or Jordan imagine. Though severely restricted, they are in a state of neither ignorance nor innocence. Like the Nambikwara chief, Dessa questions Nehemiah's note-taking and is amazed at what it can do. Listening to Nehemiah reading some of her comments, '[s]he was entranced' (45). But Dessa is not naïvely open to every manipulation. When she asks further about the purpose of the notes, Nehemiah justifies the activity to her: 'I write what I do in the hope of helping others to be happy in the life that has been sent them to live' (45). After telling him something of her terrible life, Dessa responds: 'You think ... what I say now going to help peoples be happy in the life they sent? If that be true ... why I not happy when I live it?' (50). Dessa discerningly sees that it is not herself or the slave population generally that is being helped by Nehemiah's plundering of her narrative for the writing of his management manual. Grace, at first, is somewhat soothed by Jordan's note-taking since it is so much less aggressive than the courtroom interrogation. But, she adds that 'underneath is another feeling, a feeling of being wide-eyed awake and watchful ... . And underneath that is another feeling still, a feeling like being torn open' (69). Both Dessa and Grace understand how writing functions not from any 'instantaneous' comprehension but from their experience of symbolic violence. Deborah McDowell comments on the frequency of writing metaphors in *Dessa Rose*, the use that Harker, the organiser of the escape, makes of his own form of notation and Dessa's fascination with the contents of a printer's shop.[21] Similarly, Grace is highly aware of her own textual production, at one moment scoffing at the things that had been written about her, at another deliberately composing herself to play the role the narrative demands. Furthermore, the convincing details of Grace's account that so impress Jordan may spring from newspapers and other publications. As her lawyer remarks: 'Criminals will read about themselves endlessly, if given the chance. They are as vain in that way as authors' (373).

Dessa and Grace are not corrupted by the writing but are able either to use the master's tools against him or, at least, to render those tools less oppressive.[22] Ill at ease in his situation, Nehemiah's notes are 'hastily scratched' (18) and his journal entries show errors in understanding and an uncertain attempt to reproduce Dessa's voice 'as though he remembered every word' (18). Grace notices the sporadic nature of Jordan's note-taking and how it is most vigorous when she is recounting tragic or salacious details. In the end, Jordan's notes come to nought. He never does write the scientific papers or the report that could have helped free Grace and, indeed, he cannot even reply to the letters from the importunate Mrs Humphrey; those replies come from Jordan's formidable mother. But Grace does write, 'although not much accustomed to it' (422), and we can read her letter to Jordan in 1859 and her letter to Jeremiah in 1861. Jeremiah had sent her a button of the same pattern as some he had given her many years before when she was a free woman. Though Grace ostensibly never seemed to understand the association of the objects Jordan had brought her, she has no problem in decoding the meanings of the button as both a remembrance of Jeremiah and a warning to keep things 'buttoned up'.

At the conclusion of *Dessa Rose*, Nehemiah's 'book' is merely scattered pages on the floor and it is Dessa who will tell the story through a fusion of oral and written modes. Speaking as an old woman, Dessa recalls the process of her narration:

> And my mind wanders. This why I have it wrote down, why I has the child say it back. I never will forget Nemi trying to read me, knowing I had put myself in his hands. Well, *this* the childrens have heard from our own lips. (236)

In this conjunction is an 'undecidability' that makes it impossible to prioritise either speech or writing. Though Derrida warns of the ethic of speech as 'the *delusion* of presence mastered' (139), there is value in the fact that the children have heard the story not through Nehemiah's malicious distortion but from the lips of Dessa and the other ex-slaves. Telling from the lips has the 'benefit of a teacher's instruction', a wisdom coming from lived experience, which Plato in the *Phaedras* believes is one of the advantages of speech over writing.[23] Significantly, in this instance, the teacher is not the philosopher master but the woman who has suffered. Dessa's fear of having 'put myself in his hands' reminds us of Lévi-Strauss's scribe who 'has a hold' over the illiterate and innumerate. Here, though, the relations are different. Parts of Dessa's story are memorised by her children and enter the oral tradition; parts are written down. In this case, the scribe is the child who writes within a loving, filial relationship, within a known community and, unlike Nehemiah, with an open ear, 'a keen ear' which 'will have managed to receive the message', the same open ear that Grace had for Jeremiah but not for Jordan. Dessa also retains some control of the writing through the reading back. It is important not to idealise the conjunction of the oral and the written, to see it as 'uncontaminated' or expressive of Dessa's full presence or as *the* strategy for giving voice to the illiterate.[24] However respectful the reading of the work, it will '*lead it off* elsewhere, so running the risk of *betraying* it, having to betray it in a certain way so as to respect it, through the invention of another signature just as singular'.[25] But, in this particular instance and at this particular moment, Dessa is satisfied that her story is being told in the way she would want and the *pharmakon* of writing reveals itself as more cure and remedy than poison. Dessa's friend, Cully, had told her once how his old slave master had tried to bring him up as both slave and son, 'teaching him to read but not to write, to speak but daring him to think' (169). Dessa realises that she must not resist writing, be 'sensible', as Lévi-Strauss says; instead she has to do it all – read, write, speak, think and, we could add, hear.

Power in the margins: *Foe* and *Dessa Rose*

Q: How do these reflections bear on your own position as a successful author?

COETZEE: 'Successful author' is a barbed phrase here, a highly barbed phrase. Foe in the book, or Daniel Defoe in 'real' life, is the type of the successful author. Am I being classed with Foe, though my interest clearly lies with Foe's foe, the *un*successful author – worse, author*ess* – Susan Barton? How can one question power ('success') from a position of power? One ought to question it from its antagonist position, namely the position of weakness. Yet once again, in this interview, I am being installed in a position of power – power, in this case, over my own text.

Tony Morphet 'Two Interviews with
J. M. Coetzee, 1983 and 1987'[26]

Coetzee is a notoriously difficult interviewee.[27] In this extract he does not like being identified as a 'successful author' and sees his 'interest' as lying with Susan, the failed author. What can the word 'interest' mean in this context – finding the character interesting or having some common identification or having some vested interest? Leaving aside the fact that one is fictional and the other living, the possibility of a common interest is difficult to hold since Susan – female, poor, outside the public domain – has the markers of a marginal cultural figure while Coetzee – male, white, middle class, internationally recognised, fêted with literary prizes – has all the markers of cultural success. Susan is more likely to be subjected to the vested interest of others. One can see where Morphet's question is coming from. How, then, could the 'interests' of Coetzee and Susan be aligned? Coetzee believes that through the interview process he is, against his will, being 'installed in a position of power' but we know that even if the interview had never happened, that power, secured by a history, a particular gendered and raced identity, material comfort and symbolic capital, would still be in place. To question power, one has to get outside power, says Coetzee. Gayatri Chakravorty Spivak offers the same advice: 'I think in the language of commercials, one would say: Try it, you might like it. Try to behave as if you are part of the margin, try to unlearn your privilege. This, I think, would be a lesson one could draw, in a very crude way, from the post-structuralist enterprise.'[28] But, for the privileged, how can that be done in anything more than a gestural way? How can the privileged, even if in critical relation to the centre, stand in a 'position of weakness'?

These questions – and nobody is more aware of them than Coetzee and Spivak – suggest that the margins may be a broad space and that distributions of power within the margins are as complex as between margin and centre. Susan, for instance, is both the victimised woman, sexually vulnerable, subject to Cruso's control and excluded from literary history *and* the self-made woman, implicated in the colonial enterprise and, whether she likes it or not, a slave owner. She is increasingly troubled by her ownership of Friday but could one go so far as to say that her 'interest clearly lies' with him, as Coetzee says of Susan? And, if not, do we then conclude that it is race rather than gender that is the most divisive factor? Susan is in the margin but in sight of the centre, in negotiation with the centre. She is, as David Attwell says, 'the colonial storyteller seeking authorization through the metropolis'.[29] If events had taken a slightly different turn, she could have become the successful author of 'The Female Castaway. Being a True Account of a Year Spent on a Desert Island. With Many Strange Circumstances Never Hitherto

Related' (67). However, Friday is, in Spivak's words, 'the unemphatic agent of withholding' and 'the curious guardian at the margin', 'guardian' presumably in the sense that he protects the margin from the all-conquering knowing of the centre.[30] Susan's concern for Friday has succeeded no better than Cruso's indifference and only in the most approximate way can we, well-meaning readers, behave as if we are part of Friday's place in the margin.

It is through her meditations and her discussions with Foe on language, writing, publication and authorship that Susan traverses the margins from her own position with its reformist potential to join the centre to Friday's position out in the far reaches. In so doing she realises the impossibility of any unproblematic 'common interest' between herself and Friday. Initially, Susan is convinced of the importance of language in both speech and writing. She values 'the fullness of human speech' (8), the civilising 'pleasures of conversation' (22) and she is surprised that Cruso has not kept a journal which could have acted as a memorial to him. She believes that writing is important as a defence against the fallibility of memory; to forget is to lose the significance and the singularity of one's life while remembering is essential in establishing truth. She believes that signs are meaningful and that 'if we wait long enough we are bound to see that design unfolding' (103). She tells Friday about the magic of writing, how, if written about, one can live forever; in deference to Foe, she acknowledges the labour of writing; and, with an eye to fortune, she thinks of the economic gains to be had from publishing.[31] In short, Susan is a wonderful advocate for an intelligible universe, for the capacity of language and writing to reveal 'truth', for the sociality of language – 'a bridge of words' (60) – and for the writer's ability to give 'substance' to the human subject.

The words 'substance' and 'substantial' recur repeatedly in Susan's letters to and discussions with Foe. Susan pursues Foe because she believes he can make her 'substantial'; her own storytelling reduces her to 'a being without substance' (51). If she is 'a being without substance' she is a ghost, another term that is repeated in the novel, particularly with reference to the girl whom Foe insists is Susan's daughter or, as Susan calls her, paradoxically, 'a substantial ghost' (132). But, at other times, Susan resents being seen as 'but a house of words, hollow, without substance' (131). She fears that she is losing her materiality, like Alice's Cheshire Cat, and gradually fading away into textuality. As Derek Attridge remarks, 'she attempts to resist, as she must, what is implied by this self-perception: that her story is determined not by herself but by the culture within which she seeks an identity' and, thus, she continues to affirm that she is 'a substantial being with a substantial history in the world'.[32] With the exception of a short comment to Foe, it is a resolute insistence on substance that forms Susan's final words in the book:

> No, she is substantial, as my daughter is substantial and I am substantial; and you too are substantial, no less and no more than any of us. We are all alive, we are all substantial, we are all in the same world. (152)

Attridge responds at this point – 'For us, of course, that world is the world – substantial or insubstantial? – of Coetzee's novel' (178) – while Foe replies: 'You have omitted Friday' (152). Susan's insistence on substance does not solve the problem as we are still caught up in textuality and Friday remains excluded both materially and in terms of representation. As Coetzee says in another response to Morphet, 'I wonder only whether Friday is not beyond the help of art' (463).

The unredeemable 'otherness' of Friday shatters all Susan's humanist beliefs about language, 'truth', writing and authorship. Language can enable a free social interchange but it is also, as Susan realises, 'the shortest way to subject him to my will' (60) and, as Foe points out to her, the slaver – for which we can read anyone in a position of power – has an investment in keeping the subordinated silent. Friday without language has no substance, 'no defence against being re-shaped day by day in conformity with the desires of others' (121). Words are meaningless to Friday. All Susan's attempts at writing lessons, trying to link signifier and signified, fail; unlike the Nambikwara chief, this native has no interest in emulating the white man – or woman. But then Friday's signs – the humming, the dancing, the music, the scattering of petals, his hieroglyphic writing, the impenetrable silence – are opaque to Susan. The difference is that Susan keeps trying to decode his sign system while Friday remains impervious. Susan, like Jordan with Grace, is tormented by not hearing, by not knowing the truth, sometimes almost to the point of violence: 'So I knew he knew something; though what he knew I didn't know' (45). She keeps constructing interpretations of Friday which, whether well intentioned or not, are impositions on him. And, the reader/critic, slyly set up by Coetzee, does precisely the same thing. Our 'interest' is to interpret Friday within a discourse of anti-racism and anti-colonialism and to highlight his subversive potential. So the inarticulate 'Ha-ha-ha' from Friday's mutilated mouth is read as a derisory laugh and Friday's literal donning of Foe's mantle is read metaphorically as either emulation or a parody of Foe's authorship.

In discussing the various ways in which Coetzee's text might be taught, Spivak includes '[r]egistering the white woman as agent, as the asymmetrical double of the author' and she adds in brackets, 'I think the problems with the figure of "fathering" mark this asymmetry' (175). Authorship is linked to a male genealogy. The best Susan can do is to avoid the missionary position and actively beget her story by straddling Foe and becoming a dominant Muse. Her authorial position, then, has agency but is not symmetrical with Foe's and one could say that an important movement within literary feminism, since at least the eighteenth century, has been to establish the groundwork for that symmetry. The term 'asymmetrical' suggests some relationship though not of equivalence while for Friday even asymmetry is too much to claim. Attwell attributes to Coetzee a 'poetics of reciprocity' which he sees as informing all his work:

> What is distinctive in Coetzee ... is that he broaches the possibility of ethical reconstruction in a movement which begins with abnegation, with the recognition of unbridgeable historical constraints. It is a scrupulous position: more than conscious of the limits of its authority, it nevertheless anticipates a properly ethical reciprocity at some as-yet-unimagined historical moment.[33]

Iris Marion Young brings both these terms together when she talks of relations of 'asymmetrical reciprocity'.[34] She disputes Seyla Benhabib's contention that moral respect demands the recognition of other people's positions as symmetrical and reversible with one's own.[35] Instead she offers:

> an ideal of asymmetrical reciprocity. Moral respect between people entails reciprocity between them, in the sense that each acknowledges and takes account of the other. But their relation is asymmetrical in terms of the history each has and the social position they occupy. (41)

However knowledgeable we might be, however open to the tale of the other person – Young invokes Irigaray's sense of 'wonder' before the other – we can never inhabit another's history or understand the world precisely from the other's position. Recognising the difference of histories and positions does not preclude reciprocity but it does preclude 'reversibility'. Each has to acknowledge the 'otherness' of the other and have a certain humility before the other. But because we are all multiply positioned and able to learn from each other – at least those of us who

are willing to hear – and because those positions are themselves changing we can enter into relations of reciprocity with each other – with the
warning, says Young, that 'the positions cannot be plucked from their
contextualized relations and substituted for one another' (52).

 If Attwell is correct, the characters of *Foe* are still caught in 'unbridge-
able historical constraints' when the novel ends and the hope lies in
'some as-yet-unimagined historical moment'. There is some reciprocity
between Foe and Susan, brokered around certain class assumptions and
their dialogue about politics and textuality; there is none with respect to
Friday. The final dream-like sequence of the novel is divided into two
sections. Each section ends with the opening of Friday's mouth; in the
first, the 'sounds of the island' issue (154), in the second 'a slow stream'
(157). At a stage in the future Friday's story will be heard and the
possibility of reciprocity will be initiated. This process of revealing the
suppressed stories is ongoing and Coetzee's narrative of the lost story of
Susan depends on it but Coetzee is also perturbed about 'the endlessly
skeptical processes of textualization' which undermine representation
and immediately remove power from those to whom it has been given
so recently and so minimally, in this case to the white woman and the
black man. Coetzee believes the final pages of *Foe* 'have a certain power.
They close down the text by force, so to speak: they confront head-on
the endlessness of its skepticism.'[36] One would not want the little that
Susan and Foe have gained to be lost so it is with hesitation that I say,
'what about the black woman?' If the text has to be 'closed down', there
must always be countless silent others with a legitimate claim to tell
their story.

 As we have seen, the ending of *Dessa Rose* permits the story of this
particular black woman to be heard. The resolution never doubts the
continuing asymmetry of relations between black and white but, in
Williams's text, the possibilities for reciprocity are here and now not in
some imagined future. At the same time and cautiously, the text affirms
that the reciprocity is limited, fragile and has to be worked for persist-
ently.[37] As Dessa and the other slaves escape towards freedom, it is an
alliance within the margins that rescues Dessa at a most dangerous
moment. Hunted by the crazed Nehemiah, Dessa has once again been
imprisoned and Nehemiah is maintaining that it is the scars on Dessa's
body which will prove who she is. His plan is thwarted through the collusion, enabled by an asymmetrical reciprocity, between Dessa, the old
black woman brought into the jail to check Dessa's body and Rufel,
the abandoned wife of the plantation owner and now supporter of the
slaves. Seeing, speaking, reading and writing are, again, integral to

the scene. Dessa and Rufel, slowly moving to some level of understanding, 'just barely knew how to read each other's eyes' (229); Dessa tries to 'catch' the eyes of the old woman (231); and the old woman with eyes 'so milky ... she might've been blind' runs her hands over Dessa's body, but not below her waist where the scarring is, and declares, 'I ain't seed nothing on this gal's butt' (231). Rufel plays to the hilt the part of the Southern lady particularly with respect to the inviolability of the white woman's word and declares that this Dessa is not the one Nehemiah is looking for. Finally, when Nehemiah produces his book and attempts to read incriminating evidence from it, his authorial power is destroyed. Rufel's baby, who has just been passed from Rufel's arms to Dessa's, knocks the unbound book out of his hand and the pages fall to the floor. '[A]in't nothing but some scribbling on here,' says the sheriff, 'And these is blank', says Rufel (232). Ultimately Dessa emerges as a sophisticated story teller, conscious of the politics of narrative, alert to the strategies of narrative production and this is partly because her experience of asymmetrical reciprocity has enhanced her ability to see, hear and understand both the various positions within the margins and the power at the centre.

6
'A Constant State of Tension'
Academic Women Authors

> Girls who are alone too much need not suffer in this day and age. They can do research.
>
> Anita Brookner, *A Start in Life*[1]

> The spring which keeps anyone thinking and writing is fragile and utterly vulnerable to a hostile environment or indeed a calm but firm incredulity which gives you to understand that your presence here is implausible.
>
> Michèle Le Dœuff, *Hipparchia's Choice*[2]

In the second edition of *A Literature of Their Own*, Elaine Showalter comments: 'Just as the heroine of a New Woman novel in the 1890s was likely to be an artist or writer, the heroine of a New British Woman novel in the 1990s is likely to be a feminist literary critic'.[3] As Showalter's footnote makes clear, this is not solely a British phenomenon and, equally, to demark the 1990s as its period is rather too narrow. She mentions literary examples from the United States – Gail Godwin's *The Odd Woman*, published in 1974, and *Death in a Tenured Position*, published in 1981 by Amanda Cross, pen name of Carolyn Heilbrun; from France, she includes Julia Kristeva's *Les Samouraïs*. Some of the texts we shall be looking at in this chapter would add other examples to Showalter's selection – David Lodge's *Nice Work* and Antonia Byatt's *Possession: A Romance* – while Sarah Maloney in Carol Shields's *Mary Swann*, whom I discussed in Chapter 4, would also fit this category of successful feminist literary critic.[4] We could further expand Showalter's claim. Sometimes the literary academic heroine, though deeply involved in her subject, is not writing from a feminist position: Anita Brookner's heroines, Ruth Weiss in *A Start in Life* or Kate Maule in *Providence*, are experts in French literature or, as a slightly earlier example, there is Rosamund Stacey who, in the course of Margaret Drabble's *The Millstone*, acquires an illegitimate baby, a Ph.D. in sixteenth-century poetry and an academic post at a new university. Sometimes the character is a feminist academic but not literary and not necessarily the heroine: Jean Hastie, the feminist theologian, in Emma Tennant's *Two Women of London* or Beth, the Women's Studies lecturer and ex-wife of Larry, in Carol Shields's *Larry's Party* or Olivia, the feminist historian in Stevie Davies's *Impassioned Clay*.[5] Exceptionally, a character's name might carry an allusion to a 'real life' feminist literary critic. Commenting on the intertextuality of J. M. Coetzee's *The Lives of Animals*, Marjorie Garber writes:

> There is a scholar named Elaine Marx ... who is not the same as Elaine Marks, the translator of *Modern French Feminisms* but is instead the chair of the English department, a feminist who writes about women's fiction – a description that might fit Princeton English professor (and former department chair) Elaine Showalter.[6]

And Garber's own name and situation gets strangely tied up with fiction. She recalls how several people sent her copies of Cross's *Death in a Tenured Position*, a detective novel about the suspicious death of the first tenured female professor in the English department at Harvard, after she took up precisely that appointment. She adds wryly: 'I would like to believe they came from well-wishers.'[7]

Whatever the qualifications, Showalter's basic claim is well made: the academic woman author features widely in contemporary fiction and the feminist literary critic is part of a significant subset. In exploring the figure of the academic woman author, I shall consider, first, the awkward configuration of intellectualism, femininity and feminism that the academic woman author confronts. My title for this chapter, 'a constant state of tension', comes from Simone de Beauvoir. Even someone of her exceptional ability, it seems, feels the contradictions.[8] Second, I shall discuss the danger for the intellectual woman of what Michèle Le Dœuff calls 'erotico-theoretical transference' relations, an unconscious projection of desires from the female academic junior to the male intellectual father.[9] This transference can be seen as an attempt to ease one of the points of tension in the coming together of intellectualism, femininity and feminism, namely, that between intellectualism and femininity. The transference should enable the female academic to be recognised as a woman (feminine) and as an academic author (intellectual). But the resolution is illusory and often has detrimental intellectual, emotional and social effects.[10] Though the possibilities – or not – of authorship constitute an element in the lives of all these academic women, I want to focus, finally, on the specific significance of 'the literary' in the figure of the feminist literary critic. My example here is, Maud Bailey, the author of feminist studies on the Victorian poet, Christabel LaMotte, in Byatt's *Possession*. Her problematic situation as a feminist literary critic – intellectual, feminine and feminist – is resolved in some measure through negotiations within literary theory and literary form.

Intellectualism, femininity, feminism

Karen Horney wrote in 1934 of a 'common present-day feminine type'; she faces the 'conflict which confronts every woman who ventures upon a career of her own and who is at the same time unwilling to pay for her daring with the renunciation of her femininity'.[11] In 1949, Simone de Beauvoir characterised the independent woman as 'torn between her professional interests and the problems of her sexual life'. She continues with the phrase I have just noted: 'it is difficult for her to strike a balance between the two; if she does it is at the price of concessions and sacrifices which require her to be in a constant state of tension'. Michèle Le Dœuff has commented in *Hipparchia's Choice* that the price for her was a 'kind of mutism'.[12] Antonia Byatt recalls wondering as a young woman, how to be 'both at once, a passionate woman and a passionate intellectual, and efficient'.[13] What is common to all these remarks is a sense of the intellectual woman as impossibly divided; success as an intellectual is predicated on failure as a woman and vice versa. Around the concept of 'the intellectual' clusters a number of problems. We need not rehearse the misogynistic history that sees women as irrational and incapable of intellectual work or how, in some respects, even in the contemporary period, women still have to strive for access to the academy and, once within, have difficulty in being accepted as 'intellectuals'.[14] Though studies of individual intellectual women have been written – Mary Wollstonecraft, Margaret Fuller, George Eliot, Eileen Power, Simone de Beauvoir, to name just a few – women barely feature in cultural histories of 'the intellectual'; there the names of Benda, Althusser, Gramsci, Sartre, Foucault are much more likely to appear. Even when the sympathetic are aware of her exclusion, the woman intellectual never seems to take centre stage. In his 1993 Reith lectures, *Representations of the Intellectual*, Edward Said draws attention, on more than one occasion, to her absence but his own argument across six lectures, referenced with a hugely impressive historical and international range of figures, discusses only one woman intellectual, Virginia Woolf, and her mention is just over a paragraph in length.[15]

The problem is three-fold: women's difficulty in defining themselves as 'intellectuals' given their historical exclusion from academic and public life; linked to that, the absence of a speaking position for women because of the lack of discursive representation; and, conversely, women's understandable reluctance to identify with a role which has been so male-defined. In addition, many feminists would be reluctant to identify as 'an intellectual' because of the connotations of elitism. Bruce Robbins in the Introduction to *Intellectuals: Aesthetics, Politics, Academics*, his edited collection of essays on the figure of the intellectual, regrets his own failure to find a gender balance among the essays – 'The subject of intellectuals', he remarks, 'has been about as gender-neutral as pro football'. He adds on the issue of women's reluctance:

> If women have not been invited into the conversation about intellectuals, they have also had good cause to feel that the conversation had nothing to offer them. A discussion centered on the ideal of universality without ties, on intellectuals as unattached and disembodied (Benda himself specified that the mission of transcendence precluded marriage and family) could easily appear to occupy a realm of male fantasy.[16]

Where feminists *have* felt more connected to the role of the intellectual it has been through a position of critical independence (Virginia Woolf's 'outsider' in *Three Guineas*) or through a position of 'dissidence' (Julia Kristeva's 'A New Type of Intellectual: The Dissident').[17] Said's concept of the intellectual as a representative figure who is prepared to take a stand also speaks to feminism's sense of commitment and action. But, even here, the social role of women and their corporeality need to be more fully considered. Part of the quality of Woolf's work is that she constructs the role of the critical, female 'outsider' in the context of the social and psychic constraints on a middle-class woman of that period.

At the shoulder of every intellectual woman author is the fearful spectre of the New Woman, the scribbling woman, *la femme savante*, the Female Wits, the bluestocking and their collective associations with unattractiveness, sterility, domestic chaos and risible pretensions. In recent academic satires the humour that has been directed against the clever woman is redirected and the focus becomes the anxious man and his fears of castration. In David Lodge's *Nice Work*, Vic Wilcox, MD of an engineering firm, is appalled to find that his 'shadow' for an Industry

Year link between his firm and the nearby university is '[n]ot just a lecturer in English Literature, not just a *woman* lecturer in English Literature, but a trendy, leftist feminist lecturer in English Literature! A *tall* trendy, leftist feminist lecturer in English Literature!' (116). Whereas within the academy Robyn's femininity is a problem, from outside it is seen as entirely appropriate. Vic's rigid adherence to a philosophy of separate spheres positions intellectual work as both feminine and effeminate – 'it's all right for girls ...[and] nancy boys', he says (114). What Vic relishes when entering his factory is 'the soothing satisfying sound of men at work' (38). But feminist literary critic Robyn Penrose crosses these distinctions. Not only does she refuse to behave 'like a girl', she brings all her disruptive notions, culled from a reading of nineteenth-century industrial novels, into the male heartland of the factory. In Byatt's *Possession*, Roland Michell, although a fellow academic, also fairs badly on first meeting Maud Bailey. He is overwhelmed by the complexity of one of her essays that he reads on his way and the Maud he meets is taller than him, unsmiling, has a patrician voice that unnerves him and, humiliatingly, she tries to carry his bag. In both cases the woman's intellectualism, competence, her refusal to use a masquerade of deference or charm and her intimidating height have an unmanning effect. At these points, the focus of the humour might be the men's anxieties but this is possible only because the figure of the academic woman as a castrator still holds cultural credibility and, from a reactionary position, the title 'feminist' simply confirms the castrating role. Though Robyn and Maud are published authors and exude intellectual confidence, though both are convinced that the university is a place where they should be, both continue to find it difficult to reconcile their intellectualism, femininity and feminism.

Undoubtedly, feminism has supported women in their intellectual aspirations and validated women's entry into the university specifically as intellectual *women*. For all the fictional feminists listed at the start of this chapter, feminism has been essential to their sense of legitimacy as academics and authors. Intellectualism and femininity have also been brought together within the discourse of feminism and, thus, feminism has provided a way for the intellectual woman to understand her difficult position. Moreover, in recent years, feminism has carried an intellectual currency that has given the feminist academic author some status within the university. At the same time, though, a feminist commitment demands as well a constant questioning of one's position; it weighs on the woman intellectual an obligation to confront sexism, institutional or personal, blatant or more subtle and intellectualised; it obliges her to take a position and to be seen by others as 'representative' of a group or a cause; it also leads her to question the relation between intellectualism and activism, between feminism and femininity. In short, feminism does not always make it any easier to be an academic woman author.

Little wonder, then in the face of this impossible configuration that Janet Mandelbaum, an outstanding seventeenth-century scholar and the dead body in Amanda Cross's *Death in a Tenured Position*, takes an understandable but futile route and tries to reject both feminism and femininity to preserve inviolate a 'pure', male-identified intellectualism.[18] Her strategy is literally lethal. As the new incumbent of a Chair in English at Harvard, funded by a beneficent millionaire with the proviso that the holder of the post must be female, she is cold-shouldered by most of the department and deeply resented by some male staff and students. Although very beautiful, she is in no way conventionally feminine or, even, particularly humane. She has little contact with her family, no emotional ties, no children, no friends. There is also no allegiance to feminism. She certainly does not want to be seen as a representative woman interested in women's issues; she is intolerant of any feminist or female support; and she is ashamed of the malicious association of her with a women's commune and its connotations of lesbianism. Kate Fansler, Professor of Literature at a New York university and the literary sleuth who will solve the mysterious death, discusses Janet's position with Joan, a member of the commune. It is Janet's denial of both femininity and feminism that they note:

> 'Janet was never a feminist,' Kate said.
> 'I wouldn't say that.' Joan reinforced the sarcasm with her gestures.
> 'She was never a *woman*, professionally speaking.'
> 'I know,' Kate said. 'I assumed that was why Harvard had taken her. She had also had a hysterectomy, when young, and could therefore be guaranteed not to have a menopause, during which all women go mad, as everyone knows.' (12)

Janet aims to identify not so much 'as a man' but as an asexual, disembodied brain. She was what the ruthlessly misogynistic head of the search committee wanted, a 'dame [who] ought to be well established and, if possible, not given to hysterical scenes' (3). But, ultimately, even such a woman is not satisfactory; her brain might be good, her antagonism to feminism all that is expected, but the bodily expression of her femininity is a constant affront.

Not only in fiction but also in women's memoirs about gaining access to male domains it is notable how often the difficulty in accommodating the woman and her intrusive corporeality is expressed in the trope of the toilet.[19] The first real indication that things have gone awry for Janet Mandelbaum is when she is discovered drunk in an old bath, part of the women's toilets in the building that houses the English department; her drink had been spiked at a departmental party. Subsequently, her dead body is found in a stall in the men's toilets. What Kate reveals is actually a case of suicide. Through her understanding of the patriarchal politics of Harvard and the severe pressures on the isolated intellectual woman and through her critical analysis of the reading Janet was doing before her death, she unlocks Janet's state of mind – desperate to be accepted by the male establishment which hated her, contemptuous of the women's movement that could have offered her support, anguished at being thought a lesbian. Kate's detecting is both womanly and intellectual. As she discovers, Janet's body had been moved and it is Allen Clarkville, Chair of the English Department, who had put her in the men's toilets. The convulsed position of Janet's body as a result of taking cyanide had suggested to Clarkville a figure sitting on a toilet. Like excreta, women are disgusting, shockingly misplaced in the academy and must be expelled. Though Kate interprets Clarkville's moving of the body as a grotesque comment on the invasion of men's territory by academic women, Janet's real place of death was an equally telling location; she had actually chosen to die in Clarkville's own office.

'Erotico-theoretical transference'

In her essay 'Long Hair: Short Ideas', Michèle Le Dœuff suggests that in relating the feminine to the intellectual many academic women are hindered by their involvement in 'erotico-theoretical transference' relations, a dangerous 'confusion of [the] amorous and [the] didactic' (104). Le Dœuff's argument is grounded in philosophy but the mention of 'transference' indicates how she draws on the insights of psychoanalysis. The process whereby the analysand transfers emotions from her/his relations with other people onto the analyst and, conversely, the process of counter-transference from the analyst to the analysand can be replicated in the teaching situation, as commentators have pointed out.[20] 'What distinguishes psychoanalysis from other relations', claims Jane Gallop, 'is the possibility of analysing transference, of being aware of the emotions as a repetition, as inappropriate to context'.[21] What might distinguish psychoanalysis does not necessarily distinguish teaching. Le Dœuff is concerned about the lack of awareness in the teaching situation of the workings of transference and counter-transference; she is concerned also with the form this transference and counter-transference can take and, within the context of gender, of the potentially damaging consequences for the female student of the male teacher.

To be caught up in a process of 'erotico-theoretical transference' may, at first, seem attractive in that it allows the girl or woman to pursue, to some extent at least, her intellectual interests while maintaining a proper feminine attachment to a 'superior' man. In this way it could relieve the unbearable tension of which de Beauvoir speaks. As countless female students, research assistants and junior staff have discovered it can also be exciting since, in one sense, the relationship crosses all kinds of boundaries though, in another sense, the gender and power relations are usually utterly conventional. The teacher becomes 'the professor' (sometimes actually *is* the professor), 'the intellectual master' and 'the father-figure' but also, rather confusingly, 'the lover'. The reverence and devoted admiration that the pupil has for the intellectual master, 'the subject supposed to know', as Lacan would say, can equally be present in the male pupil.[22] We can all name from our own experience many male Lacanians, Foucauldians, Derrideans and so on, all obsessively tied to his master's voice. But, generally, it is easier for men to pass through the transference relation and move beyond the initial affiliation to a more autonomous position in the intellectual field. The disappointment of the male pupil in finding the master inadequate produces, Le Dœuff argues, 'a radical lack which the Other cannot complete' (107). Trying to fill this radical lack encourages critique, the pursuit of knowledge and independence though – and again we could all give examples – the male disciple may simply move into another transference relation with another master who also in time 'fails'.

Le Dœuff believes it is more difficult for the female student to break that relationship of tutelage because of the erotic attraction. She is, of course, talking here in the context of heterosexual relations and there is a whole other story to be told with respect to gay and lesbian relations.[23] The female student becomes emotionally and intellectually bound to the male teacher – a *devotée*, a handmaiden or, like Marie-Louise in Michèle Roberts's *The Looking Glass* (chapter 8), she may be the keeper of the sacred flame. Men have had greater access to the institutions of education, employment, publishing which can act as 'the third factor' (106) to break the intense relationship and to enable the man to enter a wider critical field than the master's own. The knowledge the chosen male pupil gets from the master is not only an education into certain theories, beliefs and practices but is involved, as Pierre Bourdieu would suggest, with the transmission of forms of capital – cultural, symbolic, social. The woman is more likely to be bound in a 'definitive fealty to one particular form of thought' (107), that of her intellectual mentor. For the intellectual father, the daughter's devotion is extremely pleasurable and, hence, the lure towards counter-transference: 'How can it not be gratifying to be seen as a plenitude when one is oneself caught in incompleteness and disappointment?' (107). If the intellectual daughter remains devoted, the father does not have to face the anguish of Oedipal rivalry and of being supplanted by the son when the grateful *protégé* becomes the competitor in the field. The daughter too has the rewards of being indispensable and favoured but at the price of existing only in the margins of the institution and, as Elizabeth Grosz has pointed out, of sometimes becoming a victim of sexual exploitation when the fantasy erotic relationship becomes real.[24] One way of understanding issues of sexual harassment within the academy and the often-damaging consequences for women and, indeed, for the men who become subject to disciplinary procedures is within the context of unresolved transference and counter-transference relations. No wonder Freud advised that anyone going into education should undergo psychoanalytic training.

We see some of these dynamics at work in the careers of Beatrice Nest, the old-school, literary critic in *Possession* and Vinnie Miner, the professor of children's literature in Alison Lurie's *Foreign Affairs*.[25] Both Beatrice and Vinnie are involved in 'erotico-theoretical transference' relations with significant males, damagingly for Beatrice's writing, not at all for Vinnie's. As an undergraduate Beatrice had focussed all her intellectual aspirations and her sexual longing on the Victorian poet, Randolph Henry Ash:

> Reading these poems, she obscurely knew, offered her a painful and as it seemed illicit glimpse of a combination of civilised talk and raw passion which everyone must surely want, and yet which no one, as she looked round her small world, her serious Methodist parents, Mrs Bengtsson running her University Women's Tea Club, her fellow-students agonising over invitations to dance and whist – no one seemed to have. (114)

The unattainable ideal to be found in a combination of 'civilised talk and raw passion' is a peculiarly academic erotic fantasy. The fact that Ash is long-dead does not prevent him from functioning as a transferential love object. Conveniently, his death allows Beatrice the promise of passion without any of the problems of pursuit or consummation that would challenge her conventional social world; in this respect, absence is better than presence. Less conveniently, though, death freezes in aspic Ash's idealised status. Beatrice is not permitted even the role of handmaiden. Her desires are stifled by her supervisor who believes Ash to be beyond her research capabilities; how could a young woman produce any significant 'Contribution to Knowledge' (114) about the mind of a great man? By excluding Beatrice from the study of Ash, her supervisor maintains the value of the subject and his ownership of it. Beatrice is blocked in both her 'erotico-theoretical transference' relations and her access to the institution. Her supervisor steers her towards the 'modestly useful, manageable' (114) journals of Ash's wife, Ellen.

Beatrice's only output over the next twenty-five years is, appropriately, a slim volume about the dutiful wives of important men, and her institutional position remains resolutely marginal. Excluded in the early days from the Senior Common Room and the decision-making in the pub, despised in later years by many of her male co-researchers and regarded unsympathetically by even the feminist critics who occasionally visit her archive in the basement of the British Museum, Beatrice has defensively entombed herself: 'In an inner room, beyond the typewriter cubicle, was a small cavern constructed of filing cabinets, inhabited by Dr Beatrice Nest, almost bricked in by the boxes containing the diary and correspondence of Ellen Ash' (27). The final line of defence which, at the same time, declares her impossible femininity is Beatrice's own large breasts. Though she had at first hoped that she could retain contact with Ash through Ellen's writing – 'some intimacy with the author of the poems, with that fine mind and passionate nature' (114) – that was not to be. Gradually she becomes involved in Ellen's life, supportive of her dutifulness, her complaints, her protective silence. The narrator's comment – 'There was no PhD in all this' (115) – confirms Beatrice's inferior status within the discipline and the institution. Yet, though stowed away in the British Museum, Beatrice does not bury herself in the institution in quite the way Le Dœuff fears. What concerns Le Dœuff is the intellectually conformist woman who invests all her energies in the institution, volunteers for every committee, identifies with institutional goals; she makes the institution a substitute for the man. Beatrice, however, is obdurate and uncooperative. Through a mode of deliberate obfuscation which parallels the obfuscation of Ellen's journal, she is involved in her own small rebellion against the university and the field of literary criticism which disdains her anti-theoretical research.

For Vinnie Miner the intellectual situation, if not the emotional, is more optimistic. She does not have a theoretical dependence on any master and with her Ivy-league job and her publications she has a firm place in the institutions of the university and the field of literary criticism. Although she has had quite an active sex life, with the passing of time the possibility of reconciling a successful femininity and a successful intellectual life becomes less likely. Now middle-aged, she is cast in the role, she realises, of a rather tetchy 'Spinster Professor' (198). The 'erotico-theoretical transference' relations she enjoys are compensatory and act as a salve to the hurts in her academic life and her carefully managed emotional life. As with Beatrice, her relationships are imaginary. Over the years she has had a series of fantasy liaisons with a long list of American men-of-letters from the post-war world: 'Daniel Aaron, M. H. Abrams, John Cheever, Robert Lowell, Arthur Mizener, Walker Percy, Mark Schorer, Wallace Stegner, Peter Taylor, Lionel Trilling, Robert Penn Warren, and Richard Wilbur.'[26] The narrator goes on to comment: 'As the list shows, she rather preferred older men; and she insisted on intellectuals' (74). Though the older intellectual suggests the father and the mentor, Vinnie's relation to her fantasy figures is not one of tutelage. On the contrary, there is a narcissistic element in her ideal figures. We hear that she has 'always preferred in men an elegant slimness, fair fine hair and skin, small well-cut features – the sort of looks that are an idealized male version of her own' (11). Similarly, the attraction of the men of letters is that they alone can perceive *her* quality, 'her wit, charm, intelligence, scholarly achievement, and sexual inventiveness' (75). Thus, their approval is the only one worth having. In one sense the fantasy gratifyingly proves to her that she can master the masters but it is also a defence against her insecurities. These are the usual intellectual insecurities – she is much bothered by a bad review from Prof L. D. Zimmern – and her particular erotic insecurities – she has always been the undemanding pal who, at heart, felt she never could be loved. If the love object is unattainable then he will never confirm her inadequacy.

As a senior academic and established author herself, though not as senior as the men about whom she fantasises, there is little danger of sexual exploitation. When she actually meets any of the men she is always disappointed. Vinnie discovers 'the radical lack' which Le Dœuff says the male pupil often finds in the master and simply shifts to the next name on the list. The length of the list indicates the 'unsatisfiable' character of desire and its impersonality; any man of a certain type could fill this space. Its alphabetical arrangement suggests something of Vinnie's desire to order her emotional and sexual life. As the possibility for a fulfilled femininity declines, her intellectual/professional needs loom larger than the emotional. She notices how increasingly her fantasies are of 'public bodies rather than private ones', 'in a vertical rather than a horizontal position' and that she is dressed 'not in her best black nightgown but in the black gown and colored silk hood appropriate to the recipient of various prizes and honorary degrees' (111). The narrative twist is that when Vinnie really falls in love it is, very reluctantly and unexpectedly, with a man far from her idealised love object – Chuck Mumpson, an engineer from Tulsa specialising in waste-disposal systems, 'a person without inner resources who splits infinitives' (68).

Beatrice's involvement in Ellen's life suggests a different mode of identification for the intellectual woman author. What are the consequences of transference onto a woman rather than a man? Becoming involved in Ellen's life moves Beatrice away from an idealisation of 'the subject who is supposed to know'. Ellen has little in terms of 'civilised talk and raw passion' so she cannot elicit a starry-eyed admiration from Beatrice. A different kind of identification takes place as Beatrice recognises a sister, easily dismissed like herself and in need of fierce protection. But, as Alison Lurie shows in *The Truth about Lorin Jones*, these sisterly identifications can be just as unsatisfactory.[27] Polly Alter is writing a biography of the artist Lorin Jones and wants to portray her in heroic terms, her genius betrayed by a cruel patriarchy and sadly dying before feminism was around to rescue her. The interpretation fits Polly's circumstances. Never quite recovered from her father's abandonment of the family when she was a child, recently divorced and heavily reliant on Jeannie, Lurie's cardboard version of a radical-lesbian, Polly is only too ready to believe in a female 'subject who is supposed to know'. She also wants to believe the best about Lorin because she is, as her surname suggests, Lorin's *alter ego*. Not only does Polly deduce all manner of correspondences in their lives but Lorin is also the artist Polly desperately wants to be. So closely does Polly identify with Lorin that on occasions she finds herself repeating moments from Lorin's life and acting in ways she is sure Lorin would want her to act. At the end of the book, she is thinking of returning to the Florida Keys where Lorin lived, moving in with Lorin's ex-lover and returning to painting.

The predictable emotional and intellectual journey Polly takes is to discover that Lorin is neither as flawless nor as manipulated as she thought. That view could only be maintained through deceit. As unwelcome information is revealed about Lorin, Polly's files labelled 'DOUBTFUL and NOT TO BE USED' begin to grow (208). Thinking about her research while in the dentist's chair, Polly concludes that she is 'probing for the diseased roots in Lorin Jones's life' but also admits that she is 'planning to fill them up with cement and cover the whole thing with a shiny white deceptive surface' (170). By the end of the novel, the interview material she has rejected as compromising or prejudiced is reinterpreted as inevitably disparate and partial. Polly has broken through her limiting identification with Lorin and has recognised Lorin's lack, the 'diseased roots'. She understands also something of her own investment and strategies in wanting Lorin to be both victim and genius and herself to be the rescuer. Every interviewee had their own story and their own view on others' stories. At the risk of angering or disappointing everybody, Polly concludes that the only way to write the biography would be through the different stories to find a fuller 'truth about Lorin Jones'.

There is a danger here of replacing the flawed heroine with another fantasy of completeness, that of a totalised historical knowledge recoverable by the careful researcher. Beatrice's hero, Randolph Henry Ash, has warned us that the past and the truth are not fully recoverable: 'A lifetime's study will not make accessible to us more than a fragment of our own ancestral past' (104).[28] Beatrice and Polly's struggles for a different relation to the production of knowledge indicate a formidable challenge for contemporary feminism. How might the woman become an intellectual and an author in her own right and cast off deference to the master? How can the intellectual woman already within the academy enable that development without replacing the patriarchal structures of master/pupil with similarly hierarchical mistress/pupil relations? How can the intellectual woman author defend her history while being necessarily critical and suspicious of that history?

The function of the literary

Le Dœuff has another important warning for the academic woman. She comments on how sometimes the female student in philosophy escapes the intellectual mentor in the form of the professor only to find fellow male students pressing on her the same relation of tutelage. The male student who is seen as more brilliant than her offers to become her guide and protector and the 'erotico-theoretical transference' starts again. It is the relationship of Sartre and de Beauvoir which is much in Le Dœuff's thoughts at this moment. In 'Long Hair: Short Ideas' she mentions the sentence from de Beauvoir's *Memoirs of a Dutiful Daughter* when Sartre, on telling de Beauvoir that she had passed the *agrégation*, remarks, 'From now on I will take you in hand' (119). The control element here is reminiscent of the Dessa-Nehemiah relationship where

Dessa worries, as we saw in Chapter 5, about putting herself in the hands of Nehemiah. Le Dœuff repeats Sartre's comment in *Hipparchia's Choice* and discusses also the scene in the Luxembourg Gardens, again from *Memoirs of a Dutiful Daughter*, when the young de Beauvoir argues philosophy with the equally young Sartre and declares herself 'beaten' (135–8). Toril Moi describes this as a 'primal scene' for de Beauvoir: 'In the course of three hours in the Luxembourg Gardens Simone de Beauvoir has indeed been transformed: if she arrived as a woman with a philosophical project of her own, the elaboration of a new ethics, she leaves as a woman undone, or to put it differently: as a *disciple*.'[29] As Moi indicates, Sartre's intellectual mastery of de Beauvoir is like a defloration and, equally, the desire of the woman caught in 'erotico-theoretical transference' 'turns the man into philosophy: his body comes to represent phallic knowledge to her' (18).

In *Possession*, Maud Bailey's relationship with Fergus Wolff, her colleague and ex-lover, has already been an education for her in the dangers of 'erotico-theoretical transference'. If Maud gave an inch, Fergus could so easily become the Sartre to her de Beauvoir. In the historical and political contexts in which they work – late twentieth century, theoretically conscious, alert to feminism – he would not dare to offer himself as Maud's mentor but he does delight in suggesting that Roland Michell, with whom Maud is working, is her intellectual inferior while he is her intellectual equal. At another point he gives Maud a Lacanian reference which Maud with irritation tracks down, the irritation coming through her awareness of the threat posed by Fergus's knowledge and 'helpfulness'. Fergus produces papers of consummate theoretical aplomb – 'The Potent Castrato: the phallogocentric structuration of Balzac's hermaphrodite hero/ines' (57). He later plans to give a paper on the Victorian poet Christabel LaMotte who is the subject of Maud's research; having lost Maud he pursues her work instead. Fergus writes to Maud: 'Would you be pleased to hear I have decided to give a paper on Christabel at the York conference on metaphor. I thought I'd lecture on The Queen of the Castle: What is kept in the Keep? How does that strike you? Do I have your imprimatur? Might I even hope to be able to consult your archive?' (138). Fergus's lecture plans carry their own metaphorical associations. Maud with her room at the top of Tennyson tower is like the Queen of the Castle; exploring the secrets of the keep and the archive could have penetrative connotations. Everything can be accommodated within Fergus's 'slippin-an-slidin' theoretical interests. His unctuous manner and his 'apparently' feminist argument are but the sheepish exterior that hides a wolfish heart. His approach of false deference, wiliness and opportunism signifies, in a text highly conscious of literary form, both the rapacious fairy tale wolf and the villain of a Victorian melodrama, in each case homing in on their innocent prey.[30]

Maud's problem, then, like Byatt's mentioned at the start of this chapter, is how to be 'both at once, a passionate woman and a passionate intellectual, and efficient'. Fergus seems to offer erotic passion at the expense of intellectual independence. Byatt's hope as a young woman was to 'switch gear from one to another' since the danger was that 'if you let them all run together organically, something messy would occur and you would get overwhelmed'.[31] Hitherto, Maud has circumvented the dilemma by reinforcing her intellectualism and efficiency, the grounds for her writing and academic achievement generally, and repressing her 'passionate femininity'. Like Christabel LaMotte, she is a 'chilly mortal' who needs 'quiet and nothingness' (285–6) so as to focus on her work.[32] Her long blonde hair, variously signifying the sexual, the frivolous, an anti-feminist preoccupation with female beauty, has to be kept covered. Though accepting of herself as 'intermittent and partial', Maud finds it much more difficult to accommodate her body, '[t]he skin, the breath, the eyes, the hair, their history, which did seem to exist' (251). The research discoveries about Christabel are also a confrontation with the difficult materiality of the female body, what it might mean to be a brilliant, Victorian woman poet who is also a middle-class unmarried mother.

Byatt explores the problem of intellectual and sexual containment through the figure of the egg. Maud identifies with Christabel's metaphor of the unbroken egg and its connotations of the self-contained, particularly when she recalls the disturbing image she associates with her liaison with Fergus: 'Her mind was full of an image of a huge, unmade, stained and rumpled bed, its sheets pulled into standing peaks here and there, like the surface of whipped egg-white' (56). The egg white suggests both semen stains and the loss of the egg's sealed autonomy. When Fergus offers his tit-bit of Lacanian knowledge it is the egg image which once more returns to Maud's mind: [t]he tormented bed rose again in her mind's eye, like old whipped eggs, like dirty snow' (141). Maud's unease about the relation between the sexual and the intellectual extends into the terrain of literary theory. One reason why Beatrice gives Maud access to the Ellen Ash journal is because Maud understands her antipathy to the contemporary critical preoccupation with sexuality: Maud thinks of 'the whole tenor and endeavour of twentieth-century literary scholarship' and then of 'a bed like dirty egg-white' (221–2).

Consequently, to bring together Maud and Roland Michell in the narrative's twentieth-century romance, to unite the sexual and the intellectual without slipping into something messy and overwhelming, to allow
Maud to continue as the academic author she wishes to be requires some
nifty footwork on Byatt's part. First, it is essential that Maud does not
enter into an 'erotico-theoretical transference' relation with Roland.
Having evaded Fergus's strategies she must not fall for anybody else's.
This does not seem likely since Maud is of a higher social class than
Roland, professionally more secure and intellectually more confident
than him – hence, as we saw, her castrating role. But Maud does have to
find some way of maintaining her intellectual independence while giving full expression to her 'passionate femininity'. Meanwhile, Roland
has to be rescued from his castrated, inferior position and his intellectual status recognised while ensuring that he does not take up the position of the intellectual master.[33] It is fortunate that Roland is happy
about Maud's need for separateness, in large part because he has the
same need. Worn down by his relationship with the embittered Val,
Roland tells Maud of his vision of 'the white bed' (270). On the research
trails in Yorkshire and Brittany, Maud and Roland have separate rooms
'with the requisite white beds' (421).[34] Their carefully restrained speech
and physical contact both heighten their awareness of sexual potential
and give back 'their sense of their separate lives inside their separate
skins' (424); as Maud had commented earlier, 'Celibacy as the new
volupté. The new indulgence' (271).

Roland, the Knight, eventually breaks through the metaphorical
hymen, the 'Thresholds. Bastions. Fortresses' (506) that have been the
focus of Maud's literary research, and captures his Princess, taking 'possession of all her white coolness' and promising to take care of her (507).
At this precarious moment, Maud remembers once again Christabel's
unbroken egg and '[h]er self-possession, her autonomy' (506). The 'taking possession' and the 'taking care of' have worrying connotations of
domination. We could imagine Fergus acting and promising similarly
for his own corrupt reasons and Roland's words sound very close to
Sartre's promise to 'take (de Beauvoir) in hand'. The 'taking possession'
and the 'taking care of' could shade into the messy and the overwhelming.
There is no effusion in Maud and Roland's declarations of love; rather
the language is hesitant, staccato, at times briskly practical. Maud finally
commits to Roland only when she is sure that he 'would never – blur the
edges messily' (506) and at consummation there can then be a willing
fusion on Maud's part as 'her white coolness ... grew warm against him,
so that there seemed to be no boundaries' (507).

Following Le Dœuff again, we could say that one aspect of the 'third factor' that breaks any damaging dependence on Maud's part is expressed through Byatt's deployment of literary theory and literary forms. A self-consciousness of 'the literary' is evident in many of the texts listed at the start of this chapter. It is not simply that author characters proliferate. Texts are replete with literary allusions; chapters are introduced with literary epigraphs; plots, characters, events in the contemporary narratives echo those in literary texts from the past; critical reading is a key element in the detective work of the literary sleuths; contemporary texts speak to, sometimes pastiche, literary forms and styles; texts debate literary problems about authorship, fictionality, closure; particularly in the satire and the knowing jokes, texts show their awareness of the working of the literary field. Byatt's construction of the relationship of Maud and Roland in terms of a negotiation on theory and form allows the personal relationship to be established in a way that enables both intellectual independence and erotic fulfilment. For the intellectual woman, and in a book so theoretically knowing, resolution cannot be only a matter of sexual politics. It must also be theoretical; literary theory is part of the problem for the academic woman author and part of the solution.

Maud is at first included by Byatt in her satire of contemporary critical theory. For instance, she features as one of the authors in an edited collection on LaMotte:

> They wrote on 'Ariachne's Broken Woof: Art as Discarded Spinning in the Poems of LaMotte.' Or 'Melusina and the Daemonic Double: Good Mother, Bad Serpent.' 'White Gloves: Blanche Glover: occluded Lesbian sexuality in LaMotte.' There was even an essay by Maud Bailey herself on 'Melusina, Builder of Cities: a Subversive Female Cosmogony'. (37–8)

It is not only the subject matter of the essays or the critical vocabulary indicated in 'subversive' and 'occluded' and 'cosmogogny' but the actual form of the titles with the obligatory colon – in one case, two colons – that Byatt mocks. Yet, as the heroine of the contemporary romance, Maud has to be saved from being merely an object of satirical derision and this requires careful placing in the critical field. She has to be distanced from what Byatt sees as the follies of contemporary critical theory, particularly feminist critical theory. Hence, Maud's alliance with Beatrice Nest, her cautions about the determination of the loud, flamboyant, bisexual Leonora Stern to see everything as related to sexuality and her antipathy to the theoretically cutting-edge but, in truth, amoral and apolitical interventions of the oleaginous Fergus Wolff. Byatt's dislike of the theoretical positions Leonora and Fergus represent is writ large but she also dislikes their methodology, their freewheeling mode of association. What unites Maud and Ariane Le Minier, 'a passionate precision in their approach to scholarship' (334), is much more to Byatt's taste.[35]

The romance dictates a working through of the theoretical differences that separate Maud and Roland. Signs are not auspicious at first. Maud, with her work on feminism, psychoanalysis and Winnicott is theoretically sophisticated; Roland describes himself as 'an old-fashioned textual critic' (50). Yet, it is Roland who initiates the research endeavour with Maud and who convinces her that there is something significant to be discovered in the relationship of Ash and LaMotte. As they work together intellectual relations develop. Though the theoretical frameworks are different, Maud's 'passionate precision' in her intellectual work is not far removed from Roland's close textual analysis and Maud does describe herself as a 'textual scholar' (211). Roland has similar reservations about Leonora. Reading her Irigarayan essay on the relation between imagined landscapes and the female body he feels that her emphasis on sexuality homogenises everything. Both have an initial aversion to biography. Maud dislikes feminist interest in private lives and claims that '[y]ou can be psychoanalytic without being *personal*' (211). Both want to focus on the author's mind rather than the details of their lives; both, like their nineteenth-century counterparts, Ash and LaMotte, give priority to 'the Life of Language'.[36]

Towards the end of the book, Roland embraces with increasing confidence critical positions that Maud would question. He finds his own liminal space on the border between criticism and poetry and begins to write 'lists of words that resisted arrangements into the sentences of literary criticism' (431).[37] He also questions the lessons he had learned from poststructuralism:

> He had been taught that language was essentially inadequate, that it could never speak what was there, that it only spoke itself.
>
> He thought about the death mask. He could and could not say that the man and the mask were dead. What had happened to him was that the ways in which it could be said had become more interesting than the idea that it could not. (473)

Byatt's phrasing is careful here. It is not that Roland is reinstating a fixed relation between the signifier and the signified, rather that such a hypothesis is a fruitful notion to explore, particularly for the poet. Similarly, Roland's reaffirmation of 'the author' – 'He could hear, or feel, or even almost see, the patterns made by a voice he didn't yet know, but which was his own' (475) – has a complex relation to the self.[38] Though this is not Maud's theoretical position, it is no bad thing for the resolution of the romance that Roland has staked out a territory which is different from, though compatible with, Maud's and, potentially, of equal status to Maud's. Byatt has transposed a nineteenth-century notion of separate spheres to the intellectual field of the twentieth century.

Moreover, though Maud is absorbed in theory, it is wrong to see Roland as a theoretical *ingénu*. For example, he endorses, as Maud would, anti-essentialist concepts of the subject but then both have to reappraise the theory. If in 'erotico-theoretical transference' relations the theoretical leads somewhat problematically to the erotic, Maud and Roland learn how it is also possible for the theoretical to lead to an impasse in the erotic. If you know everything about sexuality theoretically but, like Prince Charles when marrying Lady Diana, you distrust the idea of being 'in love', if you reject a notion of your essential self or anybody else's, if you have no belief in coherence or resolution, if everything is constructed and plotted and nothing innocently chosen, how will boy ever meet girl and live happily ever after? For theoretically conscious literary critics the words of love have no authenticity and can exist only in the context of a postmodern irony or, as we saw earlier, an awkward hesitancy. We shall see in the following chapter how problematic are the words of love even for the authors of romantic fiction also.

Finally, it is inevitable that Byatt has to reclaim older narrative forms and techniques to provide the resolution the romance demands. Roland is speaking for Byatt when he thinks of coherence and closure as 'deep human desires that are presently unfashionable. But they are always both frightening and enchantingly desirable' (422). Byatt embraces realist and anti-realist positions, exposing the constructedness of literature and history while at the same time convincingly recreating a period and a literature and evoking in the reader a nostalgia for the satisfactions embedded in that literature. The text also resurrects the omniscient narrator. The narrative voice that emerges in 'Postscript 1868' tells of things that 'leave no discernible trace' but it is also quite absolute that '[t]his is how it was' (508). There is no parodic edge to this voice. Rather the bitter-sweet story that is told of love and loss, as Ash meets his daughter, recognises her and sends a message to Christabel which the child loses, has the deep affective power on the reader that Byatt and Roland recognise as so pleasurable. Byatt reveals both intellectual interest and satirical distance as she plays with postmodern fragmentation, uncertainties and discontinuities but the stronger, more deeply held narrative drive is to connection, resolution and closure. To achieve this, Byatt must reinstate the narrative modes of the realist novel and turn away from satire. As David Lodge reminds us when talking of his own satirical romance, *Small World: An Academic Romance*, a novel which like Byatt's both questions and employs realist conventions, 'satire is the antithesis of romance, because romance is ultimately about the achievement of desire; satire is saying you won't get what you desire, you don't deserve it'.[39]

Maud and Roland's tentative optimism for the future is supported by a shrewd management of literary form. Roland is aware that he is operating in 'a vulgar and a high Romance simultaneously' (425). He is a Knight wooing his Princess; he is searching for the Holy Grail; he is, also, a lower-middle-class academic, hoping for a decent job and in love with a woman who is socially and, perhaps, intellectually above him. 'Reader, I married him', concludes Jane Eyre; 'Reader, I have admitted my love for Roland but will maintain my autonomy while Roland can commute between Lincoln and his new job, perhaps in Amsterdam' is – roughly – Maud's guarded modern equivalent. Byatt looks to her heterosexual romance to reconcile oppositions, male and female, poet and critic, erotic and intellectual; her play with form allows the reader to 'feel the passion' and 'do the standing back and thinking';[40] and the hope is that Maud's plan will enable her to be both the passionate woman and the passionate feminist academic author without an unhealthy dependence on Roland. In trying to reconcile everything, though, the novel inevitably invokes the terms that could split the resolution apart. It is, as its subtitle tells us, a romance and its balancing act constructed within a liberal-humanist discourse is cheering but suspect. As romance is the antithesis of satire, so Roland realises that it is also the antithesis of social realism. The novel must end before social realism can kick in, before, for example, Maud has experienced motherhood and the strains that can put on the independent woman. What Roland Barthes calls 'the N.W.P.', that is the 'non-will-to-possess', can be 'a tactical notion' in which possession is secured by apparently renouncing it or 'a final snare' in boosting one's virtuous self image.[41] At some stage, quite unexpectedly, Maud might find herself in a position of economic and emotional dependence; in such circumstances she could find her intellectual autonomy and her writing career difficult to maintain and Roland could then be cast as the new *paterfamilias* taking everything in hand.

7
Finding the Right Words
Authors of Romantic Fiction

At the best of times, love is absence.

Elizabeth Wilson, *Hallucinations*[1]

It's possible to speak ironically about romance, but no adult with any sense talks about love's richness and transcendence, that it actually happens, that it's happening right now, in the last years of our long, hard, lean, bitter, and promiscuous century.

Carol Shields, *The Republic of Love*[2]

Roland Barthes in *A Lover's Discourse* disparages the love story. He sees the lover's discourse as possessed by 'figures' like Greek Furies that disturb and clash but have no narrative order. Fashioning a love story, believes Barthes, is to subjugate the excessive disorder of love; it is 'the tribute the lover must pay to the world in order to be reconciled with it'.[3] If this is so, it is curious how unsuccessful romantic fiction is in putting desire in its place. Although everyone in romantic fiction is sincerely looking for 'true love', it seems difficult to find even in the narrative form dedicated to providing it. Desire is tied to the impossibility of fulfilment. As the narrator claims in Anita Brookner's *The Bay of Angels*, 'Even a happy ending cannot always banish a sense of longing'.[4] Freud's suggestion is that the cause here is two-fold. First, 'that something in the nature of the sexual instinct itself is unfavourable to the realization of complete satisfaction'.[5] It is not merely that obstacles in the course of love – missed meetings, misunderstandings, partings, prohibitions and so on – increase desire, they are essential to creating it. Failing to find love is at once a torment, a pleasure and a confirmation of the love object's ideal status. Second, since the original object of desire is the forbidden parent, the subsequent focus for desire has to be a substitute and, hence, unsatisfying. Thus romantic love, in Elizabeth Wilson's words, 'represents longing, represents a desire for something (someone) who stands in for that which was always lost' (143). We are, therefore, in the impossible position of being driven to fulfil our desires and, yet, unable to fulfil them since desire demands failure and the success that is most secretly desired is unattainable. The saturation of our culture by narratives of romantic love, from high opera to soap opera, from epic poetry to TV jingles, signifies at one level a desperate replaying of the problem in the hope of, somehow, filling the gap.

Catherine Belsey points us to another way in which loss and failure are at the centre of desire, namely in the difficulty for romantic love in finding a language equal to its own importance. There is a profound irony in the nature of desire, that while being intense, personal and urgent, it is also 'allusive, derivative, citational'.[6] The experience that feels so powerful that it must be exceptional actually has no originality. Belsey cites Jeanette Winterson to this effect: ' "I love you" is always a quotation', acknowledges the narrator of *Written on the Body*; nevertheless, "the most unoriginal thing we can say to one another is still the thing we long to hear" ' (76).[7] Within the first two pages of Winterson's novel, the narrator offers us two contrary readings of the problem. Clichés of love are imprecise; unable to give expression to the overwhelming power of desire *and* the comforting familiarity of clichés is just what is needed when love threatens. Their predictability defuses the unmanageable intensity of desire; a cliché is all one can cope with. Desire might be suggested, as Belsey shows, through well-worn, often catastrophic, metaphors such as surging seas and leaping flames; similarly, Mary Evans remarks on the metaphors of illness and disease when love is represented as 'a feeling that "infects" and "disturbs" the orderly presentation of the self'.[8] Desire is implied in the clichés of love ('I love you'; 'Will you always be mine?' etc.), through the numerous cultural representations of love, or through citing what are seen as appropriate texts. Commenting on a passage from Barbara Cartland, Belsey illustrates how the heroine makes incoherent noises, supposedly indicative of desire without any real words, while the hero quotes an ancient Chinese poem. She remarks:

> [A]s the metaphors themselves also indicate, in order to speak, to ground itself at the level of the signifier, love can only quote, and preferably from a text which is virtually without origin and thus transparent. Desire alludes to texts – but in order to efface its own

citationality. It thus draws attention to its elusiveness, its excess over the signifier. Desire is what is *not* said ... (17)

On its own account, in its own voice, 'desire hardly speaks at all', says Belsey (17). Yet, to return to Freud, the impediment, the 'not-saying', enhances the desire. We see this within romantic fiction as the heroine endlessly interprets the brooding silences or the occasional terse comment of the hero, or in the hero, inflamed by the inexplicable tears or the hesitancies of the heroine. We experience it also as the reader: 'by citing, by evading, by teasing, [the texts] elicit the desire of the reader, thus demonstrating the degree to which desire is an effect of the signifier' (19).

For the 'adult with any sense', as Shields remarks, the words of romantic love have been particularly awkward. Traditionally, the critical reader has denied any personal involvement with romance. Tania Modleski has spoken of the most frequent response to popular feminine narratives (romance, Gothic, soap opera) as 'a flippant kind of mockery'.[9] She refers to George Eliot's 'Silly Novels by Lady Novelists' as an early example and footnotes Germaine Greer's *The Female Eunuch* as a more contemporary one. Who can forget Greer's description of romantic fiction as 'dope for dopes'. More recently, however, the critic has recognised the power of the illicit in romantic fiction – reading romantic fiction as something done in private with a consenting adult (oneself) – and negotiated the relation between pleasure and guilt, a negotiation in which she herself is embroiled rather than intellectually apart.[10] The critic knows the interpretive community inhabited by the common reader and understands, if not actively shares, its values.[11] For her, the memory of a younger, less sophisticated, less analytic self generates a mood of nostalgia, a droll humour, a twin sense of distance and engagement.

Yet, still, there is a problem of language. That negotiation between past and present, innocence and knowing can take place only through a theoretical vocabulary. As Shields's epigraph indicates, the transcendent language of love is today more out of place than ever. There is something embarrassingly naïve, déclassé in talking about love and romance in a non-theoretical way. '[Y]ou're far too intelligent a woman to be having a romance', says Bev to her friend, Fay, the folklorist heroine in Shields's *The Republic of Love*. 'Only deeply fluffy people have romances'. Fay responds by pondering the question: 'Is it possible to have an intelligent love affair?' (250). Maurice Zapp in David Lodge's *Small World* would think not. He is exasperated that Philip Swallow, in love with Joy Simpson, has failed to appreciate the discursive, chimerical nature of desire and sunk to the level of the man in the street:

> Hasn't he learned by now that this whole business of being 'in love'
> is not an existential reality, but a form of cultural production, an
> illusion produced by the mutual reflections of a million rose-tinted
> mirrors: love poems, pop songs, movie images, agony columns,
> shampoo adds, romantic novels?[12]

Swallow, Professor of Literature no less, can do no better than the most
hackneyed phrase, 'madly in love'. Zapp's comment indicates that the
problem lies not simply in the banality of the words of love but in a
particular academic discourse that has invalidated love as heart-stopping
romance. Academics may speak of desire or the erotic within the param-
eters of psychoanalysis; they can speak of romance as a literary convention within culture, high or popular; they can subject the discourse
to a deconstructive analysis.[13] And the end result is that in moments of
intimacy, there is just nothing possible to say. Thus feminist literary
critic, Robyn Penrose, uncompromisingly explains to factory owner,
Vic Wilcox in Lodge's *Nice Work*.

> 'I've been in love with you for weeks.'
> 'There's no such thing,' she says. 'It's a rhetorical device. It's a bour-
>   geois fallacy.'
> 'Haven't you ever been in love, then?'
> 'When I was younger,' she says, 'I allowed myself to be constructed by
>   the discourses of romantic love for a while, yes.'
> 'What the hell does that mean?
> 'We aren't essences, Vic. We aren't unique individual essences
>   existing prior to language. There is only language.'
> 'What about this?' he says, sliding his hand between her legs.[14]

In the *Postscript to The Name of the Rose*, Umberto Eco confronts this
problem of inappropriate words between clever people and provides a
solution for his academic audience. A man can't say the words 'I love
you madly' to 'a very cultivated woman', claims Eco, without invoking
Barbara Cartland and so undermining the effectiveness of his words.[15]
Eco's answer again turns on citation. The only thing to do, he thinks, is
deliberately to cite Barbara Cartland. This recognises that there is no way
of speaking innocently but, at the same time, enables the declaration of
love and a pleasurable and knowing irony between the lovers. The issue
is similar to that discussed in the previous chapter concerning the

relationship of Maud and Roland in Byatt's *Possession*. Here too was a man and 'a very cultivated woman' in love, neither of whom can say the words 'I love you madly' since they 'mistrusted love, "in love", romantic love, romance in *toto*'.[16] In that instance the solution is not a postmodern irony, though that strategy is considered in the novel, but, as we saw, a series of abrupt, incomplete interjections within which Maud and Roland finally realise the sincerity of their own and the other's feelings. But the words of love remain impossible to say in any easy way. Maud and Roland convey their meanings to each other in the unspoken gaps, in their anxiety and through a joint awareness of their history rather than in the words themselves. In this chapter, the authors struggle to find the right words, reject the words of love or opportunistically employ the words of love. They also understand their own role as authors of romantic fiction textually and construct themselves in relation to cultural signs, literary references, varied literary forms and cultural myths. The problem is, how can love be both textual and lived, both fiction and true?

Hotel du Lac: 'Desire is what is *not* said'

In Anita Brookner's *Hotel du Lac*, romantic fiction author, Edith Hope, has been temporarily 'banished' by her friends to a Swiss hotel, having committed the worst of social gaffs in not turning up for her own wedding.[17] Edith takes with her to the hotel two folders to accommodate two writing activities – one for her letters to her married lover, David, the other containing the first chapter of her latest romantic fiction, *Beneath the Visiting Moon*. Edith services David sexually, though the only sign of physical contact in the book is a surreptitious holding of hands; maternally by feeding him school-boy food of eggs and chips and beans or, even, nursery food, plates of egg custard; and emotionally in that she always rises to the challenge of his opening gambit – 'Well, darling, what news from Cranford?' – and provides humorous anecdotes to soothe David's spirit returning from work or his own domestic fray (114). Edith tries to construct the letters to David in Cranford-style, which is bright and entertaining with sharp perceptions about the social world of the hotel. The unspoken, one-sided agreement between herself and David that ensures she makes no untoward demands also makes the speaking of love impossible. Yet the letters escape her control. She repeatedly aborts them or feels she has to cross out sentences or she leaves them for later revision. What are censored are words of feeling, complaints directed at David, longing for him, pity for herself, 'coarse and mean thoughts' (81). When she writes her last letter to him to tell of her proposed marriage to Mr Neville whom she has met at the hotel, we discover that none of the others have been sent. In this last letter the words of passion and loss are finally spoken – 'You are the breath of life to me' (179); 'I lived for you' (180) – but then, on deciding not to marry Mr Neville, that letter too is destroyed. The only communication actually sent to David is a telegram with the single word, 'Returning'. Even here Edith has edited her words; her first attempt read 'Coming home' (184).

Isobel Armstrong finds in Brookner a 'poetics of loss', a 'desire of lack' and a 'poetics of lack' while also suggesting an 'implicit political analysis in her novels'.[18] The differing responses are two sides of the same coin. The hope pushes against all manner of repressions and constraints and even the acceptance of those constraints with full knowledge of the consequences doesn't entirely invalidate the possibility of hope. Edith's love for David is associated with domesticity and part of her pain at her banishment to the Hotel du Lac lies in the loss of her home and her anxiety as to whether she will ever be able to 'come home' in the fullest sense. What she offers David during those occasional evenings of food and diverting conversation is partly a conscious construct in response to his need and partly an enacting of her genuine longing for domestic compatibility. 'My idea of absolute happiness,' says Edith, 'is to sit in a hot garden all day, reading, or writing, utterly safe in the knowledge that the person I love will come home to me in the evening. Every evening' and the activities of that evening will not be unbridled lust but: 'An evening walk, arm in arm, in fine weather. A game of cards. Time for idle talk. Preparing a meal together' (98). Belsey refers to the domestic as what 'fills the gap' between two desiring subjects, 'gives this reciprocal love a being, endowing it with substance, referentiality' (31). But in Edith's situation even this decorous, proper domesticity, so removed from any passionate eroticism, so attenuated is excessive. It isn't reciprocal but only gleaned in the moments when David comes to play his domestic game.[19]

Edith's other writing activity as the author of romantic fiction is also censored but this time by Brookner rather than Edith. Eco's clever, citational solution is not possible. Edith, also 'a very cultivated woman', makes clear that far from despising the words of love in her novels or writing with irony or subtle cynicism, she actually writes with total conviction: 'I believed every word I wrote' (181). Brookner, however, has no way of showing the reader Edith's writing since, like her heroine, she is deeply antithetical to postmodern irony as a narrative strategy and so could not shape Edith's writing in the way Eco suggests and she cannot cite purple passages from Edith's novels without contaminating her own text and undermining the tragic status of her heroine. In interview with Shusha Guppy, Brookner has spoken of a distinction between what she calls 'the genuine Romantic novel' where there is a 'confrontation with truth' and 'the "romance" novel' which deals with 'a surrogate, plastic version of the truth'. Edith, says Brookner, 'is not a twentieth-century heroine, she belongs to the nineteenth century'.[20] Edith's anomalous position, it seems, is having the sensibility of a 'Romantic' novelist in a period where all one can write are 'romance' novels of the Barbara Cartland, Mills & Boon variety. She is historically out-of-sync. Very occasionally a self-conscious wryness about romantic fiction surfaces in Brookner's text. For example, Edith describes her typical heroine as 'the mouse-like unassuming girl who gets the hero, while the scornful temptress with whom he has a stormy affair retreats baffled from the affray, never to return' (27) and the titles of Edith's books – not only *Beneath the Visiting Moon* but also *The Stone and the Star* and *The Sun at Midnight* – carry in their elemental associations a trace of citational irony. But, generally, Brookner's and Edith's position is that the words of love are better to remain silent if they can only be trite or dissembling or parodic.

What we discover from Edith, therefore, are not the words she actually writes but her understanding of the situation of a romantic fiction author and in this account we see Edith caught between rational and impassioned responses. On the one hand, she is aware of all the frequent anti-romance arguments and, to an extent, agrees with them. The narrator's comment on romance as a 'daily task of fantasy and obfuscation' (50) or, like the production of a drug, 'that illicit manufacture of a substance not needed for survival' (120) could be the words of Edith. She agrees with Mr Neville that her engagement with romantic fiction encourages her to be evasive, to become 'secretive, self-effacing, perhaps dishonest' (100). Talking to her agent, Edith also shows herself alert to changing markets and how she positions herself within them. Yet, from another perspective this rational understanding is completely irrelevant. Edith is impelled to write. The tug between the rational and the irrational is also a replaying of her childhood relationship with her parents which is again for Edith a problem of language – her father's wise, cautious precepts on the one hand, her mother's cries of rage and thwarted desire on the other. But, partly too, the writing of romantic fiction has a darker edge. It can elicit in her 'a disgust, as if something orgiastic had taken place, while the children were coming home from school' (120).

The writing is like a sexual assault from which Edith emerges exhausted, dazed and grubby to reassemble her lady-like, public identity.[21]

We learn about Edith's writing day, something of her eye for character and event, occasionally the technical problems she has to handle but nothing of the plot of her novels and, as in the communication with David, no words of love. Brookner does cite texts but, unlike Barbara Cartland, not those that are supposed to signify passion. On the contrary, the texts alluded to situate Edith in her public persona as an educated, cultured woman, precisely the woman who can't say the words of love. Writing to David, she paraphrases T. S. Eliot and Stevie Smith; in conversation with Mr Neville she mentions Proust; thinking of her own writing she remembers Tennyson; as we have already seen, the private joke between herself and David is about Mrs Gaskell. Moreover, the extended allusion throughout the book is between Edith and Virginia Woolf in her 'Bloomsburian' looks and manner and her use of Vanessa Wilde as her pen name. The only possible indication of desire entering Edith's choice of texts is when, to calm her distress, she chooses to read Colette's *Ces plaisirs, qu'on nomme, à la légère physiques* over Henry James.[22]

Thus one of the fascinations of *Hotel du Lac* is how a book about a writer of love who is herself deeply in love can speak so few words of love. Desire is coiled tight, distilled within silence and restraint and unspoken longing. The silence signifies in a number of ways. Silence has been an oppressive constraint imposed upon Edith:

> [S]he seemed to look back into the past, to other times when silence had been her lot. When she had stood at the window of her house, listening to the vanishing hum of David's car. When, wordless, she had watched her father tidy his desk for the last time, or meekly taken her mother's spilt coffee back to the kitchen. (182)

She lives a life of exquisite tact and it is difficult to break through the barrier of silence since speaking can be dangerous. She knows the destabilising effect of words, how the sign can slide so easily and alarmingly from 'pear' to 'fear'. She realises the falsity of the effusions of Mrs Pusey, who is also staying in the hotel, and the closeness of love to the hackneyed and insincere. Eventually, she sees through the corrupt, clever eloquence of Mr Neville. Edith's sympathy for the wordless and silent – the taciturn gardener, the child with a speech-defect, the stone-deaf Mme Bonneuil – comes from her own youth spent in 'silence and warinesss' (174). In this world of suspect speech, silence or reticence or the judicious choice of words becomes the sign of authenticity. The words of love are valued so highly, one shouldn't be profligate with them. Perversely then, one declares true love by saying virtually nothing at all.

The Life and Loves of a She Devil: the tortoise, the hare and fish

Dismissing her agent's view that she should adapt her writing to suit the Cosmopolitan reader, Edith affirms that, on the contrary, she is writing for the tortoise market. Like, Aesop, she provides consolation in a world where, in reality, it is the hare not the tortoise who always wins. Edith totally identifies with a tortoise/hare structure of romance and sees herself as a tortoise. She waits longingly for a sign from David, for example, and she describes the passivity of her confinement in the Hotel du Lac as a state of 'pure tortoisedom' (30). The seriousness of Brookner's writing about romance relates to the tragedy of the tortoise when not rescued by the hare and unable or unwilling to break out of this particular structure of romance on her own initiative. In Edith's – and Brookner's – fiction, the best the woman can hope for is to become the hare's consort. Mary Fisher, the romantic fiction author in Fay Weldon's *The Life and Loves of a She Devil*, produces her fiction from what Edith would see as a degraded version of romance. She is a hare who masquerades as a tortoise. She has carefully cultivated the looks and manner of the romantic heroine, that is a delicate, blonde prettiness and a tendency to cry and faint and she affects an admiring docility towards the dominant male. Beneath this façade, Mary Fisher is a high-achieving, self-centred hare or, to take a different metaphorical turn, she has followed Christ's instruction to St Paul and become a fisher of men.

Unlike Edith, Mary's romantic ethic is manipulative. There is no hesitation or rectitude in Mary's citing of the words of love. Indeed, she employs the clichés of love with instinctive calculation. Here she is persuading Bobbo, her accountant and latest lover, to leave his wife and children:

> Love is outside our control. We fell in love: it is no one's fault. Not yours. Not mine. ... You acted out of kindness when you married her, and I love you for it, but now, my love, be kind to me. Live with me. Here, now, for ever! ... [T]he children are Ruth's crown and jewels. They are her comfort. She is so lucky. I have no children. I have no one except you.[23]

In some respects, Weldon and Brookner are in accord. Weldon, like Brookner, recognises the consolatory function of romantic fiction – what Bridget Fowler calls 'fiction as a technology of "coping" ' – and Mary's work sells well on the impoverished estate of Bradwell Park.[24] Brookner, like Weldon, recognises how women's attachment to romance can be devious. Mrs Pusey, in Brookner's novel, is clearly of the same school as Mary Fisher and cites to her own satisfaction and advantage the conventional terms of romance:

> I'm afraid I'm a romantic … .You see I was brought up to believe in the right values … Love means marriage to me … Romance and courtship go together. A woman should be able to make a man worship her … .Well, perhaps I've been fortunate … My husband worshipped me. (73–4)

With a nice touch on Brookner's part, Mrs Pusey then calls upon one of Edith's novels as supportive evidence for her own vanity: 'This is the sort of story I enjoy' (74). On the other hand, Weldon has none of Brookner's indulgence towards romance. Her savage indictment of the romance ethic and of romantic fiction as the narrative form that sustains it determines that her own author-heroine must be satirised and brought down. Equally, the self-abnegating heroine of Brookner's fiction finds no sympathy in Weldon. What Brookner sees as gallant, stoic and honourable, Weldon sees as masochistic.[25]

All aspects of Mary Fisher's consummate management of her life – her finances, household, aged mother, personal relations, the discourses of love themselves – collapse under the double impact of love and revenge: she really falls in love with her accountant, Bobbo, and she becomes a victim of Ruth, Bobbo's avenging wife. Chaos, excess, pain flood in and Mary turns into a rather desperate tortoise. She doubts herself, she clings to Bobbo, she becomes vulnerable: 'The less he loves, the more she will,' says the narrator, a perfect example of the elusive dynamics of desire (143). Significantly, she also loses her touch with her writing; the language will no longer say what she wants it to say. Her publishers are unimpressed with *The Far Bridge of Desire* and *Ace of Angels*; *The Gates of Desire* is popular but all the royalties are confiscated because of Bobbo's embezzlement conviction, orchestrated by Ruth; *The Pearly Gates of Love* sells poorly. Susceptible to men in a way she has never been before, Mary tries to follow the spurious literary advice of Bobbo and Father Ferguson and can no longer easily reproduce the romance formula. Her writing veers between romance, gritty realism, fable and, under the influence of

Father Ferguson, what the bookseller refers to as a 'load of religious twaddle' (215).

Ruth represents the diabolic revenge of the tortoise on the hare; 'Ruth' becomes 'ruthless'. Through scheming, financial acumen and drastic plastic surgery, she reverses positions with Mary Fisher. As Mary dies of cancer, Ruth is re-born looking exactly like Mary, living in her house with a broken Bobbo, leading her life-style and writing a romantic fiction novel which Mary's publishers are keen to publish. Significantly, this is not an opportunity Ruth wants to pursue. She has learned from Bobbo's and Ruth's lips that the words of love are deceitful. Ruth's intervention into textuality, then, is not through an engagement with language but through an audacious authorising of herself and this has been accomplished by a creative plundering of a whole range of cultural figures, genres and narrative forms. Ruth becomes her own text. In Edith's or Mary's fiction, women are allowed one transformation, from mousy girl to wife of the desired man, and one move, from her lonely home to his domestic idyll. Ruth, however, undertakes multiple transformations and moves. She is the ultimate shape-shifter and, having cast off the role of oppressed wife and mother, she embarks on a kind of picaresque journey through the underbelly of contemporary life.[26] She becomes the seducer of old and unattractive men, then a nurse at a care home for the aged; she transforms into Vesta Rose, working at a prison for the criminally insane and, subsequently, sets up the Vesta Rose secretarial agency; she is Polly Patch when cleaning for the sadistic Judge Bissop, Molly Wishart when housekeeper to Father Ferguson, Georgiana Tilling to her cosmetic dentist, Millie Mason when she joins the 'wimmin's' commune and Marlene Hunter when she enters the clinic for her plastic surgery. Like the devil she is, she can perceive everyone's secret desires and adopt any form in the pursuit of her own fiendish plans.

Lorna Sage comments on the 'confrontation between genres' in Weldon's novel, Gothic versus romantic fiction, and how the confrontation 'makes novelistic conventions themselves the protagonists'.[27] The involvement of the avenging Ruth could only be with a romance of the Gothic variety with Ruth actively creating the Gothic rather than being the victim of it. But there is more than Gothic and romantic fiction in the frame. Ruth in her recreation of herself must cut herself off from the old stories and figures of femininity, like those of romance, that tie women to compliance and subordination. As she sets out on her journey to put herself and others to right, the cultural figures that she actively adopts or implicitly suggests are those of determination and power – not only the she devil and the shape-shifting trickster but the ruthless avenger of a Jacobean drama, a female version of the self-made man, the female grotesque and, to counter the Olympian delusions of Judge Bissop, the oracle of Hades.[28] The question that Ruth confronts is that of Ann Marie Hebert: 'Oppressed by the performative weight of the feminine script, how can women escape the plot and live to tell the tale?'[29] Ruth escapes through a combination of masculine self-determination and feminine monstrosity.

Ruth's self-authorising also demands a reworking of various creation myths. Ever since Ruth expelled herself from Eden/Eden Grove it was clear that she would have the determining role. However, the plastic surgeons, Mr Ghengis (perhaps suggestive of Ghengis Khan) and Dr Black, like to see themselves as the creators and with a brutal instrumentality they construct a model of Ruth so as to experiment with their new techniques and materials:

> [T]hey played with it, pinching out flesh here, adding it there, working their way to perfection. They thought they might have to alter the position of the kidneys, so that they lay one above the other, not side be side. It was easy enough. The working parts of the body must be properly linked; their actual position was immaterial. (233)

Predictably, they are attracted to those myths in which an inanimate woman is revivified. Mr Ghengis's clinic is named after Hermione who in *The Winter's Tale* reappears to her husband, Leontes, looking like a statue and is then revealed to be the living woman, and the model of Ruth that the surgeons create is like Galatea, the beautiful sculpture that comes to life through the prayers of the sculptor. Mr Ghengis believes that he can act as Ruth's Pygmalion in remodelling her. When Ruth refuses to be grateful to him he, then, wonders if he must pray to Aphrodite to bring Ruth to a warmer, more responsive life as she did for Pygmalion's statue of a maid. Dr Black believes Ruth is more like Venus fresh from the waves; Mrs Black wonders if she isn't, rather, Frankenstein's monster, an opinion that Dr Black comes to agree with when Ruth rejects his advances.

The final, dangerous stage of Ruth's surgery is both a play on Mary Shelley's *Frankenstein* and like a scene from a Hammer horror as the forces of good and evil battle it out. An earthquake splits along the San Andreas fault, electrical storms cut the power supply, the day darkens, no regenerative rain falls. Ruth makes clear that she, not God nor Mr Ghengis nor Dr Black, is the author of her own creation: 'God's angry,' said Mr Ghengis ... .'Of course He's angry,' said Ruth. 'I am remaking myself' (249). Like Hans Anderson's Little Mermaid, Ruth has to suffer for her new legs – she feels always as if she's treading on knives – but Ruth joyfully embraces the suffering of creation. Inevitably, Ruth's authorising of herself within masculine narratives of activity and control imposes its own restrictions. There is, for instance, no place for the maternal in the highly individualistic narratives that now motivate Ruth. Painfully but, ultimately, successfully she crushes all her maternal feelings and she offers similar advice to the women she meets along the way, even suggesting to welfare mother, Vickie, 'a modest proposal', namely sell her children to rich adoptive parents and start again. By the end, Ruth is not imprisoned in the High Tower that Mary once owned but ruling it. She has controlled nature itself in the form of her own body and, to get one over on King Canute, in controlling the waves below her tower. Ultimately, she can forgive Ruth everything – except, of course, her disempowering novels.

Lady Oracle: excess and instability

If Edith Hope's relation to the narratives and language of romance is marked by restraint, Mary Fisher's by calculation and Ruth's by rejection, Joan Foster's response in Margaret Atwood's *Lady Oracle* is largely that of excess and lack of control.[30] Largely, but not entirely. There are ways in which Joan, an author of Costume Gothics, shows herself to be precisely aware of publishers' demands, readers' needs and the aesthetic conventions of the form. She soon learns from her lover, the Polish Count – alias 'Mavis Quilp', author of nurse romances – that publishers buy this material more or less by the yard for a set fee and she readily fulfils the expectations. She already knows from her own life the anaesthetising qualities of romantic fiction and about her audience's need for escape, the longing to be a heroine and to succeed at femininity. Recounting her narratives, she reels off the improbable plots, the stock scenes, the familiar tropes, the characters straight from central casting with full recognition of their formulaic quality. The passages quoted from her novel-in-production, *Stalked by Love*, or her earlier publication, *Escape from Love*, show how she has internalised the hectic pacing, the overblown style, the clichés, and the conveying of 'period' by a few obvious markers. But in this she is not motivated by the cold opportunism of Mary Fisher; she does write for money but, like Edith Hope, unfortunately she believes every word.

In Joan's world, though, there are just too many words, signs and narratives. She is unanchored amongst what Elisabeth Bronfen refers to as 'the general rulership of signs as the agency that dictates the way we perceive our world over and beyond any phenomenological reality'; indeed, the pressing problem for Joan is the tentativeness of her contact with a 'phenomenological reality'.[31] Having faked her death in Canada, she arrives in Terremoto and tries to construct a life incognito. This involves a range of consumer products – Maximum Protection sun cream, White Rose Gasoline, a Fiat car, Band-aids, Peek Frean biscuits, Glad Bags and Cinzano; her situation suggests to her a number of cultural forms and events – Fellini films, Walt Disney cartoons, the Metropolitan Opera, True Love stories, a Greyhound Bus trip; she imagines herself in several performances – as a Mediterranean beach belle, as the heroine in a romantic balcony scene, as the terrified victim, making a fast getaway from an approaching killer. And all these are mentioned within a single reverie during Joan's second afternoon in Terremoto. Joan is adrift in a Baudrillardian universe where not only is the distinction between reality and image, depth and surface, industry and art obliterated but also that between image and image. '[S]igns will exchange among themselves exclusively,' says Baudrillard, 'without interacting with the real'.[32] Joan's recall moves indiscriminately across forms, modes, cultural hierarchies, historical periods, visual and verbal. There is no resistance to, critical distance from or little ordering of the signs that surround her. She is, as Baudrillard comments, in a 'schizophrenic vertigo of these serial signs, for which no counterfeit, no sublimation is possible, immanent in their repetition – who could say what the reality is that these signs simulate?'[33] Furthermore, if there are no fixed distinctions between sign systems, then the serial can, on occasions, find unexpected links. So the inscrutable comments of the Gothic hero – is he sympathetic or is he sinister? – are not that different from the perplexing oracular remarks of Joan's Aunt Lou and of Leda Sprott, head of the Spiritualist church, which, in turn, are also rather like the sibylline utterances in Joan's volume of avant-garde poetry, which is then reviewed as 'gnomic'. The title of the poetry volume, *Lady Oracle*, loops us back to Aunt Lou and Leda Sprott and, surprisingly, to the book we are reading.

Coral Ann Howells remarks that the Gothic images in the 'Lady Oracle' title poem 'display an excess of signification which hints at the complex energies incompletely understood by the subject herself for most of the novel'.[34] This is certainly the case but that 'excess of signification' is there in everything Joan writes, thinks, does or is. She is not without self-awareness on this matter; she recognises how her life has 'a tendency to spread, to get flabby, to scroll and festoon like the frame of a baroque mirror'.[35] Her very body as a fat child and teenager was 'a huge, edgeless cloud of inchoate matter' (67); her feelings are expressed as 'a burlesque of grief, an overblown imitation' (10). As Baudrillard would argue, Joan's emotion, already a burlesque and an imitation, 'bears no relation to any reality whatever: it is its own pure simulacrum'. Rather than 'signs which dissimulate something', her emotions are 'signs which dissimulate that there is nothing'.[36] Since Joan has no sense of boundaries, her identities multiply.[37] Changing body shape, clothes, makeup, wigs, hair length and colour, names, bank accounts and addresses, she is, either consecutively or simultaneously, fat girl and thin woman, mothball and butterfly, a freak and a dancing girl, best friend and 'duplicitous monster' (95), Joan Delacourt, Joan Foster and Louisa K. Delacourt, faithful wife and scandalous lover, alive and dead. Identities are assembled and disposed of according to the whims or exigencies of the moment. Named by her mother after Joan Crawford, the 1940s film star, Joan comes to realise that even Joan Crawford isn't Joan Crawford; she is actually Lucille LeSueur and, any-way, which Joan Crawford was she named after, the hardworking actress, the screen image or the thin body?

Joan is not the postmodern subject in the sense of being disengaged and morally empty and her world of consumer signs is pretty shabby, not one of status symbols. She is also looking for meaning: 'if I could only turn the next corner or the next … I would find the thing, the truth or word or person that was mine, that was waiting for me' (221). Furthermore, Joan's turbulent propulsion through and across identities is very different from Ruth's carefully staged shape-shifting.[38] Joan is looking for completeness because she is so at risk of fragmentation. Ruth's frighteningly strong ego determines her every move, and her control is also the underlying reason for her rejection of the publisher's offer. Writing, particularly fantasy writing, would open her up to the irrational, to vulnerability and incompleteness, at the very moment when her rational ego must be unthreatened if her revenge is to succeed. Though Ruth and Joan live in some of the same literary forms and figures – not only the Gothic but the Oracle, the female grotesque, trick-ster fiction and Hans Anderson's 'Little Mermaid' – Ruth is motivated by a driving purpose, Joan by her unresolved past.

Joan is lost in a plethora of signs, lost in the labyrinth of the uncon-scious, particularly in her tortured relationship with her mother, and lost in the mazes, puzzles and suspicions of the Gothic romance. Baudrillard asks: 'who could say what the reality is that these signs simulate?' In one sense we could say there is a reality that underpins the

Gothic. Joan's experience as a child with the daffodil man who is certainly a flasher but may also be her rescuer when tied up by her Brownie friends is the origin, or one of the origins, for her Gothic hero/villain whose motivation is unclear but always associated with sexual threat. Joan's mother is the 'other woman' of Gothic fiction who stands between the heroine and her hero/father; the Brownies also are a form of that jealous, competitive, powerful female other. Joan's transformation from fat girl to thin, beautiful woman is both 'real' and replicated in every romance transformation from plainness and insignificance to glamour and power. The Gothic, then, is an expression of the female condition. But this 'reality' is always framed by signs – her mother's warnings about bad men, the films Joan sees with Aunt Lou, the myths and fairy tales of her childhood reading, her visits to the Canadian National Exhibition.[39] Joan moves between the Gothic in life and the Gothic in fiction. She constructs the real world in Gothic terms and, conversely, finds her daily life seeping into the Gothics. So every man she meets is a Gothic hero until, that is, he turns into the Gothic villain and the most transitory interchange is refashioned into a dark drama. Thus when a man sits at her table in an Italian restaurant, Joan immediately concludes:

> In his eyes our clothes fell to the floor, we fell to the floor, the white glass-topped table overturned and there was broken glass everywhere. Don't move, Signora, not even your hand with the wedding ring, where is your husband? Or you will cut yourself and there will be a lot of blood. Stay here on the floor with me and let me run my tongue over your belly. (184)

Joan had just been reading a *fotoromanzo*. Condensed in this image are a number of textual references, the broken glass of the Lady of Shalott's mirror, the blood on the painful feet of the Little Mermaid or on the dancing feet in Anderson's 'The Red Shoes', but there are also associations with real people and events – Arthur, the husband she has left behind or Joan's bloody belly when she makes love to the Royal Porcupine – and the associations move both backward and forward as, later in the book, we learn that Joan does really dance on broken glass and gets bloody feet.[40] As Joan's life spirals increasingly out of control, more preposterous details find their way into the Costume Gothic – Aunt Lou's fox fur, Arthur's turtleneck sweater, the dancer's tights and tutu. These details can represent metonymically the significant people and events from Joan's life and the associated fears and desires while, equally, they parody the costume trope. Joan thinks that her *Lady Oracle* poems are 'a Gothic gone wrong' and an 'upside down' Gothic but, then, so is her life (232).

Atwood believes that authors are always double: 'The author is the name on the books: I'm the other one'.[41] In *Lady Oracle* the doubleness is such that nobody knows for sure who is 'the author' and, even those who think they might be 'the author', have little in the way of authorial control, either in name or over the production or dissemination of the work. The Polish Count publishes under a pseudonym; Aunt Lou publishes advice for young girls on menstruation under her own name but doesn't write the copy; and Joan writes her Gothic romances under Aunt Lou's name while *Lady Oracle* is written under what Joan at first thinks of as her own name and then admits is actually Arthur's. Meanwhile, *Reject*, the literary magazine published by Joan's blackmailer, Fraser Buchanan, fails because no one wanted to be known as a rejected author and the political pamphlets of Arthur collapse in disarray, along with the groups they publicise, so none of those authors ever see the light of day either. Though Joan, as we have seen, is aware of the conventions of the form she uses, the actual writing is barely a conscious undertaking. The romances are usually written with her eyes shut, writing blocks are dislodged by acting out scenes and *Lady Oracle* is the product of an exercise in automatic writing. Her writing is, then, a form of possession rather than authorising and Joan's effectiveness as a writer is another manifestation of what Leda Sprott sees as Joan's talent as a medium. When Joan sends her *Lady Oracle* manuscript to publishers Morton and Sturgess, everything in terms of title, editing, cover image and marketing moves decisively beyond her reach.

Sonia Mycack's Kristevan reading of Joan's authorship views both of Joan's modes of writing, the trashy bodice-rippers and the high-art poetry, as telling the same story about 'a form of regression to the archaic maternal space and reinvestment of that energy into adult symbolic existence'. In her writing, Joan attempts to 'create a new position for herself, a position that does not negate the maternal but nevertheless assures her a symbolic identity' and in this Mycack believes she is successful, citing as evidence Joan's eventual understanding of the unappeasable demands of her mother and her decisions to give up the Costume Gothics and to return to Canada to resolve the mess she left behind.[42] But Mycack achieves this resolution only by ignoring other textual details. This final crisis has come about because Joan is – yet again – playing out a Gothic scene; she has just knocked unconscious with a Cinzano bottle a journalist whom she imagines to be the Gothic villain. She *does* decide to give up Costume Gothics but thinks she might take up another fantasy form, science fiction. She *is* going to go back to Canada but '[r]ight now ... it's easier just to stay here in Rome' (345). And she is still looking for the Romantic hero; if the reporter doesn't have the aquiline nose of her ideal, at least 'there is something about a man in a bandage' (345). If we relate our authors' positions to Baudrillard's four phases in the succession of the image, Joan, by the end of the book, remains in the order of simulation and finds it difficult to 'separate truth from false, the real from its artificial resurrection' even though she has made some advances in understanding her situation (174). If Ruth had written her romantic fiction, the narrative would express, from her deeply anti-romantic position, Baudrillard's third phase and simply disguise 'the *absence* of a basic reality'; certainly, this is what Ruth believes the cynical Mary Fisher does. From Edith Hope's perspective, Mrs Pusey's engagement in romance links to Baudrillard's second phase. It is one that 'masks and perverts a basic reality'; Mrs Pusey's false, narcissistic love speaks louder than true, altruistic love. Only Edith holds on to the belief that the image is 'the reflection of a basic reality' (173). She still has faith in the real (as does Brookner, if we take the evidence of her earlier comments on the opposition of true and 'plastic' versions of romance) and she has faith – sadly, valiantly, perhaps anachronistically – in the possibility of hearing the words of true love.

8
The Reluctant Author

> Such decisions to destroy, to hide, the records of an exemplary
> life are made in the heat of life, or more often in the grip of
> immediate *post-mortem* despair, and have little to do with the
> measured judgment, and desire for full and calm knowledge,
> which succeed these perturbations.
>
> A. S. Byatt, *Possession: A Romance*[1]

The above epigraph is from chapter 26 of Mortimer Cropper's *The Great Ventriloquist*, his study of the Victorian poet, Randolph Henry Ash. It is one of the many fictional intratexts of Antonia Byatt's novel. Even these few lines give us a sense of Cropper's fulsome, self-satisfied prose; further acquaintance reveals that his research has little to do with 'measured judgment' or a 'desire for full and calm knowledge' and much to do with his own tortuous psyche. At the end of the book, Cropper does, indeed, 'come a cropper' when he is caught plundering the grave of Ash to retrieve the material that has been buried with him. The impulse to destroy or hide is evident in the texts that feature in this chapter. In Jane Gardam's story, 'The Sidmouth Letters', Annie, the author heroine, inherits some lost love letters of Jane Austen and with complete 'measured judgment' destroys them, unread. In Ursula Le Guin's short story, 'Sur', a group of South American ladies reach the South Pole three years in advance of the Norwegian explorer, Roald Amundsen. One writes a report about the trip but doesn't publish it. In Michèle Roberts's *The Looking Glass*, a number of potential female writers hesitate about writing and publishing.[2] If the figure of the woman author in contemporary fiction has demanded access to the cultural sphere and support for her role as author, she has also on occasions expressed considerable doubt about what she is getting into. The question this chapter explores is

'Why?' Why might a woman with the possibility of a publishing coup or with a wonderful story to tell or with literary talent and inclinations worth developing draw back from writing and publishing, resist the knowing and possessing that motivate Cropper, construct strategies of silence and secrecy to hide her work or be, at best, a reluctant author? The most obvious reason is that writing isn't easy and there are numerous examples of author heroes and heroines with writers' block or disabling scruples about their work. The reasons discussed in this chapter, however, lie elsewhere – in the women's fear of male retribution if they do publish, in the women's attachment to a different economy of authorship which is unconcerned with fame and, in Roberts's novel, in a resistance among some of the women to the very act of writing itself.

The female masquerade: 'Sur' and 'The Sidmouth Letters'

The reluctance to publish is not an empty negative. The opening words of Le Guin's story indicate the possibility of authorship but are, in fact, predicated – at least for the moment – on secrecy and reluctance:

> Although I have no intention of publishing this report, I think it would be nice if a grandchild of mine, or somebody's grandchild, happened to find it some day; so I shall keep it in the leather trunk in the attic, along with Rosita's christening dress and Juanito's silver rattle and my wedding shoes and finneskos. (255)

The reference to 'finneskos', boots made of tanned reindeer skin, sits oddly with the other contents of the trunk, tokens of a respectable, bourgeois wifehood and motherhood. We read on to find an explanation and discover an amazing, unpublished account of heroic female achievement. Virginia Woolf in her essay 'Professions for Women' offers one possible explanation for women's reluctance to publish in suggesting that women writers are 'impeded by the extreme conventionality of the other sex'.[3] This is certainly the case for the women in Le Guin's story. The narrator discretely leaves out the surnames of her companions; the women remain silent about the name of their benefactor; they swear to secrecy the captain of the ship which takes them to Antarctica; they devise pretexts to cover their absences – a retreat in a Bolivian convent or the winter season in Paris – and the reason for all this, the narrator tells us, is 'lest embarrassment or unpleasant notoriety ... be brought upon unsuspecting husbands, sons etc.' (258). Evidently, even when women are not talking about sex, which was the focus of Woolf's remark, the delicate sensibilities of men have to be protected; everything from slightly unconventional behaviour to historic achievement is a threat. As Woolf shows in *A Room of One's Own* that sensitivity can in certain circumstances become violent. Professor von X, writing *The Mental, Moral and Physical Inferiority of the Female Sex*, stabs the virgin page with his phallic pen 'as if he was killing some noxious insect as he wrote'.[4] Who knows what would happen if the Professor had to write of an incident where women were mentally, morally and physically superior – for example, being the first to discover the South Pole. No wonder the women of 'Sur' decide to leave no mark in the public domain, whether on the land they explored, in historical record or as a personal narrative.

Woolf's comments link readily with those of Joan Riviere whose essay, 'Womanliness as a Masquerade', was published in 1929, the same year as *A Room of One's Own*.[5] Riviere's essay sprang from her psychoanalytic practice – in fact, also from her own biography – and focussed on case studies of professional women whose uncertainty about their public roles and their reception by male colleagues had resulted in some distressing psychic symptoms.[6] Riviere deduces that 'women who wish for masculinity may put on a mask of womanliness to avert anxiety and the retribution feared from men' (35), the retribution of which Professor von X is clearly capable. The women of 'Sur' act similarly and profit from the masquerade. The pretexts, the narrator's care to keep the account secret, their conventional behaviour (the story indicates that the expedition was the only occasion on which they acted independently) ensure that they can maintain a mask of appropriate femininity and, hence, male retribution is kept at bay. The account ends with a note added in 1929, once again the year of Woolf and Riviere:

> We are old women now, with old husbands, and grown children, and grandchildren who might some day like to read about the Expedition. Even if they are rather ashamed at having such a crazy grandmother, they may enjoy sharing in the secret. But they must not let Mr Amundsen know! He would be terribly embarrassed and disappointed. There is no need for him or anyone else outside the family to know. We left no footprints, even. (273)

The story of the expedition can be revealed only in old age and only within the confines of the family. The threat it embodies to the male reader will there be transformed into harmless eccentricity and years of playing the role, as Riviere describes it, of 'merely a castrated woman', 'masquerading as guiltless and innocent' (38) will defuse the danger. With age, respectability and a suitably self-deprecating manner comes limited licence. Carolyn Heilbrun could have been talking of the grand-mothers of 'Sur' when she wrote: 'It is perhaps only in old age, certainly past 50, that women can stop being female impersonators, can grasp the opportunity to reverse their most cherished principles of "femininity" '.[7] It is not surprising that Woolf, Riviere and the reluctant author of 'Sur' should fit together so neatly. Though Woolf and Riviere are concerned with women who are moving into what at that time was seen as an almost exclusively male sphere of intellectual pursuits while the women of 'Sur' want to usurp the father's place as adventurer, discoverer, sur-vivor, the texts bring together the common problems of male power and female powerlessness and the common defensive ploy of silence, secrecy and reticence played out as part of the female masquerade.

In another way, though, the women of 'Sur' differ from Riviere's case studies since they display none of the disturbing symptoms of those women. This is, I believe, for three reasons. First, though the women explorers are looking to break out of the private sphere, albeit temporar-ily, they are not concerned about recognition in the public sphere. For Riviere's women it is the public exhibition at the lecture podium or in writing or in giving instructions that render what Riviere sees as their 'masculine' desires impossible to accommodate. Second, Le Guin's nar-rator shows, in Riviere's words, 'a high degree of adaptation to reality' (36). For her 'the capacity for womanliness' is more than simply 'a device for avoiding anxiety' (38). Nor does her life consist 'alternately of masculine and feminine activities' (38). Apart from this one momen-tous occasion the narrator seems to be in happy acquiescence with her lot. The pleasure she can take in her position as wife, mother and grand-mother, together with her middle-class status, may convince her that she has more invested in maintaining the *status quo* than challenging it. In this respect, the narrator of 'Sur' is close to Irigaray's description of the masquerade as 'what women do in order to recuperate some element of desire, to participate in man's desire, but at the price of renouncing their own'.[8] The women of 'Sur' are never seen as threateningly 'having the phallus'; instead the masquerade enables them to continue 'being the phallus'.[9] Yet, from a third perspective, the masquerade might work in their interests. Rather than being its victims or unconsciously caught up in its workings, they use the masquerade as a conscious and highly effective strategy to reclaim something of their own desires, using it, as Mary Ann Doane believes Riviere failed to do, for 'joyful or affirmative play'.[10] Judith Butler talks of the 'undecidability' of gender, 'neither a

purely psychic truth, conceived as "internal" and "hidden," nor ...
reducible to a surface appearance'. This play between psyche and
appearance is 'regulated by heterosexist constraints though not ... fully
reducible to them'.[11] In Le Guin's story the undecidability of, specifically, the masquerade, regulated by heterosexism but not reduced to it,
can produce both conservative and subversive effects that can be
exploited by the women. Hence, the retreat in a convent or a season in
Paris is for their husbands and sons evidence of what women are really
like, either virtuous or vain (conservative) while for the women it is a
calculated deployment of femininity to enable them to fulfil their own
desires (subversive). The masquerade ensures that they retain a feminine
and private subjectivity (conservative) but the masquerade might also
enable new meanings for femininity (subversive). It prevents the publication of the text (conservative) but it also maintains the possibility of
the revelation of the text (subversive).

Jane Gardam's story, 'The Sidmouth Letters', shows how the reluctance
to publish may come not from a fear of retribution – indeed Annie, the
author heroine, has much to gain from publishing Jane Austen's lost love
letters – but from a second concern, doubts about the workings of the literary market and a regard for the privacy of the author. The letters were
written by Austen in Sidmouth in 1801 to a man with whom she had
fallen in love and who, three weeks after being called away on family
business, suddenly died.[12] Annie, the narrator of the story, had written a
short piece about the Sidmouth incident while studying at an American
university, a piece that was subsequently plagiarised by her professor,
Shorty Shenfold. Years later, by which time Annie herself has become
a respected author, she meets Shorty again at the Royal Society of
Literature. Shorty asks Annie to accompany him to Jane Austen's house
in Chawton to photograph some handwriting but the real intention is
that Annie should keep an eye on his alcoholic wife, Lois. The day after
the Chawton visit and the sudden death that night of Lois, Annie agrees to
Shorty's request to go to Sidmouth so as to fetch the lost Austen letters
that Shorty has tracked down and has been negotiating to buy. The photographing of the handwriting had evidently been for verification purposes. Amidst all his adroit scheming, Shorty has forgotten one vital
piece of information, namely that Annie comes from Sidmouth, and is
unaware of another – the Austen letters, the very ones that had inspired
her student essay and that he is now planning to buy, are owned by her
family. During the visit, Annie's ancient aunt gives her the letters as her
inheritance. Annie sits on the beach at Charmouth Bay, a favourite spot
of Jane Austen's, and burns them. Shorty never knows the truth and,

undaunted, continues his pursuit of both literary triumphs and beautiful, unstable and extremely wealthy wives.

Unlike the account in 'Sur', there may have been nothing in Austen's
letters to challenge the dominant gender ideology and, hence, nothing
to disturb the conventional male reader and, as they are over two hun-
dred years old, probably nothing to disturb any descendants. Although
Annie feels no sense of indulgence towards Shorty, no desire to ward off
his retaliation through flirtation or charm as do Riviere's women, she
does, like the women of 'Sur', use the masquerade for her own purposes.
She seems to concur with Shorty's schemes and she takes on various
subservient roles with respect to him, acting as gopher and as companion to Lois, while at the same time embarking on a prudent undermining of Shorty's plans. Annie avoids a direct confrontation not so as to
protect Shorty from disillusion or herself from retribution but as the
most productive means of protecting Jane Austen and, along the way, of
offering support to Lois. She understands the secrecy of the letters as
something chosen by Jane Austen, 'chosen' within the expectations of
the period that is, rather than an imposition on her. Austen's instruction
to her sister, Cassandra, to burn her papers after death links reluctance
with privacy and propriety. Annie honours Austen's wish and takes on
Cassandra's sisterly duty.

Economies of authorship:
'Sur' and 'The Sidmouth Letters'

Barthes talks in *A Lover's Discourse* of '[e]xchange, gift, and theft' as 'the
only known forms of economy'.[13] The term 'economy' is not limited to
monetary or property transactions but encompasses social relations, the
organisation of the psyche, the linguistic and, for our purposes, authorship and the production and circulation of writing. Hélène Cixous both
genders the term and stresses its wide relevance to 'a whole huge system
of cultural inscription':

> The (political) economy of the masculine and the feminine is organized
> by different demands and constraints, which, as they become social-
> ized and metaphorized, produce signs, relations of power, relation-
> ships of production, a whole huge system of cultural inscription that
> is legible as masculine or feminine.[14]

Her reference to masculine and feminine economies has no absolute link
to male and female people though, from a psychoanalytic perspective,

the effects of the castration complex and, from a socio-political context, the workings of patriarchy, render it more likely for men to inhabit a masculine economy and women, a feminine.[15] The involvement of authors in economics in a narrow way by gaining monetary wealth through writing or trading books or, to use Bourdieu's extension of the economic, by gaining symbolic capital through becoming a famous author is, in the texts under consideration here, largely a male pursuit. But even in the broader understanding of the term that Cixous indicates it is the men again who are tied to an economy of profit and loss. The women are, in varying degrees, excluded from, indifferent to and suspicious of literary production as it is conventionally understood and the texts they produce gain nothing in terms of the market economy; they are written for private circulation, hidden and, as in the case of 'The Sidmouth Letters', destroyed. Moreover, though the women authors are involved in the exchanges, gifts and thefts that Barthes mentions, here with relation to literary material, their understanding of profit and loss in these transactions often differs from the men's. The women are not averse to the triumphs of presence, visibility and ownership but, equally, they do not hunger for them and are not dismayed by absence, invisibility and forfeiture.

The new order envisaged by Barthes and Irigaray seems more to their liking. Barthes imagines an economy not of exchange or gift or theft but 'simultaneous proffering' which 'relapses nowhere and whose very community abolishes any thought of reservation' (151). Irigaray has also looked to ' "another" kind of commerce' among specifically women which she characterises as: 'Exchanges without identifiable terms, without accounts, without ends ... . Without additions and accumulations, one plus one, woman after woman ... . Without sequence or number. Without standard or yardstick' (197). Both of these are economies where relations of profit or loss, gain or withholding have no place. In our texts it is the women who are more open to such possibilities but they are also more open to working across different economies. The extent to which one can be indifferent to the dominant economy without becoming its victim has to be carefully calculated and the women sometimes have to intervene in the dominant economy to protect their interests. Indeed, the very language of 'calculation' and 'interests' reveals how impossible it is to escape the terms of that economy.

Masculine and feminine economies, structured around problems of authorship, are largely set in opposition in the stories of Le Guin and Gardam. In both instances a masculine economy based on performance, recognition, gain and possession clashes with a feminine economy associated with discretion, giving, sharing, even self-denial. In 'Sur' the feminine economy operates not only with respect to the production and circulation of the report. Buried beneath the ice is a cave of ice sculptures carved by Berta which will 'last as long as stone' (265). Once again the text is hidden but could later be revealed. The women's organisation of the expedition itself is distinguished from that of the male explorers in its respectful, creative, at times playful attitudes towards the land and the process of exploration. They have no interest in colonising the land; their mapping consists of making up funny names for the places they discover and the arrival at the South Pole is marked not by the raising of a flag but by the brewing of a cup of tea. Le Guin marries green politics with the practice of prudent housekeeping; not for these women the disarray of empty meat tins, broken biscuits and dog turds that surround the camp that Scott and Shackleton had used. The women's practical good sense copes with everything including a pregnancy and birth. The social relations they establish of openness and ease, the chain of command that they set up but, significantly, never use, their under-cutting of any pretension question the male heroic ethic of leadership and individualism and, equally, are a long way from the female rivalry that Riviere associates with the masquerade.

In 'The Sidmouth Letters', the contrary responses of Annie and Shorty to the Austen letters, with opposing notions about the ownership and circulation of texts, expose, as Cixous indicates, the gap between masculine and feminine economies as cultural inscriptions. At every level – economic, social, linguistic, psychic – Shorty and Annie are at odds. Gardam structures these differences in terms of both gender and national identity. Annie's decorous English femininity is set against Shorty's self-seeking American masculinity. Like that other careerist American critic, David Lodge's Maurice Zapp, Shorty is seeking to augment his reputation through the literary texts of Jane Austen.[16] He tours the world accruing cultural capital, funded by the economic capital of a succession of rich wives and supplemented by the symbolic capital acquired through 'his grants and scholarships and awards' (132). Shorty is no disinterested aesthete; he is very preoccupied with hard cash and, with respect to the Austen letters, he has been carefully assessing the market, working out the odds and positioning others to advance his ends. He is a kind of literary shyster. Thus he has already involved a newspaper which is paying all the expenses – 'so you can make 'em high' (137) – and sorted out the American and British rights. With Lois's 'inconvenient' death and the cost of the funeral to worry about, Shorty is bothered that he might not get the return he wants on his investment; at a stroke he could lose both the Austen letters and a chunk of Lois's money. Hence, Annie is dispatched to get the letters with a cheque that Shorty has predated so as to ensure that it does not have to be included in Lois's estate.

An economy of giving, of generosity is genuinely distressing for Shorty. Annie's refusal of payment produces a look of 'utter hatred' (139) but he is also upset because events have forced him to use Annie as his agent and, thus, she will be the first to see and touch the Austen letters, to have a pleasure that should, he thinks, be his. The inability to give is further evident in his use of language. His predilection for the peremptory, short words and phrases, clipped instructions, ensures that there is no excessive expenditure. He says only what needs to be said to get what he wants. In writing too he is known for short literary studies. Shorty doesn't need the mammoth productions of Maurice Zapp, who is planning to write the ultimate version of Jane Austen criticism after which nothing more could be said – or from an earlier period we could think of Causaubon's *Key to All Mythologies* in George Eliot's *Middlemarch*; instead, Shorty acts out his phallic desire for a total control of knowledge within a miraculously small space. The attention to detail, which serves him so well in his economic activities, operates similarly in his writing. His books are 'magnificently thorough', noted for their 'accuracy and exhaustiveness' and produce a return in that he masters all his competitors – 'no scholar could fault them' (130). But Shorty's inability to leave anything open or tentative produces depressing literary effects; his writing is both exhaustive and exhausting. Just as his wives always look tired, so his lectures and books are wearisome to the audience. Personal relations and literary productions are all 'bludgeoned' (133) into submission by his powerful personality that has no space for the other and permits no access.

What *is* at play in Shorty's writing is only a crude suggestiveness that belittles his subjects. Annie's plagiarised essay has been reproduced verbatim by Shorty 'with just the added hint that the lover's disappearance was a little mysterious, more of a getaway than a death' (132). His writing is the product of a sublimated sadistic sexual energy: 'Excitement means the pen' (132). His large, ebullient, bullish physicality and sensibility – 'a bull's neck, a bull's crinkly chunk of hair, a bull's manners and a bull's dangerousness' (130-1) – works on the author most noted in the popular imagination for lady-like decorum; it is a form of literary rape. The writing he produces for a more popular market has 'the tang of something rather nasty about it' (130). Annie knows that Jane Austen's letters too would have been written up for this market with hints and innuendo of a titillating, salacious nature. As in Austen's own novels, it is a finely wrought, feminine sensibility which triumphs over the brutally masculinist. Annie picks up clues and nuances in a way that Shorty, despite his thorough research methods, is unable to do. When being told about the Chawton trip she senses 'the slightest pause' (134) in Shorty's speech; hidden from Shorty and the literary editor accompanying them to Chawton, she hears the editor say, 'My dear – this is going to be *utterly* exciting' (135); she notices the repeated 'quick uneasy look' (137) as Shorty tells her about the letters.

The difference between masculine and feminine literary economies is most tangible in the contrary responses to Austen's handwriting, the closest we can now get to the embodied presence of Austen. The trip to Chawton and the photographing of the handwriting is, in Shorty's schema, for practical purposes and to ensure for himself a lucrative gain. Annie, on the other hand, is thrilled 'to hold the MSS, touch the old writing paper, smell it, look closely at the lovely, diamond-sharp, unmistakable hand' (134). Such a sensuous apprehension is not unknown to Shorty. When sending Annie to claim the letters she perceives that 'he was genuinely longing to see the bundle, to be the first to hold the beautiful, live writing in his hand' (138). Annie recognises that longing but she and the other women of her family don't feel impelled to possess and to know in the same way as Shorty. 'You don't read other folk's letters', says Annie's aunt; 'I've read the fronts of the envelopes, that's all' (145). Annie reads the envelopes, opens them and confirms the signatures on the letters but goes no further. Though texts like letters, diaries, journals (unpublished material generally) inhabit an ambiguous ground between public and private, the tentative suggestion by Enid, Annie's cousin, that perhaps Austen's genius should have given Cassandra, and by implication future owners of the letters, the freedom to countermand Austen's request is rejected out of hand – 'I said I didn't think that would have made the least difference' (147) – and Enid is not keen to press the point. Unlike Shorty, and unlike Maud Bailey who, when faced with the locked box Cropper has stolen from Ash's grave, comments, 'But we *must* look', Annie and the women in her family can resist both looking and the profit motive.[17] As Auntie says in giving the letters to Annie, 'Not to sell, mind. We've never sold them. It's a tradition. And it's a tradition we've never looked at them' (145).

Masculine and feminine economies are not, however, entirely separate and, as I have indicated, the subordinated need to understand the workings of the dominant economy. Annie is capable of working within a market economy – she is, after all, a successful author in her own right – and at various points in the story has been as canny as Shorty but her end purpose is not increased economic, cultural or symbolic capital. Her actions in disposing of the letters are not rational within the terms of the market economy but there is a return as the actions are deeply satisfying to her. Reflecting on her destruction of the letters, Annie remarks: 'I have felt very happy ever since that I of all people have had the chance of paying back a little of a great debt' (148). Those terms, 'paying back' and 'debt', are terms of the dominant economy, suggesting a relation of profit and loss, debit and credit, but the sentiment that governs Annie's action is not financially motivated. Cixous rightly comments:

> Really, there is no 'free' gift. You never give something for nothing. But all the difference lies in the why and how of the gift, in the values that the gesture of giving affirms, causes to circulate; in the type of profit the giver draws from the gift and the use to which he or she puts it.[18]

We have already seen in earlier chapters how there is sometimes an imperative to keep women's cultural production out of the market economy. For example, Mama in Alice Walker's 'Everyday Use' gives the quilts to Maggie just as Auntie gives the letters to Annie. Both Maggie and Annie have the greater need, each is the better custodian and, if the quilts disintegrate through everyday use or the letters are destroyed, it is a price worth paying. The lack of a financial return is of little consequence since, in both instances, there is a more important political, ethical and emotional return.

Across the centuries a connection is established between the two women authors, Jane Austen and Annie. Both have written a handful of novels; both have been unhappy in love and remained unmarried – indeed, Annie's aunt hints that both were in love with sailors; both have a supportive coterie of female family members. Both have also felt caught between independence and attachment to that home and family. Annie's life has been dogged by an Austenesque doublet, Love and Privacy. It was the title she gave to her student essay in which she had recognised how Austen had wanted her privacy to be maintained by hiding her unfulfilled love. Now in destroying the Sidmouth letters the two terms are brought into relation; the love will remain private and Annie shows her love for Jane Austen by ensuring her privacy. But the two terms also illustrate a successful resolution between two economies, one of love with the associations of openness, giving forth, a movement outwards towards the other and another of privacy with its associations of inwardness and retreat. It is part of the ironic humour of the story that a generosity of giving to the memory of Jane Austen and a rejection of monetary self-interest is fulfilled through a characteristic English, Austenesque femininity of reticence, discretion, holding-back. The story supports Cixous's comment and indicates how the difference between feminine and masculine economies lies not in an unqualified opposition between giving and taking but in the motives, values, types of profit and effects that surround the transactions.

The impossibility of writing: *The Looking Glass*

Recognising Shorty's longing to see the Austen letters for the first time is the single, brief moment in the story when Annie feels any sympathy for him. On the other hand, Gérard Colbert, the famous, early twentieth-century writer in Michèle Roberts's *The Looking Glass*, is surrounded by women who are only too happy to lavish attention on him in every possible way. Moreover, they are themselves deeply involved in storytelling and varied forms of writing. Geneviève, illegitimate and placed in an orphanage, comforts herself with daydreams and tells stories to the other children. She listens to the lives of saints told by the nuns but is more taken with the fantastic folk tales told by her first employer and surrogate mother, Madame Patin. She later becomes Gérard's servant and sleeps with him. Millicent, the Colbert's English governess, writes a rather adolescent, priggish and xenophobic diary but also amuses herself by composing in her head endings to the stories she reads in *La Mode Illustrée*. Infatuated by Gérard, she visits him at night in his room. Later she starts writing poetry. Isabelle, Gérard's mistress, writes him short letters but also long letters that she never sends and invents stories to hide their affair: 'loving Gérard,' she says, 'has turned me into a writer' (187). Marie-Louise, Gérard's niece, becomes the guardian of the sacred flame and writes a memoir of her uncle which, like the narrator's in 'Sur', is kept hidden in a box in the attic. Yvonne, Marie Louise's childhood acquaintance, is the only one out of the orbit of Gérard and she gives a critical account of him to a male researcher which reads like the harbinger of feminist literary analysis. In this narrative of abundant female literary activity, the one writer whose literary ability is brought to its publishable potential is, predictably, male, white and middle class, though even Gérard is cut short by premature death in the First World War.

Not only are the female writers and storytellers numerous and the literary forms diverse but the discourses suggested in the text on the meanings and functions of writing and storytelling are multiple. In the orphanage, Geneviève wards off danger by her nightly instalments that keep the bullies in their place; like Offred, she uses the strategy of Scheherazade. But she is also the Pied Piper, spellbinding the other children and leading them 'into a world where [she] ran on just ahead, towards the unknown' (10). To the nuns such storytelling is simply lying; for Yvonne too all art is close to deceit; to Geneviève, though, Isabelle's creative re-tellings of events are not lies but a sign of how memories change. Geneviève, Isabelle and Millicent all fall in love with Gérard through his poetry. In particular, Millicent's literary and intellectual pretensions lead her to a naïve, romantic idealisation of 'the poet' whom she describes in a series of clichés – 'a poet, who can voice the deepest wishes of the human heart. A poet must not be kept silent. He must sing. He must fly ...' (111). Yvonne, though, maintains an emotional distance which renders her suspicious of both art and masculinity and enables her to develop a sexual politics of authorship. She recognises the imbalance of power that underpins the production of texts since much of Gérard's folkloric material came, uncredited, from Geneviève; she disputes the effectiveness of Gérard's female poetic voices and suggests that several female poets of the period were superior writers; she points out how in Marie-Louise's careful staging of the poet's study for public view the pornography collection has been omitted; she notes how Gérard's behaviour, despite its bohemian dimension, fits prevailing norms of bourgeois masculinity.

A further elaborated discourse in the book links writing with desire. Through her reading of her uncle's poetry, Marie-Louise believes she can reclaim him and her childhood and she develops a theory of writing as the relation between memory and desire. In writing, the absence on the white page is invaded, even impregnated, by the presence of the past '[s]o to remember and to write seems to mean to be haunted, and simultaneously to feel fertile' (237). The image she has of herself as a writer – 'a bareback rider standing astride two galloping steeds: memory and desire' (236) – recalls the excited, fervid games which, as a child, she played each night on Gérard's knee, games which Madame Colbert always stopped. Isabelle produces a further psycho-sexual analysis of Gérard's writing. In their lovemaking Isabelle and Gérard construct an equation between sex and poetry which Isabelle extends to include dressmaking. In each activity you practise your techniques, sensitise yourself to another's needs. Isabelle comes to realise, though, how the elimination of woman is essential to Gérard's writing, how the removal of her materiality permits her aestheticisation and how, in turn, this process is linked to his unresolved Oedipal relation with his dominant mother. His writing, she believes, is the product of loss and unfulfilled desire. There is, then, pleasure in sexual abstinence since the absence of the loved one produces the writing. The mother too is wanted and rejected while his prostitutes are a comfort precisely because they are not loved, not wanted and, therefore, can be rejected without guilt. Interestingly, as Isabelle takes on both the guise of a writer and a new sexual freedom through her relationship with Gérard, so she approximates a position of masculinity. She becomes, on an occasional basis, a *flâneuse*, picking up the men she wants when she wants. She also learns to relish Gérard's absence as an impetus to her love. But Isabelle can only play with the position. The conditions of the period do not permit her adopting either the freedom of sexual licence or the authority of authorship.

Despite the intense involvement in many literary forms, these potential women authors find not only publishing impossible but, in some cases, writing itself. As in 'Sur', this reluctance is linked to the accepted social norms in terms of femininity. Both texts are situated in the early years of the twentieth century within conventional, bourgeois, Roman Catholic cultures. But, in Roberts's novel, the reluctance springs also from a psychic resistance to linguistic structuring. Some of the women in *The Looking Glass* feel their words have to remain secret or unarticulated since they are both excessive and too precious. Isabelle and Marie-Louise, for instance, believe their writing cannot be confined to an established syntax. For Isabelle it is the language 'that can flow and does not have to stop; a long cry uttered in silence' (187); for Marie-Louise it is writing 'that sprawls and dashes about all over the place, that wants to be given its head and won't stay tidy, within the bounds of some logical narrative of what happened next' (237). Geneviève knows that she must tell her story but is unnerved by the process. On the one hand, she fears retribution, the response to things 'I hardly dared say' (274) but, on the other hand, she fears that language is inadequate to the task and to tell her story will entail a loss and a limitation: the story is 'smoothed, flattened and straightened' (275). The problem is both lexical and syntactical. What Geneviève perceives at the moment is 'hardly words at all' (274) and they form no linear structure; rather they exist as 'a comforting soup ... melting, mixed up with each other' (274) or 'a mad circling dance' (275). There is no 'I', no speaking subject, no distinction between subject and object and the temporality she experiences is not of a beginning, middle and end but of 'an eternal now', 'wholly present in just one second' (275). From this perspective, Eve's punishment was to *have* to speak, to become a storyteller. Paradise needed no language; it was 'the shimmering eternal moment which was outside time ... when no one could separate us (Geneviève and Madame Patin) and when we didn't have to speak to know we were happy' (275).

Julia Kristeva's theory of the relation between the semiotic and the symbolic, the libidinal and the linguistic, can help us to understand the predicament of Isabelle, Marie-Louise and, particularly, Geneviève and it gives a further inflection to the meaning of 'economy'. The symbolic order, explains Elizabeth Grosz, 'organises the libidinal drives according to a phallic sexual economy, a normative and generative linguistic structure (including grammar, logic, syntax, and access to the shifter "I", which gives the subject access to appropriating discourse as its own, as referring to itself), and a subjective and social identity'.[19] Geneviève fears that the phallic sexual economy will condemn her as an improper woman but, equally, the mastery of language and the achievement of 'a subjective and social identity' are at a cost, namely the repression of the semiotic and the undifferentiated unity with the maternal body, that 'shimmering, eternal moment'. 'The speaking subject,' Grosz adds, 'must "pay" for the unity and certainty of its position, its "mastery", with the renunciation of its maternal pleasures and the sacrifice of its oedipal, incestual attachments' (49). For Geneviève, Madame Patin's stories, particularly those about the silent, dangerous, seductive mermaid, are disturbing. Listening to them offers a retreat to childhood and a maternal connection but they also suggest new possibilities which her burgeoning sexuality recognises but cannot put into words. As a child, Geneviève is overwhelmed by Madame Patin's voice. When listening to her stories she says: 'I could not resist her deep voice beginning: once upon a time, long, long ago' (27). According to Cixous, what she hears is 'the voice of the mother, passing on what is most archaic. The most archaic force that touches a body is one that enters by the ear and reaches the most intimate point'.[20] But, warns Kristeva, 'the call of the mother ... generates voices, "madness", hallucinations'. The love which ties the little girl to the mother is like 'black lava', sucking her away from the symbolic, paternal order.[21] Geneviève is torn between semiotic and symbolic dispositions, at one moment moving away from the maternal body towards the paternal, at the next turning back. If, as Kristeva says, 'through identifying with the father, she strives for access to the Word and to time', Geneviève also longs for the mother and wants to reject both Word and time (41).

Responding to Kristeva's warning about the danger of a symbiotic union with the mother, Makiko Minow-Pinkney remarks: 'If this is indeed so in the case of our present mode of subjectivity, then it is all the more urgent to pursue the project of forging a new kind of subjectivity for which the call of the mother and the fall of the paternal order would *not* mean its foundering'.[22] The novel ends with both the promise and the undermining of such an aspiration. Geneviève imagines her return to the sea at Blessetot and to her surrogate mother, Madame Patin. The text hints at a new relationship, different from her earlier desire to fuse with the mother. Central to this is an acceptance of 'the Word'. She remembers the voices of the orphans and she hears the voices of their parents, 'crying for their lost ones to come home again. Crying out for all their lost words to return' (277). Perhaps the lost child, herself, can come home only if she accepts the 'lost words'. The sea at Blessetot expresses the impossible duality. It links to the mother, the semiotic with its rhythmical pulsations, 'back and forth, back and forth', but within that movement the salt foam is 'tracing filigree lines of script onto the loose shingle' (277), a suggestion of the demands of the symbolic. This script, we could call it 'the Word' or the 'lost words', is uncertain, constantly eradicated but, equally, constantly re-written. And the historical moment is also uncertain. The final words of the novel, which date Geneviève's situation, are 'this early summer of 1914' (277). She is creating a new link with the mother at the same time as she will experience a terrible tremor in the paternal order.

It is Madame Patin's stories that Geneviève in turn tells to Gérard and, again, water imagery is uppermost. Millicent surprises them in the kitchen when the words are 'pouring out' of Geneviève towards Gérard, like 'a leaping fish spouting jets of water' or a 'rushing stream of talk' and Geneviève is in a 'swimmy trance' (112–13). Cixous, we remember, talks of the movement of the feminine text as one of outpouring, flow, disgorging, vomiting.[23] The imagery might suggest as well a reversal in gender roles. Geneviève is 'tipping herself into him' (113) and Gérard responds with 'his whole body shaped into an attitude of listening, as though he had curved himself into a great ear, a great shell' (113). His ear is the orifice into which Geneviève pours but in addition the image harks back to the deep, troubled waters of the mermaid and the voice of the mother spilling into the ear. In a later image Gérard 'swallowed (the stories) with gusto, tipping them down his throat like oysters' (162). The link to water is still present but the image has a sophisticated, metropolitan association. He consumes the stories with the same relish as a good meal in a Parisian restaurant.

The traversing of economies in the telling and circulation of the mermaid tales is complicated. When Madame Patin tells the stories to

Geneviève they sit by the fire, doing mending or knitting, while Geneviève sometimes brushes Madame Patin's hair. These are moments of ease and intimacy, separate from the strenuous aspects of the domestic economy but also linked to that economy since, for Geneviève, the house, the objects in it, their daily activities are all 'saturated ... with the most tender feelings and memories, my earliest experiences of joy' (39).[24] This could be Barthes's 'simultaneous proffering' or Irigaray's 'exchanges without identifiable terms'. When Millicent recounts the storytelling incident in the kitchen between Gérard and Geneviève, she sees it as a scene of 'giving and capturing' (113), a phrase which suggests generosity on the part of one, an eager taking by the other. The problem is the nature of that giving and taking: to what extent is that generosity freely given or is it compromised and is the taking mutually sanctioned or is it exploitative? Yvonne's interpretation is that the stories that find their way into Gérard's volume, *Men and Mermaids*, indicate the expropriating ploys of the bourgeois male who will claim as his own whatever he wants; in short, they are theft. Geneviève's own understanding of the scene is more nuanced and has a history. Gérard had rescued her from an attempted suicide by drowning and given her a job. She recognises that a gift is never without obligation and, at first, feels resentment towards him. In deciding to give him something in return, it is her class interests that are to the fore – 'to give him something back ... to make sure there was nothing too condescending about his visits, no being kind to the poor orphan who nearly died' (162). The return for the gift is a repayment but it also deepens the relation between them and alters the power balance slightly. Eventually she admits she enjoys the conversations in the kitchen: 'I ended up wishing to join in, to reciprocate in some way' (162) and she tells him Madame Patin's stories. The transaction moves more towards an exchange, particularly in the word 'reciprocate'. Of course, this is not an exchange between equals as the fundamental class and gender differences are unchanged. Geneviève remains the servant, 'giving' her domestic labour in return for minimal economic capital and no symbolic capital. But she is aware of what she is doing and uses her assets as best she can. She trades the stories for the pleasure of conversation and contact; she knows she is valued by Gérard and has some leverage over him; she enjoys his kindness and his gifts of books and magazines.

The dangerous pleasures of reluctance

There might be dangers for women in the fall of the paternal order but there are many delights in secretly chipping away at its foundations.

Mr Amundsen never knows how misplaced is his sense of heroism; Shorty never knows how he has been out-manoeuvred by Annie; and the great lover, Gérard, is unaware of the final transaction in which he plays a part – Isabelle, Millicent and Geneviève, drunk after a morning on calvados, cut cards to see which of them is going to claim sole rights to him; now it is the man who has become an object of exchange. At the same time it is from the perspective of pleasure that the women's reluctance to be authors or to enter into the literary field can begin to look less of an imposition, less of a necessary strategy and, perhaps, less noble. In 'Sur', for example, the old-fashioned charm of the narrator hides a more complex structure of feeling and relationship. Her remarks about not wanting to embarrass men, about protecting Mr Amundsen, the decision to leave no mark at the South Pole lest 'some man longing to be first might come some day, and find it, and know then what a fool he had been, and break his heart' (270), her understanding that 'the backside of heroism is often rather sad' (263) all reveal her as conscious of the limitations of male heroism and yet tolerant of them. The narrator expresses both kindness and a knowingness and all the women of 'Sur', it appears, act as mothers, indulging the boys' games and safeguarding from attack the tender psyches of their menfolk through a process of ingenious plotting, humouring and, if necessary, 'wretched contrivances and downright lies' (258). Men might do brave things, the story indicates, but they are emotionally insecure; women are emotionally strong and flexible, adept at coping. Thus, they can at once admire men and trivialise them. They can remain inside the dominant order, living out their subservience with true womanliness, and act outside the dominant order in their critique of it. The masquerade hides their critique but it also enables the men to retain their phallic display.

What the women *refusniks* of our narratives never admit to is how this knowingness and indulgence can be linked to a sense of superiority over the men. As Stephen Heath has remarked, among the many possible interpretations of the masquerade is 'subjection to the male régime of "the woman" ' but also 'derision of that régime'.[25] Le Guin's comments on her own work illustrate this range of responses. She describes the writing of 'Sur' as 'one of the pleasantest experiences of my life'; she shows a protective indulgence in wanting 'to subvert as much as possible without hurting anybody's feelings' but then a sense of superiority in her response to male exploration: 'So I go on loving Shackleton, but with the slightest shade of contempt for his having boasted'.[26] Almost all the women of these narratives see the male régime as risible, so easily fooled. The open display of derision causes problems. For example,

Riviere's client who cannot prevent herself from interspersing her lecture with jokes and flippant remarks receives in return 'comment and rebuke' from her male colleagues (39). Secret derision, though, shared within a chosen circle, has none of the threat and all of the pleasure and a key reading effect of these narratives is to extend that complicit pleasure from author to characters to female readers. We are encouraged to feel superior to the men who are caught in the absurdity of the bubble of a self-regarding masculinity and their values are devalued; we feel good about the women characters and, perhaps, endow them with a superiority they themselves don't want; we also might feel good about ourselves, not only in possessing the superior values but in being privy to this secret circumvention of male power and in remembering with some glee our own similar circumventions.

'The sacrifice of pleasures is of course itself a pleasure,' says Fleur Talbot in Muriel Spark's *Loitering with Intent*.[27] What this pleasure in exclusion, silence or reluctant engagement might imply for the politics of feminism is a crucial question. Is it, for example, implicated in a form of *ressentiment*? The slave, Nietzsche tells us, 'has a perfect understanding of how to keep silent, how not to forget, how to wait, how to make himself provisionally small and submissive'.[28] In these texts much of the pleasure of the narratives lies in the not acting out, in the secrecy around these events, in savouring the possibility of a future, explosive revelation if the narrator of 'Sur' or Annie ever publish what they know or in a rewriting of literary history if the potential of the women in Roberts's novel finds an outlet. In short, the pleasure is in silence, not forgetting, waiting, appearing submissive. This is the 'imaginary revenge' Nietzsche talks of which compensates those 'to whom the real reaction, that of the deed, is denied' (22). The *ressentiment* encouraged in these texts is not of the corrosive, rancorous, poisonous, vindictive, cunning nature that Nietzsche discusses in epithets that are nothing if not trenchant; it is debunking, full of fun, a necessary defence. But, then, one may never fully know the forces of repression at play that can lead one to mask pain and rage behind humour and gentle mockery. Reluctance, withdrawing, silence and secrecy can be at once self-protecting and self-defeating. As Véronique Machelidon says of Riviere's project: 'Riviere's artistic creativity and rebelliousness has been subdued into a masquerade that exposes, mocks, but ultimately does not threaten established gender hierarchies and psychoanalytic authorities'.[29] If the pleasures of secrecy, of collusion and conspiracy can lead us, as Nietzsche says, to 'imaginary revenge', then they can also lead us away from action, to 'the magnificence of self-abnegating, calm, and patient virtue', even to a fear of freedom (30). Barbara Johnson comments:

> There seem, then, to be two things women are silent about: their pleasure and their violation. The work performed by the idealization of this silence is that *it helps culture not to be able to tell the difference between the two.*[30] (Italics in original.)

The problem also is that it helps women specifically not to tell the difference between the two. Ultimately, the danger is not only that women are prohibited or constrained from full involvement in the cultural sphere but that women might find pleasure in the prohibition.[31] The secret pleasure then becomes disabling and ties us to the constraints.

Afterword

> May she get out of booby-trapped silence! And not have the
> margin or the harem foisted on her as her domain!
>
> Hélène Cixous, 'Sorties'[1]

Hélène Cixous's hope stands in contrast to the secrecy and subterfuge
that attracted the women authors in the previous chapter. She would say
to those reluctant women, 'And why don't you write? Write! Writing is
for you, you are for you; your body is yours, take it'.[2] Her laughing
Medusa who, in the 1970s and 1980s, became an exemplary figure for
the writing woman is ebullient, irreverent and unconstrained, full of
revolutionary potential. According to Cixous, she must write 'a *new
insurgent* writing which, when the moment of her liberation has come,
will allow her to carry out the indispensable ruptures and transformations in her history' (250). Cixous imagines women's return 'from
"without", from the heath where witches are kept alive; from below,
from "beyond" culture; from their childhood' (247). The place of
women, it seems, was everywhere except here at the heart of the culture.
But their time has come. Cixous positions her comments at what she
sees as a moment of transformation: it has not yet arrived; she cannot
name the date but it is 'just on the point of being discovered' (245).
Women are opening up to a 'vatic bisexuality' (254) and Cixous encourages them to this utopian future.

Looking back nearly thirty years to when Cixous's essay was first
translated into English, the fiction of authorship that has been produced
during that time contains sadly little of Cixous's optimism. Created in
realist and, as in Margaret Atwood's *The Handmaid's Tale*, dystopian
modes rather than utopian, the figure of the woman author that has
emerged continues to be caught in old problems about access to cultural

production and anxiety about the kind of values she might be forced either to forfeit or to embrace in the process. Even the shape-shifting Joan in *Lady Oracle* or Ruth in *The Life and Loves of a She Devil* or the playful Fleur in *Loitering with Intent* have not escaped a consciousness of themselves as *women* writers and a sense of the strains that category imposes on them. The disruptive strategies of these author figures have been vital to the women involved but, far from having a revolutionary effect, they have been small-scale and unknown to history.

Two strands draw together many of the texts I have considered in this study. On the one hand, there is a sense of the woman author's vulnerability in the public sphere – for example, in the work of Gardam or Coetzee or Williams. On the other, there is the care with which she needs to negotiate the private sphere. This is evident not only in the humouring of male sensibilities which we saw in Le Guin or Roberts but in the persistence of problems surrounding maternity. In Antonia Byatt's 'Art Work', Debbie gives up her creative work to become mother, homemaker and breadwinner. In both *Possession* and David Lodge's *Nice Work*, we leave the heroines before motherhood is on the agenda as if the resolution achieved in these novels could not withstand the disturbance of maternity. In Lodge's later novel, *Thinks ...*, Robyn Penrose returns. Although she is now both professor and mother, the two are hard to reconcile. At an after-lecture dinner, even Robyn has little interest in the content of the talk she has just given and prefers to discuss childhood illnesses and nursery schools. Her fierce intellectual energy has, to some extent, evaporated. Carol Shields, one of the few authors, who has consistently placed her author-heroines within domestic settings and portrayed them as 'jobbing' authors, sorting literary problems alongside the washing, has paid the price by being critiqued for cosiness.

The longevity of the figure of the woman author is evidence of the unresolved nature of the problems she embodies, both political and cultural. Peggy Kamuf's query in 1980, which I noted in the Introduction, that feminist concern with the author would encourage 'the reduction of the literary work to its signature and to the tautological assumption that a feminine "identity" is one which signs itself with a feminine name', has, on the whole, proved not to be substantiated.[3] Feminism has not closed the argument but has continued to worry about what the signature suggests with respect to gender and difference generally, what meanings and potential lie in the identity, 'the woman author', and what constitutes the past, present and future of this figure. And even beyond feminism the author seems to be on the verge of another resurrection. Indeed Seán Burke goes so far as to assert that 'the reconstruction of the political may depend in considerable measure upon the rematerialisation of the author'. The author does not reinforce the coherent, unitary subject; instead, 'the retracing of the work to its author is a working-back to historical, cultural and political embeddedness'.[4] This is not far from the point that Nancy Miller was making fourteen years earlier when, as I pointed out in Chapter 2, she insists on complicating Barthes's generic concept of 'the Author' through the corporeal, historical and political figure of the woman author. In a period in which there has been such a high level of uncertainty about the significance and status of the author, in which the figure repeatedly re-emerges at the centre of cultural and political debates, in which the ethical and political responsibilities of authorship have been brought home by some striking *causes célèbres* and in which gender has entered the discussion in a decisive way, it is inevitable that the figure of the woman author should feature so often in fiction as problem or irritant, as focus for struggles, as an expression of desire, as loss or as a harbinger of change. Because this figure has remained so in dispute, so she has remained alive.

Notes

1 Introduction: Birth, Death and Resurrection

1. Seán Burke, *Authorship: From Plato to the Postmodern. A Reader* (Edinburgh: Edinburgh University Press, 1995), p. 145.
2. Carol Shields, *Mary Swann* (London: Flamingo, 1993); Muriel Spark, *Loitering with Intent* (Harmondsworth, Middlesex: Penguin, 1995); Antonia Byatt *Possession: A Romance* (London: Vintage, 1991).
3. Sherley Anne Williams, *Dessa Rose* (London: Virago Press Ltd., 1998); Margaret Atwood, *Lady Oracle* (London: Virago Press Ltd., 1982); Ursula Le Guin, 'Sur', *The Compass Rose* (London: Victor Gollancz, 1983).
4. Alice Walker, 'Everyday Use', *In Love and Trouble* (London: The Women's Press Ltd., 1984); Antonia Byatt, 'Art Work', *The Matisse Stories* (London: Vintage, 1994).
5. The history and etymology of the term, 'author', are usefully discussed in Donald E. Pease, 'Author', in Frank Lentricchia and Thomas McLaughlin (eds) *Critical Terms for Literary Study* (Chicago, IL and London: University of Chicago Press, 1990), pp. 105–117.
6. See, for example, Grace Stewart, *A New Mythos: The Novel of the Artist as Heroine 1877–1977* (Montreal, Canada: Eden Press Women's Publications, 1981); Linda Huf, *A Portrait of the Artist as a Young Woman* (New York: Frederick Ungar Publishing Co., 1983); Rachel Blau DuPlessis, *Writing Beyond the Ending: Narrative Strategies of Twentieth-Century Women Writers* (Bloomington, IN: Indiana University Press, 1985); Gayle Greene, *Changing the Story: Feminist Fiction and the Tradition* (Bloomington, IN: Indiana University Press, 1991); Lisa Maria Hogeland, *Feminism and Its Fictions: The Consciousness-Raising Novel and the Women's Liberation Movement* (Philadelphia, PA: University of Pennsylvania, 1998).
7. Ruth Parkin-Gounelas, *Fictions of the Female Self: Charlotte Brontë, Olive Schreiner, Katherine Mansfield* (London: Macmillan, 1991), p. 2. Note also the significant number of texts, particularly in the second half of the 1970s and into the 1980s, whose titles turn on notions of silence, breaking through silence, finding words, speaking out and so on.
8. Carol Shields, *Unless* (London: Fourth Estate, 2003), p. 208. Further references appear in the text.
9. Sandra Gilbert and Susan Gubar, *The Madwoman in the Attic: The Woman Writer and the Nineteenth-Century Literary Imagination* (New Haven, CT: Yale University Press, 1979). See Chapter 2.
10. Lorna Sage, *Women in the House of Fiction* (London: Macmillan, 1992).
11. See Jenny Hartley, *Reading Groups* (Oxford: Oxford University Press, 2001); the *Survey of the English Curriculum and Teaching in UK Higher Education* (Report Series No. 8: English Subject Centre, 2003) shows that in terms of the popularity of optional courses women's writing is on a par with Shakespeare

and second only to contemporary writing courses on which women writers tend to feature prominently as well.

12. Roland Barthes, 'The Death of the Author', in Stephen Heath (selected and trans.), *Image–Music–Text* (London: Fontana, 1977).

13. Barbara Smith, 'Toward a Black Feminist Criticism', *Conditions: Two* 1, No. 2 (1977); Luce Irigaray, *Ce sexe qui n'en est pas un* (Paris: Minuit, 1977); Elaine Showalter *A Literature of Their Own* (Princeton, NJ: Princeton University Press, 1977); Hélène Cixous, 'The Laugh of the Medusa', *Signs*, Vol. 1, No. 4 (Summer, 1976); Marxist–Feminist Literature Collective, 'Women's Writing: *Jane Eyre, Shirley, Villette, Aurora Leigh*', in Francis Barker, John Coombes, Peter Hulme, Colin Mercer and David Musselwhite (eds) *The Sociology of Literature 1848* (Essex: University of Essex, 1978); Gilbert and Gubar, *The Madwoman in the Attic*.

14. Eugen Simion, *The Return of the Author* (1981) ed. and intro. James W. Newcomb; trans. James W. Newcomb and Lidia Vianu (Evanston, IL: Northwestern University Press, 1996), p. 111.

15. Sage, *Women*, p. 168. Gilbert Adair, *The Death of the Author* (London: Minerva, 1993).

16. See Burke's essay, 'The Ethics of Signature', in *Authorship*, pp. 285–91.

17. The writer as Jekyll and Hyde is explored by Margaret Atwood in *Negotiating with the Dead: A Writer on Writing* (London: Virago Press Ltd., 2003). Examples of the author taking over the identity of another would include Bernice Rubens, *Autobiopsy* (London: Sinclair-Richardson, 1993) and John Colapinto, *About the Author* (London: Fourth Estate, 2002).

18. Linda Hutcheon, *Narcissistic Narrative: The Metafictional Paradox* (London: Methuen, 1984). Hutcheon makes clear that she is using the term with respect to the narrative text and not the author. I would suggest that where the author figure features significantly in the text the term could be extended to include the author also.

19. J. M. Coetzee, *Foe* (Harmondsworth, Middlesex: Penguin, 1987).

20. I am following the Barthesian convention of using the upper-case 'A' when talking about the author of origin and legal and social status and the lower-case 'a' when referring to the published writer generally.

21. Peggy Kamuf, 'Writing Like a Woman', in Sally McConnell-Ginet Ruth Borker and Nelly Furman (eds) *Women and Language in Literature and Society* (New York: Praeger, 1980), pp. 285–6.

22. Carol Shields, 'Absence', *Dressing Up for the Carnival* (London: Fourth Estate, 2000).

23. Margaret Atwood, *The Handmaid's T*ale (London: Virago Press Ltd., 1987).

24. Nancy Miller, 'The Text's Heroine: A Feminist Critic and Her Fictions', *Subject to Change: Reading Feminist Writing* (New York: Columbia University Press, 1988), p. 71.

25. Most especially Bourdieu has written on Flaubert. See *The Field of Cultural Production: Essays on Art and Literature*, ed. and intro. Randal Johnson (Cambridge: Polity Press, 1993) and *The Rules of Art: Genesis and Structure of the Literary Field*, trans. Susan Emmanuel (Cambridge: Polity Press, 1996). For examples of a Bourdieuian analysis of women's writing, see Bridget Fowler, *The Alienated Reader: Women and Popular Culture in the Twentieth Century* (Hemel Hempstead, Hertfordshire: Harvester Wheatsheaf, 1991) and *Pierre*

Bourdieu and Cultural Theory (London: Sage Publications, 1997). Toril Moi's essays on appropriating Bourdieu for feminism in *What Is a Woman?* (Oxford: Oxford University Press, 1999) are also relevant and a Bourdieuian approach influenced her *Simone de Beauvoir: the Making of an Intellectual Woman* (Oxford: Blackwell Publishers, 1994).

26. Raymond Williams, *The Long Revolution* (Harmondsworth, Middlesex: Pelican, 1965).

27. Margaret Atwood, *Alias Grace* (Toronto, Ontario: McClelland & Stewart Inc., 1996).

28. Salman Rushdie, *Shame* (London: Jonathan Cape, 1985), p. 116.

29. Claude Lévi-Strauss, 'A Writing Lesson', *Tristes Tropiques*, trans. John and Doreen Weightman (London: Jonathan Cape, 1973), pp. 294–304; Jacques Derrida, *Of Grammatology*, trans. Gayatri Chakravorty Spivak (Baltimore, NY and London: The Johns Hopkins University Press, 1976).

30. Gayatri Chakravorty Spivak, 'Theory in the Margin: Coetzee's Foe Reading Defoe's Crusoe/Roxana', in Jonathan Arac and Barbara Johnson (eds) *Consequences of Theory: Selected Papers from the English Institute, 1987–88* (Baltimore, NY and London: The Johns Hopkins University Press, 1991); David Attwell in interview with Coetzee, in David Attwell (ed.) *J. M. Coetzee, Doubling the Point: Essays and Interviews* (Cambridge, MA: Harvard University Press, 1992); Iris Marion Young, *Intersecting Voices: Dilemmas of Gender, Political Philosophy, and Policy* (Princeton, NJ: Princeton University Press, 1997).

31. Elaine Showalter, *A Literature of Their Own*, 2nd ed. (London: Virago Press Ltd., 1999), p. 321.

32. David Lodge, *Nice Work* (Harmondsworth, Middlesex: Penguin, 1989); Alison Lurie *Foreign Affairs* (London: Abacus, 1986); Alison Lurie, *The Truth about Lorin Jones* (London: Michael Joseph, 1988); Amanda Cross, *Death in a Tenured Position* (New York: Ballantine Books, 1981).

33. Michèle Le Dœuff, *The Philosophical Imaginary*, trans. Colin Gordon (London: The Athlone press, 1989) and *Hipparachia's Choice: An Essay Concerning Women, Philosophy, etc.*, trans. Trista Selous (Oxford; Blackwell, 1991).

34. Anita Brookner, *Hotel du Lac* (London: Granada publishing Co. Ltd., 1985); Fay Weldon, *The Life and Loves of a She Devil* (London: Sceptre, 1984).

35. Sue Vice, 'Addicted to Love', in Lynn Pearce and Jackie Stacey (eds) *Romance Revisited* (London: Lawrence & Wishart, 1995), pp. 122–3.

36. Catherine Belsey, *Desire: Love Stories in Western Culture* (Oxford: Blackwell, 1994).

37. Jane Gardam, 'The Sidmouth Letters', *The Sidmouth Letters* (London: Abacus, 1981).

38. Michèle Roberts, *The Looking Glass* (London: Little, Brown and Company, 2000).

39. Joan Riviere, 'Womanliness as a Masquerade', Victor Burgin, James Donald and Cora Kaplan (eds) *Formations of Fantasy* (London: Methuen & Co. Ltd., 1986).

40. Hélène Cixous, 'Sorties', in Cixous and Catherine Clément *The Newly Born Woman*, trans. Betsy Wing (Manchester: Manchester University Press, 1986).

41. Friedrich Nietzsche, *On the Genealogy of Morals*, trans. Douglas Smith (Oxford: Oxford University Press, 1996).

2 Feminism and the Death of the Author

1. Julie Birchall, *The Guardian* 26 October 2002.
2. Carol Shields, 'Absence', *Dressing Up for the Carnival* (London: Fourth Estate, 2000). Further references appear in the text.
3. Jorge Luis Borges, 'Borges and I', *Labyrinths* (Harmondsworth, Middlesex: Penguin, 1970), p. 283.
4. Virginia Woolf, *A Room of One's Own* and *Three Guineas* (Harmondsworth, Middlesex: Penguin, 1993), p. 90. See also Woolf on the relation between 'I' and egotism in essay writing in 'The Decay of Essay-writing', in Andrew McNeillie (ed.) *The Essays of Virginia Woolf: Volume 1 1904–1912* (London: The Hogarth Press, 1986), pp. 24–7.
5. Maxine Hong Kingston, *The Woman Warrior: Memoirs of a Girlhood among Ghosts* (London: Picador, 1981), p. 49. Further references appear in the text.
6. Roland Barthes, 'The Death of the Author', in Stephen Heath (selected and trans.) *Image–Music–Text* (London: Fontana, 1977), p. 142. Further references appear in the text.
7. Michel Foucault, 'What is an Author?', in Josué V. Harari (ed.) *Textual Strategies: Perspectives in Post-Structuralist Criticism* (Ithaca, NY: Cornell University Press, 1979), p. 160. Further references appear in the text.
8. In addition to the essays to be discussed here, see also Peggy Kamuf, 'Replacing Feminist Criticism', *Diacritics*, Vol. 2, No. 12 (Summer, 1982), pp. 42–7; Kamuf, *Signature Pieces: On the Institution of Authorship* (Ithaca, NY and London: Cornell University Press, 1988); Kamuf and Nancy Miller, 'Parisian Letters: Between Feminism and Deconstruction', in Marianne Hirsch and Evelyn Fox Keller (eds) *Conflicts in Feminism* (New York: Routledge, 1990), pp. 121–33. Kamuf's 'Replacing Feminist Criticism' and Miller's 'The Text's Heroine: A Feminist Critic and Her Fictions' are also anthologised in the Hirsch and Fox Keller volume.
9. Nancy Miller, 'The Text's Heroine: A Feminist Critic and Her Fictions', *Subject to Change: Reading Feminist Writing* (New York: Columbia University Press, 1988), p. 75.
10. Peggy Kamuf, 'Writing Like a Woman', in Sally McConnell-Ginet *et al.* (eds) *Women and Language in Literature and Society* (New York: Praeger Publishers, 1980), p. 286.
11. Miller, 'Changing the Subject: Authorship, Writing, and the Reader', *Subject to Change*, p. 107.
12. Ibid., p. 106.
13. Miller, 'The Text's Heroine: A Feminist Critic and Her Fictions', p. 69.
14. Ibid., p. 67.
15. Reina Lewis 'The Death of the Author and the Resurrection of the Dyke', in Sally Munt (ed.) *New Lesbian Criticism: Literary and Cultural Readings* (Hemel Hempstead, Hertfordshire: Harvester Wheatsheaf, 1992), p. 18.
16. Toril Moi, *What is a Woman? And Other Essays* (Oxford: Oxford University Press, 1999), p. 57.
17. Lorna Sage, 'Death of the Author', *Granta 41: Biography* (London: Granta Publications, 1992), p. 235. Further references appear in the text.
18. Marina Warner's Introduction to Lorna Sage, *Moments of Truth: Twelve Twentieth-Century Women Novelists* (London: Fourth Estate, 2001), p. xvi.

19. On the de Man scandal, see Christopher Norris, *Paul de Man: Deconstruction and the Critique of Aesthetic Ideology* (London: Routledge, 1988); David Lehman, *Signs of the Times: Deconstruction and the Fall of Paul de Man* (New York: Poseiden Press, 1992); Martin McQuillan, *Paul de Man* (London: Routledge 2001).

20. John Banville, *Shroud* (London: Picador, 2002), p. 285. This novel also uses the Paul de Man story as one of its intertexts. The hero, Alex Vandler, is a successful academic who has hidden his collaborationist past.

21. Gilbert Adair, *The Death of the Author* (London: Minerva, 1993). Further references appear in the text.

22. De Man's wartime writings were discovered by a research student, Ortwin de Graef.

23. Seán Burke, *The Death and Return of the Author: Criticism and Subjectivity in Barthes, Foucault and Derrida* (Edinburgh: Edinburgh University Press, 1992), p. 175, n. 8.

24. Paul de Man, 'Autobiography as De-Facement', *The Rhetoric of Romanticism* (New York: Columbia University Press, 1984), p. 77. Further references appear in the text.

25. Margaret Atwood, *The Handmaid's Tale* (London: Virago Press Ltd., 1987). Further references appear in the text. As a further example of a Barthesian reading of Atwood's novel, see Elisabeth Mahoney's 'Writing so to Speak: the Feminist Dystopia', in Sarah Sceats and Gail Cunningham (eds) *Image and Power: Women in Fiction in the Twentieth Century* (London: Longman, 1996), pp. 29–40. Here *The Handmaid's Tale* is discussed with reference to Barthes's *The Pleasure of the Text*.

26. Kamuf, 'Writing Like a Woman', p. 297. Further references appear in the text.

27. Of related interest are Jessie Givner's comments on the gaps in the text between sign and signified, name and person. See 'Names, Faces and Signatures in Margaret Atwood's *Cat's Eye* and *The Handmaid's Tale*', *Canadian Literature*, Vol. 133 (Summer, 1992), pp. 56–75.

28. See Foucault, *Language, Counter-Memory Practice: Selected Essays and Interviews*, Donald Bouchard (ed.); trans. Donald Bouchard and Sherry Simon (Ithaca, NY: Cornell University Press, 1977). Anthologised in Séan Burke (ed.) *Authorship from Plato to the Postmodern: A Reader* (Edinburgh: Edinburgh University Press, 1995).

29. Roland Barthes, 'From Work to Text', in *Image–Music–Text*, p. 142. Further references appear in the text.

30. See Chapter 5 for further comment on the relation of women's authorship to oral narratives. See also Linda Hutcheon, *The Canadian Postmodern: A Study of Contemporary English–Canadian Fiction* (Oxford: Oxford University Press, 1988), Chapter 3 for a discussion of the oral/written opposition in Canadian postmodern novels.

31. The process here of constructing Offred's text could be compared with the discussion in Chapter 4 of the literary history of Swann's poetry in Carol Shields's, *Mary Swann*.

32. See Jonathan Bignell, 'The Lost Messages: *The Handmaid's Tale*, Novel and Film', *British Journal of Canadian Studies*, Vol. 8, No. 1 (1993), pp. 71–84. Bignell's comments on Pieixoto's use of historical data as a further way of restraining Offred's narrative and fixing the generic possibilities are particularly relevant here.

33. See Sharon Rose Wilson, *Margaret Atwood's Fairy-Tale Sexual Politics* (Jackson, MS: University Press of Mississippi, 1993) for a full and interesting account of Atwood's use of fairy-tale and myth, though Wilson doesn't actually refer to the Orpheus and Eurydice myth in her comments on *The Handmaid's Tale*. Some comparison between Orpheus and Pieixoto is made by Brian Johnson in 'Language, Power, and Responsibility in *The Handmaid's Tale*: Toward a Discourse of Literary Gossip', *Canadian Literature*, No. 148 (Spring, 1996), pp. 39–55.

34. Margaret Atwood, *Selected Poems II: Poems Selected and New, 1976–1986* (Boston, MA: Houghton Mifflin Co., 1987), p. 107. Further references appear in the text.

3 Playing the Field: Women's Access to Cultural Production

1. Tom Stoppard, *Travesties* (London: Faber & Faber, 1975), p. 28.
2. Alice Walker, 'Everyday Use', *In Love and Trouble* (London: The Women's Press Ltd., 1984); A. S. Byatt, 'Art Work', *The Matisse Stories* (London: Vintage, 1994). Further references appear in the text.
3. Randal Johnson's Introduction to Pierre Bourdieu, *The Field of Cultural Production: Essays on Art and Literature* (Cambridge: Polity Press, 1993) provides helpful explanations of the key terms in Bourdieu's work.
4. Pierre Bourdieu, *The Rules of Art: Genesis and Structure of the Literary Field*, trans. Susan Emmanuel (Cambridge: Polity Press, 1996), p. 229.
5. Pierre Bourdieu, *On Television and Journalism*, trans. Priscilla Parkhurst Ferguson (London: Pluto Press, 1998), p. 71. Further references appear in the text.
6. Elsewhere Bourdieu points out how the acquisition of wealth can be linked to a loss of prestige. See 'The Field of Cultural Production, or: The Economic World Reversed', in *The Field of Cultural Production: Essays on Art and Literature*; also 'An Economic World Turned Upside Down' and 'The Literary Field in the Field of Power', in *The Rules of Art: Genesis and Structure of the Literary Field*. Note also Elizabeth W. Harries's questioning of this thesis when applying it to earlier periods in ' "Out in the Left Field": Charlotte Smith's Prefaces, Bourdieu's Categories, and Public Space', *Modern Language Quarterly*, Vol. 58, No. 4 (December, 1997), pp. 457–73.
7. For further references on Bourdieu's concept of the field in general and the artistic field in particular, see Pierre Bourdieu and Loïc J. D. Wacquant, *An Invitation to Reflexive Sociology* (Cambridge: Polity Press, 1992), p. 94, fn. 42.
8. See, for example, Pierre Bourdieu, *Sociology in Question*, trans. Richard Nice (London: Sage Publications, 1993), p. 34 and Bourdieu and Wacquant, *An Invitation to Reflexive Sociology*, p. 98.
9. Bertolt Brecht, 'On Rhymeless Verse with Irregular Rhythms', *Poems 1913–1956* (London: Eyre Methuen Ltd., 1976), p. 465.
10. Pierre Bourdieu, *Distinction: A Social Critique of the Judgement of Taste*, trans. Richard Nice (London: Routledge, 1986), p. 86.
11. Bourdieu, *The Field of Cultural Production*, p. 58.
12. Similar sentiments are evident in Walker's poem 'For My Sister Molly Who in the Fifties', *Revolutionary Petunias* (New York: Harcourt Brace Jovanovich, 1973), p. 17. This is also about the sister who 'escapes'.

13. Bourdieu, *The Rules of Art*, p. 219.
14. Bridget Fowler, *Pierre Bourdieu and Cultural Theory* (London: Sage Publications, 1997), p. 137. Fowler is discussing here Bourdieu's comments on Virginia Woolf's *To the Lighthouse* in his 'La Domination Masculine', *Actes de la Recherche en Sciences Sociales*, Vol. 84 (1990), pp. 2–31.
15. Bourdieu, *Distinction*, p. 31.
16. Ibid., p. 56.
17. Ibid., p. 91.
18. Ibid., p. 511.
19. Beate Krais, 'Gender and Symbolic Violence: Female Oppression in the Light of Pierre Bourdieu's Theory of Social Practice', in Craig Calhoun, Edward LiPuma and Moishe Postone (eds) *Bourdieu: Critical Perspectives* (Cambridge: Polity Press, 1993), p. 172.
20. See Toril Moi's comments on Simone de Beauvoir as a *miraculée* in *Simone de Beauvoir: The Making of an Intellectual Woman* (Oxford: Blackwell Publishers, 1994), particularly p. 186 and chapter 2 for an analysis of Beauvoir's speaking position.
21. See Rozsika Parker and Griselda Pollock, *Old Mistresses: Women, Art and Ideology* (London: Routledge and Kegan Paul, 1981), pp. 70–81 for a comparable discussion of the invisibility of the quilt makers in an exhibition at the Whitney Museum in 1972.
22. See 'The Production of Belief: Contribution to an Economy of Symbolic Goods', in *The Field of Cultural Production*, particularly pp. 76–7 and 'But Who Created the "Creators"?', in *Sociology in Question*, pp. 139–48.
23. Bourdieu, *Distinction*, pp. 34 and 35.
24. Bourdieu, *The Rules of Art*, p. 216.
25. Bourdieu, *Distinction*, p. 34.
26. Ibid., pp. 487–8.
27. Ibid., p. 34.
28. Ibid., p. 30.
29. Ibid., p. 53.
30. John Frow, 'Accounting for Tastes: Some Problems in Bourdieu's Sociology of Culture', *Cultural Studies*, Vol. 1, No. 1 (January, 1987), p. 62.
31. Following his comment above, Frow critiques Bourdieu for confirming an opposition between 'art' and 'real life', precisely the opposition Mama rejects. This aspect of Bourdieu's thinking is also critiqued in Richard Shusterman, *Pragmatist Aesthetics: Living Beauty, Rethinking Art* (Oxford: Blackwell Publishers, 1992), pp. 192–8.
32. Another current example is the work of Toni Morrison. Lauded by the dominant, speaking for the dominated, she has received both the Nobel Prize for Literature and huge commercial success and 'fandom' through Oprah's Book Club.
33. Bourdieu, *Distinction*, p. 40.
34. 'Womanist' is defined by Walker at the start of *In Search of Our Mothers' Gardens* (New York: Harcourt Brace Jovanovich, 1983), p. xi–xii.
35. Walker, 'In Search of Our Mothers' Gardens', p. 239.
36. Elaine Showalter, *Sister's Choice: Tradition and Change in American Women's Writing* (Oxford: Oxford University Press, 1991), p. 164.
37. Bourdieu, *Distinction*, p. 569, fn. 81.

38. Pierre Bourdieu and Alain Darbel (with Dominique Schnapper), *The Love of Art: European Art Museums and their Public*, trans. Caroline Beattie and Nick Merriman (Cambridge: Polity Press, 1991), p. 37.
39. Bourdieu, *Distinction*, p. 267.
40. Bourdieu, *The Field of Cultural Production*, p. 121.
41. Toril Moi, 'Appropriating Bourdieu: Feminist Theory and Pierre Bourdieu's Sociology of Culture', *New Literary History*, Vol. 22, No. 4 (Autumn, 1991), p. 1019. This essay was subsequently included in Moi *What Is a Woman? And Other Essays* (Oxford: Oxford University Press, 1999). The comment is on p. 268.
42. Lawrence Gowing, *Matisse* (London: Thames & Hudson, 1979).
43. Jean Baudrillard, 'Symbolic Exchange and Death', in Mark Poster (ed.) *Jean Baudrillard: Selected Writings* (Cambridge: Polity Press, 1988), p. 147.
44. One could compare here Tracy Chevalier's *Girl With a Pearl Earring* (London: HarperCollins Publishers, 1999). Such is the aesthetic perception of Vermeer's maid, later model, that she is able to suggest improvements to his pictures and discern what needs to be done before he has realised it.
45. Virginia Woolf, *A Room of One's Own* and *Three Guineas*, ed. Michèle Barrett (Harmondsworth, Middlesex: Penguin, 1993), p. 184.
46. Luce Irigaray, *This Sex Which Is Not One*, trans. Catherine Porter (Ithaca, NY: Cornell University Press, 1985), p. 197.
47. Bourdieu, *Distinction*, p. 228.
48. Beverley Skeggs, *Formations of Class and Gender: Becoming Respectable* (London: Sage Publications, 1997), p. 91.
49. Bourdieu, *Sociology in Question*, p. 74.
50. Note Toril Moi's claim that the force of Bourdieu's work lies in its resistance to any opposition between voluntarism and determinism. See 'The Challenge of the Particular Case: Bourdieu's Sociology of Culture and Literary Criticism', *Modern Language Quaterley*, Vol. 58, No. 4 (December, 1997), pp. 497–508. This essay was subsequently included in Moi, *What Is a Woman?*, pp. 300–11.
51. Bourdieu and Wacquant, *An Invitation to Reflexive Sociology*, p. 199.

4 Lost and Found: The Making of the Woman Author

1. Muriel Spark, *Loitering with Intent* (Harmondsworth, Middlesex: Penguin, 1981), pp. 19–20. Further references are included in the text.
2. Muriel Spark, *Curriculum Vitae* (Harmondsworth, Middlesex: Penguin, 1993), p. 213. Further references are included in the text.
3. Carol Shields, *Mary Swann* (London: Flamingo, 1993), p. 26. Further references are included in the text.
4. Note that Lang complains at the end of *Mary Swann*, not that the love letters have been stolen but the love *poems* (see p. 309). This may be a typographical error or yet another example to add to the multiple losses.
5. Not all the losses are literary. Josh Flanner, a Nobel Prize winner is also 'a smuggler of rose cuttings' (p. 75) – so someone, somewhere is losing them – and a number of losses are bodily: Sarah's mother has an operation and loses her lump; Rose suffers from fibroids and loses blood, worries about it and loses weight.

6. Pierre Bourdieu, *In Other Words: Essays Towards a Reflexive Sociology*, trans. Matthew Adamson (Cambridge: Polity Press, 1990), pp. 110–11.

7. On the possibility of Susanna Moodie, a long-term interest of Shields's, as a more convincing antecedent to Swann, see Clara Thomas, 'Reassembling Fragments: Susanna Moodie, Carol Shields, and Mary Swann', in W. H. New (ed.) *Inside the Poem* (Toronto, Ontario: Oxford University Press, 1992), pp. 196–204 and Faye Hammill, *Literary Culture and Female Authorship in Canada 1760–2000* (Amsterdam: Rodopi, 2003). See also Shields's own comment later in text.

8. Michel Foucault, 'What Is an Author?', in Josué V. Harari (ed.) *Textual Strategies: Perspectives in Post-Structuralist Criticism* (Ithaca, NY: Cornell University Press, 1979), p. 150. Further references are included in the text. For a further discussion of Mary Swann with reference to Foucault's author-function see Brian Johnson, 'Necessary Illusions: Foucault's Author Function in Carol Shields's *Swann*', *Prairie Fire*, Vol. 16, No. 1 (Spring, 1995), pp. 56–70.

9. Pierre Bourdieu, *The Field of Cultural Production: Essays on Art and Literature*, ed. Randal Johnson (Cambridge: Polity Press, 1993), p. 77.

10. Pierre Bourdieu and Loïc J. D. Wacquant, *An Invitation to Reflexive Sociology* (Cambridge: Polity Press, 1992), pp. 120–1.

11. Pierre Bourdieu, *In Other Words*, p. 108.

12. Pierre Bourdieu, *The Logic of Practice*, trans. Richard Nice (Cambridge: Polity Press, 1999), p. 73.

13. Carol Shields in interview with Eleanor Watchel in *Room of One's Own*, Vol. 13, Nos 1&2 (July, 1987), pp. 30–1. Also relevant is Shields comment on her later creation, Daisy Goodwill in *The Stone Diaries* (1993): 'the really tricky part was to write about a woman thinking her autobiography in which she is virtually absent'. Quoted in Joan Thomas, ' "The Golden Book." An Interview with Carol Shields', *Prairie Fire*, Vol. 14, No. 4 (Winter, 1993–4), p. 58.

14. Pierre Bourdieu, *The Rules of Art: Genesis and Structure of the Literary Field*. trans. Susan Emmanuel (Cambridge: Polity Press, 1996), pp. 244, 245.

15. Roland Barthes, 'The Death of the Author', in *Image–Music–Text*, ed. Stephen Heath (London: Fontana, 1977), p. 147.

16. Malcolm Bradbury, *No, Not Bloomsbury* (London: Andre Deutsch, 1987), p. 271–2. Peter Kemp makes a similar remark when he talks of Spark's work bringing together 'temporary spuriousness and eternal verity, to amalgamate metaphysics and derision in a tense and tightly plaited structure'. See *Muriel Spark* (Novelists and Their World Series) (London: Elek, 1974), p. 142.

17. Muriel Spark, 'Edinburgh-born', *New Statesman*, Vol. 64 (10 August 1962), p. 180. Spark talks here of the use of this word in the Edinburgh of her childhood, how it implies a particular way of thinking and the pronounced impact it had on her writing and her conversion to Catholicism.

18. Bryan Cheyette, *Muriel Spark* (Tavistock, Devon: Northcote House, 2000), p. 23.

19. Martin McQuillan (ed.) *Theorizing Muriel Spark: Gender, Race, Deconstruction* (London: Palgrave, 2003), p. 90. Further references are included in the text.

20. Spark is answering her own critics here since she is often accused of being cool, if not cold, in her writing. Note also the riposte on p. 37 about fiction being exaggerated.

21. Muriel Spark, 'The Desegregation of Art', The Annual Blashfield Foundation Address, Proceedings of the American Academy of Arts and Letters and the

National Institute of Arts and Letters (2nd Series) (New York: Spiral Press, 1971), p. 24. Further references are included in the text.

22. John Glavin interestingly relates this elliptical method to an *unknowing* which counters the *knowing* of the phallogos. See 'Muriel Spark's Unknowing Fiction', *Women's Studies: An Interdisciplinary Journal*, Vol. 15, Parts 1–3 (1988), pp. 221–41.

23. Emily Dickinson, Poem 1129, *The Poems of Emily Dickinson*, ed. Thomas H. Johnson (Cambridge, MA: The Belknap Press of Harvard University Press, 1951); Virginia Woolf, *A Room of One's Own*, in Michéle Barrett (ed.) *A Room of One's Own* and *Three Guineas* (Harmondsworth, Middlesex: Penguin, 1993), p. 77.

24. Virginia Woolf, *Three Guineas*, in *A Room of One's Own* and *Three Guineas*, p. 310.

25. Elizabeth Dipple, *TheUnresolvable Plot: Reading Contemporary Fiction* (New York: Routledge, 1988), p. 151.

26. Dominick LaCapra, 'Trauma, Absence, Loss', *Critical Inquiry*, Vol. 25 (Summer, 1999), p. 712. Further references are included in the text.

27. Spark, 'Edinburgh-born', p. 180.

5 Tell Me a Story: Women Oral Narrators

1. J. M. Coetzee, *Foe* (Harmondsworth, Middlesex: Penguin, 1987), pp. 71–2. Further references are included in the text. Note that Coetzee uses the name 'Foe', an earlier version of Daniel Defoe's name though, obviously, also connoting 'enemy'. 'Cruso' is spelt in Coetzee's novel without the 'e'.

2. Michèle Roberts, *In the Red Kitchen* (London: Minerva, 1991), p. 133.

3. On the significance of Susan 'fathering' her story, see Gayatri Chakravorty Spivak, 'Theory in the Margin: Coetzee's *Foe* Reading Defoe's *Crusoe/Roxana*', in Jonathan Arac and Barbara Johnson (eds) *Consequences of Theory: Selected Papers from the English Institute, 1987–88* (Baltimore, NY and London: The Johns Hopkins University Press, 1991).

4. For a discussion of the relevance of Defoe's *Roxana* to Coetzee's text, see David Attwell, *J. M. Coetzee: South Africa and the Politics of Writing* (Berkeley, CA and Los Angeles, CA: University of California Press, 1993).

5. Of course in another re-writing of *Robinson Crusoe* a different story might be told by making use of recent research on the role of early-modern women in publishing, manuscript circulation, the book trade and so on. See Josephine Donovan, *Women and the Rise of the Novel 1405–1726* (New York: St. Martin's Press, 1999), Elizabeth Egar, Charlotte Grant, Clíona Ó Gallchoir and Penny Warburton, *Women, Writing and the Public Sphere 1700–1830* (Cambridge: Cambridge University Press, 2001), Margaret J. M. Ezell, *Social Authorship and the Advent of Print* (Baltimore, NY: Johns Hopkins University Press, 1999), Paula McDowell, *The Women of Grub Street: Press, Politics, and Gender in the London Literary Marketplace 1678–1730* (Oxford: Clarendon Press, 1998).

6. Sherley Anne Williams, *Dessa Rose* (London: Virago Press Ltd., 1998), p. 19. Further references are included in the text.

7. Susan VanZanten Gallagher, *A Story of South Africa: J. M. Coetzee's Fiction in Context* (Cambridge, MA: Harvard University Press, 2001), p. 178.

8. Margaret Atwood, *Alias Grace* (Toronto, Ontario: McClelland & Stewart Inc., 1996), p. 403. Further references are included in the text.

9. Deborah E. McDowell connects the visual and looking as systems of representation largely with section two of the novel, 'The Wench', though, as is evident here, they do operate throughout. See *'The Changing Same': Black Women's Literature, Criticism, and Theory* (Bloomington, IN: Indiana University Press, 1995).

10. Margaret Atwood, 'In Search of *Alias Grace*: On Writing Canadian Historical Fiction', *American History Review*, Vol. 103 (1998), p. 1515.

11. Mae G. Henderson discusses what she terms Dessa's 'strategies of narrative insurgency' in her essay on Williams's 'Meditations on History', the novella that Williams later developed into *Dessa Rose*. See '(W)Riting The Work and Working The Rites', in Linda Kauffman (ed.) *Feminism and Institutions: Dialogues on Feminist Theory* (Oxford: Basil Blackwell, 1989), pp. 10–43.

12. All Grace's strategies can be seen in other ways. See, for example, Coral Ann Howells's discussion of Grace's 'double voicing' which can be interpreted as a subversive, defensive strategy or as a sign of Grace's innocence or of her mental illness or that she is a charlatan: *Contemporary Women's Fiction: Refiguring Identities* (Houndmills, Basingstoke: Palgrave Macmillan, 2003), pp. 32–6.

13. See Henderson, '(W)Riting The Work and Working The Rites', p. 34 on the call-response interchange in the black oral tradition.

14. Jacques Derrida, *The Ear of the Other: Otobiography, Transference, Translation*, trans. Peggy Kamuf; ed. Christie McDonald (Lincoln, NE and London: University of Nebraska Press, 1988), p. 50. Further references are included in the text.

15. Trinh T. Minh-ha, *Woman, Native, Other: Writing Postcoloniality and Feminism* (Bloomington, IN: Indiana University Press, 1989), p. 101.

16. Anne E. Goldman, ' "I made the Ink": (Literary) Production and Reproduction in *Dessa Rose* and *Beloved'*, *Feminist Studies*, Vol. 16, No. 2 (Summer 1990), pp. 325–6.

17. Claude Lévi-Strauss, *Tristes Tropiques* [1955] trans. John and Doreen Weightman (London: Jonathan Cape, 1973), pp. 294–304. Further references are included in the text.

18. Note how slavery and 'the Abolition question' feature as a sub-text in *Alias Grace* and how in Jordan's increasingly fervid imagination Grace becomes the slave. He imagines kissing her and pressing his mouth to her throat 'like a brand' (389). Jordan eventually becomes a Military Surgeon for the Union cause in the Civil War.

19. Jacques Derrida, *Of Grammatology*, trans. Gayatri Chakravorty Spivak (Baltimore, NY and London: The Johns Hopkins University Press, 1976), p. 101. Further references are included in the text.

20. Christopher Norris glosses this term as 'everything that escapes the ethos of nature, origins and presence and is thus metaphorically or covertly placed on the side of a bad, unnatural writing' and, thus, not corrupted. See *Derrida* (London: Fontana Press, 1987), p. 131. Further references will be included in the text.

21. Deborah E. McDowell, *'The Changing Same'*, pp. 151–2.

22. I am conscious here of Audre Lorde's essay 'The Master's Tools Will Never Dismantle the Master's House', in *Sister Outsider* (Trumansberg, New York: The Crossing Press, 1984), pp. 110–13.
23. Quoted in Jacques Derrida, *Dissemination*, trans. Barbara Johnson (London: The Athlone Press, 1981), p. 102.
24. Sherley Anne Williams also writes of a conjunction between the oral and the written in 'The Blues Roots of Contemporary Afro-American Poetry', *Massachusetts Review*, Vol. 17 (1977), pp. 542–54. In this instance, it is the tradition of Afro-American blues and European literary poetry.
25. Jacques Derrida, *Acts of Literature*, ed. Derek Attridge (New York and London: Routledge, 1992), p. 69.
26. Tony Morphet, 'Two Interviews with J. M. Coetzee, 1983 and 1987', in David Bunn and Jane Taylor (eds) *From South Africa: New Writing, Photographs and Art* (a special issue of *TriQuarterly*, Northwestern University, 1987), p. 462. Further references will be included in the text.
27. Coetzee talks about his disquiet in *Doubling the Point: Essays and Interviews*, ed. David Attwell (Cambridge, MA: Harvard University Press, 1992), pp. 64–6. See also Austin Briggs's account of an abortive attempt to engage Coetzee in conversation in 'Who's Who When Everybody's at Home: James Joyce/J. M. Coetzee/Elizabeth Costello', in the *James Joyce Literary Supplement* (Spring, 2002), p. 11.
28. Gayatri Chakravorty Spivak, *The Post-Colonial Critic: Interviews, Strategies, Dialogues*, ed. Sarah Harasym (New York and London: Routledge, 1990), p. 30.
29. J. M. Coetzee, *Doubling the Point*, p. 10.
30. Spivak, 'Theory in the Margin', pp. 172, 157. Further references will be included in the text.
31. I differ here from Benita Parry who sees Susan as more concerned with speech and Foe with writing. Susan seems to me to be fully involved with the possibilities and limitations of both. See Parry, 'Speech and Silence in the Fictions of J. M. Coetzee', in Graham Huggan and Stephen Watson (eds) *Critical Perspectives on J. M. Coetzee* (London: Macmillan, 1996).
32. Derek Attridge, 'Oppressive Silence: J. M. Coetzee's *Foe* and the Politics of Canonisation', in Huggan and Watson (eds) *Critical Perspectives on J. M. Coetzee*, p. 177. Further references are included in the text. Section III of Attridge's essay (pp. 174–8) is devoted to this issue of 'substance'/'substantial'. Similar comments appear in Kim L. Worthington, *Self as Narrative: Subjectivity and Community in Contemporary Fiction* (Oxford: Clarendon Press, 1996), pp. 267–70.
33. See Coetzee, *Doubling the Point*, p. 12. Attwell mentions the phrase 'poetics of reciprocity' on p. 58.
34. Iris Marion Young, *Intersecting Voices: Dilemmas of Gender, Political Philosophy, and Policy* (Princeton, NJ: Princeton University Press, 1997), chapter 11 is entitled 'Asymmetrical Reciprocity: On Moral Respect, Wonder, and Enlarged Thought' (pp. 38–59). Further references will be included in the text.
35. Young is referring to Seyla Benhabib, *Situating the Self* (New York: Routledge, 1991).
36. Coetzee, *Doubling the Point*, p. 248.
37. In a comparable way and using the work of Mikhail Bakhtin, Mae Gwendolyn Henderson suggests how the black women authors are

' "privileged" by a social positionality that enables them to speak in dialogically racial and gendered voices to the other(s) both within and without' (18). See 'Speaking in Tongues: Dialogics, Dialectics, and the Black Woman Writer's Literary Tradition', in Cheryl A. Wall *Changing Our Own Words: Essays on Criticism, Theory, and Writing by Black Women* (London: Routledge, 1990).

6 'A Constant State of Tension': Academic Women Authors

1. Anita Brookner, *A Start in Life* (Harmondsworth, Middlesex: Penguin, 1991), p. 23.
2. Michèle Le Dœuff, *Hipparchia's Choice: An Essay Concerning Women, Philosophy, etc.*, trans. Trista Selous (Oxford: Blackwell, 1991). Further references are included in the text.
3. Elaine Showalter, *A Literature of Their Own*, 2nd ed. (London: Virago Press Ltd., 1999), p. 321.
4. David Lodge, *Nice Work* (Harmondsworth, Middlesex: Penguin, 1989); Antonia Byatt, *Possession: A Romance* (London: Vintage, 1991). Further references to both are included in the text.
5. Further examples can be found in what Hilary Radner calls 'the dissertation novel' and what Suzanne Keen terms 'romances of the archive': Radner, 'Extra-Curricular Activities: Women Writers and the Readerly Text', in Mary Lynn Broe and Angela Ingram (eds) *Women's Writing in Exile* (Chapel Hill, NC and London: The University of North Carolina Press, 1989); Keen, *Romances of the Archive in Contemporary British Fiction* (Toronto, Ontario: University of Toronto Press, 2001).
6. J. M. Coetzee, *The Lives of Animals* (Princeton, NJ: Princeton University Press, 2001), pp. 78–9.
7. Ibid., p. 77.
8. Simone de Beauvoir, *The Second Sex*, trans. and ed. H. M. Parshley (Harmondsworth, Middlesex: Penguin, 1972), p. 705.
9. Michèle Le Dœuff, 'Long Hair: Short Ideas', *The Philosophical Imaginary*, trans. Colin Gordon (London: The Athlone Press, 1989), p. 104. Further references are included in the text.
10. There is an element of erotico-theoretical transference in Astrid's attitude to Sfax in chapter 2 and the consequence on this occasion is certainly disasterous.
11. Karen Horney, 'The Overvaluation of Love' (1934) in *Feminine Psychology* (New York: W. W. Norton & Co., 1967), pp. 182, 183. See also Helene Deutsch, *The Psychology of Women*, Vols 1 & 2 (New York: Grune & Stratton, 1944 and 1945), particularly 'The "Active" Woman: the Masculinity Complex', *The Psychology of Women*, Vol. 1; also *Confrontations with Myself: An Epilogue* (New York: W.W. Norton & Co., 1973).
12. Michèle Le Dœuff, *Hipparchia's Choice: An Essay Concerning Women, Philosophy, etc.*, trans. Trista Selous (Oxford: Blackwell, 1991), p. 31. Further references are included in the text.
13. Nicolas Tredell, 'A. S. Byatt in Conversation', *P. N. Review*, Vol. 17, No. 3 (January/February 1991), p. 27. The comments of Joan Riviere in Chapter 8 would furnish a further example.

14. See, for instance, Louise Morley and Val Walsh (eds) *Feminist Academics: Creative Agents for Change* (London: Taylor & Francis, 1995); Nadya Aisenberg and Mona Harrington, *Women of Academe: Outsiders in the Sacred Grove* (Amherst, MA: University of Massachusetts Press, 1988) and Susan Gubar, 'The Graying of Professor Erma Bombeck', *Critical Condition: Feminism at the Turn of the Century* (New York: Columbia University Press, 2000).

15. Edward Said, *Representations of the Intellectual: The 1993 Reith Lectures* (London: Vintage, 1994), pp. 25–6.

16. Bruce Robbins (ed.) *Intellectuals: Aesthetics, Politics, Academics* (Minneapolis, MN: University of Minnesota Press, 1990), pp. xvii–xviii.

17. Virginia Woolf, *Three Guineas*, in Michèle Barrett (ed.) *A Room of One's Own* and *Three Guineas* (Harmondsworth, Middlesex: Penguin, 1993); Julia Kristeva, 'A New Type of Intellectual: The Dissident', in Toril Moi (ed.) *The Kristeva Reader* (Oxford: Basil Blackwell, 1986).

18. Amanda Cross, *Death in a Tenured Position* (New York: Ballantine Books, 1981). Further references are included in the text. Relevant in this context is Susan Weisman's essay on Susan Sontag who, it could be argued, does just the same: ' "Femininity" and the Intellectual in Sontag and Cixous', in Helen Wilcox, Keith McWatters, Ann Thompson and Linda R. Williams (eds) *The Body and the Text: Hélène Cixous, Reading and Teaching* (Hemel Hempstead: Harvester Wheatsheaf, 1990), pp. 98–113.

19. See, for example, Susan Gubar's account of joining the English department of Indiana University in 1973 in *Critical Condition*, p. 91.

20. See, for instance, Roland Barthes, 'Writers, Teachers, Intellectuals', in Stephen Heath, selected and trans. *Image–Music–Text* (London: Fontana, 1977), pp. 190–215; Shoshana Felman, *Jacques Lacan and the Adventure of Insight: Psychoanalysis in Contemporary Culture* (Cambridge, MA: Harvard University Press, 1987); Arthur W. Frank, 'Lecturing and Transference: The Undercover Work of Pedagogy', in Jane Gallop (ed.) *Pedagogy: The Question of Impersonation* (Bloomington, IN: Indiana University Press, 1995), pp. 28–35.

21. Jane Gallop, 'Keys to Dora', in Charles Bernheimer and Claire Kahane (eds) *In Dora's Case: Freud–Hysteria–Feminism*, 2nd ed. (New York: Columbia University Press, 1990), p. 212.

22. Jacques Lacan, *The Four Fundamental Concepts of Psychoanalysis*, trans. Alan Sheridan (New York: W. W. Norton & Co., 1977).

23. Just how difficult that story can be is evident in Jane Gallop, *Feminist Accused of Sexual Harassment* (Durham, NC: Duke University Press, 1997); Jane Gallop, 'Resisting Reasonableness', *Critical Inquiry*, Vol. 25, No. 3 (Spring 1999), pp. 599–609 and the Critical Responses to Gallop in both that issue and *Critical Inquiry*, Vol. 26, No. 3 (Spring 2000).

24. Elizabeth Grosz, *Sexual Subversions* (St Leonards, NSW: Allen & Unwin, 1989), p. 206.

25. Alison Lurie, *Foreign Affairs* (London: Abacus, 1986). Further references are included in the text.

26. One of the names on this list, Lionel Trilling, featured prominently in the life of Carolyn Heilbrun. This relationship could be taken as another example of 'erotico-theoretical transference'. See Heilbrun's comments on the difficulty of the relationship or, in Trilling's eyes, non-relationship in *Reinventing Womanhood* (New York: W. W. Norton & Co., 1979) and the relevant chapter

from Susan Kress's *Carolyn G. Heilbrun: Feminist in a Tenured Position* (Charlottsville, VI and London: University Press of Virginia, 1997), significantly entitled, after Heilbrun, 'The Unwilling Mentor'.

27. Alison Lurie, *The Truth about Lorin Jones* (London: Michael Joseph, 1988). Further references are included in the text.

28. Note how frequently academic fiction plays with this fantasy – for example, when the critics in *Possession* pool their knowledge and their critical methods to discover the story of Ash and LaMotte or when the symposium members in Carol Shields's *Mary Swann* (see chapter 4) piece together the poetry of Mary Swann.

29. Toril Moi, *Simone de Beauvoir: The Making of an Intellectual Woman* (Oxford: Blackwell, 1994), p. 17. Further references are included in the text. See also on the de Beauvoir/Sartre relationship, Alice Jardine, 'Death Sentences: Writing Couples and Ideology', in Susan Rubin Suleiman (ed.) *The Female Body in Western Culture: Contemporary Perspectives* (Cambridge, MA: Harvard University Press, 1986), pp. 84–96.

30. Of course, 'Wolff' also suggests – with terrible irony – 'Woolf' as in 'Virginia'.

31. Tredell, 'A. S. Byatt in Conversation', p. 27.

32. Though not the focus of this particular chapter, Christabel LaMotte's story could also be discussed with reference to 'erotico-theoretical transference' relations.

33. This is rather like the problem Charlotte Brontë faces in *Shirley* when the tutor Louis has, somehow, to be made worthy of the masterful Shirley. However, Brontë's power reversal would not suit a contemporary audience.

34. For further discussion of the meanings of whiteness, see Jennifer M. Jeffers, 'The White Bed of Desire in A. S. Byatt's *Possession*', *Critique: Studies in Contemporary Fiction*, Vol. 43, No. 2 (Winter 2002), pp. 135–47.

35. See also Christien Franken, *A. S. Byatt: Art, Authorship, Creativity* (London: Palgrave, 2001), p. 135, n. 22. Franken notes how Byatt positions Maud at some distance from what is in Byatt's view Leonora's over-identification with gender and in agreement with Ariane's interest in moving beyond gender-identification.

36. In this respect it is not always helpful to see the male and female critics in the book as in opposition as Elisabeth Bronfen does in her essay, 'Romancing Difference, Courting Coherence: A. S. Byatt's *Possession* as Postmodern Moral Fiction', in Rüdiger Ahrens and Laurenz Volkmann (eds) *Why Literature Matters: Theories and Functions of Literature* (Heidelberg: Universitätsverlag C. Winter, 1996), pp. 117–134.

37. See Byatt's comments in her interview with Tredell on her own parallel experience, 'A. S. Byatt in Conversation', p. 27.

38. See Frederick M. Holmes, *The Historical Imagination: Postmodernism and the Treatment of the Past in Contemporary British Fiction* (Victoria, BC, Canada: University of Victoria, 1997), pp. 72–3 for similar comments. Note how Holmes finds here a link with Romanticism which Roland earlier rejected. See also Byatt's essay, 'Identity and the Writer', in Lisa Appignanesi (ed.) *Identity: The Real Me*, ICA Documents 6 (London: Institute of Contemporary Arts, 1987), pp. 23–6.

39. See John Haffenden's interview of David Lodge in *Novelists in Interview* (London: Methuen, 1985), p. 159.

40. Tredell, 'A. S. Byatt in Conversation', p. 25. See also Byatt's essay, 'People in Paper Houses: Attitudes to "Realism" and "Experiment" in English Post-war Fiction', in *Passions of the Mind: Selected Writings* (London: Chatto and Windus, 1991), pp. 165–88 and Bronfen's interesting comments on the essay, 'Romancing Difference, Courting Coherence,' pp. 120–1.
41. Roland Barthes, *A Lover's Discourse: Fragments*, trans. Richard Howard (Harmondsworth, Middlesex: Penguin, 1990), p. 233.

7 Finding the Right Words: Authors of Romantic Fiction

1. Elizabeth Wilson, *Hallucinations: Life in the Post-Modern City* (London: Radius, 1988), p. 142. Further references are included in the text.
2. Carol Shields, *The Republic of Love* (London: Fourth Estate, 2001), p. 248. Further references are included in the text.
3. Roland Barthes, *A Lover's Discourse: Fragments*, trans. Richard Howard (Harmondsworth, Middlesex: Penguin, 1990), p. 7.
4. Anita Brookner, *The Bay of Angels* (London: QPD, 2001), p. 21.
5. Sigmund Freud, *On Sexuality: Three Essays on the Theory of Sexuality and Other Works*, ed. Angela Richards; trans. James Strachey. The Penguin Freud Library, Vol. 7 (Harmondsworth, Middlesex: Penguin, 1977), p. 258.
6. Catherine Belsey, *Desire: Love Stories in Western Culture* (Oxford: Blackwell, 1994), p. 81. Further references are included in the text.
7. The comment from Winterson is from *Written on the Body* (London: Vintage, 1993), p. 9.
8. Mary Evans, *Love: An Unromantic Discussion* (Cambridge: Polity Press, 2003), p. 27.
9. Tania Modleski, *Loving with a Vengeance: Mass-Produced Fantasies for Women* (London: Routledge, 1982), p. 14.
10. For instance, Mary Evans writes in her Acknowledgements, 'I have very much enjoyed writing this book' (*Love: An Unromantic Discussion*, p. viii) and Catherine Belsey opens her web-based article on writing *Desire: Love Stories in Western Culture* with the words 'I am writing a book about desire. I can't now remember why I ever wanted to write about anything else' (http://www.arts.gla.ac.uk/SESLL/STELLA/COMET/glasgrev/issue2/belsey.htm; accessed 9.6.04). Often what is desired is not so much the dashing hero or the magical transformations of romance but that younger self in the first flush of romantic desire. Her youthful excitement is looked on tenderly and ruefully.
11. Example of such communities can be seen in Janice Radway's study *Reading the Romance* (Chapel Hill, NC: University of Carolina Press, 1984) and Bridget Fowler's *The Alienated Reader: Women and Popular Romantic Literature in the Twentieth Century* (Hemel Hempstead, Hertfordshire: Harvester Wheatsheaf, 1991).
12. David Lodge, *Small World: An Academic Romance* (London: Secker & Warburg, 1984), p. 249.

13. See Stevi Jackson on the lack of attention in sociology to love as an emotion: 'Even Sociologists Fall in Love: An Exploration in the Sociology of Emotions', *Sociology*, Vol. 27, No. 2 (May, 1993), pp. 201–20.
14. David Lodge, *Nice Work* (Harmondsworth, Middlesex: Penguin, 1989), p. 293.
15. Umberto Eco, *Postscript to The Name of the Rose*, trans. William Weaver (New York: Harcourt Brace Jovanovich, 1984), pp. 67–8. This fascinating passage has been frequently referred to in texts on postmodernism and romance. See Maroula Joannou, 'Essentially Virtuous? Anita Brookner's *Hotel du Lac* as Generic Subversion', in Lynne Pearce and Gina Wisker (eds) *Fatal Attractions: Rescripting Romance in Contemporary Literature and Film* (London: Pluto Press, 1998), pp. 84–97; Jackie Buxton, ' "What's love got to do with it?" Postmodernism and *Possession*', *English Studies in Canada*, Vol. 22, No. 2 (June 1996), pp. 199–219; Diane Elam, *Romancing the Postmodern* (London: Routledge, 1992), pp. 45–8.
16. Antonia Byatt, *Possession: A Romance* (London: Vintage, 1991), p. 423.
17. Anita Brookner, *Hotel du Lac* (London: Granada Publishing Co., 1985), p. 114. Further references are included in the text.
18. Isobel Armstrong, 'Woolf by the Lake, Woolf at the Circus: Carter and Tradition', in Lorna Sage (ed.) *Flesh and the Mirror: Essays on the Art of Angela Carter* (London: Virago Press Ltd., 1994), pp. 258, 265, 267, 258–9. Clare Hanson indicates a similar conjunction when she brings together Edith's personal aspiration and 'a strongly social and ethical dimension'. Hanson interestingly relates this utopian principle to the work of Ernst Bloch. See *Hysterical Fictions: The 'Woman's Novel' in the Twentieth Century* (London: Macmillan, 2000).
19. Though 'home' is here related to a domestic idyll, it also often signifies, in romantic fiction, the Gothic and threatening and, for the heroine, the possibilities of a rise in social status as she becomes mistress of the house. I am grateful to Susan Watkins for reminding me of this.
20. Shusha Guppy, 'The Art of Fiction XCVIII: Anita Brookner', *Paris Review* (Fall, 1987), p. 161.
21. One can link here with two scenes with Mr Neville (read 'evil' and 'devil') where during highly charged conversations Edith removes the restraining pins from her hair: pp. 99, 168.
22. Brookner has commented on both authors in interviews though not, I have to say, in the context of more desiring and less desiring. See, for instance, John Haffenden, 'Playing Straight: John Haffenden Talks to Anita Brookner', *Literary Review* (Sept., 1984), pp. 25–30 and Guppy, 'The Art of Fiction XCVIII', pp. 146–69.
23. Fay Weldon, *The Life and Loves of a She Devil* (London: Sceptre, 1984), p. 41. Further references are included in the text.
24. Bridget Fowler, *The Alienated Reader*, p. 15.
25. Note how Brookner has spoken positively of Weldon's work. In an interview with John Haffenden, she commends Weldon for being 'savage' and 'sprightly rather than stoic'. See 'Playing Straight', p. 29.
26. See Julie Nash, ' "Energy and Brashness" and Fay Weldon's Tricksters', in Regina Barreca (ed.) *Fay Weldon's Wicked Fictions* (Hanover and London: University Press of New England, 1994), pp. 93–103 on Ruth as a shapeshifting trickster.

27. Lorna Sage, *Women in the House of Fiction: Post-War Women Novelists* (London: Macmillan, 1992), p. 158.

28. See Sara Martin, 'The Power of Monstrous Women: Fay Weldon's *The Life and Loves of a She-Devil* (1983), Angela Carter's *Nights at the Circus* (1984) and Jeanette Winterson's *Sexing the Cherry* (1989)', *Journal of Gender Studies*, Vol. 8, No. 2 (July 1999), pp. 193–210 on the grotesque in Weldon. Martin also mentions Weldon's novel with reference to the picaresque, science fiction and fairy tales. For a linking of Weldon's novel to contemporary horror writing see Gina Wisker, 'Demisting the Mirror: Contemporary British Women's Horror', in Emma Parker (ed.) *Contemporary British Women Writers* (Cambridge: D. S. Brewer, 2004).

29. Ann Marie Hebert, 'Rewriting the Feminine Script: Fay Weldon's Wicked Laughter', *Critical Matrix*, Vol. 7, No. 1 (1993), p. 25. Susan Sellers makes use of Hebert's comment on Weldon's scripts in *Myth and Fairy Tale in Contemporary Women's Fiction* (London: Palgrave, 2001).

30. For a discussion of excess with respect to multiple subjects and plots, see Susanne Becker *Gothic Forms of Feminine Fictions* (Manchester: Manchester University Press, 1999).

31. Elisabeth Bronfen, 'Romancing Difference, Courting Coherence: A. S. Byatt's *Possession* as Postmodern Moral Fiction', in Rüdiger Ahrens and Laurenz Volkmann (eds) *Why Literature Matters: Theories and Functions of Literature* (Heidelberg: Universitätsverlag C. Winter, 1996), p. 121.

32. Jean Baudrillard, 'Symbolic Exchange and Death', in Mark Poster (ed.) *Jean Baudrillard: Selected Writings* (Stanford, CA: Stanford University Press, 2001), p. 128.

33. Jean Baudrillard, *Simulations*, trans. Paul Foss, Paul Patton and Philip Beitchman (New York: Semiotext[e], 1983), p. 152.

34. Coral Ann Howells, *Margaret Atwood* (London: Macmillan, 1996), p. 73.

35. Margaret Atwood, *Lady Oracle* (London: Virago Press Ltd., 1982), p. 7. Further references are included in the text.

36. Baudrillard, 'Simulacra and Simulations', in Poster (ed.), p. 173. Further references are included in the text.

37. Feminist critics have made frequent use of Nancy Chodorow's work as a way of explaining the uncertain boundaries between mother and daughter. For an application of Chodorow to *Lady Oracle* see Susan Watkins, *Twentieth-Century Women Novelists: Feminist Theory into Practice* (London: Palgrave, 2001). Note also how the female of the female grotesque 'fails' in the terms of the dominant order to know her boundaries – see Mary Russo, 'Female Grotesques: Carnival and Theory', in Teresa de Lauretis (ed.) *Feminist Studies: Critical Studies* (Bloomington, IN: Indiana University Press, 1986), pp. 213–29 – and feminist interest in the female body as uncontained, 'volatile' and 'leaky'.

38. Note Gillian Beer's more positive take on Joan as a shape-shifting trickster in 'Narrative Swerves: Grand Narratives and the Disciplines', *Women: A Cultural Review*, Vol. 11, Nos 1–2 (Spring/Summer 2000), pp. 2–7. She sees Joan's movements across boundaries as subversive and pleasurable.

39. On the various cultural forms and figures reworked by Atwood, see Barbara Hill Rigney, *Margaret Atwood* (London: Macmillan Education Ltd., 1987) and Eleonora Rao, 'Margaret Atwood's *Lady Oracle*: Writing against Notions of Unity', in Colin Nicholson (ed.) *Margaret Atwood: Writing and Subjectivity*

(London: Macmillan, 1994), pp. 133–52. Gayle Greene is particularly good on the mythological associations; see *Changing the Story: Feminine Fictions and the Tradition* (Bloomington, IN: Indiana University Press, 1991).

40. For an extensive survey of Atwood's use of fairy-tale motifs, see Sharon Rose Wilson, *Margaret Atwood's Fairy-Tale Sexual Politics* (Jackson, MS: University of Mississippi Press, 1993).

41. Margaret Atwood, *Negotiating with the Dead: A Writer on Writing* (London: Virago Press Ltd., 2003), p. 32. Doubleness is linked not only to authorship but to the construction of the subject generally: Joan's father is both a killer and a saviour; the Royal Porcupine is also suburban Chuck Brewer; Leda Sprott is also E. P. Revele and so on. And other characters are more than double: Arthur, Joan's husband, is multiple but sequential while her mother is three-headed when looking in her triple mirror but also endlessly reflected when the mirrors are so positioned.

42. Sonia Mycak, *In Search of the Split Subject: Psychoanalysis, Phenomenology and the Novels of Margaret Atwood* (Toronto, Ontario: ECW Press, 1996), p. 75.

8   The Reluctant Author

1. Antonia Byatt, *Possession: A Romance* (London: Vintage, 1991), p. 445.

2. Jane Gardam, 'The Sidmouth Letters', *The Sidmouth Letters* (London: Abacus, 1981); Ursula Le Guin, 'Sur', *The Compass Rose* (London: Victor Gollancz Ltd., 1983); Michèle Roberts, *The Looking Glass* (London: Little, Brown and Company, 2000). Further references are included in the text.

3. Virginia Woolf, 'Professions for Women', in Rachel Bowlby (ed.) *The Crowded Dance of Modern Life: Selected Essays Vol. 2* (Harmondsworth, Middlesex: Penguin, 1993), p. 105.

4. Virginia Woolf, *A Room of One's Own* and *Three Guineas*, Michèle Barrett (ed.) (Harmondsworth, Middlesex: Penguin, 1993), p. 28.

5. Joan Riviere, 'Womanliness as a Masquerade', in Victor Burgin, James Donald and Cora Kaplan (eds) *Formations of Fantasy* (London: Methuen & Co. Ltd., 1986). Further references are included in the text.

6. For discussion of Riviere's work in relation to her biography, see Janet Sayers, *Kleinians: Psychoanalysis Inside Out* (Cambridge: Polity Press, 2000).

7. Carolyn Heilbrun, *Writing a Woman's Life* (London: The Women's Press Ltd., 1989), p. 126.

8. Luce Irigaray, *This Sex Which Is Not One*. trans. Catherine Porter with Carolyn Burke (Ithaca, NY: Cornell University Press, 1985), p. 133. Further references are included in the text.

9. This application of Lacan to Riviere's essay appears in Jean Walton's 'Re-Placing Race in (White) Psychoanalytic Discourse: Founding Narratives of Feminism', *Critical Inquiry*, Vol. 21 (Summer 1995), pp. 775–804.

10. Mary Ann Doane, *Femmes Fatales: Feminism, Film Theory, Psychoanalysis* (New York: Routledge, 1991), p. 38.

11. Judith Butler, *Bodies that Matter: On the Discursive Limits of 'Sex'* (London: Routledge, 1993), p. 234.

12. The biographical evidence for this is slight, only an account told by Cassandra when an old woman to her niece, Caroline, and with no mention of letters. But the possibility of discovering lost Austen texts seems to stir the

imagination of critics and readers. For instance, in Byatt's *Possession*, Maud Bailey uses an analogy to impress on her relatives the significance of the Christabel La Motte letters – 'It's as though you've found – Jane Austen's love letters?' (p. 89). The Brontës intrigue in a similar way. See Stevie Davies's *Four Dreamers and Emily* (London: The Women's Press Ltd., 1996) and Michèle Roberts's *The Mistressclass* (London: Little, Brown, 2003), both working on the trope of lost or unsent letters.

13. Roland Barthes, *A Lover's Discourse: Fragments*, trans. Richard Howard (Harmondsworth, Middlesex: Penguin Books, 1990), p. 151. Further references are included in the text.

14. Hélène Cixous, 'Sorties', in Cixous and Catherine Clément, *The Newly Born Woman*, trans. Betsy Wing (Manchester: Manchester University Press, 1986), pp. 80–1. Further references are included in the text.

15. See Susan Sellers, *Hélène Cixous: Authorship, Autobiography and Love* (Cambridge: Polity Press, 1996) and Judith Still, *Feminine Economies* (Manchester: Manchester University Press, 1997), particularly chapter 8 'The Question of the Gift in the late Twentieth Century: Cixous, Derrida, Irigaray', pp. 149–80 for excellent discussions of these issues.

16. David Lodge, *Changing Places* (Harmondsworth, Middlesex: Penguin, 1978).

17. Byatt, *Possession: A Romance*, p. 498. The texts of Byatt and Gardam make an interesting comparison in terms of literary economies, particularly in the conflicts around privacy, possession and renunciation.

18. Cixous, 'Sorties', p. 87.

19. Elizabeth Grosz, *Sexual Subversions: Three French Feminists* (St. Leonards, NSW: Allen & Unwin, 1989), p. 48. Further references are included in the text.

20. Hélène Cixous, 'Castration or Decapitation?', trans. Annette Kuhn *Signs: Journal of Women in Culture and Society*, Vol. 7, No. 1, Autumn, 1981, p. 54.

21. Julia Kristeva, *About Chinese Women* [1974], trans. Anita Barrows (London: Marion Boyars, 1977), p. 39. Further references are included in the text.

22. Makiko Minow-Pinkney, *Virginia Woolf and the Problem of the Subject* (Brighton, Sussex: Harvester Press Ltd., 1987), p. 196.

23. Cixous, 'Castration or Decapitation?', p. 54.

24. On the particular relation between food and the maternal in Roberts's work, see Sarah Sceats, *Food, Consumption and the Body in Contemporary Women's Fiction* (Cambridge: Cambridge University Press, 2000).

25. Stephen Heath, 'Joan Riviere and the Masquerade', *Formations of Fantasy*, p. 47. Within the critical field, Jane Gallop has spoken of her own 'matronizing' relation to Roland Barthes as a way of establishing a position of superiority. See 'Precursor Critics and the Anxiety of Influence', *Profession* (The Modern Language Association of America, 2003), pp. 105–9.

26. Ursula Le Guin, *Dancing at the Edge of the World* (London: Paladin, 1992), pp. 172, vii and 174.

27. Muriel Spark, *Loitering with Intent* (Harmondsworth, Middlesex: Penguin, 1995), p. 69.

28. Friedrich Nietzsche, *On the Genealogy of Morals*, trans. Douglas Smith (Oxford: Oxford University Press, 1996), p. 24. Further references are included in the text.

29. Véronique Machelidon, 'Masquerade: A Feminine or Feminist Strategy?', in Peter L. Rudnytsky and Andrew M. Gordon (eds) *Psychoanalyses/Feminisms* (New York: State University of New York, 2000), p. 106.

30. Barbara Johnson, *The Feminist Difference: Literature, Psychoanalysis, Race, and Gender* (Cambridge, MA: Harvard University Press, 1998), p. 137.

31. Relevant here is feminist work on women's relation to pain and suffering. See Wendy Brown, *States of Injury: Power and Freedom in Late Modernity* (Princeton NJ: Princeton University Press, 1995); Vikki Bell, *Feminist Imagination: Genealogies in Feminist Theory* (London: Sage Publications, 1999); Sara Ahmed, 'Feminist Futures', in Mary Eagleton (ed.) *A Concise Companion to Feminist Theory* (Oxford: Blackwell Publishing, 2003), pp. 236–54. Also relevant is feminist work on women's relation to care. For an excellent introduction to this area see the review essay by Diemut Bubeck, 'Ethic of Care and Feminist Ethics', *Women's Philosophy Review*, No. 18 (Spring, 1998), pp. 22–50.

Afterword

1. Hélène Cixous, 'Sorties' in Cixous and Catherine Clément, *The Newly Born Woman*, trans. Betsy Wing (Manchester: Manchester University Press, 1986), p. 93.

2. Hélène Cixous, 'The Laugh of the Medusa' in Elaine Marks and Isabelle de Courtivron (eds) *New French Feminisms* (Brighton: Harvester Press Ltd., 1981), p. 246. Further references appear in the text.

3. Peggy Kamuf, 'Writing Like a Woman', in Sally McConnell-Ginet *et al.* (eds) *Women and Language in Literature and Society* (New York: Praeger, 1980), pp. 285–6.

4. Seán Burke, *The Death and Return of the Author: Criticism and Subjectivity in Barthes, Foucault and Derrida* 2nd ed. (Edinburgh: Edinburgh University Press, 1999), pp. 201, 202.

Bibliography

Primary sources

Adair, Gilbert, *The Death of the Author* (1992) (London: Minerva, 1993).
Atwood, Margaret, *Lady Oracle* (1976) (London: Virago Press Ltd., 1982).
Atwood, Margaret, *The Handmaid's Tale* (1985) (London: Virago Press Ltd., 1987).
Atwood, Margaret, *Alias Grace* (Toronto, Ontario: McClelland & Stewart Inc., 1996).
Brookner, Anita, *Hotel du Lac* (1984) (London: Granada Publishing Co., 1985).
Byatt, Antonia, *Possession: A Romance* (1990) (London: Vintage, 1991).
Byatt, Antonia, 'Art Work', *The Matisse Stories* (1993) (London: Vintage, 1994).
Coetzee, J. M., *Foe* (1986) (Harmondsworth, Middlesex: Penguin, 1987).
Cross, Amanda, *Death in a Tenured Position* (New York: Ballantine Books, 1981).
Gardam, Jane, 'The Sidmouth Letters', *The Sidmouth Letters* (1980) (London: Abacus, 1981).
Le Guin, Ursula, 'Sur', *The Compass Rose* (London: Victor Gollancz, 1983).
Lodge, David, *Nice Work* (1988) (Harmondsworth, Middlesex: Penguin, 1989).
Lurie, Alison, *Foreign Affairs* (1984) (London: Abacus, 1986).
Lurie, Alison, *The Truth about Lorin Jones* (London: Michael Joseph, 1988).
Roberts, Michèle, *The Looking Glass* (London: Little, Brown and Company, 2000).
Shields, Carol, 'Absence', *Dressing Up for the Carnival* (London: Fourth Estate, 2000).
Shields, Carol, *Mary Swann* (1987) (London: Flamingo, 1993).
Spark, Muriel, *Loitering with Intent* (1981) (Harmondsworth, Middlesex: Penguin, 1995).
Walker, Alice, 'Everyday Use', *In Love and Trouble* (1973) (London: The Women's Press Ltd., 1984).
Weldon, Fay, *The Life and Loves of a She Devil* (1983) (London: Sceptre, 1984).
Williams, Sherley Anne, *Dessa Rose* (1986) (London: Virago Press Ltd., 1998).

Secondary sources

Ahmed, Sara, 'Feminist Futures', in Mary Eagleton (ed.) *A Concise Companion to Feminist Theory* (Oxford: Blackwell Publishing, 2003).
Aisenberg, Nadya and Mona Harrington, *Women of Academe: Outsiders in the Sacred Grove* (Amherst, MA: University of Massachusetts Press, 1988).
Armstrong, Isobel, 'Woolf by the Lake, Woolf at the Circus: Carter and Tradition', in Lorna Sage (ed.) *Flesh and the Mirror: Essays on the Art of Angela Carter* (London: Virago Press Ltd., 1994).
Attridge, Derek, 'Oppressive Silence: J. M. Coetzee's *Foe* and the Politics of Canonisation', in Graham Huggan and Stephen Watson (eds) *Critical Perspectives on J. M. Coetzee* (London: Macmillan, 1996).
Attwell, David (ed.) *J. M. Coetzee, Doubling the Point: Essays and Interviews* (Cambridge, MA: Harvard University Press, 1992).

Attwell, David, *J. M. Coetzee: South Africa and the Politics of Writing* (Berkeley, CA and Los Angeles, CA: University of California Press, 1993).

Atwood, Margaret, *Selected Poems II: Poems Selected and New 1976–1986* (Boston, MA: Houghton Mifflin Co., 1987).

Atwood, Margaret, 'In Search of *Alias Grace*: On Writing Canadian Historical Fiction', *American History Review*, Vol. 103 (1998), pp. 1503–16.

Atwood, Margaret, *Negotiating with the Dead: A Writer on Writing* (London: Virago Press Ltd., 2003).

Banville, John, *Shroud* (London: Picador, 2002).

Barthes, Roland, *Image–Music–Text*, selected and trans. Stephen Heath (London: Fontana, 1977).

Barthes, Roland, *A Lover's Discourse: Fragments* (1977), trans. Richard Howard (Harmondsworth, Middlesex: Penguin, 1990).

Baudrillard, Jean, 'Symbolic Exchange and Death', in Mark Poster (ed.) *Jean Baudrillard: Selected Writings* (Cambridge: Polity Press, 1988).

Baudrillard, Jean, *Simulations*, trans. Paul Foss, Paul Patton and Philip Beitchman (New York: Semiotext[e], 1983).

Becker, Susanne, *Gothic Forms of Feminine Fictions* (Manchester: Manchester University Press, 1999).

Beer, Gillian, 'Narrative Swerves: Grand Narratives and the Disciplines', *Women: A Cultural Review* Vol. 11, Nos 1–2 (Spring/Summer 2000), pp. 2–7.

Bell, Vikki, *Feminist Imagination: Genealogies in Feminist Theory* (London: Sage Publications, 1999).

Belsey, Catherine, *Desire: Love Stories in Western Culture* (Oxford: Blackwell, 1994).

Benhabib, Seyla, *Situating the Self* (New York: Routledge, 1991).

Bignell, Jonathan, 'The Lost Messages: *The Handmaid's Tale*, Novel and Film, *British Journal of Canadian Studies* Vol. 8, No. 1 (1993), pp. 71–84.

Birchall, Julie, *The Guardian* 26 October, 2002.

Borges, Jorge Luis, *Labyrinths* (Harmondsworth, Middlesex: Penguin, 1970).

Bourdieu, Pierre, *Distinction: A Social Critique of the Judgement of Taste*, trans. Richard Nice (London: Routledge, 1986).

Bourdieu, Pierre, *In Other Words: Essays Towards a Reflexive Sociology*, trans. Matthew Adamson (Cambridge: Polity Press, 1990).

Bourdieu, Pierre, *Sociology in Question*, trans. Richard Nice (London: Sage Publications, 1993).

Bourdieu, Pierre, *The Field of Cultural Production: Essays on Art and Literature*, ed. and intro. Randal Johnson (Cambridge: Polity Press, 1993).

Bourdieu, Pierre, *The Rules of Art: Genesis and Structure of the Literary Field*, trans. Susan Emmanuel (Cambridge: Polity Press, 1996).

Bourdieu, Pierre, *On Television and Journalism*, trans. Susan Emmanuel (Cambridge: Polity Press, 1998).

Bourdieu, Pierre, *The Logic of Practice*, trans. Richard Nice (Cambridge: Polity Press, 1999).

Bourdieu, Pierre and Alain Darbel (with Dominique Schnapper), *The Love of Art: European Art Museums and their Public*, trans. Caroline Beattie and Nick Merriman (Cambridge: Polity Press, 1991).

Bourdieu, Pierre and Loïc J. D. Wacquant, *An Invitation to Reflexive Sociology* (Cambridge: Polity Press, 1992).

Bradbury, Malcolm, *No, Not Bloomsbury* (London: Andre Deutsch, 1987).

Brecht, Bertolt, 'On Rhymeless Verse with Irregular Rhythms', *Poems 1913–1956* (London: Eyre Methuen Ltd., 1976).

Briggs, Austin, 'Who's Who When Everybody's at Home: James Joyce/ J. M. Coetzee/Elizabeth Costello', *James Joyce Literary Supplement* (Spring 2002), p. 11.

Bronfen, Elisabeth, 'Romancing Difference, Courting Coherence: A. S. Byatt's *Possession* as Postmodern Moral Fiction', in Rüdiger Ahrens and Laurenz Volkmann (eds) *Why Literature Matters: Theories and Functions of Literature* (Heidelberg: Universitätsverlag C. Winter, 1996).

Brookner, Anita, *A Start in Life* (Harmondsworth, Middlesex: Penguin, 1991).

Brookner, Anita, *The Bay of Angels* (London: QPD, 2001).

Brown, Wendy, *States of Injury: Power and Freedom in Late Modernity* (Princeton, NJ: Princeton University Press, 1995).

Bubeck, Diemut, 'Ethic of Care and Feminist Ethics', *Women's Philosophy Review* No. 18 (Spring 1998), pp. 22–50.

Burke, Seán, *Authorship: From Plato to the Postmodern. A Reader* (Edinburgh: Edinburgh University Press, 1995).

Burke, Seán, *The Death and Return of the Author: Criticism and Subjectivity in Barthes, Foucault and Derrida* (Edinburgh: Edinburgh University Press, 1992; 2nd ed. 1999).

Butler, Judith, *Bodies that Matter: On the Discursive Limits of 'Sex'* (London: Routledge, 1993).

Buxton, Jackie, ' "What's love got to do with it?" Postmodernism and *Possession*', *English Studies in Canada*, Vol. 22, No. 2 (June 1996), pp. 199–219.

Byatt, A. S., 'Identity and the Writer', in Lisa Appignanesi (ed.) *Identity: the Real Me*, ICA Documents 6 (London: Institute of Contemporary Arts, 1987).

Byatt, A. S., *Passions of the Mind: Selected Writings* (London: Chatto and Windus, 1991).

Chevalier, Tracy, *Girl With a Pearl Earring* (London: HarperCollins Publishers, 1999).

Cheyette, Bryan, *Muriel Spark* (Tavistock, Devon: Northcote House, 2000).

Cixous, Hélène, 'The Laugh of the Medusa', in Elaine Marks and Isabelle de Courtivron (eds) *New French Feminisms* (Brighton: Harvester Press Ltd., 1981).

Cixous, Hélène, 'Castration or Decapitation?', trans. Annette Kuhn, *Signs: Journal of Women in Culture and Society*, Vol. 7, No. 1 (1981), pp. 41–55.

Cixous, Hélène, 'Sorties', in Cixous and Catherine Clément *The Newly Born Woman*, trans. Betsy Wing (Manchester: Manchester University Press, 1986).

Coetzee, J. M., *Doubling the Point: Essays and Interviews*, ed. David Attwell (Cambridge, MA: Harvard University Press, 1992).

Coetzee, J. M., *The Lives of Animals* (Princeton, NJ: Princeton University Press, 2001).

Colapinto, John, *About the Author* (London: Fourth Estate, 2002).

Davies, Stevie, *Four Dreamers and Emily* (London: The Women's Press, 1996).

De Beauvoir, Simone, *The Second Sex* (1949), trans. and ed. H. M. Parshley (Harmondsworth, Middlesex: Penguin, 1972).

De Man, Paul, 'Autobiography as De-Facement', *The Rhetoric of Romanticism* (New York: Columbia University Press, 1984).

Derrida, Jacques, *Of Grammatology*, trans. Gayatri Chakravorty Spivak (Baltimore, NY and London: The Johns Hopkins University Press, 1976).

Derrida, Jacques, *Dissemination*, trans. Barbara Johnson (London: The Athlone Press, 1981).

Derrida, Jacques, *The Ear of the Other: Otobiography, Transference, Translation*, trans. Peggy Kamuf (ed.) Christie McDonald (Lincoln, NE and London: University of Nebraska Press, 1988).

Derrida, Jacques, *Acts of Literature*, ed. Derek Attridge (New York and London: Routledge, 1992).

Deutsch, Helene, *The Psychology of Women* Vols, 1 & 2 (New York: Grune & Stratton, 1944 and 1945).

Deutsch, Helene, *Confrontations with Myself: An Epilogue* (New York: W. W. Norton & Co., 1973).

Dickinson, Emily, *The Poems of Emily Dickinson*, Thomas H. Johnson (ed.) (Cambridge, MA: The Belknap Press of Harvard University Press, 1951).

Dipple, Elizabeth, *The Unresolvable Plot: Reading Contemporary Fiction* (New York: Routledge, 1988).

Doane, Mary Ann, *Femmes Fatales: Feminism, Film Theory, Psychoanalysis* (New York: Routledge, 1991).

Donovan, Josephine, *Women and the Rise of the Novel 1405–1726* (New York: St. Martin's Press, 1999).

DuPlessis, Rachel Blau, *Writing Beyond the Ending: Narrative Strategies of Twentieth-Century Women Writers* (Bloomington, IN: Indiana University Press, 1985).

Eco, Umberto, *Postscript to The Name of the Rose*, trans. William Weaver (New York: Harcourt Brace Jovanovich, 1984).

Egar, Elizabeth, Charlotte Grant and Clíona Ó Gallchoir and Penny Warburton *Women, Writing and the Public Sphere 1700–1830* (Cambridge: Cambridge University Press, 2001).

Elam, Diane, *Romancing the Postmodern* (London: Routledge, 1992).

Evans, Mary, *Love: An Unromantic Discussion* (Cambridge: Polity Press, 2003).

Ezell, Margaret J. M., *Social Authorship and the Advent of Print* (Baltimore, NY: Johns Hopkins University Press, 1999).

Felman, Shoshana, *Jacques Lacan and the Adventure of Insight: Psychoanalysis in Contemporary Culture* (Cambridge, MA: Harvard University Press, 1987).

Foucault, Michel, *Language, Counter-Memory, Practice: Selected Essays and Interviews*, Donald F. Bouchard (ed.) trans. Donald F. Bouchard and Sherry Simon (Ithaca, NY: Cornell University Press, 1977).

Foucault, Michel, 'What is an Author?', in Josué V. Harari (ed.) *Textual Strategies: Perspectives in Post-Structuralist Criticism* (Ithaca, NY: Cornell University Press, 1979).

Fowler, Bridget, *The Alienated Reader: Women and Popular Romantic Literature in The Twentieth Century* (Hemel Hempstead, Hertfordshire: Harvester Wheatsheaf, 1991).

Fowler, Bridget, *Pierre Bourdieu and Cultural Theory* (London: Sage Publications, 1997).

Frank, Arthur W., 'Lecturing and Transference: The Undercover Work of Pedagogy', in Jane Gallop (ed.) *Pedagogy: The Question of Impersonation* (Bloomington, IN: Indiana University Press, 1995).

Franken, Christien, *A. S. Byatt: Art, Authorship, Creativity* (London: Palgrave, 2001).

Freud, Sigmund, *On Sexuality: Three Essays on the Theory of Sexuality and Other Works*, the Penguin Freud Library, Vol. 7, trans. James Strachey and ed. Angela James (Harmondsworth, Middlesex: Penguin, 1977).

Frow, John, 'Accounting for Tastes: Some Problems in Bourdieu's Sociology of Culture', *Cultural Studies*, Vol. 1, No. 1 (January, 1987), pp. 59–73.

Gallagher, Susan VanZanten, *A Story of South Africa: J. M. Coetzee's Fiction in Context* (Cambridge, MA: Harvard University Press, 2001).

Gallop, Jane, 'Keys to Dora', in Charles Bernheimer and Claire Kahane (eds) *In Dora's Case: Freud–Hysteria–Feminism*, 2nd ed. (New York: Columbia University Press, 1990).

Gallop, Jane, *Feminist Accused of Sexual Harassment* (Durham, NC: Duke University Press, 1997).

Gallop, Jane, 'Resisting Reasonableness', in *Critical Inquiry*, Vol. 25, No. 3 (Spring 1999), pp. 599–609.

Gallop, Jane, 'Precursor Critics and the Anxiety of Influence', *Profession* (The Modern Language Association of America, 2003), pp. 105–9.

Gilbert, Sandra and Susan Gubar, *The Madwoman in the Attic: The Woman Writer and the Nineteenth Century Literary Imagination* (New Haven, CT: Yale University Press, 1979).

Givner, Jessie, 'Names, Faces and Signatures in Margaret Atwood's *Cat's Eye* and *The Handmaid's Tale*', *Canadian Literature*, Vol. 133 (Summer, 1992), pp. 56–75.

Glavin, John, 'Muriel Spark's Unknowing Fiction', *Women's Studies: An Interdisciplinary Journal*, Vol. 15, Parts 1–3 (1988), pp. 221–41.

Goldman, Anne E., ' "I made the Ink": (Literary) Production and Reproduction in *Dessa Rose* and *Beloved*', *Feminist Studies*, Vol. 16, No. 2 (Summer, 1990), pp. 313–30.

Gowing, Lawrence, *Matisse* (London: Thames & Hudson, 1979).

Greene, Gayle, *Changing the Story: Feminist Fiction and the Tradition* (Bloomington, IN: Indiana University Press, 1991).

Grosz, Elizabeth, *Sexual Subversions: Three French Feminists* (St Leonards, NSW: Allen & Unwin, 1989).

Gubar, Susan. *Critical Condition: Feminism at the Turn of the Century* (New York: Columbia University Press, 2000).

Guppy, Shusha, 'The Art of Fiction XCV111: Anita Brookner', *Paris Review* (Fall, 1987), pp. 149–69.

Haffenden, John, 'Playing Straight: John Haffenden talks to Anita Brookner', *Literary Review* (September, 1984), pp. 25–30.

Haffenden, John, *Novelists in Interview* (London: Methuen, 1985).

Hammill, Fay, *Literary Culture and Female Authorship in Canada 1760–2000* (Amsterdam: Rodopi, 2003).

Hanson, Claire, *Hysterical Fictions: The 'Woman's Novel' in the Twentieth Century* (London: Macmillan, 2000).

Harries, Elizabeth W., ' "Out in the Left Field": Charlotte Smith's Prefaces, Bourdieu's Categories, and Public Space', *Modern Language Quarterly*, Vol. 58, No. 4 (December, 1997), pp. 457–73.

Hartley, Jenny, *Reading Groups* (Oxford: Oxford University Press, 2001).

Heath, Stephen, 'Joan Riviere and the Masquerade', in Victor Burgin, James Donald and Cora Kaplan (eds) *Formations of Fantasy* (London: Methuen & Co. Ltd., 1986).

Hebert, Ann Marie, 'Rewriting the Feminine Script: Fay Weldon's Wicked Laughter', *Critical Matrix*, Vol. 7, No.1 (1993), pp. 21–40.

Heilbrun, Carolyn, *Reinventing Womanhood* (New York: W. W. Norton & Co., 1979).

Heilbrun, Carolyn, *Writing a Woman's Life* (London: The Women's Press, 1989).

Henderson, Mae G., '(W)Riting The Work and Working The Rites', in Linda Kauffman (ed.) *Feminism and Institutions: Dialogues on Feminist Theory* (Oxford: Basil Blackwell, 1989).

Henderson, Mae G., 'Speaking in Tongues: Dialogics, Dialectics, and the Black Woman Writer's Literary Tradition', in Cheryl A. Wall (ed.) *Changing Our Own Words: Essays on Criticism, Theory, and Writing by Black Women* (London: Routledge, 1990).

Hogeland, Lisa Maria, *Feminism and Its Fictions: The Consciousness-Raising Novel And the Women's Liberation Movement* (Philadelphia, PA: University of Pennsylvania, 1998).

Holmes, Frederick M., *The Historical Imagination: Postmodernism and the Treatment of the Past in Contemporary British Fiction* (Victoria, BC, Canada: University of Victoria, 1997).

Hong Kingston, Maxine, *The Woman Warrior: Memoirs of a Girlhood among Ghosts* (London: Picador, 1981).

Horney, Karen, 'The Overvaluation of Love' (1934), in *Feminine Psychology* (New York: W. W. Norton & Co., 1967).

Howells, Coral Ann, *Margaret Atwood* (London: Macmillan, 1996).

Howells, Coral Ann, *Contemporary Women's Fiction: Refiguring Identities* (London: Palgrave Macmillan, 2003).

Huf, Linda, *A Portrait of the Artist as a Young Woman* (New York: Frederick Ungar Publishing Co., 1983).

Hutcheon, Linda, *Narcissistic Narrative: The Metafictional Paradox* (London: Methuen, 1984).

Hutcheon, Linda, *The Canadian Postmodern: A Study of Contemporary English–Canadian Fiction* (Oxford: Oxford University Press, 1988).

Irigaray, Luce, *Ce sexe qui n'est pas un* (Paris: Minuit, 1977).

Irigaray, Luce, *This Sex Which Is Not One*, trans. Catherine porter with Carolyn Burke (Ithaca, NY: Cornell University Press, 1985).

Jackson, Stevi, 'Even Sociologists Fall in Love: An Exploration of the Sociology of Emotions', *Sociology*, Vol. 27, No. 2 (May, 1993), pp. 201–20.

Jardine, Alice, 'Death Sentences: Writing Couples and Ideology', in Susan Rubin Suleiman (ed.) *The Female Body in Western Culture: Contemporary Perspectives* (Cambridge, MA: Harvard University Press, 1985).

Jeffers, Jennifer M., 'The White Bed of Desire in A. S. Byatt's *Possession*', *Critique: Studies in Contemporary Fiction*, Vol. 43, No. 2 (Winter 2002), pp. 135–47.

Joannou, Maroula, 'Essentially Virtuous? Anita Brookner's *Hotel du Lac* as Generic Subversion', in Lynne Pearce and Gina Wisker (eds) *Fatal Attractions: Rescripting Romance in Contemporary Literature and Film* (London: Pluto Press, 1998).

Johnson, Barbara, *The Feminist Difference: Literature, Psychoanalysis, Race and Gender* (Cambridge, MA: Harvard University Press, 1998).

Johnson, Brian, 'Necessary Illusions: Foucault's Author Function in Carol Shields's *Swann*', *Prairie Fire*, Vol. 16, No. 1 (Spring, 1995), pp. 56–70.

Johnson, Brian, 'Language, Power, and Responsibility in *The Handmaid's Tale*: Toward a Discourse of Literary Gossip', in *Canadian Literature*, No. 148 (Spring, 1996), pp. 39–55.

Kamuf, Peggy, 'Writing Like a Woman', in Sally Mc Connell-Ginet, Ruth Borker, Nelly Furman (eds) *Women and Language in Literature and Society* (New York: Praeger, 1980).

Kamuf, Peggy, 'Replacing Feminist Criticism', *Diacritics*, Vol. 2, No. 12 (Summer, 1982), pp. 42–7.

Kamuf, Peggy, *Signature Pieces: On the Institution of Authorship* (Ithaca, NY and London: Cornell University Press, 1988).

Kamuf, Peggy and Nancy Miller, 'Parisien Letters', in Marianne Hirsch and Evelyn Fox Keller (eds) *Conflicts in Feminism* (New York: Routledge, 1990).

Keene, Suzanne, *Romances of the Archive in Contemporary British Fiction* (Toronto, Ontario: University of Toronto Press, 2001).

Kemp, Peter, *Muriel Spark* (Novelists and Their World Series) (London: Elek, 1974).

Krais, Beate, 'Gender and Symbolic Violence: Female Oppression in the Light of Pierre Bourdieu's Theory of Social Practice', in Craig Calhoun, Edward LiPuma and Moishe Postone (eds) *Bourdieu: Critical Perspectives* (Cambridge: Polity Press, 1993).

Kress, Susan, *Carolyn G. Heilbrun: Feminist in a Tenured Position* (Charlottsville, VI and London: University Press of Virginia, 1997).

Kristeva, Julia, *About Chinese Women*, trans. Anita Barrows (London: Marion Boyars, 1977).

Kristeva, Julia, 'A New Type of Intellectual: The Dissident', in Toril Moi (ed.) *The Kristeva Reader* (Oxford: Basil Blackwell, 1986).

Lacan, Jacques, *The Four Fundamental Concepts of Psychoanalysis*, trans. Alan Sheridan (New York: W. W. Norton and Co., 1977).

LaCapra, Dominick, 'Trauma, Absence, Loss', *Critical Inquiry*, Vol. 25 (Summer, 1999), pp. 696–727.

Le Dœuff, Michèle, *The Philosophical Imaginary*, trans. Colin Gordon (London: The Athlone Press, 1989).

Le Dœuff, Michèle, *Hipparchia's Choice: An Essay Concerning Women, Philosophy, etc.*, trans. Trista Selous (Oxford: Blackwell, 1991).

LeGuin, Ursula, *Dancing at the Edge of the World* (London: Paladin, 1992).

Lehman, David, *Signs of the Times: Deconstruction and the Fall of Paul de Man* (New York: Poseiden Press, 1992).

Lévi-Strauss, Claude, *Tristes Tropiques*, trans. John and Doreen Weightman (London: Jonathan Cape, 1973).

Lewis, Reina, 'The Death of the Author and the Resurrection of the Dyke', in Sally Munt (ed.) *New Lesbian Criticism: Literary and Cultural Readings* (Hemel Hempstead, Hertfordshire: Harvester Wheatsheaf, 1992).

Lodge, David, *Changing Places* (Harmondsworth, Middlesex: Penguin, 1978).

Lodge, David, *Small World: An Academic Romance* (London: Secker & Warburg, 1984).

Lodge, David, *Nice Work* (Harmondsworth, Middlesex: Penguin, 1989).

Lodge, David, *Thinks ...* (London: Secker & Warburg, 2001).

Lorde, Audre, *Sister Outsider* (Trumansberg, NY: The Crossing Press, 1984).

Machelidon, Véronique, 'Masquerade: A Feminine or Feminist Strategy?', in Peter L. Rudnytsky and Andrew M. Gordon (eds) *Psychoanalyses/Feminisms* (New York: State University of New York, 2000).

Mahoney, Elisabeth, 'Writing so to Speak: the Feminist Dystopia', in Sarah Sceats And Gail Cunningham (eds) *Image and Power: Women in Fiction in the Twentieth Century* (London: Longman, 1996).

Martin, Sara, 'The Power of Monstrous Women: Fay Weldon's *The Life and Loves of a She-Devil* (1983), Angela Carter's *Nights at the Circus* (1984) and Jeanette Winterson's *Sexing the Cherry* (1989), in *Journal of Gender Studies*, Vol. 8, No. 2 (July, 1999), pp. 198–210.

Marxist–Feminist Literature Collective, 'Women's Writing: *Jane Eyre, Shirley, Villette, Aurora Leigh*', in Francis Barker, John Coombes, Peter Hulme, Colin Mercer and David Musselwhite (eds) *The Sociology of Literature 1848* (Essex: University of Essex, 1978).

McDowell, Deborah E., *'The Changing Same': Black Women's Literature, Criticism, and Theory* (Bloomington, IN: Indiana University Press, 1995).

McDowell, Paula, *The Women of Grub Street: Press, Politics, and Gender in the London Literary Marketplace 1678–1730* (Oxford: Clarendon Press, 1998).

McQuillan, Martin, *Paul de Man* (London: Routledge, 2001).

McQuillan, Martin (ed.) *Theorizing Muriel Spark* (London: Palgrave Publishers Ltd., 2002).

Miller, Nancy, 'The Text's Heroine: A Feminist Critic and Her Fictions' and 'Changing the Subject: Authorship, Writing, and the Reader', in *Subject to Change: Reading Feminist Writing* (New York: Columbia University Press, 1988).

Minow-Pinkney, Makiko, *Virginia Woolf and the Problem of the Subject* (Brighton, Sussex: Harvester Press Ltd., 1987).

Moi, Toril, *Simone de Beauvoir: The Making of an Intellectual Woman* (Oxford: Blackwell Publishers, 1994).

Moi, Toril, *What Is a Woman? And Other Essays* (Oxford: Oxford University Press, 1999).

Modleski, Tania, *Loving with a Vengeance: Mass-Produced Fantasies for Women* (London: Routledge, 1982).

Morley, Louise and Val Walsh (eds), *Feminist Academics: Creative Agents for Change* (London: Taylor & Francis, 1995).

Morphet, Tony, 'Two Interviews with J. M. Coetzee, 1983 and 1987', in David Bunn and Jane Taylor (eds) *From South Africa: New Writing, Photographs and Art* (a special issue of *TriQuarterley* , Northwestern University, 1987), pp. 454–64.

Mycak, Sonia, *In Search of the Split Subject: Psychoanalysis, Phenomenology and the Novels of Margaret Atwood* (Toronto, Ontario: ECW Press, 1996).

Nash, Julie, ' "Energy and Brashness" and Fay Weldon's Tricksters', in Regina Barreca (ed.) *Fay Weldon's Wicked Fictions* (Hanover and London: University Press of New England, 1994).

Nietzsche, Friedrich, *On the Genealogy of Morals*, trans. Douglas Smith (Oxford: Oxford University Press, 1996).

Norris, Christopher, *Paul de Man: Deconstruction and the Critique of Aesthetic Ideology* (London: Routledge, 1988).

Norris, Christopher, *Derrida* (London: Fontana Press, 1995).

Parker, Rozsika and Griselda Pollock, *Old Mistresses: Women, Art and Ideology* (London: Routledge and Kegan Paul, 1981).

Parkin-Gounelas, Ruth, *Fictions of the Female Self: Charlotte Brontë, Olive Schreiner, Katherine Mansfield* (London: Macmillan, 1991).

Parry, Benita, 'Speech and Silence in the Fictions of J. M. Coetzee', in Graham Huggan and Stephen Watson (eds) *Critical Perspectives on J. M. Coetzee* (London: Macmillan, 1996).

Pease, Donald E. 'Author', in Frank Lentricchia and Thomas McLaughlin (eds) *Critical Terms for Literary Study* (Chicago, IL and London: University of Chicago Press, 1990).

Radner, Hilary, 'Extra-Curricular Activities: Women Writers and the Readerly Text', in Mary Lynne Broe and Angela Ingram (eds) *Women's Writing in Exile* (Chapel Hill, NC and London: The University of North Carolina Press, 1989).

Radway, Janice, *Reading the Romance* (Chapel Hill, NC: University of Carolina Press, 1984).

Rao, Eleonora, 'Margaret Atwood's *Lady Oracle*: Writing against Notions of Unity', in Colin Nicholson (ed.) *Margaret Atwood: Writing and Subjectivity* (London: Macmillan, 1994).

Rigney, Barbara Hill, *Margaret Atwood* (London: Macmillan Education Ltd., 1987).

Riviere, Joan, 'Womanliness as a Masquerade' (1929), in Victor Burgin, James Donald and Cora Kaplan (eds) *Formations of Fantasy* (London: Methuen & Co. Ltd., 1986).

Robbins, Bruce (ed.), *Intellectuals: Aesthetics, Politics, Academics* (Minneapolis, MN: University of Minnesota Press, 1990).

Roberts, Michèle, *In the Red Kitchen* (London: Minerva, 1991).

Roberts, Michèle, *The Mistressclass* (London: Little Brown, 2003).

Rubens, Bernice, *Autobiopsy* (London: Sinclair Richardson, 1993).

Rushdie, Salman, *Shame* (London: Jonathan Cape, 1985).

Russo, Mary, 'Female Grotesques: Carnival and Theory', in Teresa de Lauretis (ed.) *Feminist Studies: Critical Studies* (Bloomington, IN: Indiana University Press, 1986).

Sage, Lorna, *Women in the House of Fiction: Post-War Women Novelists* (London: Macmillan, 1992).

Sage, Lorna, 'Death of the Author', *Granta 41: Biography* (London: Granta Publications, 1992).

Said, Edward, *Representations of the Intellectual: the 1993 Reith Lectures* (London: Vintage, 1994).

Sayers, Janet, *Kleinians: Psychoanalysis Inside Out* (Cambridge: Polity Press, 2000).

Sceats, Sarah, *Food, Consumption and the Body in Contemporary Women's Fiction* (Cambridge: Cambridge University Press, 2000).

Sellers, Susan, *Hélène Cixous: Authorship, Autobiography and Love* (Cambridge: Polity Press, 1996).

Sellers, Susan, *Myth and Fairy Tale in Contemporary Women's Fiction* (London: Palgrave, 2001).

Shields, Carol, *The Republic of Love* (London: Fourth Estate, 2001).

Shields, Carol, *Unless* (London: Fourth Estate, 2003).

Showalter, Elaine, *A Literature of Their Own: British Women Novelists from Brontë to Lessing* (Princeton, NJ: Princeton University Press, 1977); (2nd ed., London: Virago Press Ltd., 1999).

Showalter, Elaine, *Sister's Choice: Tradition and Change in American Women's Writing* (Oxford: Oxford University Press, 1991).

Shusterman, Richard, *Pragmatist Aesthetics: Living Beauty, Rethinking Art* (Oxford: Blackwell Publishers, 1992).

Simion, Eugen, *The Return of the Author* (1981) ed. and intro. James W. Newcomb; trans. James W. Newcomb and Lidia Vianu (Evanston, IL: Northwestern University Press, 1996).

Skeggs, Beverley, *Formations of Class and Gender: Becoming Respectable* (London: Sage Publications, 1997).

Smith, Barbara, 'Toward a Black Feminist Criticism', *Conditions: Two*, Vol. 1, No. 2 (1977), pp. 25–44.

Spark, Muriel, 'Edinburgh-born', *New Statesman*, Vol. 64 (10 August 1962), pp. 271–2.

Spark, Muriel, 'The Desegregation of Art', The Annual Blashfield Foundation Address, Proceedings of the American Academy of Arts and Letters and the National Institute of Arts and Letters (2nd Series) (New York: Spiral Press, 1971).

Spark, Muriel, *Curriculum Vitae* (Harmondsworth, Middlesex: Penguin, 1993).

Spivak, Gayatri Chakravorty, *The Post-Colonial Critic: Interviews, Strategies, Dialogues*, ed. Sarah Harasym (New York and London: Routledge, 1990).

Spivak, Gayatri Chakravorty, 'Theory in the Margin: Coetzee's *Foe* Reading Defoe's *Crusoe/Roxana*', in Jonathan Arac and Barbara Johnson (eds) *Consequences of Theory: Selected Papers from the English Institute, 1987–88* (Baltimore, NY and London, The Johns Hopkins University Press, 1991).

Stewart, Grace, *A New Mythos: The Novel of the Artist as Heroine 1877–1977* (Montreal, Canada: Eden Press Women's Publications, 1981).

Still, Judith, *Feminine Economies* (Manchester: Manchester University Press, 1997).

Stoppard, Tom, *Travesties* (London: Faber & Faber, 1975).

Survey of the English Curriculum and Teaching in UK Higher Education (Report Series No. 8: English Subject Centre, 2003).

Thomas, Clara, 'Reassembling Fragments: Susanna Moodie, Carol Shields, and Mary Swann', in W. H. New (ed.) *Inside the Poem* (Toronto, Ontario: Oxford University Press, 1992).

Thomas, Joan, ' "The Golden Book." An Interview with Carol Shields', *Prairie Fire*, Vol. 14, No. 4 (Winter, 1993–4), pp. 121–31.

Tredell, Nicholas, 'A. S. Byatt in Conversation', *P. N. Review*, Vol. 17, No. 3 (January/February 1991), pp. 24–8.

Trinh T., Minh-ha, *Woman, Native, Other: Writing Postcoloniality and Feminism* (Bloomington, IN: Indiana University Press, 1989).

Vice, Sue, 'Addicted to Love', in Lynne Pierce and Jackie Stacey (eds) *Romance Revisited* (London: Lawrence & Wishart, 1995).

Walker, Alice, *Revolutionary Petunias* (New York: Harcourt Brace Jovanovich, 1973).

Walker, Alice, *In Search of Our Mothers' Gardens* (New York: Harcourt Brace Jovanovich, 1983).

Walton, Jean, 'Re-Placing Race in (White) Psychoanalytic Discourse: Founding Narratives of Feminism', *Critical Inquiry*, Vol. 21 (Summer 1995), 775–804.

Warner, Maria, 'Introduction', in Lorna Sage, *Moments of Truth: Twelve Twentieth-Century Women Novelists* (London: Fourth Estate, 2001).

Watchel, Eleanor, 'Interview with Carol Shields', *Room of One's Own*, Vol. 13, Nos 1&2 (July, 1987), pp. 5–45.

Watkins, Susan, *Twentieth-Century Women Novelists: Feminist Theory into Practice* (London: Palgrave, 2001).

Weisman, Susan, ' "Femininity" and the Intellectual in Sontag and Cixous', in Helen Wilcox, Keith McWatters, Ann Thompson and Linda R. Williams (eds) *The Body and the Text: Hélène Cixous, Reading and Teaching* (Hemel Hempstead: Harvester Wheatsheaf, 1990).

Williams, Sherley Anne, 'The Blues Roots of Afro-American Poetry', *Massachusetts Review*, Vol. 17 (1977), pp. 542–54.

Williams, Raymond, *The Long Revolution* (Harmondsworth, Middlesex: Pelican, 1965).

Wilson, Elizabeth, *Hallucinations: Life in the Post-Modern City* (London: Radius, 1988).

Wilson, Sharon Rose, *Margaret Atwood's Fairy-Tale Sexual Politics* (Jackson, MS: University Press of Mississippi, 1993).

Winterson, Jeanette, *Written on the Body* (London: Vintage, 1993).

Wisker, Gina, 'Demisting the Mirror: Contemporary British Women's Horror', in Emma Parker (ed.) *Contemporary British Women Writers* (Cambridge: D. S. Brewer, 2004).

Woolf, Virginia, 'The Decay of Essay-writing', in Andrew McNeillie (ed.) *The Essays of Virginia Woolf: Volume 1 1904–1912* (London: The Hogarth Press, 1986).

Woolf, Virginia, *A Room of One's Own* and *Three Guineas*, ed. Michèle Barrett (Harmondsworth, Middlesex: Penguin, 1993).

Woolf, Virginia, 'Professions for Women', in Michèle Barrett (ed.) *The Crowded Dance of Modern Life: Selected Essays Vol. 2* (Harmondsworth, Middlesex: Penguin, 1993).

Worthington, Kim, *Self as Narrative: Subjectivity and Community in Contemporary Fiction* (Oxford: Clarendon Press, 1996).

Young, Iris Marion, *Intersecting Voices: Dilemmas of Gender, Political Philosophy, and Policy* (Princeton, NJ: Princeton University Press, 1997).

Index